A LONG TIME DEAD

SAMARA BREGER

Bywater
BOOKS

2023

Bywater Books

Copyright © 2023 Samara Breger

Print ISBN: 978-1-61294-265-0

Bywater Books First Edition: May 2023

Printed in the United States of America on acid-free paper.

Cover designer: TreeHouse Studio

Bywater Books
PO Box 3671
Ann Arbor MI 48106-3671

www.bywaterbooks.com

For Alessandra, who deserves the world.

There she sees a damsel bright,
Drest in a silken robe of white,
That shadowy in the moonlight shone:
The neck that made that white robe wan,
Her stately neck, and arms were bare;
Her blue-veined feet unsandl'd were,
And wildly glittered here and there
The gems entangled in her hair.
I guess, 'twas frightful there to see
A lady so richly clad as she—
Beautiful exceedingly!

Mary mother, save me now!
(Said Christabel) And who art thou?

—Samuel Taylor Coleridge, *Christabel*

Part I

Somewhere foggy, 1837

Chapter 1

Poppy was well rested and warm, which meant something was wrong. Neither state was easily acquired in London's limpid early spring, the lengthening, foggy days offering up exhaustion and cold in clammy handfuls. This wretched March huddled sheepishly in the damp, unmanning non-season between the body-heat-hungry snow and the eager, pollen-stained warmth to come, when men would bang down Poppy's door, reawakened, ready to split the earth like tulips from their bulbs. Until that time, until Green Park was yellow with daffodils and the sun burned away the last wisps of fog, she would bed down beside hunger and chill.

She recognized the weakness in her bones—that at least was familiar, as good rest had been hard to come by, what with Minna turning her out in one of her inscrutable changes of mood. But beyond the weakness there was something else—a thirst like she had never encountered, burning from throat to eyeballs. She thought first of water, and her stomach roiled. No, water wouldn't do at all. There was something else, something terribly vital, and if she could only figure out what it was she would shout its name.

"Here."

Someone shoved a goblet in Poppy's hand and she drank down its contents greedily, the smell awakening her brain like a lightning strike. It was warm and viscous, savory with a sweet iron tang. She moaned into the goblet, the sound echoing back against the metal in feral harmony.

"Fucking hell," she gasped when the goblet was empty. "Fucking *hell*."

"Quite."

Her eyes snapped open. "Who are you?"

The woman beside her was turned away, baring the back of her bonnet

3

and frock. She wore heaps of gray fabric. In the dim candlelight, she was a brooding pigeon constructed entirely of rags. "I'm no one. Do you need more?"

Poppy blinked down into the empty goblet, licking her sticky lips. "What *was* that?"

"Blood."

"Naw. Pull the other one."

"I'm not deceiving you." The woman spoke pristinely, with what might have been the fading hint of an Irish lilt. "It was rabbit's blood. Not the most fresh but needs must."

"Why are you giving me blood? This some sort of, what do you call it, demonic practice?"

The woman sighed, finally turning to reveal her face. Her eyes were the strangest hue, a deep, cool iron-gray that grabbed Poppy and held her. Poppy was typically one for riotous color, spending her meager earnings on richly dyed lengths of ribbon to wind around the pale curls that framed her heart-shaped face. How, she wondered in this never-ending moment, could a pair of eyes entirely devoid of color captivate her so completely?

The woman, Poppy realized after a few moments, was speaking.

"Your life will be different now, I'm sorry to say. I hope you don't have a large family awaiting your return, because you'll never be able to—"

"Wait." Poppy held up a hand. "What's your name?"

The woman blinked. "My name?"

"It's not an unreasonable question."

"It's not. Of course. I—"There was a brief second in which the woman appeared flustered, before a careful blankness overtook her face. "My name is Roisin."

"Roisin." Poppy let the syllables roll over her tongue, smooth as treacle, just to see if she could crack that steely facade. It didn't budge. "I'm Poppy."

"Yes. I'm aware. Now if we could return to the matter at hand . . ."

Had she been abducted? She wasn't chained, of course, but there were other ways to keep a cat like Poppy against her will. Taking her away from London would be enough, particularly in this state; she wore only her chemise, with no stockings nor shoes, and had no idea where those needments might be. She took a peek around, discovering she was in a bedchamber, and that she sat on a bench at the foot of a looming, behemoth four-poster. The room was dim, lit only by two thin tapers in heavy brass sconces. Yet despite the lack of light, her eyes could easily discern details. She could see each twist in the mouldering wallpaper, which might have begun as any color, but was now a garden of wilted grays and dust-caked browns. The planks below her naked feet were warped beyond repair. The whole place smelled of disuse, a relic of riches long gone.

"Poppy?"

She jolted to attention. Roisin had been speaking. She wasn't any longer. Now, she stared, silent, concern hewing her features from granite, carving her cheekbones and chipping lines into her forehead.

"I'm well," Poppy said. "I don't know why I'm here, is all."

"Oh, yes." Roisin winced. "Terribly sorry about that. There's much to explain. Though, you seem to be taking this very well."

"Taking, erm, what exactly?"

Roisin frowned. "What I've been—" Comprehension dawned slowly, widening her eyes. "Don't tell me you weren't listening."

"I won't." Poppy wiped an itch from her chin. "Tell you, that is."

Roisin made an aborted movement toward her nose, likely to pinch the bridge. "I'll say it once more: several nights ago you made the acquaintance of a woman named Cane. She probably plied you with alcohol and payment, as well as, more than likely, a good deal of mesmerism. She drank your blood, and you hers, and now you are a creature of the night. An immortal. A vampire if you'd rather. You will not hunger for food—it will sicken you. You will not thirst for ale—it will taste of filth. The sun will sting your skin. The blood of humans will tempt you to drink. You will not age. You will remain young, healthy, and beautiful for the rest of your days." Roisin eyed her warily, braced for a reaction. "Do you have any questions?"

Poppy felt the tears welling. "No more food?"

"I—*what?*"

"No more sausages? Pints? No more *jellied eels?*" She swiped carelessly at her eyes. "Are you telling me I can't have my spoonful of treacle before bed?"

"I'm telling you that you will no longer need to *sleep.*"

She batted that away. "It's for my health, yeah? The treacle. Surely I can have that. It's *medicinal.*"

The blankness on Roisin's face was no longer careful. She looked stunned beyond the capacity for thoughtful physical reaction. "No."

Poppy dropped her head to her hands. Her mother had often told her to slow her eating, that her body was becoming too round and too soft, that there was far too much of her. That had never bothered her; food was a pleasure, and the full breasts and dimpled buttocks she earned therefrom were pleasures in themselves. Her bedfellows had certainly never minded. One of her regular partners had often remarked that Poppy's entire body felt like a breast, and that could only be a good thing. Therefore nothing could stop Poppy from the joys of her delicacies, when she had the dosh for them. Nothing but *this*. Gone were the days of tasting. No more rice milk, thin and sugary and oh so warm. No more bone broth, hearty and fatty and bolstering on those long nights walking the cobbles. No more cottage loaf or stout or sharp wedges of cheese toasted on the hearth. No more of these lovely things she so enjoyed putting in her mouth. And to that end . . .

"How will I make my living?"

Roisin was staring at her. "You earn money by eating?"

"Sucking pricks, you dolt. Am I meant to take a pay cut because I can't swallow?"

Roisin stilled. Her lips thinned into the familiar expression of someone caught between bemusement, disgust, and the first wisps of real alarm. "I've told you that you'll outlive everyone you've ever met, and you're concerned about swallowing *seed?*"

"Oi! Not all of us are dealt the same lot. I won't have you judging me for my living, not when I don't know a damn thing about you."

"Sorry, sorry." She frowned, tight and small. This expression, too, was a familiar friend: the face of someone reluctantly amused by Poppy and irritated about it.

Roisin had a strong, patrician nose—now vaguely twitching—chiseled out above a mouth entirely devoid of smile lines. Her cheekbones could shelter mice in a rainstorm. It was her eyes that gave her away; they crinkled sweetly at the corners, and in those tiny fronds of mirth Poppy counted her victory.

Her favorite sort of people were like that. Schoolmistresses, priests, the ladies who handed out pamphlets on the perils of vice while Poppy was attempting to earn an honest day's wage. The sort of people who didn't

6

dole out smiles easily. The type that required coaxing. Their pleasure, when received, was never false, never meant to flatter. When a man generous with smiles paid for Poppy's time, she knew he'd disappear the moment he was spent, in a muttered flurry of apologies and buttons. But the frigid, icy ones would always return—the sort from whom she had to drag high spirits kicking and screaming. Like Clive, who hired rooms, allowing Poppy to sleep in blissful solitude when her work was through. Or Henry, who brought her little cakes and treats, and in return she'd make him laugh and laugh. Those men had wanted her, valued her, and not for the fucking. Well, not *entirely* for the fucking. In the end, all anyone wanted was to laugh. It was as much a service as a pull on the old arbor vitae, and just as rewarding.

"All right, all right," Poppy allowed. "I'll figure something else out, shall I?"

"I don't know the answer. I never—" Roisin shook her head, brow creased in genuine consideration. "I know who to ask. I'll write a letter."

Poppy pressed her lips together and swallowed a laugh. In its absence, she realized she was absurdly touched. "Thank you."

"But your stomach will rebel against human food. Your, uh, *other faculties* will be intact." Roisin turned her face away at that, apparently in discomfort. "The rest of your body, aside from your digestion, will function as it always has. Better, in fact. You'll never be ill. You'll run faster. You'll be far stronger. You may . . . I couldn't say. I ought to dress." Roisin rose, just a touch unsteadily. Poppy spared a wisp of curiosity for what the woman wore when she was comfortable. If she were ever comfortable.

"And," Roisin went on, "I suppose you'd like a minute with your thoughts? I daresay I've given you a great deal to mull over."

"Yes, that would be welcome." No, it wouldn't. Poppy never enjoyed quiet moments with her own mind. She preferred the joviality of drink and company, the din of a public house gilding the dark edges of her private thoughts. But there was no route nor reason to express any of that to Roisin. Roisin would dress, and then she'd come back. The stiff ones always came back.

Roisin hesitated by the entrance. "If you have any questions . . ."

"I'll think some up." She pulled a reassuring smile from her well-worn collection. "Don't worry."

At the click of the closing door, Poppy groaned, the silence of the dust-choked room swallowing the sound. Any reasonable person would doubt what Roisin had just told her. She ought to grasp at an earthly explanation for why a woman like Roisin might try to convince Poppy she had become an impossible thing. But Poppy couldn't deny the change in her own body. Her sight, even in this dim room, carried farther than it had since her thirteenth summer, when a passing doctor recommended spectacles her family could ill afford. Her skin was smooth, the little rose garden of nicks and imperfections around her nail beds gone fallow. And the *smells*. Outside the heavy drapes, greenery forced its way in, stubborn and wet, teeming with fresh, split-leaf fragrance. In her improved ears, Poppy heard the familiar notes of a cricket orchestra.

She wasn't in London. At least that was certain.

She rubbed her face, piecing together shards of memory. There had been a woman. A tall, beautiful, unquestionably wealthy woman, who had pressed a pouch of coins into Poppy's hand and asked, unsubtly, for her company over the nearest pint. Stares greeted them as they tromped into the local, the woman dressed as though she were asking for her pockets to be thoroughly and mercilessly picked. Fortunately, the landlady was well acquainted with Poppy's odd range of companions, and managed to act as though nothing was amiss, leading the assembled patrons to follow suit. Still, Poppy felt the press of a dozen gazes. If the roughs had their way with the strange lady's belongings—well, it hadn't been Poppy's idea to dress like that, had it? Any grown woman should have known not to wear silk in this part of the city, least of all for the puddles of mysterious filth that a floor-length frock would soak up like bread in broth.

Despite the ignorant dress and the—oh hell, those jewels had to be paste, hadn't they?—the woman had a fearsomeness to her. Her fingers were slim but strong, with long, well-kept nails. Her collarbone was hewn from marble, her neck like a swan's. Swans, Poppy knew, were not to be crossed. They didn't honk; they hissed.

"Thank you for bringing me here," the woman cooed. Her voice was as low and husky as fog. "It's a lovely spot."

"'Tisn't."

The woman laughed easily. "I was being polite."

"Of course. You're a lady." Poppy showed off her most knowing smirk.

"And so am I."

"Then perhaps we should have met at a teahouse." The woman raised a manicured eyebrow. "Or at a more appropriate hour."

"You chose the hour, mate. Not me."

The woman's dark eyes traveled up Poppy's body, spending a long, leisurely moment on her breasts. It raised the hair on the back of her neck, just as it sent a pleasant rush between her legs.

"You may call me Cane."

Poppy wasn't entirely sure how or when it had happened, but she suddenly discovered a pint of bitter sweating before her. She reached out to take a bracing sip.

"Like the Bible?"

"The very same. Though spelled differently. *C-A-N-E.*"

"Of course." Poppy couldn't read much beyond her own name. It wasn't for lack of trying—she'd had schooling. The letters just had a pesky habit of darting beyond her reach. "*C-A-N-E.*"

"Well done, you."

Poppy didn't enjoy condescension, but she loved praise. Her body warred with itself, revulsion and attraction warming her skin in equal measure.

"You'll find I have many skills," Poppy told her, attempting to regain her composure. She realized, distantly, that she was sweating.

"I don't doubt that. You're a clever little thing, aren't you?" Cane snapped her fingers and Poppy stood, not bothering to wonder why she did so, why it required so little thought. "Come along. We have places to be."

The memories flitted through her skull like butterflies, landing for only seconds at a time. Poppy was in a lush set of rooms, Cane's lady's maid squeezing her body into a frock that was just slightly too small, her breasts spilling out of the top. Cane watched, silent and assessing, and Poppy had never felt more exposed, more vulnerable. Her skin crawled, but her quim was wet and aching to be touched. Cane rose and pinched a nipple through the soft fabric of the garment and Poppy couldn't hold back her ragged, wanton moan.

Poppy sat in a chair at a chophouse, or music hall, or private parlor—there was no way of knowing. There were people all around, well dressed and perfumed, but Poppy had eyes only for Cane. Cane's fingers, delicately holding a champagne flute, tipping it into Poppy's open mouth.

"Drink. Good girl. Drink it all. You want to please me, don't you?"

Poppy was in someone's arms, her back to their front. It was Cane. She whispered in Poppy's ear as her deft hands traveled across Poppy's naked body.

"Please!" Poppy wailed, bucking into Cane's teasing fingers. "*Harder.*"

"Hush, now. I'll take my time with you."

And so she did, graduating from teasing circles to firm, punishing strokes, coaxing crisis after crisis out of Poppy's tingling, throbbing body.

"Good girl. But we aren't finished yet."

And then she bit Poppy where neck met shoulder, flesh yielding to Cane's sharp teeth and clever tongue, and Poppy came so hard her vision blackened, screaming and writhing, warm spend gushing from between her legs in wave after unceasing wave.

"Oh, you're a sweet thing. Far too fun to drain. I think I'll keep you around for a bit longer, shall I?"

More impressions, more ragged bits of memory. Being fed raspberries from Cane's chilled hands. Wrapped in a blanket and bundled into a coach. Cane whispering "Hush, now," and "More sleep, I think." More coupling, more powerful, terrifying bites and their ensuing, earth-shattering pleasure. And then, this bed.

"Quickly." The cool flesh of a split wrist, sticky with blood, pressing against her slack lips. "Quickly, drink of me."

Then, only pain. Blistering hot in one moment, freezing cold the next. Her bones had ached like they yearned to force their way out of her body, tearing muscle and tendon and skin. Her fingers and feet had gone numb, then stinging, then screaming pain, needles scraping and poking her flesh. Her muscles had locked and released, seized and spasmed and twisted. Her organs had become a frightened mouse, her body the powerful snake digesting it. She had screamed, her voice a ragged, baleful thing, shaking the walls and the floor.

But she hadn't been alone.

Someone had stroked her hair. Someone had watched over her. Someone had held and bathed her, dressed her in the clean, unfamiliar chemise she currently wore. Someone had stripped the bed and taken the bloodied sheets away. Someone had run their fingers over her burning eyelids and said, "It's all right. It's nearly over."

That someone hadn't been Cane.

Poppy stumbled to her feet, realizing as she did so that she was shaking. She peered out the window. It was night. The curtains were heavy, perfect to block out a sun that stung. She wondered whether, in time, she'd grow to miss the sun. Luckily, she had always been a night creature, ever since her childhood on the pig farm, sneaking out to stare at the endless stars. Then in London, starless nights working and fucking and laughing, drinking and swearing and, on occasion, running and fighting. The night was when people like Poppy could thrive, those who were never meant to clerk or serve or marry. The debauched found a home in the night, and Poppy prided herself on being as thoroughly debauched as a girl of her station could possibly manage.

She slipped from the chamber into a wide, dingy hallway. A cheerful little bouquet of larkspur and geranium sat in a pot beside the door. There must be gardens here, wherever "here" was. She had never been inside the stately country home that her family's pig farm supplied, but she had imagined it might look something like this, with paneled wood walls and ornate rugs covering the floor. The master of that big house—Poppy had only seen him up close on the one occasion her father brought her along while he paid his rent—probably wouldn't have allowed his home to become as shabby as this one. That landlord had been stuffy and fastidious, unmoved by Poppy's father's emotional pleas. He had so carefully turned up his nose at the pig farmer's hungry daughter, used as an ultimately ineffectual prop. Poppy had imagined he treated his home as he did his tenants: without compromise.

His nibs would not have abided the dust graying the mounted portraits, nor the wayward eye of the pathetically decayed taxidermy fox. His drapes would have been drawn in the day and shut at night, tassels tied away, not hanging loose with the air of a farmhand on break. He wouldn't have looked at his bare feet and thought, as Poppy did now, that it would have been wise to wear shoes, lest one split one's foot open on an errant, filthy nail and succumb to infection.

Although—hadn't Roisin told Poppy she'd now be free from disease? Bolstered, she plodded on barefooted.

11

As expected, there were no maids to encounter in the innumerable rooms into which Poppy poked her head. No signs of life at all, for that matter. Instead, she spotted a moldy library that smelled of the forest and a garderobe that might have been one of Dante's more macabre imaginings. A brace of unused bedchambers huddled uncertainly at the top of a stairway, as though even they couldn't recall their intended purpose. Eventually, she wound up in the kitchen, which was as derelict as one might expect in a home where no one ate food. On the far wall, an open door let in a sliver of moonlight.

Roisin was crouched on the ground outside. She startled as Poppy approached.

"Oh," Poppy breathed. "*Oh.*"

Roisin's eyes were wide and frightened, her unsmiling mouth smeared lurid red. She hunched over the unfortunate form of a dead hare, its blood dripping from her bared teeth. Quickly, she schooled her face and snapped her mouth shut.

"Pardon me," she stammered, reaching into her pocket for a handkerchief and wiping her lips. "That was most unbecoming."

"No, please, don't stop on my account. It was—" Odd. There had been a bare second before Roisin had fully awoken to Poppy's presence, in which she had been as an animal, feral and wild. Not eating, but *feeding*. It had been horrible, but entrancing. Frightfully beautiful and beautifully frightful, like watching a goshawk swoop down and snatch a field mouse. Poppy lived to see the buttoned-up unbutton, to unleash the wild, incautious beast that slumbered within every human soul. Roisin's beast was almost beyond imagining, and even now, just moments after watching it slip away, Poppy longed for it to return.

"You can keep going," Poppy whispered into the reverent night. "I didn't mean to interrupt."

"No, no, it's unseemly."

"Please." Poppy stepped forward. The clover was dew-damp and midnight-chilled, but the cold barely touched her. "I want to watch."

Roisin's mouth fell open, exposing the white points of fangs just past the reddened flesh of her upper lip. She looked stunned, transfixed. Bathed in moonlight, she was an apparition pulled out of time, fixed in a moment that stretched on for decades.

"Y-you want . . ."

"To watch." She watched the shiver run from Roisin's lifted shoulders to her swaying knees. "If you'll let me."

Roisin's steel eyes flicked to the ground. Her knees softened once, twice, and then—

"No, not tonight." She swallowed thickly, straightening her clothes. "It's, uh, impudent."

"Of course." She brushed off the disappointment, making a note to ask again, once she'd fully endeared herself to this woman. "You've changed your clothes I see."

"What? Oh. Yes." Roisin wore men's clothes: simple breeches, shirtsleeves, and a waistcoat, a watch chain peeking out from the left pocket. Like Poppy, Roisin wore no shoes. Her hair, which had previously hid under a bonnet, was now tied in a low queue. It was wet-earth-dark and bone straight, glistening and touchable under the stars. "I prefer to dress casually while I'm here."

"Where is 'here'?"

"Covenly. The family seat."

In the dark, the grounds stretched on and on, clover and wildflower and overgrown shrub, with forest encroaching at all sides. The stars fought their way through shifting fog, winks of diamond in wool. "Whose family?"

"Yours, as it happens." Roisin lowered herself to the ground and tossed the remains of her hare into the underbrush. She hesitated before tapping the space beside her in invitation. "Both of ours. Creatures in our line—of our sire and hers before her—have used this house for centuries."

"It doesn't seem like anyone is using it now," Poppy observed, finding a seat on the springy earth.

"Well, there are far fewer of us than there once were." Roisin placed her hands behind her, tilting her face to the sky. "It's a long life. Between long-held grudges, the odd tontine, and the world-weariness, many of us were lost."

"Tontine?"

"A betting scheme. The last one living gets the pot."

"So, among immortals . . ."

"Murder is incentivized, yes." She let out a long breath. "It's all very juvenile, of course. Most vampires, if they've been alive for centuries, are wealthy. Some merely adequately, some blindingly. All it takes is a single monetary investment and a bit of patience. And even so, they're placing bets on their lives."

"Why?"

"To feel. To remember that life isn't meant to . . ." She broke off. Her neck was long and slender, and Poppy watched it shift as she swallowed. "It's difficult for one to find meaning when one's life is this long. A life this long is unnatural."

"And you?" Poppy asked, bristling slightly at the caustic tone in which Roisin said *unnatural*. "What do you do with your very long life?"

"Me?" Roisin smiled weakly. It didn't turn up at the corners, more slid from one side of her face to the other. "Right now, my only occupation is to teach you how we live. Come. It's nearly dawn."

Roisin led her through the creaking halls, back to what Poppy had already begun to think of as her bedchamber—she had had so many homes in so few years, the habit of nestling into a new burrow had turned into a reflex. There was a chest with fresh linens up against a wall, beneath a sconce housing a candle burned down to the socket. Together, they made up the bed.

"It looks lovely," Poppy remarked. "But you did say neither of us will be sleeping in it."

"Not *sleeping*, no."

Poppy raised an eyebrow. Roisin's eyes widened, and she frantically shook her head.

"No! No, no, no, I meant—oh, saints." She ran her hands over her restrained hair. "Yes, yes, laugh at me. I deserve it. No, I meant, well, we don't need to sleep. But the day does weaken us, and it isn't natural for a creature to live without any sort of rest. When you've grown a bit used to being a vampire, you can do as you please during the day. But now, as you are a newborn, I suggest we enter a trance."

"What's that mean?"

"I'll show you." Roisin considered for a moment, then sat on the bed. "I suspect you won't mind us sharing, will you?"

Poppy smirked, flopping down beside her. "I promise I won't attempt anything untoward."

"Yes, well. See that you don't." Roisin's jaw shifted, her tight expression valiantly fending off a reaction, and Poppy's stomach flipped for the smile huddled under Roisin's tongue. "None of the other beds are in any sort of fit state, and I'm far too coddled to go back to the coffins."

"*Coffins?*"

"Yes, coffins. It isn't as dire as it sounds. Coffins block out the sun and they're conveniently person-shaped. And we can enter trances for long periods of time, so a vampire may choose a coffin to travel."

"Avoid the boat fare?"

"Yes, actually, and the questions. Imagine sailing the Atlantic, attempting to explain to the passengers and crew why you spend the whole day shut up in your cabin and the whole night competing with the ship's cat for rats."

"Vampires drink from *rats?*"

"Vampires drink from *people*, but some animals serve as a decent substitute. Oh, come now, what did I say about looking at me like that? Rats are a far less horrific choice than humans."

Poppy shivered. "I'd prefer a hare."

"As would I," Roisin replied, with some approval. "Luckily, the grounds are absolutely riddled with them. Come now. Stop distracting me and lie down, please."

It was the less appealing of two options, but Poppy did as bid, shimmying so her head rested on a pillow. The last thing she saw before closing her eyes was Roisin peering down at her.

"Good," Roisin murmured. The bed dipped, and Poppy knew that they were lying side by side. Comically stiff with a good twelve inches of space between them, but still somehow intimate. "Now try to empty your mind."

"Believe you me, it's sufficiently empty. I have my old schoolmistress's good word on the subject."

"Hush. Empty it of *thoughts*, I mean."

"Again, my schoolmistress would—"

"*Hush.*" Poppy hushed. "Imagine your mind as a blank space, maybe a silent street filled with fog, or a cloudless stretch of sky. When a thought arrives, acknowledge it, then gently push it away. Feel your body, cloth against your skin, the blanket below you. Loosen your limbs, your jaw, your fingers. Let all tension go, and float away."

Poppy was not a swift learner, and thusly prepared to face this *trance* business with some frustration. To her surprise, it was laughably easy. One minute she was imagining a pale stretch of blankness, and the next, she had entered a twilight state, somewhere between sleeping and wakefulness. She was aware of the room around her, the bed underneath, the weight of Roisin beside her—and yet, she was elsewhere, softly bolstered by Roisin's sonorous voice, and, when it went silent, by nothing at all. The drapes were drawn tight, but somehow she knew that the sun rose outside, hot as sizzling butter in a skillet, then set. She knew that other creatures left their warrens and returned, rabbits and foxes, birds and other things that flew and chittered and vomited up worms for their young. She knew, when the night crawled beneath her skin and tugged, that it was time to rise.

Chapter 2

Poppy woke, and her throat burned.

"Roisin?" she croaked, but she was alone. "Roisin!" She needed, oh *god*—

Thirst overcame her, demanding satiation. Her skin was hot and cracked, her mouth a salivating, dripping mess. She ached for blood, craved it, a desire as fundamental as a heartbeat. And it was urgent, a single-minded drive propelling her up and out.

She raced down the halls and through the kitchen, bursting from the house. The moon was full-bellied and bright, lending its light to the overgrown wildness of the grounds, limning the clover in silver. She was as one with everything that grew, wild as the dandelion between her toes, seeding the earth, unpruned and unstoppable. She fell to all fours, sniffing the air. Nothing for a moment, and then—in the distance, something rich and red, shifting and shuffling in the gorse needles. Her legs moved without thought. She careened into waxy leaves and biting thorns she barely felt. Her hands grappled with something warm and furred. She felt an aching pressure in her gums, licked at the pointed tip of a dropped fang. She was made for this, built to hunt and kill and feed. She raised her mouth and dropped her teeth into the hare, hearing the plaintive squeals just as her mouth filled with hot, sweet blood. She moaned, drinking desperately, sticky heat dribbling down her chin. Not enough, not *enough*. The second one was easier to find; she caught in a single fist and thoughtlessly tore the creature in twain, salving the horrible burn. Pleasure ripped through her, shivering and terrible, and she wanted more, *needed* more. To feast on the earth's creatures, to fill her swelling belly with their red, flowing vitality. To

17

dig her flesh into the earth, to take it as a lover, to bear its children and devour them like a hungry god. A third hare—a fat one, greasy and rich, and she gorged herself upon it. A fourth. A fifth. A sixth. A seventh. More, *more*, she needed—

"Poppy?"

A voice, somewhere in the distance. She lifted her head, ear cocked like a wild dog.

"Poppy, are you out here?"

She knew that voice, and she liked it. Yes, *yes*, it was a voice she liked. She rose, stumbling after the sound.

"Poppy, is that—*Poppy!*" Hands on her, touching her hair and face, lifting her blood-sodden chemise over her head and tossing it away. "Are you hurt? How many did you eat? Oh, this is my fault. All my fault. I'm so, so sorry. Poppy, I'm so *sorry*."

"Roisin," Poppy slurred. She blinked her vision clear. Tuppence-silver eyes filled with concern swam before her, tucked under a furrowed brow. She gazed down; her breasts and belly were smeared with blood. "I'm nude."

"Very good. Well spotted. Saints, this is all my—oh, dear, let's get you inside, shall we?"

Poppy toddled toward the house, supported by Roisin's arm wrapped around her middle. Inside, Roisin dumped her in a large, comfortable chair by the kitchen hearth. Poppy didn't need the warmth, but the crackle and smell of the fire were something of a comfort.

The kitchen was a largish room, stone-floored and high-ceilinged. Several iron rods ornamented the hearth, perfect for hanging pots and pans, had they any. On the other side of the room, a shelf, presumably intended for more kitchenware, was piled with a haphazard assortment of books. A hulking wooden table stood in the center of the space, scarred with burns and gouges, accompanied by two long bench seats. The armchairs by the hearth were perhaps newer than the rest of the items in the house, but not by much. They were mismatched, one striped, the other solid, each festooned with what had to have been the world's least necessary antimacassar. A basket of blankets waited by Poppy's chair, moth-eaten and dingy from ash.

"Don't move," Roisin intoned. "I'll be right back." She bolted out the

18

door. When she returned, it was with a wet cloth in her hands.

"Where's water?" Poppy asked.

"Don't try to talk just now."

"It was a-a question. That's wet." She pointed at the rag, now dripping onto the flags. "Where's water?"

"Oh! A well. Just round the other side. May I . . ." She gestured at Poppy's body, a gory wreck of blood and turned earth.

Poppy's mouth was sticky and buzzing numb. "Please."

Gently, almost reverently, she washed the blood off of Poppy's soft body. Poppy watched in helpless silence as Roisin went about her careful ministrations, dragging the rag across Poppy's shivering skin. When she was done, she wrapped Poppy in a blanket from the basket—more for decency than comfort, Poppy imagined, as temperature no longer bothered her. She nearly laughed—how many London nights had she spent trembling against the icy sleet? Now she was as immune to a winter's night as a statue.

"Feeling better?" Roisin asked.

"A b-bit. What *was* that?"

Roisin took the chair on the other side of the flickering hearth. The fire lit her face, casting shadows against all of those stark angles.

"A frenzy, I'm afraid. I should have known."

"You . . ." Her mouth was numb, her words clumsy.

"Don't try to talk. It's all right. You're very young, and your thirst for blood is very strong."

"I'm t-twenty."

A tight nod of acknowledgment. "So you are. But as a vampire, you're a newborn. The best way to keep your wits is to drink carefully. Otherwise, you'll go a bit, erm, feral, I'm afraid."

She *had* been feral. It was terrifying in her recollection, how she had so carelessly discarded her humanity. And yet, it had been transcendent. She had relinquished her so-called *wits* in favor of something more pure, more essential. This must have been how Adam and Eve lived before the curse of the apple, without shame or language or waistcoats or any of the myriad tidy things people used to reassure one another they were anything other than beasts.

Roisin was eying her knowingly. "You enjoyed it, didn't you?"

She shrugged, too spent to bother with whether she ought to be ashamed.

"It's understandable, you know. I've liked it too, in my way." This appeared difficult to admit, delivered though the tight anus of a pursed mouth. "Though, you're more of an earthly pleasures-type person than I am. I'm not surprised it took you so quickly. *Oh.*" She pulled absently at her queue. "This is all my fault. I meant to drain a rabbit for you last night, but you startled me and I got distracted. I'm so *sorry*, Poppy."

"No. I . . . you . . ." She lifted her hand. *Wait.* Roisin nodded, her nervous fingers pulling at her trousers. "You've been taking care of me."

"Yes."

"How long?"

Roisin blinked. "How long . . .?"

"I was . . ." She swallowed, her lips buzzing. "When I transformed. I was bit. I was in pain. And then you came. You took care of me."

Roisin's eyes darted nervously away, like she was looking for an open window to escape through. "You remember that?"

"How long?"

"I—well. Three days."

"Three *days?*" Poppy began to laugh, the sound not entirely human and completely beyond her control. "You nursed me for *three days?*"

"Well, yes. What's the matter?"

"You—you—you kept your traveling clothes on!"

Roisin had the audacity to look affronted. "You needed help! Was I meant to leave you?"

"You're a vampire! You move quickly!"

"You were in pain!" Roisin had her arms crossed tightly over her chest. "Oh, I'm *terribly* sorry for prioritizing you in your time of need! I ought to have just left you to writhe around in agony alone, is that it?"

"For the time it took to put on some buckskins?"

"You could have . . ." Roisin cribbed an answer from a dust mote. "Choked on blood."

"Is that something that happens?"

"It could be." She puffed up her shoulders, a little proud, a little dented. Then she slumped. "It isn't. But you looked so pathetic, I couldn't bear to leave you for longer than it took to fetch you some blood."

A gasp of laughter caught in her throat. "*Pathetic!*"

"Writhing around, legs up in the air, shrieking your throat to ribbons." She sniffed. "Very undignified."

"My sincerest apologies." A log cracked in the fire, a sound so intimately of home it could have pulled her anywhere—back to her parents' cottage, a frequently used bed at Minna's, her favorite chair at the pub. It left her at Covenly instead, warm and comfortable in the big kitchen. "Thank you for your care."

"No, no."

"Yes." If she had truly been as Roisin said, convulsing and unresponsive for days, then Roisin's caretaking was no small thing. "I appreciate your help."

Roisin made a strangled noise. "There is no need to thank me."

"Roisin?"

"Hm?"

"How did you know to find me?"

"Oh. Well. This is where Cane would have . . . It's the only place she would have gone."

"How did you know she had me?"

"I—" She folded her hands in her lap, pressing them between her thighs. "It's a very complicated . . . It's quite a long story."

"Are you her friend?"

"Certainly not!"

"So you're not, erm." She searched for the right words. "You're not here to clean up her mess?"

Roisin frowned, a little line appearing between her stark eyebrows. "You'd be the mess then?"

Poppy gestured to herself, cleaned of blood and wrapped in a blanket. She was certain there were leaves and twigs in her hair. "What else?"

"If I am doing that," Roisin began slowly, "if you *are* a mess, as you say, I'm not cleaning you up for her sake."

"For whose sake, then?"

"Well, yours."

"Mine?"

"Who else?"

"Why?"

"Because you need care," Roisin said, pressed, curling down into her chair.

"You don't know me."

"I don't."

"And yet."

Roisin's eyes flicked longingly to the open door. "You need it."

"Yes, but don't you have anywhere else you're supposed to be? Anyone who expects you?"

Her face drained entirely of expression. "That's not important."

"I'm sorry," Poppy said quickly. "I didn't meant to offend."

Her jaw shifted. "You didn't offend."

"Truly? You seem so—"

"It's my fault." The words were quiet. Small. "She brought you here. She bit you. But it was my actions that caused her to do so. You are my responsibility."

From what little Poppy remembered of Cane, and from what she was beginning to surmise about Roisin, this seemed rather unlikely. "Did you ask her to bring me here?"

"I . . . No."

"Did you tell her to bite me?"

"Of course I didn't!"

"Then I don't see how any of this could possibly be your influence." Poppy drew her legs up underneath her seat. "Are you the sort that claims guilt for all the world's ills?"

Roisin coughed out a rueful sound that might have been a laugh. "Oh, certainly. But not in this case."

"A bit self-aggrandizing, wouldn't you agree?"

"How so?"

"You must think you're very important, to have so much influence on the actions of others."

One cheek extended, pushed out by a twist in her mouth. "What a privilege it would be to be so unimportant."

"It isn't a picnic, mate."

"I find it very hard to believe that you would know from experience," Roisin said, and her eyes were so intense Poppy found herself heating up under her blanket.

"*I* find it hard to believe you're responsible for any of this."

"Not if you knew the things I did when I was in her company." Poppy eyed her expectantly. Roisin sighed. "You're desperate to learn how I came to know her, aren't you?"

"I haven't made any demands."

"I can see it in those big, blue eyes. You're like a kitten watching me pour cream in my tea." She shook her head. "I'm afraid you'll be displeased with me, once I've told you."

"I think you can handle my displeasure, if it comes to that."

"I'm not sure that's true." There was a touch of hesitation before the moment she gave in. Poppy could track the acquiescence in the loosening of her shoulders, the gentle wince of surrender. "I was born in Belfast, about fifteen years before the Eleven Years' War."

"Forgive me for not knowing my Irish history."

"Not much to know. Ireland, England, and Scotland fought over which god to serve. And land, of course. And pride, one imagines. You took our means of growing food, and we were hungry. Not *you*, of course. You English." She gave Poppy an absentminded wave. "My parents owned a pub. I was a barmaid."

"Did you wear an apron and little bonnet?"

"Please abstain from being lecherous for one moment." Roisin peered up, her gaze playing at frustration, though it was tinted with gratitude. Everyone came to Poppy for a laugh. "Yes," she allowed magnanimously. "I wore a very fetching bonnet. As I was saying, there was a war on and I worked in a pub. Which meant, of course, that I was constantly surrounded by young men with a fervor for bloodshed and no idea of the grim realities of war. Have you ever seen war, Poppy? No, of course you haven't. What a silly question."

"I could have," Poppy interjected. "Perhaps I fought Napoleon."

"I wasn't aware that little yellow-haired girls took up against Napoleon. More fool I. In any case, working in a pub as I did, we had all sorts coming through. Fighters, you know."

"Let me guess. You fell in love with a handsome soldier?"

Roisin scoffed. "I'm wearing a waistcoat, Poppy. Do use a bit of deductive reasoning. No, I did not fall in love with a handsome soldier. Well, not exactly." She swallowed around the memory. "There was a woman. She had come with the Scots, but once she arrived, she decided to switch sides. For fun. That's all war was to her. Fun." She paused to consider. "I suppose it wasn't too egregious. She wasn't Scottish, after all. She was from nowhere."

"Cane."

"Yes."

Poppy could imagine it. Roisin, young and overworked, serving boorish men, all of them frothy with the thought of wartime glory. And through the rabble, a woman. Tall and beguiling, with a haughty gaze and a knowing smirk that could stop time. Condescending in her bearing, like you had to work to earn her good favor. Like its earning was the greatest accomplishment.

"We left," Roisin said. "She didn't tell me what she was at first. She didn't even turn me for a decade or so. I think she didn't want to scare me off. But I was so eager to leave that pub, I would have jumped even if she had told me the truth right away. I was so young. I would have followed her anywhere." She chuckled darkly. "I did."

"Where?"

Haltingly, then less so, Roisin told her. Together, Roisin and Cane traveled to the coldest northern reaches, bathed in Scandinavia's hot springs and watched the northern lights, huddled together in the snow, immune from the icy chill. They attended Austrian opera, both of them dressed in furs and layers upon layers of skirts, hands secretly clasped through a sable muff. They journeyed through the holy land by horse and then by camel, to the Barbary coast, due west until they hit water. From there, it was Brazil, the Spanish Main, the fledgling American colonies. And then back again—Portugal, France, the Russian Empire. East, farther, climbing the mountains of Tibet and laughing at their own incredible ceaselessness.

"There were vampires everywhere we went," Roisin explained. "We didn't have to look for them; they found us. Some still adhered to the law of the Immortal Council. The slavic *vampyr* had these old customs, so proper and welcoming. The vampires were far younger in America, and particularly concerned that we had not alerted them to our arrival in advance. We had to politely explain that we could not, as we had no idea they existed at all."

"I doubt that was received very well."

"No one died, at least."

"And you just lived for pleasure?" In the dancing flames of the hearth, Poppy saw Cane and Roisin dart from world to world, moving in night's dark embrace.

"There was an expression Cane picked up in Scotland that she enjoyed repeating. 'Be happy while you're living, for you're a long time dead.' That was her credo for a while."

"*Well*." Poppy tried, in that moment, to stem a powerful rush of want. She knew better. This story could not have a happy ending.

"It wasn't all joy, you know," Roisin said, as though she had heard Poppy's thoughts. "There was nothing new under the sun for her—or moon, I suppose. Most trips were repeat visits. And it wasn't as though we could run wild. The locals would make sure, when we hunted, that we were never discovered. It was in their own interest—any commotion would make their lives infinitely harder."

A thought occurred to Poppy, dragging behind it a long train of dread. "You were drinking from humans."

"Yes." Her jaw stiffened, the bones jutting. "Cane had no compunctions regarding that behavior, and, at the time, neither did I. A vampire will be at their strongest when drinking human blood. To drink from an animal, *well*, one can live that way. But one will never be satisfied. Never be at full strength."

"She drank from me while I was still human. It didn't kill me."

"It doesn't have to. A bite here and there won't do anything. Many enjoy it, even."

A memory of blinding pleasure crashed through Poppy's mind. "Mm."

Roisin coughed. "Yes. Well. Drinking from humans is more satisfying than animals."

"What about drinking from other vampires?"

She shook her head. "Just trading your hunger for another's. For most vampires, human blood is the only choice, but its procurement has a cost, as you can imagine. I didn't even know that it was possible to drink from animals until we met a coven of Jewish estries in the Russian Empire. They were having a debate—something about their dietary laws and whether they could follow them as vampires. Jews don't consume blood, but perhaps

25

the blood of an animal they considered 'clean' would be viable under—"

"Did Cane know?"

Roisin pushed a lock of hair behind her ear. "Whether the Jewish god would allow vampires to drink cow blood?"

"You know what I meant."

"She knew. Of course she knew." Resignation flattened her words, turning them toneless and slow. "There were a great many things she didn't tell me. She was of the opinion that, as my sire, she had the right to decide what sort of vampire I ought to be."

"And what sort of vampire is that?"

"Poppy, to understand Cane . . ." She faltered. "What I mean to say is, she's very old. So old, she has no idea when she was born. Or where. She has some guesses but . . . Why should she care about humans when, to her, their lives are so short? What is the difference if a person lives to twenty years or eighty, when she has seen centuries?"

"You've seen centuries."

"A few."

"And yet . . ."

"And yet." She stared into the fire. "Once I learned the truth, it was too difficult to go back. Even though human blood was better in so many ways—the taste, the way drinking it made me feel—the whole business began to bother me. I tried to get Cane to see my side, but, well, it wasn't *done*. A being so ancient would never change to accommodate her sired. She, um . . ."

"Roisin." Roisin didn't shift, her face pinched, her sharp cheekbones protruding. "She did something to you."

She acknowledged this with a sharp jerk of her head.

"You don't have to tell me."

"No, no. You deserve to know." She looked so small in her chair. She was long, but slender. Narrow. A bit of driftwood on a wave, caught up in Cane's wild, impossible life. Poppy could see shades of Roisin at fifteen in her pointy elbows. In her bare feet. They were knobbly, her toes curled under, and they nearly broke Poppy's heart, for the leagues they had walked and the smallness of them.

There was a cost to this telling. Roisin shrank under the weight of it. Poppy's gut churned. "You don't need to tell me—"

Roisin barreled on. "I told her that, if she insisted I feed on humans, I would leave. She disagreed. She made me stay."

She made me stay. There were stories in those few words, Poppy knew. Hours and hours' worth. Days and days'.

Guilt nearly stopped her tongue, but she asked anyway, because the only thing more terrible than the truth was the hole its absence left behind. "How did she make you stay?"

"Did you notice," Roisin said slowly, "when you were with Cane, that you lost bits of time? Or you felt as though you'd been drinking bottles and bottles of wine, but you hadn't had a drop? That you couldn't tell how many days it had been?"

She had. Hours in a carriage, where Cane had commanded her to sleep. Rising when Cane snapped her fingers. Coming to awareness in a different room, a different city. Blinking her eyes open and finding herself in a strange bed with no recollection of slipping into the sheets.

Roisin took Poppy's long silence as assent. "She did that to me. Only it wasn't days. It was years."

"*Years?*"

"To Cane, I was somewhere between companion and property," Roisin explained, detached, as flat as a painted woman. "It was unimaginable that I would do anything other than exactly what she desired. It was impossible that I would leave. I was hers, through and through."

"But you did leave." Poppy swallowed thickly. "Didn't you?"

"I did."

"How?"

Roisin's lips pressed together. "I just did. One day, I . . . I discovered I could."

A careful falsehood, like a gently closed door. Poppy couldn't fault her for it. Roisin had given her so much already, so much of her sadness and peril. Perhaps the lie protected something else, something lighter and smaller and more precious.

"I'm glad for you," Poppy said. "That you got away."

"Thank you." Roisin's voice was faint and throaty. "It's been years now, of course. History. Still, you're very kind."

Kind. That she considered Poppy's care, or even her choice not to pry further, a particular kindness curdled Poppy's stomach. "I'm not, really. It's the minimum to be decent."

"Yes, well. You'd be surprised how rarely that minimum is met."

"I'm a whore in London, mate. I'm aware most people are shits."

"Of course. Erm, there's more, I'm afraid." Her body was tense. Hesitant.

"How you knew to find me here." It felt like she had asked nights ago. Like she had asked a different Roisin.

"After I left . . . The truth is, Cane doesn't take well to losing her possessions. She'll cling to anything she considers hers. She swore when I left that she would have me back, and she prefers to keep her promises."

"Did she bring you here, too?"

"No, no. She doesn't need to bring me anywhere. She doesn't need to pursue me at all." She visibly drew up the words from beneath her tightened mouth. They came out in a rush. "She finds a girl to string along for a few days. She'll make a big show of it, like she's threatening to turn her, or kill her. And, of course, I can't help but follow—just in case, this time, my being there makes the difference. That my intervention prevents Cane ending one more life. But every time it's the same: I'll arrive to a gleeful Cane and a dead girl."

Poppy's skin pebbled. "Me."

"Yes. You."

It was a smaller, pettier explanation than she had expected. She hadn't been turned on account of her own merits—her attractiveness, her charm—but because she was a tantalizing trinket made of flesh and yellow hair. Cane had dangled her over Roisin's nose like a scrap of chicken to a dog, and Roisin had come running.

Poppy had known she was unimportant, but the confirmation was a cold, lonely thing.

"Poppy?"

"Mm?"

"Are you well?"

"Yes. Of course."

Roisin's mouth moved silently, chewing over uncertainty. Poppy thought to reassure her, but found she hadn't the strength.

"Thank you for telling me," she said instead. "All of it. You and Cane—"

28

"No." Roisin closed her eyes. "I-I beg your pardon. There's no need to thank me. Or to, to discuss it any further. Come. It's nearly morning."

They silently padded back to the room they shared. Roisin had made the bed, and they crawled below the counterpane together.

Poppy couldn't conjure blankness. Instead, her mind drew up visions of her tenth summer, the one time her parents had brought her to the sea. She had always been a strong swimmer, floating easily in the lake near her home. Though the ocean was breathtakingly vast, Poppy still cavalierly stepped into the waves, expecting to float. The next thing she knew, her father was holding her in his arms, slapping her back so she belched seawater.

"The ocean is much more powerful then you'll ever be. Be humble in it," her dad had said. "And mind you take care with that body of yours. It belongs to you, and there's none like it."

The sun peeked irrepressibly through the drawn curtains, casting a puddle of encroaching light. Poppy squeezed her eyes shut. It took her a very long time to convince her mind to think of nothing.

Chapter 3

By the time the moon rose the next night, Roisin was up and dressed.

"We've done a great deal of talking," she said with forced good cheer. "Let's run tonight."

The grounds were cool and foggy. Poppy stretched out her fingers in the moonlight, blue-tinged, stroking the darkness like a lover. Roisin held out her hand and they ran and ran, their breath clean and even, gasping in the wildness of the woods around them, the crunch of clover underfoot, stiffened by a late, stubborn frost. It was easy to calm her mind in the whipping wind, to forget that she was a coincidence. That a time existed other than right now, a place other than right here.

They talked after, seated on the two armchairs by the fire, which Roisin had built and lit. The kitchen was the largest room Poppy had yet seen in Covenly, but there was a warmth to it unlike any other place in the house. The walls themselves were welcoming, the heavy drapes grateful for the company. A kitchen was built to last, to weather heat and traffic and unkind treatment. Where the rest of the house showed its age, in here it could have been any time at all.

"How did you come to live in London?" Roisin asked. "Were you born there?" Her eyelashes fluttered, gaze cast down. "Only tell me what you want, Poppy. You don't owe me anything."

"Curious."

"Hm?"

"You told me your entire life story last night, and now you're so careful with mine?"

Roisin let out an indignant little huff. "You're *owed* mine. I altered your life."

"Have I not altered yours?"

"Well, it has been a lovely few days . . ."

"Oh, stuff it. You're looking after me instead of doing whatever else it is you do out there. Is that not a change?"

"Perhaps I spend my entire life looking after newborn vampires." A flat, sliding smile-type thing. "Like a governess."

"Do you?"

"No."

"Maybe you ought to start."

The firelight cast Roisin's face in bronze. Around her was dark, cloaking her, curling over her shoulders. Poppy only knew her like this, swaddled by night. How did she look in the day, when the sun kissed the— oh, Poppy would never know, would she? There was no reason for that to feel so tragic. Only, she had the strange urge to see Roisin in every light, gas and torch and full sun, like a piece of art. Like a painting in search of a wall that best suited its colors.

The pressure behind her eyes surprised her. So silly, because who would cry over something as ridiculous as that? She barely even knew Roisin. They had only lived here briefly, just a handful of days.

And on that note—

"How long will we be here?"

Roisin winced. "I'm not sure you'll enjoy the answer."

"You can stop doing that."

"Doing what?" She leaned back in her chair, the ends of her hair sweeping the antimacassar.

"You assume I'll hate what you have to tell me."

"You very well might."

"And what if I do? Would that be so terrible?"

"I—" Her fingers curled against the armrests. "You ought to be prepared."

"I'm well prepared, mate. I don't expect everything out of your mouth to be good tidings." She weighed her words. "I won't be cross with you."

"You might be."

"And if I were?" Poppy asked. Roisin stared back, blank and taut. "Fine. What would happen if *you* were cross with *me?*"

31

"I'm not."

"Let's pretend."

Her mouth worked. "I've never had a particularly good imagination."

"*Roisin.*"

"Fine, fine." She drew an impatient breath through her nose. "Nothing would happen. Nothing, outside of the anger. I know the point you're trying to make, Poppy, but a habit isn't so neatly left behind."

"Mm." She pursed her lips. "How long will we be here, Roisin?"

"A year."

"*What?*"

"You see?" Roisin curled up, chin on her knees, long toes hanging off the seat. It struck Poppy as an odd position for Roisin, who was such a stiff and straight person. Still, she looked distressingly comfortable with her soft parts guarded, as though it were her natural state to be a snail, deep in its shell, hiding from an intruding finger.

"I knew you would be upset," said the snail.

"I'm not upset." Christ. A *year.* "Thank you for telling me. Now, if it's amenable, could you please explain to me *why* we will be here for an entire year?"

"A new vampire," Roisin mumbled into the material of her trousers, "in the presence of humans will have no choice but to drain them. New vampires are kept out of society for fear that they would cause too large of a ruckus."

"And by ruckus, do you mean mass slaughter?"

Roisin lifted her head to scoff. "I was showing tact. I recommend it. Most new vampires are shielded by their sires, who will in turn provide humans from whom to drink. After a while, a new vampire gains control of her—oh, damn it all—*Poppy*, eventually you'll get a handle on your cravings. For now, we're here."

"And that will take a year?"

"By my estimation. But in truth?" She cocked her head, silently apologetic. "I haven't a clue. I was well enough after eight months. But then, I have always been rather adept at, uh . . ." Her eyes cut down and away. "I'm very capable of restraining myself."

It didn't need to be said: Poppy would not be the same.

"So, more than eight months for me."

"I was thinking, after a six-month, we could slowly reintroduce you. Bring you closer and closer to town. Make our estimations from there." Her face was pinched, braced for a reaction. "Is that acceptable?"

It had to be. What was the use of complaining, when nothing could be changed? She thought of her friends in London, who no doubt worried over where she was. They likely feared the worst. Lizzy was sensitive, which was so impossibly lovely. A London whore, yet still so easily moved by a kind word. And she had lost so much already.

"There are some people who will miss me," Poppy said.

"Friends?"

"Yes."

"And your family?"

"All gone. They were very bright, my parents. My mother especially. She loved to learn. She wanted my life to be remarkable." She gave a watery chuckle. "I can't think of anything more remarkable than this."

"Poppy, you have to know," Roisin said with the weight of an oncoming apology, "it's not all running fast and living forever. We're relegated to the night. We crave human blood. We're not meant to exist."

"Who says?"

"The things we desire . . ."

"I've been told all my life that my desires were monstrous." The fire leapt in the hearth. Poppy found she couldn't take her eyes off it. "But I never bothered a soul with them. Never a soul, save those what wanted to be bothered."

"Poppy . . ."

"We all have desires, Roisin. Who are we hurting?"

"I've hurt . . ." Roisin swallowed. "The sun is rising. Come. Let's enter a trance."

"Convenient."

"Hm?"

Convenient that every time a difficult subject raised its head, the dawn swept Roisin to comfort and safety. But there was fear in those silvery eyes, a carefully built wall that Poppy was slowly disassembling, brick by brick.

She had never been a patient person. She remembered her father scolding her for it when he taught her how to pick her first lock. "Slow and steady, love. I know it's not your way, but give it a chance. Don't want to lose the tension."

She looked at Roisin, legs pressed together like a trussed pigeon, tuppence eyes darting from corner to corner. It appeared there was tension enough already.

"Nothing," she said, receiving a look of visible relief. "Let's go to bed."

Chapter 4

The next night, Poppy told Roisin about her life.

She talked about the pig farm and the stretches of land around it, the rolling green broken up with fences of wood and stone. She talked about her mother and father, who had wanted more for her than to be the wife of Edwin Davies, the dull sheep farmer who proudly handed over posies of wildflowers with the roots still on. She talked about the rector who had secured an education for his daughters and offered Poppy a place beside them. *What's one more?* he had asked, and Poppy's mother's eyes had filled with hopeful tears. And Poppy had tried, she *really* tried, but it was the reading that got her in the end. The schoolmistress—a pretty, stuffy thing, who Poppy couldn't help but tease for the intoxicating attention it earned—had quickly reached her fill of attempting to educate a dullard, and offloaded her dunce back onto the disappointed pig farmers who had begotten her.

Roisin made a strange little noise at this point, but she didn't comment further.

Poppy had left after that. It had been on a clear, crisp morning, her parents sending her off with a tearful embrace and a hamper full of sandwiches. She didn't know what she would do in London, but that was no matter. Perhaps she'd apprentice with a dressmaker. She could sew well enough. Roisin raised an eyebrow at that. "Yes, yes," Poppy allowed. "I was very naïve." But London was London and soon, with her meager funds dwindling to zero, she had found herself whoring.

Luckily, soon after, she discovered she didn't mind whoring. She hadn't had to make her own way for more than two nights before an ample-bosomed madam swept her from her route and deposited her in the bawdy house that would serve as her place of employment and nearest thing to home for the following five years. Minna's wasn't the finest establishment in the area, but it was far from the worst, and the girls were welcoming, uncompetitive, and the worst sort of gossips—Poppy's people down to the ground.

Minna was the only trouble. She had moods that swept in like new weather, and the girls discussed it as such—*She's stormy today, best stay outdoors.* Minna made imagined enemies of each girl in turn; they passed in and out of the abbess's favor in the manner of a quadrille. Poppy would have a bed at Minna's at one moment, and in the next she'd be tossed aside, Minna's plump hands reaching for a new dance partner to shower with compliments and easily undone promises.

When their pockets were full enough, Poppy and Lizzy and a few others would hire a room—sometimes as Minna had turfed them, other times to protect the younger girls who hadn't the dosh for a warm bed, nor the hard-heartedness required to survive being loved one moment and hated the next. So it was no trouble, in the end. Wherever she lay her head, she always had the night to receive her.

She loved the night, the sounds and smells and the way the starless sky felt low enough to touch. It bestowed riches upon her: her friends, and the men who paid well and didn't expect too much, and the bed at Minna's or elsewhere. And when the letter came—passed from hand to hand to hand in search of her—that her parents had been taken by scarlet fever, she had shoulders to cry on and warm meals to eat and time to breathe her soul back into her body before she had to work once more. And that had all been fine until a very tall woman named Cane had asked where she might get a pint.

"You aren't a dullard, you know," Roisin said when Poppy had run out of things to say.

"What?"

"What your schoolmistress said. You alluded to it the other day as well, when we were entering the trance together."

Poppy remembered. "I'm sure I didn't."

"Regardless, it's clear you believe it." Roisin's nostrils flared, and the realization struck Poppy like a hand to the face: Roisin was angry. She was angry on Poppy's behalf for wrongs committed years ago, and Poppy didn't know whether to laugh or to cry.

"I can't read, Roisin." Her nerves bubbled, and she found herself wracked with uncomfortable giggles. "I don't know what other proof you need."

"Hogwash!" Roisin declared, arms stiff at her sides. Poppy snorted. "There are plenty of people who are exceptionally clever and require different types of schooling. You could tell me how a boat is steered until you were blue in the face, but I wouldn't truly understand until I saw the oarsman myself!"

"Fine, fine," Poppy conceded, knowing that the battle was already lost. It was sweet to watch Roisin fret like this. Not that anything would come of it.

And nothing did. For three nights exactly.

Three nights of running under the innumerable stars, Roisin trying valiantly not to laugh when Poppy tripped on a rabbit hole; Roisin, after failing to stifle some escaped snorts, letting out a stream of surprisingly girlish giggles. The two of them waiting together for the first cool tinges of coming morning, side by side in a damp dew that could never bother them, their bodies too marvelous, too powerful, too eternal—to think that measly grass could chill them! They were beyond the earthbound, akin only to the stars.

Most of the time.

"I'd like to see you read, Poppy."

Poppy snorted in surprise over her goblet of blood, sending the warm, sticky liquid into her nasal cavities.

"Bugger, that's unpleasant." She wiped her face, ignoring Roisin's mouth going flat and askew. "You want me to read, eh?"

"Yes."

"We had a dog when I was growing up. A raggedy thing. All the animals bullied him. We called him Canute."

"Naturally."

"Mum was convinced that she could get Canute to say *mama* if she tried hard enough. She would go to him, 'Say *mama*, Canute. Come on, pet. *Ma-ma.*' And he'd make these godawful noises, like a very ill cow. *Mrawmraw!*" She gargled the approximate sound, sending Roisin's lips gliding toward her cheeks. "He never quite got the trick of it, but she never stopped trying."

"I assume," Roisin remarked, dry as toast, "that this Canute tale is meant to be an allegory?"

"How am I supposed to know about allegories, mate? I can't read."

She clicked her tongue. "Fine. Don't read. But tell me, as I'm interested—what, exactly, is the difficulty? Do the letters move around? Do you find yourself jumping all over the page?"

A chill trickled down Poppy's spine. "How did you know? Did I tell you and forget?"

"What? Of all the—no, Poppy. It's because you're not the first person with this particular affliction. Nor are you likely to be the last, more's the pity."

"Affliction?"

"Yes. Or, if that bothers you, we could call it a difference. You are very *different*, Poppy . . . Er, what's your surname?"

"Cavendish. And yours?"

Roisin opened her mouth, then shut it. "I took Cane's. I've forgotten mine."

Poppy knew the sudden urge to storm down to wherever Cane laid her miserable head and tear her limb from limb. The thought occurred to her—at the wrong time, and with ill grace—that it wasn't a terrible thing to take the surname of the person you loved. Wives did it every day. Perhaps the roots of marriage, as suspected, were hopelessly barbaric. That might require some extra thought. Not now, though. Now, the only thing that mattered was wiping that lost, broken look off of Roisin's face.

For the first time, the kitchen seemed too large, Roisin too far away on her armchair.

"You're welcome to my name," Poppy offered, forcing a bawdy grin. "My name, my time, my body. I'll even hunt down a rabbit for you, if you'd like."

Roisin's mouth flattened and shifted in that newly familiar way and that was enough. "I'd settle for your company. But, oh." She hurried over to the shelves, muttering all the while. They were high, even for her; Poppy suspected the ragged-edged bits of wood on the floor had once comprised a ladder. After a moment's consideration, Roisin leapt into the air, rising nearly to the ceiling. She grabbed at a book at the peak of her ascent and held on as she fell, stumbling into a safe landing.

"Incredible," Poppy breathed.

"What is?"

"*What is*. Should I not have found that jump magnificent?"

"Mag—? Oh, well." She ducked her head so Poppy couldn't see what was no doubt a bashful little twist to her pink lips. "You can do it, too. A small benefit of our condition."

"I forget, sometimes. What we are, I mean. And then." She gestured. "We're *remarkable*."

"On our best days, yes." Roisin paused by her armchair, nodded her head in silent decision, and dragged the thing beside Poppy's so that they were side by side.

"That's odd," Poppy observed as Roisin settled down beside her.

"What is?"

"You moving that chair. It's like everything's gone upside-down—you're meant to be on the other side of the hearth. The whole room is suddenly unfamiliar. Yet I turned into a vampire not a fortnight ago and it feels like I've always been that way."

"Is there a point you're meandering toward?"

"A good one, so hush. Do you think I was always meant to be like this?" When Roisin didn't answer, Poppy poked her in the meager meat of her shoulder. "Not, you know, by *fate*. But perhaps predilection? Have I become the ideal Poppy?"

Roisin rested the book on her lap, hands stiff on the cover. "I fear I'm giving you the wrong idea about what we are."

"And what idea is that?"

"That to be like us is somehow . . . desirable."

"Is it not?"

Roisin turned to her. "*Is* it?"

"Listen, mate. All I know is that not two weeks ago I was mortal and now I'm not."

"And is immortality necessarily good?" Roisin asked mildly. "What will happen when everyone you love is gone? When you're alone, and nothing matters any longer because you don't have the prospect of your own mortality to give it weight?"

"Listen, I understand you've got an argument to make, but never in my life have I thought, 'You know what really makes this lemon cake delicious? Knowing that one day I will die.'"

Roisin's expression conveyed the fond sort of irritation that felt like an achievement. "Do you know what I think?" she asked, the silver in her eyes glinting like pebbles on a river bank.

"Hardly ever."

"I think that if anyone can enjoy this life, it's you."

The sentiment was sweet, but its implication was gut-twistingly clear. Roisin still hadn't revealed what she did in her day-to-day, what sort of life she had abandoned to care for Poppy. Every day, Poppy's suspicion grew that Roisin spent much of her time alone.

"Go ahead." Poppy tapped at the book cover, because this was all too much, and she was dangerously close to weeping. She always wept too easily, too freely. It was a real pity that becoming a nocturnal, blood-drinking horror hadn't taken care of that. "Show me what you've brought me."

"Oh." Roisin snapped to alertness. "Here you are."

"Cor." Poppy received the book with the tips of her pointer finger and thumb as though it were covered in suspicious goo. "My mate Lizzy read this to me last summer. I couldn't wee by myself for weeks."

"My mistake. Should I get you something more palatable?"

"Haven't got *Gulliver's Travels* or summat? Ooh, *Fanny Hill*?"

Roisin arched an eyebrow. "You mean the banned *Fanny Hill*?"

"Oh, don't look at me like that. It's easy enough to find if you know where to look. I'd be shocked if Cane didn't keep a copy nearby."

Roisin's face drooped. "Perhaps there is one in the larder," she said, mild as milk, like that dreadful woman's name hadn't brought up her hackles. "Shall I look?"

"No!" Poppy quickly flipped open *The Monk*, willing herself not to burst into tears for the fucking tragedy of Roisin's long life. "I will read this terrifying book!"

"Poppy . . ."

"No, no. Really. It's all very well. Let's see . . . oh, bugger." Predictably, the letters danced around in their maddening jig. "S-scarcely had the abbey bell tolled for five mi—, uh, minutes and already was the ch-church of the cap, um, cap—buggering *fuck.*" She slapped the book against her thighs. "It's no use. I am a confirmed dullard. Thank you for trying."

"I didn't try anything."

"Well, perhaps you assumed that my vampiric abilities would extend to reading. Never gets cold, doesn't require sleep, thirsts for blood, has a newfound love of Gothic literature?"

Roisin snorted in a decent facsimile of irritation; Poppy knew better.

"You're impossible. Give me the book."

She futilely held it out of Roisin's reach—the woman had nine inches on her at least. "Why? What do you plan to do with my monk?"

"Nothing he hasn't already done to himself." She plucked the book from Poppy's darting grip and flipped it open. Then, with a cheeky grin, she tore out the flyleaf.

Poppy shrieked. "My monk!"

"Oh, hush. He's already in hell. Now look." Roisin held the paper up to the first printed page, hiding everything but the first line. "Are the letters dancing now?"

The answer was yes, a bit, but there was far less dance floor upon which to jig, far fewer dancers with whom to mingle. "Goodness."

Roisin appeared inordinately pleased, yet—charming to the point of *devastation,* she was—a little shy. "It won't fix everything, of course. You might want to tear a second sheet so that when you move down the page, you can see one line at a time. Everything gets better with practice, and you'll perhaps never be as fluent a reader as those with the natural facility. But it's a start."

A start.

It had recently occurred to Poppy that she didn't need to breathe anymore. She had noticed, as she was running without fatigue, that sucking in and expelling air did nothing to enhance or detract from the experience. Closing her mouth and making a concerted effort not to inhale through her nose was, admittedly, a bit uncomfortable, but certainly not stifling, nor painful. In fact, it seemed to Poppy that, if she had the desire, she could choose not to take another breath for the rest of her not-quite-life.

She breathed now. A big, hiccupping gulp of air to pair with the stinging in her eyes, the dryness in her throat.

"Oh, fuck," she said wetly. "Shit."

41

Roisin had heard Poppy say she was a dullard, but she had listened and uncovered something else entirely. And all this, after losing years to a woman's cruelty. This kindness, from a person who flinched from Poppy's anger, from even the threat of it.

It was mundane. It was magical. In twenty years of life, Poppy had never wanted to kiss someone more.

There was no sense to it, were one to take things at a distance. Roisin's clothes were plain, her visage stern and unlovely. Her colors, dark hair and gray eyes, were in the realm of dirt and dishwater. Her skin, like her shirt and buckskins, looked as though the vibrance had been drained through years of washing. Her body was composed of lines and angles, no smoothness, no elegance.

And yet this creature made of bones and care and tragedy was the most beautiful person Poppy had ever seen.

Were she in London, she would close those few inches and lay her lips on that unsmiling mouth. Feel it shift and settle. Catch the breath that followed, swallow the surprise like sweet marzipan. Lick the taste from her teeth. Poppy couldn't read a book, but the body had always been so very legible. She knew when to open wide, to lie back and let herself be ravished. She knew when a slack, wanting mouth required a firmer hand. She could have Roisin, and give her everything she wanted in return.

But something stopped her. Something that felt very much like fear.

When Poppy was very young, her mother had tried to tutor out her clumsiness by handing her freshly lain eggs and sending her off to place them in a basket by where the primrose bloomed. She tried, hands trembling, to bear her treasure over the uneven earth and through the pasture gates without tumbling to the ground. Her small, plump body would shake with the effort, her palms sweating, her elbows pointed to the sides so no bird nor beast might impede her way.

She fell every time. A molehill caught her toe. A goat hit the back of her knee. She had a song in her head and she was too busy marking its melody to see the gate in front of her. One day, she got nearly to the primroses when she tripped on nothing at all, just her own too-small feet shuffling under her round little body, conspiring in egg sabotage.

Poppy's mother had rushed up to wipe the tears from her face and the egg from her pinafore.

"Oh, love," she had said, pushing Poppy's yellow hair from her hot forehead. "We're not all suited to handle fragile things."

Roisin was staring at her. She might have been talking.

"Poppy? Are you well?"

Oh, how kindly she asked, as if they both didn't know neither of them could ever fall ill.

"Very well. Thank you."

Roisin's gaze skittered like a nervous mouse revealed under a lifted cooking pot. "Of course. It was the least I . . ." A smile, small and dear, spread across her face. "You are very welcome."

On this night, Poppy, the coward, was the one to clutch at convenience and name the rising sun.

Chapter 5

The next night, Roisin was waiting in the kitchen with a goblet of blood, a length of ribbon, and a ruler.

"I think we ought to get you some clothes," Roisin said by way of explanation. "Since we'll be here for a while."

"Why?" Poppy plunked down at the table and began to drink. The bench seat was higher than she was accustomed to, and only her toes touched the floor. She swung them like she had as a little girl, on the days her mother had sat her in the kitchen to chop the greens from carrots and slice the roots into coins. "Not that I'm complaining, but I don't see why I need anything other than a few chemises. Either vampires have no sense of smell, or I've stopped sweating entirely."

"You've *mostly* stopped sweating. And you will need to reenter society eventually. We can't have you entirely unfamiliar with how women are meant to dress, can we?"

Poppy ran a sardonic gaze from Roisin's buckskins to her shirtsleeves. "Women, you say?"

"I'll have you know I dress in a very convincingly feminine fashion, when required."

"Sure, mate. Let's see that bonnet from your pub days then."

"I told you that bonnet was fetching. Now up, please."

Poppy obliged, holding her arms out like a scarecrow. Roisin was efficient in her ministrations, though Poppy was gratified to see her hands slip as she measured Poppy's waist and bust.

"There we are." Roisin marked some numbers on a blank page inside a beat-up volume of *Tom Jones*. "I'll run to the village at sun up. I should be back before nightfall."

"Sun up? Won't you—what happens to us in the sun? Melt like candle wax?"

Roisin winced. "It's a bit grimmer than that, I'm afraid."

"Grimmer than *melting?*"

"More like paper catching fire." She twisted her fingers in the air, like a growing flame. "*Whoosh.*"

Poppy felt ill. "And you're going *out* in it?"

"Don't be concerned. I dress for the weather."

And so she did. As morning neared, Poppy helped Roisin into a long, dark muslin dress with sleeves that went down to her wrists. She wore gloves, a bonnet ("Fetching," Poppy pronounced), and a scarf so wide it covered nearly her entire face. She carried an unfashionably large parasol; when she opened it, dust rained down. Everything was the color of the filthiest mop water—a dark, unpleasant gray, nearing black.

"You're running in *this?*"

The covered thing underneath all of the fabric might have shrugged. "I've had practice."

Poppy waved Roisin into the waxing light, watching the figure get smaller and smaller in the distance. Roisin ran lightly, her feet barely caressing the clover, her skirt whipping out behind her. The sun was an oppressive wax ball overhead, unforgiving to the shaggy grounds, casting light on the flaws gracious nighttime wove into its gentle music. In the yellowy morning, Poppy could see their home for what it wasn't: untrimmed hedges, untended flowerbeds, leaves that ought to have been swept away and turned into mulch. It was like catching Minna without her paint on and pitying the old woman for the shame her bare, painfully human face caused her. Poppy closed the door on the daytime as a mercy to the meadow, the lady of the house.

A feeling of safety overtook her at the sight of the closed door. After their time in the quiet, nighttime solitude of Covenly, the outside world was a den of asps. Aside from sunlight, there were roughs and carts and *temptations*, anything that might carry Roisin off or barrel her down or sweep her away.

The stiff ones always come back, Poppy reminded herself. Roisin would. Roisin *would*.

"She'll be back, she'll be back," Poppy muttered, lying in bed, attempting to clear her mind. Her mind, perpetually stubborn, refused to cooperate. Each time she closed her eyes, she was barraged with images of Roisin's shrinking figure, a dark splotch on a vivid bright canvas. And when she turned her mind elsewhere (she selected a remembered cake, slowly rotating, daintily covered in cherries and lines of icing), Cane forced her way in, storming up to the door of Covenly and ripping it off its hinges, demanding what was rightfully hers.

Poppy grumbled, opening her eyes to stare at the burgundy canopy. That heavy damask was her daily trancing companion, the last thing she saw before Roisin's sonorous voice lulled her into rest. It was too quiet.

"Bugger."

Roisin had said she was only going to the village, and that she would come back. Of course she would come back. But what if she craved the safety of her long, lonely existence? What if Poppy had demanded too much from her already?

What if she burst into flames like a crumpled ball of paper?

Poppy tossed off the covers, resigning herself to a restless day. Perhaps she could do a bit to improve the state of the house. They would be staying for a year, after all. It was the least she could do to make the place habitable.

She stomped off into the hallway. The flowers that had greeted her after her second birth were now wilted. She considered going into the grounds to pick some fresh replacements—she had spotted a particularly lusty crop of thrift on a previous night's run—before remembering her flammability. Ah, well. Her time would be better spent ridding the place of cobwebs.

Two hours later she was gray with dust, but feeling somewhat accomplished. She had taken care of all spiderwebs between her room and the kitchen but one: a lovely maze of a web, in which a fat, black spider languorously dined on her mummified prey. Poppy had too much respect for the beast to displace her. Besides, any place that housed vampires had to have at least one resident spider. To have none at all seemed like a dreadful omission.

She found a mostly clean rag and began to dust the portraits, straightening them as she went. They dated back to the fifteenth century, featuring pallid women in every manner of historical dress. Some women appeared in several of the paintings, hundreds of years apart. As the dates grew more current, the paintings were further spread out, like someone had taken a selection off of the wall and refused to cover the gaps. Roisin was entirely missing from the gallery, but Cane featured heavily, always heavy lidded and slyly smiling, even if the style called for a more placid expression. It took a great deal of self-control not to search the house for a knife and carve that painted smirk into ribbons.

Poppy glanced down the hall at the many shut doors. They put her in mind of "The Seven Wives of Bluebeard," a story she vehemently loathed. Why marry a man with secret doors and a history of disappearing wives? Men were tedious enough without grisly lore. Still, the story made her hesitate—only until she remembered that this home belonged to every one of her line, right down to Poppy herself. It was as much her own as it was Roisin's. If Poppy were to find a closet stuffed with murdered wives, they'd be her property by rights.

With this infallible argument in mind, she opened doors. The mulch-caked library was much the same, as were the unfortunate bedrooms and the devil's own commode. She managed to find a serviceable study, as well as a music room featuring an ornately decorated clavichord that desperately required tuning but was otherwise in working order. She made a note to return to those rooms after nightfall to open the windows and let out the stuffiness. Some fresh air would do them an absolute world of good. Not that she minded spending her time with Roisin in the kitchen, sitting together in their chairs by the hearth, bathed in the dancing orange glow—

Perhaps she would take her time with these rooms. No reason to rush.

She opened door after door, relieved to find nothing more interesting than an unnecessarily ornamented medieval solar. Of course, the last door she tried, the one hidden in shadow at the end of the hall, was locked.

Poppy knew of Pandora, of Psyche, of Bluebeard's wife—all women punished for their fatal curiosity. But this was her house and she was Poppy Cavendish. No door nor morality tale could stop her. After all, she couldn't read.

She jimmied the lock with a set of pins she found in a mouldering ladies' chamber and it gave, the door sliding open on silent hinges. This room was smaller than the rest, likely originally intended for servants or storage or, she supposed, servants' storage. There wasn't much inside, nothing but a comfortable chair and a set of paintings lined up against the wall.

Poppy knew what she would see before she looked. Still, she looked.

Roisin's face stared at her from every canvas. In the earliest, she was dressed in a lavender brocade gown, her waist nipped in whalebone stays, her hair ringleted. The painter had taken liberties with her features, softening the sharpness of her cheekbones and nose, but she still looked lovely. Untouchable and ancient, with a spark of mirth in her silvery eyes. Poppy reached out to touch before remembering herself. She scoffed, touching anyway, tracing the baby-soft cheeks of a woman she knew to be far, far sharper.

The next painting was of a salon. Only women were featured, some seated at desks, others pouring suspiciously dark red wine or chatting, their faces pressed close. Roisin was done in the style of a youth, wearing a long, frilled vest and billowing culottes. A man's wig sat atop her head, curls cascading down her back. Her fingers were rendered in exquisite detail, every bone correct as she passed a large feather quill to a smirking Cane.

Evidently, dressing as a man in paintings was a regular occurrence for Roisin, especially those she shared with Cane. She wore justaucorps and breeches, shirts with jabots, tricorns and cuffs, and even a massive Louis XIV wig that drew a reluctant giggle from Poppy. And beside her, powdered and feathered and smug, was Cane, always with a proprietary hand on Roisin's shoulder.

The last painting was the largest. In it, Roisin was styled as a centaur. Her chest was wide and without breasts, but it was undoubtedly her—it was the most accurate depiction of her face thus far, her jaw strong and cheekbones sharp. Her eyes were cast down and dazed, her mouth open in a sorrowful moue. She clutched a bow and arrow to her side. Beside her stood Cane, wreathed in laurels and holding a large, ceremonial halberd. She didn't smirk in this painting; her face was fearsome. Scolding. Her hand tangled in Roisin's hair and pulled. Roisin cowered.

"Pallas and the Centaur."

Poppy started. Roisin stood against the door frame. She still wore her long frock, but she had discarded the bonnet, gloves, shoes, and parasol. Freed from the canvas, she was painfully beautiful. There was no way a painter could capture the cleverness in those canny eyes, the charming hesitance in her gait. The length of her, tall and slender and careful.

"I'm sorry," Poppy said, hurrying toward the door. "I didn't mean—"

"You didn't do anything wrong." Roisin blocked her path with a hand. "I didn't realize these were here. I thought she had destroyed them." She stepped into the room, studying each painting in turn. She smiled at one, let out a quiet pulse of laughter. Poppy watched her look, feeling her silent heart in her throat.

Roisin stood before the final painting. "Do you recognize this?'

"Should I?"

"It's based on a Botticelli. A relatively famous painting. In the original, the centaur has a beard."

"Is there a myth?"

"Sort of." She tilted her head, gazing at the image, dispassionate and investigative. "It's more symbolic. Cane is Athena, goddess of wisdom. Centaurs are meant to be wanton. They represent wild, untamed passion."

"She's—*oh.*"

"It's not very subtle."

"Was this during . . ."

"Yes." Roisin touched the frame with a finger. It came away clean. "This was after I told Cane I wanted to stop feeding on people. This was her way of refusing."

Poppy couldn't help the sound she made. "*Roisin.*"

"It's all right, Poppy."

It absolutely was *not.* Poppy felt helpless against the magnitude of how not right it was. It was decades and decades of completely fucked, done meticulously in oils.

She crossed the room and reached for Roisin's hand. Roisin took it, fingers weaving between Poppy's. Together, they looked at the painting, Poppy's head falling to Roisin's shoulder.

"The chest looks good," Poppy observed after a few silent minutes.

"Mm. I liked looking like a man in paintings. We had talked about doing me as Dionysus, with a, um . . ." She gestured downward.

"A cock?"

"Yes." She rocked on her heels. "That. But after our fight, she decided we would do this instead."

49

"She wanted to keep you." Poppy felt her hand tightening on Roisin's but she couldn't stop it. "That's not love. That's cruelty."

"Poppy—"

"The paintings in here weren't dusty. The hinge has been oiled. She's been in here. She comes in here."

"It appears she does."

"Will she come back for you?" Fear crept up her belly. She knew a blinding, sudden urge to fell a tree, chop it into planks, and board up every door and window. She might have seen a dinged smallsword in the corner of one of the decrepit bedchambers. How hard could it be to learn, really? "I need to know. We need to be prepared."

"She won't come back here."

"You sound awfully convinced for a centaur being held by the hair."

"She won't, Poppy." Roisin drew a ragged breath. "I'll tell you, I just . . . I prepared a drink for you and made us a fire. Let's leave this place alone. Can I . . ." She laughed out a tearful bubble. "Can I call it haunted when I'm every ghost?"

Chapter 6

They adjourned to the kitchen, taking their usual seats beside the hearth. Roisin had already returned her armchair to its former home, on the other side of the fire. It felt unspeakably silly to miss the few hours the chairs had sat side by side.

There were far worse things to be than a silly girl.

Roisin handed Poppy a goblet of hare's blood. "You know, I had thought that room was locked."

"Would you like me to lie?"

"I suppose not." Her eyes glimmered in the firelight. "Is there no limit to what you can do?"

"Jimmying locks isn't anything special. All you need are a set of pins and a lack of respect for personal property."

That earned her a small smile-adjacent twitch.

"How was town?"

"Fair. I got you a few things. I'll pick them up in a week's time."

"Anything pink?"

Roisin pursed her lips. "Is that what you like?"

"Does that surprise you?"

"No, only . . ." She fidgeted. "We need to look discreet. It's best if we're not noticeable. You in pink . . ."

"Noticeable?"

"You'd turn every head."

"Flatterer. And don't lecture me on discretion. I seem to recall you leaving the house dressed as that fairytale woman. The one who likes to eat lentils from the ashes."

"She doesn't—never mind. The black doesn't reflect the sun. More protection."

"Black is a generous name for whatever that color is. You look like a spider, petal."

"I never minded spiders myself. They eat the midges. Oh, and—" She hurried away to the long table, returning with a new pen, an inkwell, a thick stack of paper, and a collection of envelopes jumbled precariously in her hands. She glanced down at them, fetched around for a nonexistent tabletop, then blinked. "Well, I ought to put these back."

"You do know I can't write," Poppy called after her.

"Yes, I know." Empty-handed once more, she plopped down in her armchair, legs curled around her, bare feet poking from the bottom of her frock. "I thought you might dictate to me. Perhaps send Lizzy a letter."

"Did I tell you about Lizzy?"

Roisin ducked her head, gaze popping this way and that. "A bit."

Only in passing. Only a mention or two. But Roisin had listened and remembered.

Under her skirt, Roisin's toes peeped like turnips ready to be pulled from the earth. Ten of them, long and slender and fair. Were Poppy an armorer, she would make tiny shields for them, molded from iron. And for her fingers, too, and for her long middle and her knobbly knees, and her whole face, a long helm to shield her cheekbones and pointed chin.

There were holes in the windows where the wind got in. More sashes were broken than not. The door had a latch lock screwed into the soft, warped wood. It wouldn't survive a good kick.

"—steel nibs are very interesting," Roisin was saying. "The last time I visited a stationer's shop, I was buying quills."

"Should we expect Cane to come here?"

Her jaw clenched. "Poppy."

"Why haven't we prepared? We've been talking and running and . . ." Looking at one another. Reading. Trancing side by side. All while a dangerous immortal woman plotted how to reclaim her greatest prize.

"We're safe for now."

"You don't know that. You *can't*." Her voice cracked. She thought the room filled with paintings, clean and comfortable and well used. Of ten minuscule shields clacking on the floor. "There must be something we can do."

"It's all right. Don't fret. I—"With what looked like great consideration, Roisin stood and lifted her arms. It took Poppy a long moment to realize that this combination of shy, averted eyes and stiff hands was an invitation to a hug. The woman looked like she had never extended such an invitation, like she didn't know how two people fit together this way. Like she had seen it in a painting once, many years ago. She wasn't human anymore—neither of them were, when one really looked at the facts—but Roisin's humanity was a further away thing, not buried deep by a cursed bite, but by utter and complete isolation.

It twisted Poppy's heart into a terrible knot. Her body moved before her mind could catch up, sprinting, unable to stop, dropping the goblet to the flags with a terrible clatter she barely heard. She crashed against Roisin, who let out a bleat of surprise, followed by a warm, put-upon chuckle. Her body was stiff, but slowly—so maddeningly slowly—she relaxed. Poppy let herself rest on Roisin's small chest, welcomed those long arms as they wrapped around her neck and held. And perhaps they were human after all, because this act felt as it always had, except a touch more solemn, a bit of weight upon Poppy's back to make it good.

After a moment, Roisin tensed up again. She gave Poppy a few careful pats, her feet dancing in centimeters toward a backward step. Reluctantly Poppy let her go. She peered up to spy the pinched face of a woman completely out of her depth.

The hug had been for Poppy of course. Roisin, mistreated by Cane for so long, wouldn't be drawn to another person for comfort in such a way. For Poppy to go back to her own seat would be a kindness.

"Thank you," Poppy said, and did the kind, horrible thing, with the ghost of Roisin's body rumbling against her skin.

Roisin sat on her heels and drew in a long breath. "I tried to kill Cane."

Poppy drew back so quickly she almost toppled off her own chair. "You *what?*"

"This. *You.* Taking you was beyond what I could stomach. I had thought about ending her life before, but I didn't have the strength. Every time I saw her with another dead woman, I would see two paths: rejoin her and live in misery, or destroy her. I could never do either. So I ran."

Poppy thought of Roisin, terrified and alone, watching Cane lick the blood from her mouth. Cane hovering above the body of another nameless young beauty. Roisin knowing that she had been too late. That she would always be too late.

"But you. When I saw what she had done . . ." Roisin's fingers pressed into her thighs. "When you were changed, I knew I couldn't stand by anymore. If I'm going to carry on living, whether or not this life is good or right or natural, it's my duty to stop her. I *will* stop her."

"Roisin." Poppy's goblet was still on the floor where she had dropped it, surrounded by a corona of blood spatter. "How do you plan to do that?"

"I'll follow her. I'll find her."

"That could take years."

"Yes," she said resignedly. "It likely will."

Oh, no. "You were with her for so long. Do you really want to spend more years making her the center of your world?"

"It's different."

It wasn't. What it was, was a fucking tragedy. "You've a while yet. Not until I'm ready to be near people, yeah? Not until I'm safe."

"Of course not. I would never want to harm you." And, god, she meant it. Feeling dripped from every word. Her eyes shone lambent in the firelight, little nimbuses of reflected flame transmuting her silver to gold.

"Good. Then we have time." Time to convince Roisin that this path was another stick she might use to beat herself bloody. "Before all that business, let's enjoy our time. You deserve a rest, don't you?"

"Do I?" Roisin murmured, a crooked, doubtful smile poking into her cheek.

"Of course, petal." Poppy bit her lip to keep from crying. When she opened her mouth, she tasted the wet salt of failure. "She's unimportant. She's nothing. It's you, Roisin. You mean the world."

"Poppy—"

"If you protest at all, if you devalue yourself in the slightest, I swear to whatever deities exist I'll make you pay."

"I didn't realize you were a polytheist."

I fancy a centaur. I'd convert for her, Poppy thought.

"If I hadn't been godless before," Poppy said instead, "becoming a blood-drinking creature of the night might do the trick, don't you think?"

Roisin pursed her lips. "You know, I was about to contradict you, but it's true that I've found more heathens than not in my travels. There are some who still find comfort in it."

"And you?"

"Me? Oh, yes, the Catholicism. Well, shall we say, I don't see the need to take communion anymore, hm?"

"Not when you'd rather skip the wine and move straight on to the blood."

Roisin regarded her, mouth tight in thoughtful, uncomfortably knowing consideration. "You make it easy."

"Make what easy?"

"Talking. I haven't made it a habit lately."

Poppy took her in, from her mussed hair to her tucked toes. "Is there somewhere safe we can go where Cane can't find us?"

"No. It isn't worth hiding. If she wanted us dead, we'd be dead. Or, rather, if she weren't afraid I would fight back and harm her, or harm myself in the process. I think the preservation of my life is almost as important to her as her own."

"Not mine."

"Oh, saints, no," Roisin said offhandedly. "She'd kill you in an instant."

"Comforting."

"Well, she's done it before."

"To the other girls she lured you with, you mean?"

"I—no. I don't mean that." She drew her knees up to her chest, folding herself up like clean laundry. "There was . . . there was someone."

Oh. Poppy could nearly taste the grief, free-floating in the air. "Who was she?"

"Just a girl." That wasn't true. No one could ever speak of *just a girl* like that. Like she remade the world. "Clover. We met her at Stonehenge. Cane was fond of the solstice celebrations, and Clover was a sort of new druid. The type that liked to read about the Celts, you know?"

Poppy had never met any such person. "Yes."

"I had been in Cane's thrall for years, just floating behind her, brainless as a cloud. And then I saw Clover, and I . . ." She stilled, then exhaled. "I came back."

Poppy tried to keep the fascination from her voice. "Just like that?"

"Just like that. Cane only planned for us to be there for a fortnight, but I snuck away to see Clover as much as I could. When I was with Cane, I pretended to be as obedient as ever, even though she could no longer access my mind. I thought she didn't notice."

Horror licked at Poppy's spine. "She did."

"She did." Roisin's fingers traveled against her shins, drawing lines and patterns that seemed somehow melancholy. "She wasn't best pleased, as you can imagine. Sh-she—"

"You don't have to." Poppy jerked forward with the urge to comfort, catching herself at the last moment. Roisin's face was turned toward the fire, orange-tinged hair mussed by a day under a bonnet. Poppy's schoolmistress had told her about women burned as witches in the time of James I. She had always imagined them like this: stoic and fearsome in the growing heat.

"I do," Roisin murmured. "I owe this much to you."

"Oh, forget what you owe me. You're in pain."

"Vampires rarely feel pain."

"Liar."

"Still. I can stomach it. If you want to know me, you need to understand . . ." She braced herself, squaring her jaw. "It was solstice night. The fortnight at Stonehenge was ending. I had talked to Clover. We made a plan. I was . . . reluctant. I begged her to let me go alone. I knew that Cane would hunt us. That she was in terrible danger. But she wanted me as much as I wanted her. Even though she knew what I was. Even though I told her I would never turn her. That our time together would be short—"

"You wouldn't turn her?"

Roisin's lower lip disappeared between her teeth. "This life. I wouldn't curse someone I loved to live this way."

Poppy had only been a vampire for a handful of nights, but it was enough to decide that Roisin's opinion was absolute shit. Roisin had traveled the world, met populations of blood-drinkers in the farthest reaches. She had lived to see kings rise and fall, to watch the Earth turn and turn and turn again. It was living, and it was a life far greater than Poppy had ever managed.

She herself had been born in a small village in the shadow of a manor house, cursed to lose her hours in pig shit and silence. Then, she moved to

London. She had assumed she'd live out the rest of her days in that wild city, drinking and dancing and fucking and laughing. Joking with other whores on the top floors of Minna's or in the shabby rented rooms they shared. It would never be a fine life, but it would always be a sensuous one—tastes and smells, sights and sounds, and the touch of a warm hand on a cold evening. London night was filthy and bursting, and she loved every fetid, rich second of it.

And now, she could have it forever.

"You wanted," Poppy said slowly, "to watch Clover age and die."

"I would have." Her chin poked out, jutting stubbornly. "She deserved a full life."

And what did you deserve? "What happened?"

"Cane had gotten her. She made me watch while she killed Clover." She spoke with a horrible dullness, her voice nearly toneless. Her toes curled under her bony feet. "She didn't do it quickly. She told me she would kill whoever took me from her. That my love was as good as a knife in the heart."

Poppy's mouth was dry. Her eyes ached. "She's a monster."

"She's lived for so long. Time has turned her this way, I believe. We all of us have it in ourselves to become monsters."

"No." Poppy wondered if vampires could vomit. "No, Roisin. People aren't that way."

"We aren't people."

I am. I'm a person. She shouldn't be arguing with Roisin over this—Roisin, still in mourning for a beautiful druidess lost to cruelty and time. Crucially, Poppy didn't have a logical leg to stand on; she had only been a vampire for a blink of an eye. How could she know more than Roisin about enduring humanity? But she had seen viciousness and kindness, and known, implicitly, that a kind person didn't have the capacity for Cane's caliber of brutality, even if they had centuries for it to foment. The vilest humans Poppy had encountered hadn't needed centuries to treat her like scum.

"You left Cane," Poppy prompted. "After that."

"I did. But I never took up with anyone, vampire or human. I knew that Cane's threats weren't empty."

"How long . . ."

"Fifty years."

Fifty years of marking time. Poppy couldn't imagine the loneliness. Nor the bravery Roisin showed now, opening her locked chest and letting all her painful, precious stories spill out like so many gold coins. She knew a desperate urge to lay Roisin in that large, shabby bed and pepper her with kisses, make her feel desired. To make certain she knew there was someone else in this world who craved her companionship. Who wanted her time. Who cared whether she lived or died, and that her life was full.

A thought occurred to her. "Cane didn't kill me."

"No."

"But she usually kills the girls she uses to bring you back."

"Yes."

"Why was it different this time?"

"I have a few theories, but mostly . . ." Roisin cringed into her seat. "You look like her."

"Like—" *Oh*. Like Clover, of course. Like the lost, lovely pagan who had reawakened Roisin's mind. Her heart.

It was a common enough occurrence, in Poppy's line of work, to be hired for the same yellow hair as Nancy, who refused, or the same soft stomach as Bess, who died. She far preferred to be wanted as herself, to hear the men sweating above her shout her own name in praise, rather than the name of a fair-haired stranger. Still, when the men who desired Bess or Nancy finished, they paid Poppy what she was owed. Nobody was paying her now.

"Oh," she said. "Oh."

"I feel truly despicable, Poppy," Roisin said wretchedly. "Like a dashed villain. You were turned because of me. Because Cane wanted to inflict pain on *me*."

"Because I look like Clover." Poppy's eyes were wet. She swiped carelessly at her face. "Because you and she both looked at me and you saw your druidess."

"I *don't*." Roisin groaned in vexation. "Is *that* what's bothering you? Not that you were turned into a vampire due to a feud between me and my sire, but that you were only turned because you have the same little nose as Clover?"

"Of course not! I don't like that my life has been irrevocably altered

58

because of Cane's pettiness. But you have to know: I don't blame you."

"You ought to."

"You didn't choose this."

"Neither did you!"

"Yes!" Poppy cried. "I don't see why you feel as though you need to shoulder the blame when neither of us chose to be turned!"

"Damn it, someone has to!" Roisin slammed a closed fist on the stuffed arm of her chair. "Don't you see, Poppy? If I had stayed with Cane, you would be mortal and Clover . . ." She choked. "She would have lived."

"Oh, you poor thing. Oh, petal. You blame yourself for Clover, too? For all of it?"

"If Cane hadn't—"

"If Cane hadn't turned you, none of this would have happened. But she did. I don't see why you have to flagellate yourself constantly, you silly Catholic. It won't punish those who deserve it. It won't balance the scales, Roisin."

Roisin wheezed out the cousin of a laugh. "It sounds so simple when you say it."

"I'm a simple girl."

"You are not." Roisin squeezed her eyes shut. When she opened them, they glistened. "You are remarkable."

A pleasant feeling bubbled up inside her, cutting a sharp line through the sorrow, making her squirm. "Well *I* know that."

"I do see you."

"What?"

She looked abashed but, to her credit, she wasn't scanning the room for an exit. "You may resemble Clover in many ways, but you're nothing like her. She was very trusting, very sweet, very naïve. You, you're—well you're sweet and, blast it all, it seems as though you trust me, though I can't imagine why. But you're so very much *yourself*. A home built of stones. No storm could fell you."

"Oh."

"I'm not done," Roisin added, too loudly and with clumsy force. "You enjoy things in a way I could never imagine. You're absolutely brimming with life, even now, after the change. You fascinate me."

Poppy's breath stuttered in her chest. "Will you take me to bed?"

She couldn't help but ask. It was as if the question had been pulled from her core by a fishing line. Six words that dropped between them like a dying fish, limp and wriggling. Roisin was staring, no warmth left in her face. She looked horrified.

"I-I meant," Poppy spluttered, "the sun is rising. We ought to go trance, oughtn't we? In the, in the bed?"

It would be hours to dawn yet, but Roisin didn't seem to notice this. No, the only thing on that poor woman's face was relief, and Poppy was disgusted in herself at the sight of it. The phantom weight of a cracked egg oozed onto her chest, the yolk dribbling down into her lap.

"Quite right." Roisin gathered herself, grimacing as she did. "Erm, Poppy? Will you help me out of this dress?"

They prepared for bed without bothering to light the candles in their dark bedroom. Poppy cursed her clumsy hands as Roisin presented her back. It was long and barely bowed, her body a single plane. Poppy moved mechanically, her mind carefully fixed on nothing at all. She thought of nothing as she moved each button through its tiny hole. She thought of nothing as Roisin's chemise was exposed. She thought of nothing, and the nothing pressed against her chest.

Her task complete, she shifted into bed, Roisin following after. Long into the day, Poppy's vision swam with terrible imaginings. Roisin weeping over one dead girl, then another. Roisin, wandering for fifty years in loneliness. Even the ancient Jews had only had to brave forty. The woman was due Ten Commandments and a fat golden calf at the very least.

Mostly, she was due rest and care—and uncomplicated friendship, which Poppy had just nearly smashed to slivers. It was clear the woman thirsted for simple companionship. This, Poppy could provide. There wasn't much else on offer. She couldn't kill an ancient vampire. She couldn't wipe years of torturous mesmerism and vicious betrayal from Roisin's history. She couldn't even keep her damned desires at bay. But she could make life a little sweeter for the woman. However long they stayed here, however long it took for Poppy to learn to control her thirst, she would endeavor to give Roisin her due.

She fell into a trance thinking of manna falling from heaven. She had always imagined it looked and tasted like sweet rolls.

Chapter 7

The following week, they sat down at the pockmarked kitchen table to pen a letter to Lizzy. It was a wet night better spent indoors, with rain so fine it could barely be recognized as falling. They sat side by side, Roisin poised primly at the bench seat, Poppy with one leg slung over either side, facing her. The short flame of a stubby candle was all they needed to light their way.

"How shall we begin it?" Roisin dipped the slender pen into ink. "Dearest Lizzy?"

Poppy shrugged. "I suppose."

"Is there something else you would prefer?"

Mostly, they called one another shitty names. *Oi, Ratbag! Lace me up. It's all them fat little fingers are good for.* "'Dearest Lizzy' is fine."

"What next?"

A terribly good question. All Poppy really wanted from this bit of correspondence was to provide comfort to a girl who no doubt expected the worst. If Lizzy were to receive a letter from a friend who she knew could barely write her own name, in formal language, and with no real specifics, it might do more harm than good.

"It's probably a waste," Poppy sighed. "Thank you for fetching the paper. And the ink, and the, you know—" She gestured to the sealing wax. "The bits."

Roisin narrowed her eyes. "The bits."

"Mm hm."

Roisin crossed her hands over the table and fixed Poppy with a gaze so knowingly stern it made her shiver.

"You know, you look just like my schoolmistress when you do your face like that."

"I don't much care for your schoolmistress." Roisin tapped the back of the pen against the table. "Be truthful. What is keeping you from writing this letter?"

"She knows I can't write. She'll think I was kidnapped by one of my men or something similarly gothic."

"Will she go to the police?"

"A missing whore with no evidence?" She let out a coarse laugh. "That's not what the Met is for, mate. They're for bashing in the heads of working men who want the vote."

"I see." Roisin pressed her lips together in thought. "What if you told her the truth about your circumstances?"

Another hard pulse of laughter. "That I'm a vampire in a mouldering estate up somewhere, with a . . ." She swallowed. "A friend."

"That you've run off with someone, and you can't tell her why or when you'll return, but you're safe and well and will endeavor to correspond with her regularly. We don't get post to the house, but perhaps she could send her letters to the posting inn in the village?"

"How am I meant to go to the posting inn?"

"I'll go to the posting inn."

"You would do that?"

Roisin managed, in the act of setting down her pen, to project the weariness of a patience mercilessly tried. "What makes you think I wouldn't?"

"Seems a bit annoying to play postman."

"Poppy, I'm already spending my days making sure you don't tear the first human you meet limb from limb. What's a run to the shops while I'm at it?"

"Kind of you." She pondered the paper. "If there's any chance of her believing it, it's got to sound like it's coming from me."

Roisin took up her pen. "Consider me your secretary."

"Dear Shit-for-Brains."

The pen didn't move. "Hm."

"Mate, if it's from me it's got to be *from me*."

"Yes, all right, all right." She drew herself up, jotting down the words in a painfully fastidious hand. "*Dear Shit-for-Brains.* Go on."

"If you've had a moment to look up from your gamahuching, you might have noticed I've fucked off."

She paused. "I'm not familiar with that word."

"It means sucking a prick."

Roisin's expression went masterfully neutral. "And how do we spell *gamahuching*, do you think?"

"*Roisin.*"

"Yes, yes. I'll get on with it. It oughtn't be terribly difficult to sound out. Feels like it should have a *u* rather than two *o's.* More elegant, don't you think?"

Poppy ignored this. "If I'd known I were going, I'd have told you in advance. But I didn't. Circumstances were well out of my control, Ratface. Don't worry about me. I'm happy." Roisin lifted the pen. "What?"

"You're happy?"

"Yes?"

"You're a vampire now."

"Yes."

"And you didn't choose to be."

"No."

"And you're trapped in a house with only me, for what we are generously estimating to be a year."

"Indeed."

She stilled for a long, blank silence before bringing her pen back down. "Go on."

"I'll keep on sending you letters," Poppy continued, because the less said about that last exchange the better. "Unless you tell me to get fucked. You can send them to the posting inn—"

"I'll handle that. Keep going."

"I hope all is well back in London. I do miss you." Her throat tightened up. She coughed a bit to clear it. "I hope you're staying warm and fed. Tell Josie and Lilly to split my men between them. Josie can get them that want to laugh, and Lilly, them who only bother with me on account of my yellow hair. They'll like her better anyway. I'm sure Maeve had her brat by now. Send news, if you can. Give the wains my love—"

Roisin flinched. "The wains."

"Oh, and I suppose you're the only Irish person to ever exist? I learned it from a Scot. And I think northerners use it, too. Don't be shocked."

"I haven't heard that word . . ." She shook her head. "It's been a while."

Poppy considered her. Her jaw was tight, her fingers wrapped fiercely around the pen's shining body. "Do you go back to Belfast much?"

"Never."

"*Never?*"

"No." Roisin stared at the table. "Never gone back to Ireland at all."

"Truly? Not in . . ." She drew up a figure. "Two hundred years?"

"One hundred and ninety-three you'll find." A thin, hoarse whisper. "One hundred and ninety-three years."

"Why not?" Poppy asked, startled into forgoing gentleness. Roisin looked like hell. Like she needed a softer hand than Poppy could easily provide.

"It . . . that's . . ." She licked her lips. "*Wains.*" The word froze on her tongue and shattered. She sat unnaturally stiff, her back ramrod straight, her hand gripping the pen, knucklebones protruding, skin tight. Her breath was coming high. The guttering candle spat wads of orange light onto her unmoving face. She opened her mouth and closed it again, her tongue darting out like a snake tasting the air.

"Roisin?" Poppy dropped a hand on her shoulder. Roisin was always cold, but she was icy now; under her shirt, her skin had a stood-out-in-the-rain chill, sucking the warmth from the room. Poppy herself hadn't felt cold since the change, but she fancied she did now, an unnatural, insistent cold. It was an unwelcome caress down her flanks, fingers on the inside of her arms. "Roisin, petal. Look at me."

She did, neck jerking, eyes full of frantic confusion. "Wha—"

"You're here with me," Poppy said, slow and calm and careful. Her ears were full of panicked roaring. "We're safe as houses, you and I. You're Roisin and I'm Poppy."

"Poppy," Roisin repeated, stunted, with thick, heavy consonants and vowels that oozed. "Poppy."

"Yes. Yes, dear heart." Oh fuck. Oh *fuck*. "It's Poppy."

"Mo waher."

"Water?" Poppy fetched desperately around before remembering. "I'm so sorry, petal. We can't have water. Shall I find you a hare?"

64

Roisin was silent. Her breathing slowed to the point of near stillness. Poppy's skin jumped. Could she fetch a doctor? But there were no doctors for vampires, were there? And even if a human doctor had been able to do something—even if she could find the village and retrieve him—one smell of rushing blood and Poppy would no doubt tear him into forcemeat. For the first time, Poppy felt the true weight of her isolation. If something happened to Roisin, she was well and truly alone.

Roisin blinked. First once, then rapidly, in a long, uninterrupted string. When she was through, awareness shone once more out of her gray eyes. "Poppy? Did you ask me something?"

"No, I—" Her hand was still clinging to Roisin's shoulder, her fingers tensed to talons. She eased off, sliding her hand down Roisin's arm as they parted. "Are you well?"

"I think so." She rubbed at her mouth. "It appears our mutual friend left me a parting gift."

"*Cane?*"

"I think it's gone now." There was a spatter of ink where she had jammed the pen into the paper, a growing void of wet darkness. Her eyes widened as she noticed. "Oh, bother. Terribly sorry. I'll copy everything on a fresh sheet."

"Roisin."

"My error, my fault," she babbled. "We have plenty of paper. You needn't fret. I'll do it just now." She reached out for the stack, but Poppy stopped her hand, trapping it against the table.

"Roisin," Poppy said, slow and careful, desperately hoping the fear she felt didn't bleed into her voice. "Something happened to you."

Roisin was warmer now, but no less tense. The candle guttered and spat and died, the fire taking its leave as though even it couldn't bear to witness this, its parting ghost a quickly dissipating stream of smoke from the dead socket.

"I know." She stared down at the place Poppy's fingers lay over her own, her voice small enough to fit in the scant few inches between her mouth and the table. She was almost angry, in her restrained sort of way. There was a hiss to her, like a coiled snake. "I know what it was. But I—oh, I really ought to rest." She rose abruptly, mussed paper crinkling in her wake. "I'll be in the music room. Why don't you run for a while? Catch something to eat? That might be a lovely, erm, a lovely . . ." She trailed off, turned, and sped down the hall with the devil on her heels, leaving Poppy alone at the table.

"Roisin!" Poppy called after her, stumbling up and catching her skirt on the seat. She toppled clumsily to the floor. "*Fuck*. Roisin!"

Roisin didn't turn. The sound of an opening door shot down the hall, followed by a booming slam.

Poppy groaned, dragging herself up off the flags. "What the *fuck?*"

The high ceiling, dusty books, and cracked windows provided no answer. She was alone. More than that, she was lonely, and she was fucking frightened. The silence was oppressive here. She had been used to the jovial din of a bawdy house filled with merriment. The tankards clanking at the pub. The guffawing of men spilling out into the street after a free and easy, rolling and cresting, an ocean wave lapping against storefronts and closed doors. Someone beside her she could turn to and say, *oi, what do you suppose that was?* Lizzy's little, dainty snores from under her sleeping mass of orange hair, her tiny freckled nose twitching through her sugary dreams.

There were no such sweet dreams here. Cane had left something lurking in Roisin's mind, a little booby trap sprung by a single word. It was an innocuous word, which Poppy had learned at fifteen, when she and Lizzy, fresh off childhood and aching for guidance, had found themselves at Minna's. Luckily, there was Iona, an older girl who eagerly took the sorry pair into her care, a big sister and mother in one. Iona had called them "wains" for years, up until she left the house to marry a clerk who had been one of her regular amours. In her absence, caring for the inexperienced girls fell to Poppy and Lizzy, and they carried on the naming convention as family tradition.

At Minna's, there had been girls with lives that rivaled Roisin's in misery. They sobbed over their stories, their wet-washing memories soggy and heavy and a trial to wear. Roisin hadn't been that way. She had sat by the fire and easily told Poppy of Belfast, of her first home, her place between the tables of a mean little pub. She spoke of seeing Cane there, following her, leaving. She had admitted to a bonnet. But even the darkest of her stories—the loss of her druidess, the stripping of her free will—were only hampered by a touch of stuttering and a roving gaze. What had Cane stolen from her? Was it the ability to long for home? And had it truly been just one word from Poppy's lips that had brought it all so violently back?

Poppy stepped through the kitchen door and into the wet night, because Roisin had proposed a hunt and she hadn't anything else to do. She cast herself through the veil of rain and bounced off the spongy earth, the brisk night air and lacy drizzle doing wonders for the residual fog in her head. It was easy to find a hare to drain, and she drank from it quickly. She had barely noticed she was thirsty, but now she was dying for a second. After the next one was dispatched, she searched for a third. She found it; a sturdy buck with wide shoulders. She snapped the poor beast's neck before carrying it into the house, letting it dangle from her fingers, its paws kissing the earth.

Roisin always prepared blood for Poppy in a goblet, but Poppy had no idea where such things were stored. After a bit of searching, she spied a small collection of mismatched drinking vessels on a tall shelf, completely out of her reach. Beside them stood an array of well-used books. On the floor beneath was the rotted remembrance of a ladder disassembled by time.

Roisin had jumped for a book. Poppy was going to jump for a cup.

After depositing the hare on the kitchen table, she positioned herself under the shelf. She bent her knees to prepare her way, then pushed with all the strength she had. The motion sent her careening upwards, bashing her head against the high ceiling. She fell even faster than she rose, hitting the ground in a groaning pile of limbs and cotton.

"Bit less force," she muttered to herself, feeling a flush; it was always harder to hide a reddened face directly after feeding. She allowed herself one moment of self-pity, then assumed the position once more. This time, her flight was more of a float, and she easily grabbed her quarry. When she landed, she cheered.

"I'm a fairy. I can *fly*."

Her introduction to her new life, as guided by Roisin, had thus far been focused primarily on the negatives. No food. No contact with the outside world. No meaning to be found in an unending life. It was easy to forget that she was magical, too. A floating bubble, who could grab cups from high shelves.

With her vessel in hand, Poppy returned to the table and considered the hare. The neck was the easiest point of entry, but it was messy. There had to be an art to decanting the thing. She opened her mouth, felt the drop of a fang, and eased her way past the fur and skin, down to the wet and crunch inside. The blood flowed easily into the cup at first, but it quickly slowed to drips.

"I recommend beheading it."

Were Poppy not holding a bleeding dead animal, she might have crossed her arms. "I was going to bring it to you. You've spoiled my plans."

"That's kind." Roisin stood in the doorway, looking tired. Her linen was wrinkled, the buttons at her throat undone. Her hair fell from its queue. "Let me show you."

She approached nonchalantly, plucking the hare and cup from Poppy's unmoving hands without waiting for a response. She then headed off toward a shut door in the corner of the room, of which Poppy hadn't previously taken note. "If you'll open that for me, Poppy. Thank you." It was a closet, with shelves running along the walls. A hook hung from the ceiling, with a small, high table underneath. On the near shelf, a set of four clean, identical goblets awaited their purpose.

"Come here." She sounded like Poppy's dad after a long day of work: tired and short and demanding, but only because there was no energy left to set wrong things right. Poppy scurried to comply. Roisin gently took Poppy's two fingers and brought them to the rabbit's shoulder. "Do you feel that? It's called the Atlas joint. It holds up the head, as Atlas holds the world."

"Yes," Poppy breathed. "I feel it."

"Here we are. Fetch a goblet for me, please, and set it right at the center of the table. And do you see that knife? I'll have that as well." Roisin drove the hook into the hare's feet, leaving it to dangle above the goblet. "The trick is to enter at the Atlas joint—" She plunged the knife in and gave it a clever twist. There was surprisingly little noise. "There we are."

The headless rabbit bled faster, but not terribly so. "How long will it be until the glass is full?"

"Perhaps an hour." She favored Poppy with the apologetic phantom of a long-dead smile. "You've done well. Thank you."

"I didn't do anything."

"You got me a hare. I would consider that a night well spent, wouldn't you?"

"Roisin, earlier—"

"Poppy." She dropped a heavy hand on Poppy's shoulder. Ink stained her fingers. "You don't need to trouble yourself with my problems."

"It isn't any trouble! You're seeing to my education."

"I owe you as much. It's my fault you were turned."

"Oh, this again." She watched the blood drip-drip-drip from the rabbit's gaping neck. "Is my company your penance?"

"Don't be silly."

"Oh, *you* don't." She pulled away and stomped back into the kitchen, knowing she was being brattish. "If you truly feel bad that I'm here and not at home in London, then at least you can provide me with some blasted entertainment."

Roisin leaned on the closet door frame. "My pain is meant to be your entertainment?"

"I didn't mean it like—"

She held up a quelling hand. "Perhaps that was glib. I'll be clearer." She squared her jaw. "I had not known Ireland existed."

"What?"

"I had not known." Her lip curled, nostrils flaring. Her anger rose quickly, a fire suddenly exposed to air. "I could tell you where I was born. I could speak about the pub. But I could not understand that Ireland was a place I could *go.*"

"You told me about it. You said the word."

"It was part of my story. It didn't exist."

"I don't . . . What does that mean?"

"It means," Roisin said, with fists tight at her sides, "it means that she prevented my returning home. Until a moment ago, I didn't know I couldn't hear my mother's voice in my memory. I can hear it now. I can fucking speak Irish again!" She slammed her fist against the wall. The cups rattled. "I have been spending years chasing that woman, trying and failing to prevent her from killing, without knowing that all this time she has denied me a home. So perhaps, Poppy, there is a good reason why I don't want to discuss this with you. Perhaps, after all that has been taken from me, I can afford to have a few things to myself!"

They stared at one another silently from across the room. Roisin's breaths scraped the ceiling, high and bright and bloody.

"I'm so sorry, Roisin." Poppy's heart didn't beat, but perhaps it could break. "I'm so sorry."

"No, no, I'm the one who should be sorry." Her shoulders drooped. She covered her eyes with a hand. "That was unbecoming."

Poppy's eyes ached. Her throat was dry. God, they were pathetic. The pair of them. "May I hold you?"

Roisin's eyes snapped up. "Wha—why?"

"To steal your pocket watch. Because you're feeling poorly and I think it might help."

"You don't need to—"

"Did you not do the same for me the other night?"

"It was what you needed."

"And what do you need?"

"A fucking pint. I haven't had a sip of ale since I was twenty-five and suddenly I'm dying for it. Do you think that was part of Cane's gift?"

"Her curse more like. Come to bed, petal. Let me tend to you."

"But the hare." She gestured listlessly to where the headless beast gave up its ichor.

"Thomas Cromwell will keep. Are you thirsty? No? Then come along."

Roisin acquiesced, doubtless spent from a night of strange surprises, hare beheading, and what Poppy imagined to have been the first healthy burst of rage the woman had managed in half a century. It was probably unfair to take advantage of the dozy cow, but a cuddle wasn't untoward and Roisin plainly needed to be touched. Poppy approached her slowly. Roisin remained slumped against the door frame, her eyes wary. Still, she offered her hand to Poppy when she reached out and allowed herself to be tugged toward the bedroom.

Poppy averted her eyes as Roisin removed her trousers with clumsy hands. She tranced in men's drawers and her linen shirt, Poppy in her chemise, the pair of them in matched white like dingy angels. Poppy settled down in the bed and reached up for Roisin, who stood beside it, arms crossed over her chest.

"Come," Poppy instructed. After a tight, unspeaking moment, Roisin did, slowly, with the bones of a much older person—or perhaps much younger, depending on how one counted.

They lay face to face. Roisin showed no sign of progressing things, so Poppy did the work for them both, bringing her hands to Roisin's shoulders and dragging her in. She was stiff as a plank, her hands folded over her chest like she lay in repose. Poppy took one and pulled it against her back, positioning Roisin so that her head lay atop Poppy's full bosom.

"Men pay a shilling for this privilege," Poppy said, and felt the warmth of Roisin's exhale against her skin. "Consider yourself lucky."

Roisin lifted her head. Her skin was reddened, her eyes wide and earnest. She stared up, brows raised at the center, mouth wet.

"I do."

Poppy squeezed her eyes shut and did her best to hold on.

Chapter 8

On a slow, dreary day, Lizzy could sometimes be prevailed upon to recount the tale of the man with the gray parrot. It was around the size of a pigeon (the parrot, of course—Lizzy could attest that the man was of average and unexceptional size) who went by the moniker Anthus. When Anthus was in company he was entirely silent, his button eyes tracking the movement of conversation as though it were a shuttlecock, pupils dilating and contracting with nauseating speed. The moment the man restrained Anthus behind a closed door, however, he began to perform an array of sounds. He mimicked the dinner bell, a knock at the door, the meow of the street cats, the spaniel's bark. And he spoke, his voice nearly identical to that of the master of the house. In this room, behind this door, he would repeat the words he had heard the master say. *Tea. Chamberpot. Luncheon. Cravat. Lizzy. Oh, good girl. Good Lizzy. Suck my cock, Lizzy. Just like that. You beautiful bugger. You are worth your weight in gold, my sweet. Lizzy! Yes!*

"He were practicing!" Lizzy would cry at the story's climax, through inevitable tears of mirth. "He were practicing in private!"

In the weeks after the rainy night when Roisin remembered Ireland, very little changed. She and Poppy still ran through the grounds together. They read books by the fireside. They talked until dawn, Poppy telling stories and Roisin asking questions, drawing her out. Poppy tried to do the same, to help Roisin open bits of herself, but Roisin always managed to deftly turn the conversation back around, shifting the focus with the skilled hand of someone well experienced in deflection.

The only noticeable change in their comfortable routine occurred in the daytime. In the morning, when they lay together to trance, Roisin would rise after she believed Poppy had drifted off and not return for hours. Poppy did not follow for a fortnight at least. Cane had torn so much from Roisin's life; Roisin deserved to treasure what remained, and treasure it alone. That righteous logic kept Poppy in bed for as long as possible, before hungry curiosity ate away at her binds. Freed, she tiptoed down the hall after Roisin, braced against her clumsiness, feet light on the creaking boards. There was sound coming from the shut music room door. She knew she shouldn't eavesdrop, but she didn't come here with any other sort of plan. What else was she meant to do?

With a hot ball of guilt in her stomach, she pressed her ear against the door. Roisin was speaking. Poppy froze in fear—who was she talking to? Was Cane somehow here? After a few tense moments, Poppy came to the conclusion that it was only Roisin's voice she was hearing. It wasn't a conversation at all, just words and phrases, repeated over and over and over again. The words were throaty and full and unrecognizable, a lilting swarm of vowels and consonants in Roisin's familiar, steady tones.

"*Dia dhuit*," she heard Roisin say, and Poppy's throat clenched with painful recognition. "*Dia dhuit*. Mo waher."

Mo waher. *Máthair*. Mother.

She were practicing in private.

Tears were rolling down Poppy's face for the sorrow of this. For Roisin, in secret and alone, practicing the language Cane had stolen from her. Roisin spoke and hummed and then, softly, she sang a tune that stopped and started, a ragged thread of dissonant notes as she tried to pull the dropped stitch from her memory. Poppy was lost to it, curled up outside the door, knees to chest. She shouldn't have come here. She shouldn't have listened. This was Roisin with no skin on, with a heart that still beat, exposed to draught and chill. Poppy couldn't move. It was as though someone had sewn her chemise to the floorboards, her back to the torn wallpaper. Her breaths shuddered through her body, and she listened, and she bore witness to this reclamation. To Roisin, who sang a song taught to her by the long dead and forgotten. To Roisin, who was not speaking her own tongue for no one to hear, so that if she perished no one would ever know. Poppy would listen and know that Roisin remembered.

The singing stopped, followed by light footsteps. Panicked, Poppy scrambled up and scurried back to the bedroom. She should have fallen down. She should have caught her foot on that hideous taxidermy fox. If there were any justice in the world, Roisin would have found her collided with some decrepit art, sprawled out onto her stomach, her chemise up to her waist, her white, wobbly arse in the air.

There was no justice. Fifteen years earlier, inconsequential eggs had been smashed by the dozen, but now Poppy made it into bed with devil-granted grace. There even was time to settle herself before Roisin joined her, silent as a ghost. Poppy stayed painfully still as Roisin closed her eyes and evened her breathing into the steady, familiar rhythm of a trance. Poppy could not follow. She stared instead at the damask canopy and tried to ignore the wetness of her pillow and the wailing, righteous anger burning in her breast.

Chapter 9

They finished *Frankenstein*.

"Oh, thank Christ," Poppy groaned, turning the final page.

Roisin wore a bemused grin. "Did you not like it?"

"No, no, it was good. Frightening."

"Too frightening?"

"Not that." She stretched her legs out in front of her, kicking away the blanket in the process. "I just fucking despised that Victor."

It was a warm night, summer rolling its languid heat over the grounds. Flowers shed their wanton odors into the thick, sweet air. Poppy and Roisin opened windows, breathing in the gentle breeze, catching wayward bees in their palms and redirecting them to their realm outside the stone walls. When they ran, their fingers and ankles were stained yellow with pollen, their palms red with blood, brown earth between their toes and green clover to soften their path. In London, the air would be stagnant, wadded handkerchiefs doing the Lord's work of sopping dirt-caked sweat. Out at Covenly, summer was clean and vibrant, a treasured promise of bounty and well-earned rest.

There was little to complain about here, even for Poppy, who was skilled in the art. The only real trouble was Roisin.

The week prior, Roisin had donned her dusty-raven-in-mourning getup and tramped back into town. She was gone for a few hours, which Poppy had spent nervously dusting corners and trying not to think of burning wads of paper. When she returned, it was with a parcel of clothes held to her chest. They were white and blue and soft downy gray, like winter cloud cover. Atop the pile lay a good length of pink ribbon. And another, a slightly different pink, the color of Poppy's flushed cheek. And a third, deeper and richer, nearly red.

"I didn't know," Roisin had said, face hidden under the brim of her sun-blocking hat. "I should have asked you about colors beforehand. But we have needles and thread, and I'm a fair hand at sewing. And you had wanted to be a seamstress, didn't you mention? I thought, perhaps, we could add a bit of your beloved pink." She had lifted her head, bashful hope writ across those charming silver eyes and Poppy, for whatever reason, had gotten a nosebleed.

Four days later, Roisin had approached with a letter, which she unceremoniously shoved into Poppy's hand. In it, a woman named Carmen assured Roisin that swallowing spend was a perfectly acceptable pastime for a vampire, were Roisin interested in taking it up. Poppy had laughed herself hoarse, despite Roisin's increasingly frequent and loud requests to "Shut up, Poppy, for the love of god." Roisin had been cranky and sullen that whole night, in a way that made Poppy want to fling herself into the other woman's lap and make herself at home, or at least prod her until she stormed off like a puffed-up pheasant. Poppy was kind, so she chose the latter.

Poppy wanted her in a painful, consuming way. Poppy couldn't have her, and that hurt too.

At least Lizzy had written back, which was a distraction. Her letter was full of the sort of angry relief that follows real fear, along with a strongly worded demand for details. Poppy gave her little. It was easier that way. And besides, she couldn't pen the sweet, florid drivel about Roisin that she would want to, were she herself holding the pen. The idea of Roisin writing her own praises was mortifying, especially when the woman gave her no indication she wanted anything from Poppy but friendship.

She supposed that wasn't entirely true. There were hints that Roisin saw her as something more than a chaste companion. Little moments of tenderness. Sweet, rare nights when Roisin gave up inches, carefully unspooling the private stories she held so close. Hungry gazes she could not entirely hide. A real smile, with teeth.

Poppy had never been called upon to exercise her patience in this way. When she wanted someone, chances were they wanted her too. And if they didn't, well, she supposed she hadn't wanted them that badly in the first place. It was easy enough to avoid a broken heart when one didn't reach for anyone who wasn't eagerly reaching back. Roisin wasn't reaching back. Not yet, at least, and it would certainly do more harm than good to nudge her hand when she balked so easily. Poppy was clumsy; if she moved too fast, she was liable to crack something. No, Poppy would have to exercise restraint, but was not used to the exertion and was therefore very sore. In the meanwhile, she would make do with Roisin's smiles, rare and precious and increasing in duration every day.

Roisin was smiling one such smile now, with Frankenstein and all his paper horrors clutched to her breast. "Is that your thesis on the novel? Frankenstein is execrable and deserves to be despised?"

"My thesis is that men who strive for greatness are hideous, self-important arses who care about nothing but their own legacy."

"I can agree with you on that point." Roisin tipped her head back against the antimacassar, regarding her. "And the monster?"

"What of the monster?"

"Was he justified in his quest for revenge? And Frankenstein, too— had he any other choice but to seek out his monster after it had killed?"

Poppy could not refrain from rolling her eyes. "Must we do this?"

"Do what?" Roisin asked, with the tiny, chagrined smirk of someone who knew she'd been caught out.

"You brought me this book to try to convince me that I should stop protesting your plan to exact revenge on Cane."

"Was I that obvious?"

"Yes. And unsuccessful."

"That can't be so." Roisin sat up, tucking her legs underneath her seat. "Was Frankenstein supposed to let a murderous beast run free?"

"A beast! I might argue that definition."

"What else?"

"A creature predisposed to love who was driven to hate!"

"You have a generous view."

"And to that end, if Frankenstein and his monster are meant to represent you and Cane, then I'm sorry to tell you this, petal, but you are the monster."

"I didn't mean it to be a direct comparison," she said, as though this were very obvious.

"But Cane created you, yes? Or at least turned you into what you now are. You may claim to be a hideous brute that humanity abhors." Poppy rolled her eyes once more, mostly for comedic effect. "I disagree, of course, but we'll say, for the sake of argument, that your predilection for human blood puts you outside of most polite society. That *is* unfortunate, don't misunderstand me. But, like the monster, all you really require is company. The reason he went bad is because he was lonely."

"I was alone for fifty years," Roisin pointed out. "I didn't murder."

"Immaterial." Poppy waved a hand. "However, if you make the argument that *you* are Frankenstein—"

"I'm neither one! If I'm anything, I'm a mixture of both. It wasn't meant to be a complete—"

"Then I suppose it *would* be your responsibility to clean up your own mess. But—and I know this is a difficult concept for you to grasp— this isn't your mess!" She held up a hand to forestall Roisin's objection. "Frankenstein had a duty to the creature he created. *You* didn't create a creature. You got bit and treated poorly and now you want to engage in an indefinite revenge plot."

"I want to prevent the murder of more women. I suppose you consider that frivolous."

Poppy was hit by a thought. "Is that why I'm here?"

"You—*what?*"

She bit her lip, homing in on an uncomfortable theory. "The monster wanted a companion. Frankenstein couldn't do the deed, but Cane could. Is that why I'm here? Was I meant to be your companion?"

Roisin stared at her like this was not only the stupidest idea she had ever heard, but also the most offensive. "No."

"I don't mind!" She thought that over and winced. "Well, I suppose I *do*, but it is a marginally better purpose than being turned because I was *there*. On that night, when she bit me, did she tell you why she intended to?"

"Oh, er . . ."

"Did you try to kill her before or after—"

Suddenly, and with a terrible jolting, Poppy's body became something new.

The red rose in her, a hot and terrible swarm of wanting. She tasted heat, her nose and mouth flooded with it. Her skin ached, each hair at attention, every pore open in hungry entreaty. She shrieked, a high, keening call to the gods. Give her this, give her this, give me, give me, give me, give, *give*.

There was a pressure atop her holding her to the floor. She hated it. She wanted to tear it to shreds. She needed to get her hands and skin and mouth on the thing, the needing thing, the blissful piece to fill the gaping, ragged hole in her empty soul. The weight prevented her, and she hated it. She growled, nails scratching on the flags, splitting, tearing down to the cuticle. The thirst was in her, on her, through her. She became it, and she was wounded to her bones that she could not give herself what she so wanted. What she needed. Give me. Give me. Give me. *Give me.*

"Give me!"

"I'm so sorry, Poppy," whispered the terrible thing pressing her to the earth. She writhed and shook against the thing. It was her jailer. Her hated restraint. Her terrible pillory, shaming her into stillness.

"Free me!" she screamed, her voice coarse and ragged and unfamiliar and *correct*, because it was strong and hearty and sang the song of red desire, heat and flame and ash. A film of crimson covered her eyes, and she blinked and she blinked and she wept. "I need it! I need it!"

"Shush, please. Please, Poppy." A hand came over her face and she bit it clean through. A yelp from above and she was free, tearing towards the door. She was hit as she grasped the handle, her head slamming into the soft wood so it cracked and splintered. The jailer grabbed and dragged her deeper into the kitchen, the mangled mess of what remained of her nails valiantly struggling against the stone, leaving trails of red. Her face was hot and sticky. Her cunt, too, and it throbbed because the red and the heat and the desire was everywhere now, a powerful longing that remade the world. She would feed, and she would become, and she would be. She would *be*.

She was crushed again to the floor, struggling and grunting for freedom, when she heard the voice of the prey floating in from the grounds outside.

"There's no smoke coming from the chimney," said something small.

"There wouldn't be smoke, idiot. It's summer," said something smaller.

"Yeah, but you said witches have cauldrons. Don't they need fire for the cauldron?"

"I never said that."

"You did."

"Well, maybe it's like how my mum doesn't light the hearth when it's hot and we just eat cold things? Bread and cheese and veg?"

"You think witches have cold summer potions?"

"Don't say it like it's silly. They're witches. They can do whatever they like."

The red smell was closer now, filling Poppy's mouth with soupy, meaty odor, savory and vital. She growled, a predator in a bush, waiting to spring. The yearning lashed her tongue, pulling it from her face. She could taste her new self in the air, the beast who fed and lived and gorged on red.

"I don't believe in witches, anyway," said the smaller thing.

"I know," replied the small thing. "You said it about a hundred times."

"But if I did—which I *don't*—I would think the lady in black is a witch."

"Which lady in black?"

"The one who goes to the posting inn and the stationer. And my mummy—I mean, my *mother* says that Louisa the dressmaker's girl said that the woman in black came in to get dresses made and they were too big and short for her. So if there's one witch, there are *two* witches."

"I thought you didn't believe in witches."

"I don't! But if I did, I would think the lady in black was one."

Poppy had no skin. No skin and no bones, nothing but snapping desire. The feeding would make her. She could not exist without the hot red in her belly. She could only see the bright bloodiness, only feel sticky longing. Her mouth opened and shut, snapping after her meal. She hissed, kicking out her legs.

"What was that?" the small thing squeaked.

"What?" demanded the smaller thing.

"I heard something."

"Oh, don't be a baby. I didn't hear anything."

"No, listen."

Poppy pressed her lips together. If she made a noise, her prey would flee, and the desire would consume her. She would be nothing, a distant star, a pinprick of empty light.

"See? Nothing. You don't have to be such a baby."

"I suppose you're right. Should we get closer?"

Above Poppy, her jailer shouted, "Leave this place!"

Rage took her and she wailed helplessly. Shrieks rang from outside, the odor growing smaller, the wanting turned to ache and weakness. She cried in desolation for this vital thing, the thing that would have made her into who she was meant to become. She would die without it. She was to die now, to be nothing, to be entirely unmade in the tragic loss of the red, the heat.

"Please!" she sobbed. "Please!"

"Shh. It's only me. This will pass. I promise."

"I hate you! I hate you!" She slammed her fist on the stone and felt bone snap. "You've ruined me! I hate you!" A hand stroked her hair and shushed her, and she reviled it. "Please! Please! Why did you do this? I want! I want!"

"I know. Just a little while yet. They're nearly gone."

The world got dark after that. Perhaps someone opened Poppy's mouth and poured in hare's blood. Perhaps she swallowed. Hands were on her body, touching and caressing and wiping a wet cloth along her skin. She opened her eyes and saw blood.

She gasped. "Did I kill—"

"No," said someone sweet. "It's come from you."

"From my eyes." She remembered the red veil in her vision. "Blood came from my eyes. Where else?"

"You need to rest."

"*Where else?*"

"Your nose, mouth, ears and quim. You bashed your scalp against the door, so there's blood there, too. There was a great deal because we fed so recently, but it wasn't just that. It was days of feedings leaving your body to make space for the human blood it wanted. I'm afraid your hair is caked in it."

"We'll get a bucket from the well." She tried to stand and found she couldn't move. Her whole body felt like tangled ropes, unraveling around the edges. It was good fortune she didn't need to breathe, because the effort might undo her. "Bugger."

"You're weak. All your strength went out with the blood. We'll see to it tomorrow. I'll bring you to bed."

81

"No." She grabbed on to what felt like a forearm. "I'll spoil our bed."

"Oh, Poppy."

"I'll spoil it. You go. Just bring me the blanket from the chair. I'll rest here."

"I'm not going to leave you."

"I must look a fright." She pried open an eye caked in blood. "Did I hurt you?"

"No, no." Roisin stood above her. Through the haze, Poppy saw a blood-spattered shirtfront.

"Did I bite you?"

"It's only a scratch." She had her hand held behind her back. Poppy tried to grapple for it, but her arms wouldn't move. "I'm worried about your fingernails. They tore."

"I bit you." Hot tears cleared her vision. Roisin stared down at her with hideous pity. Poppy wished she had gone blind. "I had no idea it would be this miserable. I wanted it with everything in me. I wanted it so much. I'm a terror. I'm weak." Sobs shook her. She curled against the ground, pulling into herself, wanting to be small. To not exist. "You'll never break me of this. You've wasted so much time. Leave me. I can't—I'm broken. I can't do this. I *can't*, Roisin."

"Shh. Oh, *mo cuishle*." Roisin lay down beside her, stroking her sticky hair and wiping her tears. Poppy was too weak to shimmy away. Pathetic. "It's my fault for not bringing you closer to humans sooner. I thought a little more time would make it easier. I was wrong and I hurt you."

"I can't do it. I'll fail. I can't do it."

"You can." Roisin caught a tear with a crooked finger. Poppy turned her heavy head, and she saw tuppence eyes. They were so close, and Poppy, so wretched, wanted to be closer. To be curled up against Roisin's skin and made good again.

"Roisin?"

"Mm?"

"I know I'm filthy, but will you h-hold me?" Worse than pathetic. A skinny worm, dried out and far from the garden.

"*Yes,*" Roisin said, and it sounded like rain. "Of course."

There were arms on her and a body beside her, and she wept for the bitter horror of this. Of remaining alive after this pain. Of knowing that there was no desire in her greater in the world than her longing for human blood.

"Don't think badly of me," she murmured into Roisin's stained linen. "I can't survive it."

After what felt like hours, Roisin said, in a voice so low it was almost inaudible, "I never could."

Chapter 10

Day passed and night fell and Poppy couldn't move. Roisin brought her a hare, which helped a bit, but only after draining three could she stand without support.

"There's nothing left in you," Roisin explained, arms outstretched, ready to catch Poppy if she fell. "But if you drink too many too fast, you'll get sick."

"Like cake," Poppy replied, half delirious. "On my birthday. I ate the cake fast and I sicked up on the egg bush. Where the primrose grows."

"Oh, did you?" Roisin spoke in the high, conciliatory tones of one dealing with an addled dowager. "That's not good at all, is it? Come with me now. We'll clean you off."

"Am I wearing anything?"

"No. Would you like to be?"

She thought for a long minute. "My birthday dress. It has daisies on."

"I'll find it for you in a moment. Let's deal with the blood first."

At the well, Roisin poured bucket after bucket on Poppy's head. She took a rag and wiped the dried blood from her face, her hair, between her legs.

"Terrible monthly I'm having," Poppy observed. "Never got it in my hair before."

"Perhaps you've had an unwise month."

"An *unwise month?*"

"Oh, erm." The hand cleaning her stomach stilled. "My mother used to say that when a woman's blood stopped in her old age, it was because she was wise. To lose a great deal was a sign of, you know, frivolity."

"*Frivolity?*"

"Yes."

"Mate," Poppy whispered conspiratorially. "Your mum might be wrong about this."

"Aren't you clever. Come back inside. I think you can handle a bit more to drink now."

After two more hares, which might have been sherry or French champagne, Poppy began to return to herself.

"Will that happen every time I'm near a human?" she asked, curled up on her chair by the fire.

"Heavens, no." Roisin sank into her own chair, having changed into fresh clothes. She tossed a pile of blood-soiled linen into the hearth. It caught and sparked. "Those children were very close. We'll stay far away."

"And do what?"

"Just sit. We'll have you out in the direction of the village and bring you closer in measures."

"What if I get too close?" She shifted, the blood sloshing in her belly. "What if I lose control and bleed out again? I don't want to hurt anyone."

Was that true? She wanted desperately for it to be true, but smelling the blood so close and so suddenly had done something to her. The aching memory of that want urged her to tear the throat of a human, drink its blood, and reach whatever potential abstaining kept her from achieving. It was becoming harder to remember that to quench this thirst was to end a person's life.

Certainly, in time and with Roisin's aid, she could stamp out the careless impulse. It was probably not worth mentioning, particularly not if it changed the way Roisin looked at her. She couldn't stomach that.

"You won't hurt anyone," Roisin assured her, blissfully oblivious. "We'll be very far away, up in a tree. I'll hold you and make sure you don't do anything rash."

"You'll hold me?"

There was a flush in Roisin's cheeks. She ducked her head. This, more than the hares, did wonders to revitalize Poppy's spirit. "I'm stronger than you are. Older vampires are stronger than young ones. I can't trust ropes, and I'm certain you wouldn't want to be restrained in that way."

"Don't make any assumptions."

Roisin's flat mouth turned down at the corners. "Poppy."

"No ropes." She held up her hands. "Your way is best."

They waited until Poppy had entirely regained her strength to begin their lessons. All in all, her recuperation took three days. It rained those days, thick, summer storms pelting the cracked windows, seeping in and wetting the stone. Roisin stubbornly kept Poppy inside, hunting for them both.

"You can't be implying that the rain will give me a chill," Poppy teased, receiving her dinner. "It's warm as a bath out there. We could run nude. Wouldn't even spoil our clothes."

"Shut up and drink your hare," Roisin said, leaving a trail of puddles as she stalked off to change her soaked linen and ruined breeches, Poppy's laughter dogging her heels.

The sky cleared on the third night, just as Roisin pronounced Poppy ready to begin her lessons. Roisin had located a cottage in the woods, two miles from the village. The tree on which they would sit was another mile or so from the cottage itself, a tall, sturdy oak with a perfect vee in its trunk to cradle them. Roisin led Poppy through Covenly's grounds and, for the first time, beyond, into a dense, small stretch of forest. It wasn't the stuff of fairytales, no creeping carpets of moss, no popping heads of speckled mushrooms, no pixy light to lead wanderers astray. It was a bland place, with a gravel made of broken twigs and stretches of unadorned dirt. Neither a welcoming nor unwelcoming wood, just fundamentally *there*, a scrubby sort of place that no one had yet had a reason to raze. The tree was taller than expected, a typical old man of the forest, with a history that must have stretched into Arthur's time. The promised vee was high up, nearly hidden in fog, roughly four Poppy-lengths from the dirt.

Poppy squinted upward, shielding her eyes with a hand out of habit. "How are we meant to get up there?"

"Climb."

"*Climb?*"

"Have you forgotten what we are? Come, hang onto my back."

Gingerly, Poppy climbed aboard. Roisin peeked over her shoulder with what might have been a smirk, then took off, scrambling up the tree at an impressive pace, fingernails finding purchase in the bark. If there were any hermits in this wood, they would have been certain they'd seen a devil, charging up the oak like an insect.

"Fucking hell, Roisin. I ought to saddle you and send you to the Royal Ascot."

"I haven't the breeding. Up you get, leg over. There we are."

She situated Poppy between her spread legs and wrapped her arms around Poppy's middle. Poppy melted into the embrace, resting her head against Roisin's shoulder. From here, all she could see was trunk and leaf and branch, barely touched by the moon's fog-impeded light. The air smelled wetter and cleaner, unsullied by humanity down below, by the filth and worry and fucking and sleeping and goings-on. Untouched by things too base for angels.

"I hardly think this restraint is necessary," Poppy said, shamelessly nuzzling deeper, hands clasping Roisin's arms, tightening the grip.

"It will be." Her lips were close to Poppy's ear, her breath stirring the small hairs. She had a deep tone, the sort of voice that traveled from the bottom of the belly to the throat. Poppy wondered how it had sounded before Cane stripped the Irish from her. Whether it skipped and jumped or rolled languidly off her tongue.

"Do you remember the smell?" Roisin asked. "The taste in the air?"

"Yes." It came back to her in a rush, the transformation, like smelling salts awakening her swooning beast. "Yes, of course."

"Catch it in the air. It's close."

It was as easy as slipping into a trance. Poppy could pinpoint the source, a wellspring of hot, red blood due north. She could run and be there in an instant. She could hop from the tree and suffer no wound. She could tear her skin to bits on the dry underbrush and be healed by the taste of the crimson thing that beckoned.

"There we are," Roisin cooed, and Poppy realized she was struggling against her bonds, her fingers attempting to pry Roisin's grip from her middle. "You're doing well."

"I want it." She writhed within her restraints, her cunt brushing the hard, unforgiving bark below her seat. It was all of a piece, the heat of the pulsing blood, the tight ring of Roisin's arm around her, the fire in her blood, her belly. "I want it. I want it."

"Breathe. Good. You're doing so well."

Praise would be her undoing. She let loose a moan that shook the trees.

"Shh. Someone will come after us if they hear you like that."

Good. Someone would come and Poppy would tear them to shreds. She would coat herself in their blood and make love to the night, and to Roisin, and they would scream themselves hoarse for the terrible pleasure of it.

"Come back to yourself, Poppy. You're in a tree with me. You're safe. The humans are as far away as they've ever been. You won't hurt anyone. Come back to me, Poppy."

"*No.*" She couldn't. She didn't want to. To do so would be to rip out a part of her, a piece of flesh that pumped and wriggled. Her fangs were so sharp. Her cunt ached, and she was close, she was *so close* . . .

"Please, Poppy. For me."

Roisin's voice washed over her, and with it, a clean wave, gray as the sea bubbling under storm clouds. Her mouth tasted of salt. She swallowed and swallowed again. Her mind housed a cool streak, trapped in the hot meat of her body. She saw trees ahead, felt her legs dangling four Poppy-lengths above dirt and twig and earth. And behind her was Roisin, steady Roisin, who held her and cared for her and wiped the blood from her body again and again, with a tenderness that brought tears to her eyes. Roisin, who had looked so panicked when Poppy tried to bring her to bed. Who was pressed so close to her now, and oh *fuck*—

"I'm sorry." Poppy gulped the air. "I'm sorry, I'm going to come. I can't stop it, *shit*—" The wave took her, pulling a groan from her throat, sending a violent tremor through her dangling legs. The shame curled around the release, the pleasure stripped humiliatingly raw. She pressed her lips together, swallowing sound, mortified heat licking her cheeks. "I didn't mean to. I don't know why that happened. I'm so sorry."

"It's quite all right." Roisin sounded stilted. Her arms were still a tight bind, but they were stiff now, too. "There is no need to apologize. It affects everyone differently." She coughed lightly. "I think that's enough for tonight. I'll demonstrate how to get down and you can follow."

Poppy didn't let herself feel hurt that Roisin didn't carry her down as she had carried her up. She watched, blinking back tears, as Roisin climbed and jumped without her, elegant and fine and so very far away.

Of course Poppy fell. Of course Roisin caught her.

"There you are." She put Poppy down and stepped away with terrible swiftness, as though Poppy were a pot right off the hearth. As though it burned to touch her.

They plodded back in silence. There was so much night yet left, the heavy moon at her very brightest. The grounds that welcomed Poppy back were alien, the kitchen askew. It seemed as though every bit of furniture had been shifted five inches to the left, the ceiling raised a foot.

"I'm sorry," Poppy said once more, wretchedly. "I've caused you discomfort."

"No, no." Roisin wouldn't meet her eyes. "Don't worry about me. Your first night was a success."

"That can't be true."

"Oh yes," Roisin told the far window. "We'll do it again tomorrow."

Poppy's stomach sank. "Should we not wait?"

"No, no. Best time for it. Best to, erm, do it while the weather is still mild."

Every sort of weather was mild for them. This was excruciating. "Roisin, I cannot apologize enough. What happened in the tree—"

"No, no." She waved off Poppy's apology with a gesture that looked nowhere near as casual as Roisin obviously intended. "There's a bit of, er, bookkeeping I need to do. I'll be off in the music room to do it. Terribly boring."

Poppy's panic was rising. "Roisin."

"Don't concern yourself with me. Perhaps you have a bit of reading you would like to do?"

"*Roisin.*"

She spun away and skittered down the hall without once turning back.

Chapter 11

Back in London, there had been women who enjoyed distributing handbills on the wages of sin. They were miserable cunts, the lot of them, but it was a laugh to tease them when there wasn't anything else to do. Over time, Poppy had developed a sort of affection for the poor mopsticks. They were so removed from their physical wants, so deeply buried within their own flesh, that it was hard not to pity the poor lambs for the frigid life they led.

These women weren't a danger, after all. They were merely misled—how could anyone in their right mind believe that Poppy's pleasure was a large enough social threat to deserve the pounds spent on paper and ink and a printer's time? In Poppy's well-educated opinion, a woman fucking for pleasure was far more virtuous than one who lay still and allowed the red-faced man who all but owned her shove his wilting member into her dry quim. These so-called moral women were laughably alien from anything truly righteous. If Poppy could only get them to see the error of their ways, maybe coax one or two of them into her bed, she'd have them seeing stars and printing pamphlets on the godliness of minetting.

But tonight, alone in a chair stained by decades of dust, next to a cold hearth, Poppy could be convinced her body was actually the sinful flesh these women condemned. Unclean, grotesque, still sticky between her legs from her rutting climax, she was no better than a dog in heat. And what's worse, she still wanted to drink that fucking blood.

Before Cane transformed her, Poppy's body and mind had worked in tandem. Now, she was separated from her thoughtful self by a body that wanted mindlessly. Dumbly. Flesh that ached for human blood. Teeth that longed to sink into a soft neck. Nipples that hardened at the sight of a woman who didn't want her. Who ran from her in true fear.

It was the sort of thing that could really topple a girl's self-regard.

She recalled the early night at Covenly when the frenzy had overtaken her and she devoured rabbit after rabbit. She had become a beast under the moon, but there had been a peace to the madness. A throwing off of restraints she hadn't realized held her down. A *relief*. She wanted that feeling again, wanted it so badly her hands shook. She was holding herself together by her fingernails. One moment of relaxation and she might spring apart.

Could this effort to keep away from human blood really be worth it? This delirious, mad ache for the stuff? This desperate control? What if—fuck, she could barely entertain the thought—but what if Cane had had the right of it? The woman was a villain, there was no question about that, but what if drinking from humans was not as terrible as Roisin made it out to be? After all, Cane hadn't had to kill Poppy to drink from her. Poppy could even envision a human asking for the bite, if it always brought on the sort of thigh-quaking climax it had given her. If she could only find a human who was willing to trade blood for pleasure, maybe an equal exchange could be made.

The bed was lumpy. The trance was reluctant. The day slogged on outside, and night rose grudgingly. Poppy didn't know whether Roisin ever joined her in bed. She hadn't noticed. She couldn't bear to think too much about it.

When she rose, Roisin was waiting at the table with a goblet of blood and a contrite expression. Poppy's traitorous stomach flipped.

"I must apologize for yesterday." Roisin pressed the goblet into Poppy's hands. "I shouldn't have run off like that."

"No. You shouldn't." Poppy drank deeply. The blood tasted weaker today. Under-steeped. "You left me to stew."

"I know. I'm so sorry."

Poppy didn't have the restraint required to be magnanimous. "Why?"

"A frightfully good question." She drew her knees to her chest, balanced on the plank of the bench seat. "I don't want you to take it personally. An, erm *climax,* isn't abhorrent to me."

She snorted into the blood. "Is it not?"

Roisin brought her forehead to her knees and groaned. "This is silly.

I'm being silly. We ought to get you back up into that tree."

"Hang on." Poppy placed the goblet on the table and held Roisin by the bare foot. "Will you talk to me?"

Roisin lifted her head slowly. Her eyes were so gray and so wet. She blinked and blinked. "I can't," she whispered.

"*Try.*" She might have been begging. "Please."

Roisin turned away, and Poppy's silent heart cracked down the center. "We ought to get in the tree."

It was a miserable night, followed by more, equal in spirit. Poppy didn't bring herself off again, but that was only through the painful force of her will, clenched teeth trapping her inside her skin. The smell of human blood was awful and wonderful in turns, a caress and a slap, whirling and shifting so all she knew was unrelenting sensation, pain and pleasure and bone-snapping misery. Each night, she sat trapped between the woman she wanted and the feast she wanted even more. The woman who did not want her and the people who would die by her teeth.

She was not improving.

"You *are*," Roisin insisted, but she couldn't meet Poppy's eyes, and that said it all really.

The air grew hotter, then cool, the summer wetness replaced by autumn wetness, dank and misty. Lizzy wrote letters and Poppy wrote back and sometimes Roisin would allow a night of reading some book or other, but the rest of Poppy's time was wasted in that tree. She lived for the moments Roisin called an end to their "lesson." Poppy could not be convinced she was learning a damned thing.

"Is there a trick to it?" Poppy asked as they lay down to trance, some time in what she might have guessed was October.

Roisin considered this. "It's a shift in you. You'll feel it. It will go from completely consuming to a low thrum, like an underground pipe."

"So even when I've controlled the urge I'll always feel it?"

"I assure you it's tolerable. I've been doing it for a century."

"We're different, you and I."

"I know," Roisin said, and rolled away.

Roisin could not hide her growing hopelessness. Despite what she had previously claimed about Poppy not being a dullard, this new struggle must have caused her to reconsider. Simple Poppy, ruled by hunger and want, writhing piteously in a tree. A creature of base animal instinct, with only the amount of self-control required to keep her from fucking a tree branch.

"Who are the people in the cottage, anyway?" Poppy growled, fighting against Roisin's terrible grip, four Poppy-lengths from freedom. *"Who are they?"*

They had no names. Their lives were short, and so small. They lived in a tiny cottage on the outskirts of a nowhere village. If only Poppy could reach the apple and bite.

"That's enough for tonight," Roisin said, and Poppy slumped home to hide from the sun.

Chapter 12

"You got a letter," Roisin said on a chilly morning. Winter was creeping up, frosting their windowpanes, turning the world quiet. It was the sort of cold that demanded a blazing fire. Tonight, the hearth was unlit—what was the point, when they would be back up in the tree in less than an hour? A waste of fuel.

"Mm." From Lizzy, of course. Her missives were stuffed with the sort of mundane nonsense that would have bored Poppy to tears were she still in London. Now, she craved each bit of correspondence. Lizzy must have known how desperate Poppy was for the little details of her repetitious days, because she relayed each and every one. Perhaps she missed Poppy as much as Poppy missed her. It wasn't worth dwelling on. Not when a trip to London was impossible.

Poppy had still made no improvement. She wasn't fucking likely to.

At least the reading had gotten easier. She tore through the envelope and pulled out the letter. A length of ribbon tumbled into her palm, along with a pretty pin. A pearl sat on the blunt end of the brass, soft and small as a soap bubble.

Dear Princess of All Rats,

Do you remember your last birthday? It was so cold I froze my knackers off—that's where they went! But you wanted to go for a promenade. The princess wanted to go for a promenade on her twentieth birthday! So I says all right, I'll take my girl where she wants to go. And then

94

all you wanted to do was see the fucking water. It was so cold there was nearly whitecaps on the Thames. But we had bone broth to drink, so it wasn't the worst I suppose. And you said to me, "This is all worth it." You remember? I thought you were talking nonsense so I checked your pockets for a bottle because if you was drinking without me I would have thrown you into the water. But you were stone sober. Pretty Poppy, no drink in her blood, talking nonsense to the river. So I said, "What are you on about?" And you stretched out your short-arse arms and talked some shite about how I was your favorite friend and this was your favorite place and there's nowhere else you would have wanted to be on your birthday. Silly cow, you made me cry then! But of course my tears froze to my face, and I said "Let's get you drunk. You want to go to the dram shop for gin and walk around more?" But you said, "Let's be around people." Thank fuck for that, as my aforementioned knackers had grown back only to turn to ice and shatter. You were drunk as a lord that night. You told everyone it was your birthday, and all the men bought pretty Poppy pints all night long until you were sick on my shoes. I had to hold back your hair in bed that night while you cast up your accounts in the chamber pot, remember? We should have hired a room, but we were in Minna's. I had the dosh for a room, but I was going to save it to buy you drinks. Silly me! We had to be so quiet because Minna would have thrown us into the street if she saw you was sick. She might have made you drink pennyroyal first, just in case. Fucking hag.

This is all to say, pretty princess Poppy, that I miss you and I hope whoever has your heart in a knot is giving you the birthday you deserve. Happy birthday, my favorite friend. I'm drinking broth by the water in your honor.

Go fuck yourself, Lizzy.

"Poppy?"

She jerked. Roisin was staring at her with a curious expression. "Sorry."

"Nothing to be sorry about." She sidled up, hands in her pockets. "Did Lizzy send you a present?"

"Oh. Yes." A pause. "It's my birthday."

"What?" Roisin squawked. "Today?"

"Not sure. What day is it?"

"November the third."

"Oh." She fingered the pearl. It really was lovely. No marks on the surface. A perfectly round ball of creamy white. "It was yesterday."

"But we should have celebrated! Twenty-one, isn't it?"

"I suppose." She flopped onto her chair with the letter in hand. She was particularly grateful today that her reading had advanced to the point where she no longer needed Roisin's assistance with letters. This wasn't for her. "You had no way of knowing."

"You didn't tell me."

"Ought I have?" she snapped.

Roisin stood in the center of the room, hands limp by her sides. "Are you upset?"

A laugh slid from her lips, dark and oily. "I could not give less of a shit that we did not celebrate my birthday."

"They're important."

"Do you celebrate yours?"

"No," she admitted. "I've forgotten mine. But you've only just changed. It's good to keep them up while you still remember."

"Mm."

"You . . ." She shuffled her feet. "You seem upset."

"Whatever gave it away?"

Roisin did not rise to the bait. "If it were me acting this way, you would say I ought to tell you how I'm feeling."

"And you wouldn't do it." Poppy shrugged. "So there we are."

"I'm sorry," Roisin said stiffly. "You're right. I have my . . . limitations. I'm not as free as you are."

"Hm."

"But we can still celebrate your birthday." Roisin edged toward her. "What would you like? A pink dress?"

She knew exactly what she would like and it sure as fuck wasn't a pink dress. She slid the pin into her hair and the ribbon into her pocket. "No." She supposed that sounded rude, so she followed it up with a terse, "Thank you."

"Poppy, if you're upset we can discuss—"

"I'm not upset!"

Silence rang out, echoing against the stone. Roisin stared, stunned.

"If I only missed Lizzy, I would be upset. If I only wished for you to speak freely with me, I would be upset. I am fucking *miserable*."

Oh, hell. Poppy had yelled. Now Roisin was frightened. Her shoulders edged up toward her ears, the coin of her center brow traveling toward her scalp. It didn't matter that it was Poppy who had shouted, that she wasn't Cane, and that she would never be Cane. All that mattered was that Roisin had heard a loud sound for which Poppy had been responsible, and it was Poppy's own damn fault that Roisin's spooked-horse breathing scalded her ears.

"I'm sorry," Roisin murmured. "I-I didn't know."

"Didn't you?" She felt her nostrils flare, the coil of anger building tension in her chest. "How else was I meant to feel, now you never speak to me anymore? We spend every night in that fucking tree. I sit there, with you at my back and the greatest thing in the world dangled in front of my face and it doesn't get any easier. It's getting worse."

"It isn't—"

"Don't lie to me!"

Roisin opened her mouth and closed it once, twice. Her face fell. "Fine. You're correct. You aren't improving as I'd hoped."

Poppy had suspected this, but to hear the truth was a despairing thing. "I'm an idiot."

"You aren't! I'm certain it will get easier."

"How can you be certain?"

Roisin looked fucking heartbroken. "Because it must." In an instant, she had knelt before Poppy's chair. Poppy curled her legs in so they didn't touch at all, and the hurt on Roisin's face at that might have turned Poppy

97

into a guilty wreck on any night but this one. "This is only a small obstacle. We have time."

"You were right."

"About . . ."

"About this life." The ashen, toothless mouth of the dead hearth gaped at her. "It's hell."

Roisin was quiet for a long moment. "I . . . well, I certainly never said it was hell." She gripped the seat of the chair, probably to mask the shaking of her hands. It didn't work. "What happened? You were so hopeful."

"I had something to be hopeful for. Now, I have no satisfaction in drinking hare's blood. Running bores me. And you." She stared down at pained gray eyes. "You run from me."

"Th-that's not . . . *Poppy*."

"You hold me for hours in that tree every night. Every night, I am forced to endure the touch of someone who would never choose to have me in her arms."

"That's not true."

"I am trapped between the woman I can't have and the blood I can't have! My desires are choking me. Have you been without a heartbeat for so many years that you no longer hunger like a human? I'm dying inside. I'm *starving*."

Roisin's brow drew down. Her face hardened. "Do you always get what you want?"

"*Pardon me?*"

"Have you ever, in your twenty-one years of life, denied yourself a single thing?"

Blood. You. "Of course I have."

"Truly?" Roisin stood up, brushed off her knees, and stalked over to her own chair across the cold hearth. She was only a few feet away. She was an ocean away. "Because it seems to me you are so unskilled in self-denial that you believe everything you desire is your due."

"You don't know what you're saying."

"Don't I?" Her mouth tightened and shrank. "I have spent decades in misery, denying myself companionship for the risk it presented. I'm sorry that running bores you, and that you can't end a human life for your supper. You want blood and you want me and when you can't have either, you throw a tantrum."

"A tantrum!"

"Yes," she said, maddeningly level. "A tantrum. Tell me: are you even trying to resist the desire to drink?"

"I . . ."

"No, I thought not. And yet, you believe you are the only one making sacrifices."

"Am I not?" Poppy asked with mock surprise, a hand to her chest. "Where else are you expected? Do your many friends miss your company?"

That did not have its intended effect. "Good show, Poppy. Hit me where it hurts."

"Why are you still here?"

"We've been through this." Roisin managed to sound both exhausted and enraged. "I'm here because you need me here."

"Go on," Poppy hissed. "Leave. You can't help me. You can't stand me. You might as well go roam the Earth somewhere else."

"You think I can't stand you?" Roisin gazed at her evenly. "You're right, Poppy. You *are* simple."

That didn't bear examination. It was far too late for that. "Why am I here?"

"You know why you're here."

"Yes, yes. Because Cane changed me. Because I look like the long-dead person you would much rather be with. Cane wanted to taunt you with me." She ignored her voice breaking. The hot tears dribbling down her face. "Did you try to kill her before or after she created another monster?"

Roisin's face went blank as waxwork. "After."

"Well, if she created me to cause you misery, then I suppose she achieved her goal. Did the sight of me brought to life disgust you so greatly you attempted to exact your revenge?"

"You can try to provoke me, Poppy, but it won't work."

Poppy didn't believe her. Not when her fingers bored so deeply into the plush arm of the chair. Not when her lips had stretched so thin, revealing her dropped fangs.

"So what was it that finally moved you?" Poppy asked, gratified to see those little points of white. "Decades of dogging that woman and only last spring were you able to raise your hand to her. What changed?"

Roisin stared, unspeaking. Her mouth worked. Her face fell, the careful blankness shattering like a dropped tea set. "I'm sorry."

"Oh," Poppy said. *Oh.* Poppy had spent enough time with Roisin now to recognize every shift of her expression, every hint of what those silvery eyes hid. There was terror in them now. Sick, agonized terror. And beyond that, a thick, shaming wash of unspeakable guilt.

"Oh. She didn't turn me. You did."

It came together in an instant. Why Roisin had been the one to tend to Poppy through her change. Why she had committed herself so fully to Poppy's care and training. Why she refused to touch Poppy, even now, with her guilty, dishonest hands. After fifty years of loneliness, Roisin had broken. She had reached for a hand and a creature reached back.

She couldn't deny it. Not when that clever face betrayed her. "I'm so sorry."

"You're *sorry?*" Poppy stood, her body filled with hot fury. "You lied to me!"

"How could I tell you the truth?" Roisin was balled in her chair, small and wretched. "It was a moment of weakness. I saw you, and you looked so much like her. And I was so lonely. I'm pathetic. I'm sorry. I'm *sorry.*"

"Shut up. Shut up!" The letter was still in her hand. She had crumpled it. Her lovely letter from Lizzy, crumpled like trash. "You hate me, is that it? You hate me because I remind you of the worst thing you've ever done. Your weakest moment?"

"I don't hate you!" She couldn't deny the rest. Of course she couldn't. "I'm sick with guilt. You deserved better than this life."

"To die by Cane's hand, you mean."

"Oh, I don't know." She rubbed her eyes. "Is it better to die young than live as a-a *thing?*"

"A thing." She was going to sick up. "What does the monster say? *Life, although it may only be an accumulation of anguish, is dear to me, and I will defend it.*"

"You're not the monster. I told you it wasn't a direct comparison."

"Shut *up.*"

"Would you call this life worth living? Answer me. Truthfully. You just told me you're unhappy."

"Because of you! Only you could find comfort in such tight restraints, petal. Not all of us seek virtue in loneliness. Only your particular mind would choose to live in a constant state of self-contempt. Only you would see being happy as some sort of moral failing."

"That isn't true!" Roisin stood now, too. She was tall, but Poppy felt taller, built high by righteous anger.

"I don't believe you."

"Fine," Roisin ground out through clenched teeth. "Would you like to hear the real reason I deny myself pleasures?" She shook her head, as if even she couldn't believe what she was about to say. Her hair was a spidery wreck, little legs and webbing pointed in all directions. Her eyes were red. Her linen was askew, untucked from her breeches. Her feet were bare, long, bony toes curled into the flags.

When she finally spoke, her voice was hoarse. "I spent fifty years alone, perfectly content, because I felt nothing. I wasn't sad. I wasn't joyous. I existed. I had to. How else was I meant to be ready whenever that woman wanted to taunt me with another girl? How else was I meant to stop her from killing? My friends—I *do* have friends, you know—offered me quarter, but if I were to rest anywhere, she would come for whoever sheltered me. So I chose not to live. If I allowed myself anything remotely human, I wouldn't be able to do it. And I had to, Poppy. For all my faults, this is the one thing I tried to make good.

"And then, you." She licked her lip, drew it into her mouth, bit. "You were bleeding. Nearly gone. But I saw you, and I thought, I have to know her. I have to see her move. I have to hear her thoughts. Yes, you look like Clover. But there was something else. I don't understand it. It's like there was a voice in my head commanding me to change you. Like I was meant to do it. Like in fifty years of running, this is what I was running to."

"Pretty words."

"Let me finish," she insisted, voice creaking through splintered, rotted wood. "From the first day I spent with you, awake and moving and so horrifically joyful, you changed me." She pressed her hands to her slim chest. "You were kind and happy and so incredibly *odd*. The greatest tragedy of your turning was that you couldn't eat food anymore. You took so much pleasure in small, silly things. You were so incredibly human. You made me remember everything I forgot. I remembered my mother because of you. My language. Do you know why?"

"I—"

"Because you reminded me what it is like to be cared for." She drew in a long, shaky gulp. "I hadn't felt like that since I was fifteen years old. I thought Cane had loved me. Even after all this time, I still thought, perhaps, in the beginning. Before I fucked it all to hell. But *you*." She pointed a shaking, accusatory finger. "You listened to me and you wanted to know me. Me! Like no one ever had. You told me that Cane's actions weren't my fault. With Cane, every mistake was my doing. But it was like you, y-you thought that at the core of me, there might be goodness."

"Roisin."

"Shut up or I won't be able to finish this." She squeezed her eyes shut, shoving the words from her mouth. "You've ruined everything. Do you know that? You've ruined me. How am I meant to hunt her after this? How am I meant to wander when every part of everything I am wants to rest with you? Of course I'm starving. Of course I'm sick. Yes, I changed you. And my punishment is that you changed me, too. You've remade me, every cell, every atom. I . . ." She sank to the floor, knees drawn up, arms wrapped around her legs. Her feet were so small, and so dear. "I am ruined."

Chapter 13

Poppy stared at her sire, curled and weeping on the flags. Anger whitened her vision, shooting down her arms and legs, lighting her up like coal gas.

"You should have said."

"I know."

"You should have given me a choice to stay."

Roisin's eyes were wet, silver coins, dropped carelessly on the street. "Would you have gone?"

"I might have demanded you leave me with someone else."

"That's your right."

The walls were closing in, the ceiling getting lower. "I'm leaving."

"Where?" Roisin's cheekbones stood out, her shoulders heaving.

"I don't know."

"Poppy, please. Let me make arrangements."

"I'm going to the cottage."

Her face went slack. "What?"

"I was turned by you. I lived by your rules, in your home."

"It's yours too," she said, gravelly and resigned.

"Perhaps in name. Just as I have freedom in name. I'm going to the cottage. I am making my own choice."

Roisin's mouth opened and shut. "It's your right."

"You're not going to try to stop me?" She resented the confused hurt between her ribs. This was freedom. Why should it matter if it tore Roisin down? Why should it matter that Roisin would not fight for what she had built?

"I wasn't honest with you. You may make your own decisions."

She drew herself up. "I will."

"Do . . ." Roisin's voice cracked. She cleared her throat. "Do you plan to return here before morning?"

"Yes." She sniffed. "And when I do, we can decide where I will go next."

Roisin stared down at her bare toes. "That's fair."

Poppy hesitated near the door, awkward and fearful and bruised. "I'm off."

"Poppy." She stood carefully. Her clothes and hair were a wreck, her face drawn. "Have a care. You've only got one body."

Poppy's throat clenched. She tore into the night. The wind was up, the sort of powerful, whipping wind that inspires stories of vengeful gods. It scattered the scent of the cottage, but after so many long nights in the tree, locating the source was as easy as breathing. There it was, the vein of ore in the stone, a glistening gift from the earth. The beast rose in her, pleased and eager. She was barefoot, clad only in her chemise, yet she felt no cold. Her long yellow hair fell down her back, the wind tossing the strands. Beneath her, rimed clover crunched and fell, earth ruined under her tread.

The woods thinned, and the cottage appeared. It was a small stone heap with a thatched roof, unremarkable in every way, except that it housed the wondrous, the food. Beside it stood a water pump and a small, fenced-in paddock, a hen house huddled in the corner. On the other side of the house was the ghost of a larger pen, the fencing worn down, a sad, empty hovel leaning listlessly on the cottage. It was just as she imagined Frankenstein's creature's shelter, and it made her giggle. Her blood was up; she was certain she had a nosebleed. Fever boiled her eyes, wriggling them. She stumbled, birthday-drunk already, into the hovel, falling onto wet, moldy straw, narrowly missing a pair of rusted-through buckets and a snapped rake.

She didn't have a peephole. She didn't need one. She could hear each individual heartbeat, four thumping rhythms, two little, two big, in blissful, oblivious sleep.

She should have drained them already. Why hadn't she drained them already?

The madness curled her toes and set her mouth watering. There was blood in her eyes. She laughed, high and trilling, and no one was startled from sleep because she might have been a bird, or a mad specter, best left alone. The scent wove through her, a river, deeper and deeper into the earth of her flesh. An underground spring.

She could eat them now. She could tear them apart.

If there were a big enough house nearby, this mean place might have been a groundskeeper's cottage. But Covenly's grounds were feral. Those that lived here were nowhere people, with a brace of chickens in their small pasture and nothing in their big one but a vampire. Maybe a cow had died here, right where Poppy sprawled. Maybe it had lain its heavy head down, bones showing from underneath splotched, powdery skin. The family might have gathered ceremoniously to see their milk-dry animal close her cloudy eyes for the last time, no meat on her, bones and hooves and nothing. She would taste of ash and disease. A stew with a name, who had chewed cud and shat and fed milk to the ones that patted her.

Blood dripped sluggishly from her eyes and mouth and nose and cunt. She picked out the dainty hiccup of three chicken heartbeats. If she ate one, there would be two, and someone would sit on the porch all night with a shotgun, peering into the yonder for foxes. For wolves. The craving for the four bleeders—two little, two big—was an underground pipe, a rush deep and contained. Above it was Poppy's dirt, thoughts squirming and chittering through the layers, dark and damp and light and dry, with gnarled roots and weeds that ate up the sun. Roisin was a deep, hard stone. The shovel clanged as it met her. To remove her would be to tear it all up, to pull the worms into the light. They had no eyes.

She gathered herself up. There was a bloodstain in the hay and she laughed at it. A blood angel, in the vague shape of her. She laughed and laughed and it hurt coming out, funny glass shards in awkward shapes.

The wood sprang up around her, the old oak doffing its crown. She nodded back. Curtsied. She asked for a lift home but he didn't know where home was, and she laughed because the blood made her chemise stick to her thighs. It was an unwise month, she told the tree, and he didn't laugh because he didn't understand. That was fine, as the moon did, and she giggled back down at Poppy and generously lit her way. She was full, that moon. She had drank up all the good blood and was tinged rose, a harvest moon, the color of a new ribbon, folded atop a stack of simple dresses by a bashful hand. The moon swallowed.

"It's safe to swallow," she whispered to the moon, and the moon sent down her thanks in cold light.

Her feet let her rest as they carried her to the grounds she knew, where she might eat a hare if only she could catch one. *But we're tired*, said her feet, which was entirely fair, so she went on her belly and gave her hands a turn. The moon bid her goodbye, and the sky turned light blue. She hadn't seen a cold, pale blue sky in so very long, the tang of it, the wet freshness. Her feet hurt, and she smelled sizzling, like roast pig. She had heard that people pissed and shat when they died. She hadn't done either in months. How interesting would it be, how novel, to do both and also die, which she had never done before—unless she'd been dead for months—but in either case, how interesting would it be to do it! How novel and new and interesting, to die, which she had never done, unless she did. Unless she died. Never. Not once, or once. And how interesting would it be to do it, or to have done it!

Perhaps a cow had died here, too. Cows had big eyes and eyelashes, like pretty girls. Silver-eyed cows dying, flat-smiled, lonely mooing things. Lying cows with bloody milk. She curled up alongside the cow's hands, her udders. Her hooves and slender fingers.

"Poppy, what have you done?" said the cow.

"Moo," said Poppy, and died.

Chapter 14

Poppy did not know how long she was dead, only that it was warm and quiet. She drank sometimes, something sweet and hot and furred. Sometimes there was bare flesh at her mouth, and different blood, or not blood at all, bright and shocking like swallowing a star.

The rector had talked about heaven. She remembered sitting with his daughters when he did, when he preached on the seraphim and the cherubim and the great honor of sitting at the side of the Lord. He had not said that heaven was dark, and that the seraphim cried sometimes, and chattered and knew her name. He had not said that the angels sang loping melodies and spoke Irish.

When a piglet is born, its eyes are closed. Five minutes later, it can see. When a puppy is born, it won't open its eyes for two weeks. After Poppy died, she opened her eyes, and it might have been five minutes or two weeks or one hundred years. She could see, and maybe it meant she was alive again.

There was damask above her and bed below. She was clean, which was funny because when piglets and puppies are born they are sticky and need to be licked. She might need to lick herself, to taste her own little hairs and salt and become clean.

The day was thick outside, its bright fingers stretched out eagerly under the drapes. The candles in the sconces had burned to nothing. She was alone. She slipped from the bed into the dark room and crept toward the door, with that familiar impulse to be quiet, because this was a sleeping place.

She nearly tripped over a mass on the floor. It was half on the rug, half off, a jumbled heap of shapes and fabric. A long woman curled in on herself, in the mussed, wrecked rest of the truly exhausted. Her clothes desperately needed brushing, coated in ash and dust and bits of rug fluff. Her dark, smooth hair had lost its luster entirely. Her face twitched as she dreamed, her fangs out, her brow knitting. Carefully, Poppy sidestepped the body, squeezed through the door, and finally exhaled.

There were two chairs by the kitchen hearth. Hers was empty. There was a woman in the other one.

"Good morning," the woman said. "I trust you're feeling better."

Poppy hadn't seen a new person in months, yet she had the instinctive awareness that this one wasn't a threat. Maybe it was the pleased expression on her face, a little wearied perhaps, but certainly relieved to see Poppy.

But appearances could be deceiving. "Who are you?"

"My name is Carmen." The woman stood, her deep blue dress blooming around her. Her skirt was wide and pleated, her arms hidden under generous leg-o-mutton sleeves. Pinned, perfect ringlets framed her long, elegant face. Her eyes were quick and knowing, her mouth painted red with what Poppy was certain was the same Turkish rouge she herself had used most nights at Minna's, the kind that tasted of vinegar. Her eyebrows were thin, plucked within an inch of their lives, in a way that emphasized their dexterousness. These eyebrows danced.

"What are you doing here?" Poppy demanded.

"A fine welcome. I'm here because Roisin asked me to come."

"Why?"

"She seemed to think I could help. Come sit. I would like to visit with you."

Poppy lowered herself into her chair, warily watching her new companion. She had never hosted someone so fine, particularly not in a place she considered her home. Her fingers itched to make tea and send for cakes. "The last rich lady I met mesmerized me, bit me, and nearly drank me dry."

"I heard." Carmen straightened her skirt with a graceful hand. Her nails were short and manicured, with little spots of color in the cuticles, like flowers growing between paving stones. "I heard a great deal about you."

"The only thing I know about you is that you—" Her words fell down on her tongue and died.

Carmen seemed to know where she was going. "Yes, I am a font of carnal knowledge. We have fun, my family and I."

She was too groggy to sidestep the bait. "Who's your family?"

"The Brood. We live in London, mostly. In Mayfair."

"Stylish."

"We travel often. Paris, Venice, Rome, Budapest—"

"Alone?"

Carmen's spare brows drew together. "As a group of course."

"No, no. Pardon me, I'm still half in a trance." She wiped the sleep from her eyes. "What I mean is, did you come here alone?"

"My man is at the inn in town." She peered distastefully at a crack in the window. "Charming place."

"Is he human?"

"Yes. We drink from humans in my family." Poppy's face must have betrayed her, because Carmen hastily held up her hands. "Oh, no, we don't kill them. We have people in our employ who enjoy the bite and are paid for their services."

An equal exchange. Just as Poppy had imagined. "Is it better than hares?"

When Camen smiled, it was with all her teeth. "Far better. We have a hutch of rabbits in the garden as supplemental food of course. You will be very comfortable with us."

Instinctive fear tightened around her chest. "I'm going with you?"

"Roisin explained the situation to me." Carmen's eyes flicked to the closed bedroom door. "I hope you don't mind."

"No." Poppy wanted to tuck her feet up underneath her, but Carmen was dressed so well and sitting so perfectly. She straightened her back instead. "How long have I been . . ."

"Out? One month."

"Oh." She swallowed to fight back a rush of fear. "Seems a bit dramatic, even for me."

She had left for the cottage on the day after her birthday. It must now be early December. Now that she knew to smell for it, there was a smoky, frosted tinge to the air, a telltale sign of approaching midwinter.

"I was told that your exit was similarly dramatic."

"Mm." Poppy shrugged. "I suppose."

Carmen regarded her for a long moment, undisguised sympathy tightening her expression. "Roisin says you resisted draining that family in the cottage, so you're probably skilled enough to travel. We can have you at the house in Wiltshire by Christmas."

"Christmas. " She let her eyes rove over the dusty books, the remnants of the ladder. The small pantry where Roisin prepared goblets of blood for her. Everything looked dingier with Carmen there, a freshly minted penny tossed amongst old coins. "Where will Roisin spend Christmas?"

"She was under the impression you wouldn't much care."

"Oh." She wrapped her arms around herself. There might be snow on the ground outside. There might be frost. "Does she want me gone?"

"May I be frank?"

"Please."

"She wouldn't leave your bedside. She gave you her own blood because she thought it would revive you. She was terrified you were gone."

Poppy's fingers pressed into her forearms. "She felt guilty for turning me without my consent."

"Yes." Carmen lifted an elegant shoulder. "You're the first person she turned. She's a paragon of self-discipline. It frightens me to think how desperate she was. It's not like her to make a mistake."

"I'm a mistake?"

Carmen's red mouth curled. "You're a mistake or she's a villain. You can't have it both ways."

"I never said she was a villain."

"What then?"

"A frightened little girl." Poppy had left her on the floor, weeping. Roisin hadn't tried to stop her. "She lied to me."

"Yes."

"She plans on finding Cane and killing her."

"I know."

"And you're going to let her?"

Carmen's slim brows ascended to nearly her hairline. "Why wouldn't I?"

"She shouldn't have to do it," Poppy snapped, a line of heat shooting through her belly.

"Poppy," Carmen intoned warningly.

"She tried to mind her business. She barely lived for years, watching

110

Cane kill girls. Staying away from her *friends*," she spat the word at Carmen, clothed in such lovely things, "for fear of getting them killed. And now she wants to waste the rest of her very long life chasing that woman. Trying to kill her. Likely getting herself killed. While you travel with your servants to Mayfair and Wiltshire and sodding *Venice*."

"You forgot a few."

"I can't leave her alone. I *can't*." She brought her hands to her face. When she peered through her fingers, Carmen was regarding her with approval. "What?"

"I agree. You ought to stay."

Poppy frowned. "So you don't want me amongst your fancy little fuckers?"

Carmen tipped her head back and cackled. "Fancy little fuckers is apt. We hold orgies."

"You never!"

"Regularly. Human and vampire. From what I hear from Roisin, you'd fit in alarmingly well."

Poppy felt her cheeks heat. "Fresh."

Carmen laughed again. It was a full, throaty laugh, the sort Poppy had always loved to draw from people. Here it sat, right under the surface, resting beneath the crinoline of this elegant woman's skirts. "I do hate to leave you here. You'd be so much fun."

Longing touched her. A little bit of hope. Maybe Carmen could buy her Turkish rouge. "After I'm well, once I'm fully trained, perhaps I could call on you?"

"I would be offended if you didn't. In the meanwhile, there is something I would like you to do for me."

"Are you paying?" She expected to be brushed off. Instead, Carmen grinned.

"Handsomely."

"Go on."

"Do not stop Roisin from hunting Cane."

"No," she said immediately. "I can't do that."

"I know you care for her," Carmen murmured with apparent sympathy. "But Cane needs to be stopped. She is a danger as long as she lives."

"So *you* kill her."

111

"Oh, that I could." Carmen gave a resigned little nod. "But Roisin has a singular skill."

"What's that?"

"She's resisted Cane's thrall." She looked away, a heaviness in her dark eyes. "Not all of us have the same facility."

"Oh."

"Indeed." Her eyelashes were dark and shining, probably daubed in castor oil. Poppy missed looking pretty like that, painted and purposefully lovely. She could have that if she went with Carmen. She could have orgies. She could see the world.

"People have tried to stop Cane before," Carmen went on. "But her gift is singular. She has a way of stopping people. Everyone but Roisin."

"Roisin thinks it's her responsibility."

"Perhaps it is. Not because of anything she's done—heaven knows she's owed her rest—but because she's the only one who can." Carmen rose and smoothed her skirts. "Smell that?"

"What?"

"My coach is without."

Sure enough, the wind brought the scent of a human approaching the house from the front entrance, along with that of a large beast. It was a frothy, gamy smell—a horse. Hoofbeats followed, accompanied by the familiar sound of wheels.

Carmen observed her. "How are you finding the craving?"

Poppy smelled the air. The red was in her, but it was deep. If she wanted, she could bring her thirst to the surface. It was no strain to resist. "I'm doing it," she said in accents of wonder. "I'm *doing* it."

"Well done." Carmen was tying a hat to her head, a sapphire concoction covered in an aviary's worth of feathers. "Of course it's just one man, but progress is progress. Do keep well, Poppy." She held out her hands. Poppy rose to clasp them, receiving a light kiss on each cheek. She hoped there would be a little Turkish rouge left behind. "Consider what I said, please. For all of our sakes, hers included. Think of how well she'll rest when Cane is gone."

"I'll . . . I suppose I will."

"Good." Carmen patted her face with a gloved hand. "And remember, you always have a place with the Brood."

Chapter 15

Poppy was staring morosely into the unlit hearth when she heard her name coming from the bedroom, high and frantic.

"In here," she called. The door banged open and Roisin bolted out, juddering to a complete, jarring stop at the kitchen entrance. Her shirt was askew, her hair loose around her shoulders. She swallowed visibly, her throat working. She stared.

"I thought you were gone," she whispered hoarsely.

"No." Poppy spread her arms. "I'm here."

"Where's Carmen?"

"Gone."

"Gone where?"

"Back to London I presume."

"London?"

"Venice, Budapest." She shrugged. "Atlantis."

Roisin blinked, uncomprehending. "You were meant to go with her."

"Well I didn't, did I?"

"No." Her brows knit. "You didn't?"

Poppy gestured impatiently toward the other chair. "Spare prick at a wedding. Come sit. You're making me nervous."

Slowly, with careful steps, Roisin made her way to the chair and sat. "You're awake."

"Clearly."

"How are your feet?"

"Fine." She peeked down at them. They were the same as always, stocky and white, as soft as they'd been since the change sloughed off the calluses. "Why?"

"They burned off."

"*What?*"

"They burned off." She carelessly pushed her filthy hair from her face. "You were out in the dawn. The light caught your feet and they burned off. I wasn't sure they were coming back."

Her stomach heaved. "That's disgusting."

"It was terrifying." Roisin's gaze was fixed somewhere indefinite, a cobweb or a mousehole or a ghost squatting in a dusty corner. "You were covered in blood. I thought it was human blood, but you smelled badly of hare. And sickness." She swallowed. "If you had killed those people, you would have made it back safely. I found you weak and drained and shriveled and thin and footless. Just two black stumps."

"Oh."

"Yes. Oh." Roisin's eyes burned into her, the tin of a kettle hung over the hearth. "I tried to feed you rabbits but you wouldn't take them. I was sure I kept a corpse in my bed, pouring blood into your open mouth. Eventually you swallowed, but that was around the same time your ribcage caved in. I started giving you my blood. Only after a week or so did you show the slightest improvement."

"You're angry," Poppy realized, with a little inexplicable skip in her stomach.

Roisin's nostrils flared. "You nearly died."

"I didn't, though."

"No. You didn't. What do you have to say for yourself?"

"I suppose I was caught flat-footed."

"Shut up. I am aware this is the second time I have brought you back from the brink of death without your permission, but you'll find I'm far less cut up about this round with the reaper."

"Terribly glad to hear I didn't further sully your pristine morals."

"Of course you did!" She threw up her hands. "Do you know how often I cursed those peasants in the cottage for still being alive? How often I scolded you for not eating them? Four souls in that house. Two children, and I still . . ." She broke off, blinking. "Why didn't you leave with Carmen?"

"I didn't like her perfume."

114

"Poppy, please. I haven't the patience."

"Oh, petal," Poppy cooed, low and snide. Roisin flinched. "You can't get rid of me as easily as that."

"I'm not trying to—" She let out a strangled noise of frustration. "What do you want, Poppy? You were through with me. You told me you were leaving. Yet you are still here, sitting in that chair like Banquo's ghost."

"Is he the one what told the son that the uncle fucked the queen?"

"*Why?*" Roisin pled. "Why would you choose to stay?"

She should have had an answer to this question. The trouble was that any uncomplicated truth sat at the bottom of a morass of weird, tangled apprehension and half-formed feelings.

Roisin crossed her arms over her chest. "Don't say it all at once."

"Give me a moment to think it over. I've only been asleep for a month."

"Sorry, sorry." She tilted her head back in her chair and closed her eyes. "If it helps, I've got a much better grasp on what it is that *I* want."

"I don't care much about what you want," Poppy lied. From the look on Roisin's face, it was a very poor lie. "Do you still think I'll need until spring to control my thirst?"

"I don't know. You nearly died last time you were near a human. That's somewhat damning evidence."

"I didn't eat anybody."

"No." She screwed up her mouth. "Do you remember the row we got in that night?"

"Why shouldn't I?"

"Because your feet burned off and you slept for a month. Forgive me for thinking you might be a little jumbled."

"I remember." Roisin in a small weeping ball on the floor, guilt twisting her face. "Why didn't you stop me?"

"It wasn't my place."

"That's bollocks!" Poppy slammed her fist on her thigh. Roisin jumped. "You had spent months telling me exactly what I should and shouldn't do, and as soon as I find out you're not morally unimpeachable, you melt. I thought you had more of a spine than that."

"See? This is it entirely." Roisin jabbed a pointed finger. "How am I supposed to do what you want when you won't tell me? You want your freedom? You want to drink from people? Feel free! It was never my place

115

to stop you. I was trying to correct a wrong. And now you're upset that I didn't continue to do the same things that bothered you in the first place!"

"They didn't *bother* me. They hurt me. You—" Her voice hitched. "You *hurt* me."

"Oh, Poppy." Roisin reached out, then drew back, balled hands pressed against her body. "I'm so sorry."

"*Sorry*," Poppy repeated mockingly, but it was entirely defanged by the snot and tears in her voice. "I thought you cared enough about me to tell me the truth."

"I should have. I should have told you right from the start."

"W-why didn't you?"

Roisin rubbed her mouth as she worked up her answer. "Shame, at first. When you woke, I could barely believe I had done it myself. It was as though, if I didn't tell you, it would be like I hadn't done anything at all. And then, when I got to know you, I was terrified that you would be angry with me."

"I'm denied the truth because you don't want me to be *cross*."

"I'm entirely aware of how selfish I've been. But Poppy, you must understand . . ." She winced, gripping her elbows. "The last time I had a companion, she severely punished any infraction or misdeed. Even when I thought I hadn't done anything that would warrant punishment, I somehow had. I had misunderstood an unspoken intention, or I had corresponded with a friend she suddenly hated. She would ignore me completely when she was upset. It was as though I were a ghost."

"I wouldn't do that," Poppy protested wetly. "Have I given you any impression that I would?"

"Of course you wouldn't. My mind knows that, but my skin." Her fingers danced over her pebbled forearms. "My lungs. It's in me. It's in my marrow. I don't think I'll ever be rid of it. And we both suffer for it."

"I hate her."

Roisin shrugged. "I don't."

"You *don't?*"

"I wish it were as simple as hating her."

"Isn't it?"

"I didn't always do the wrong thing. Sometimes I did the right thing. And when I did, it was like the sun shone again." Her half-smile, flat and

116

weak and miserable. "I still feel that when I think of her. Even after the years of mesmerism. After taking my language and my mother from me, and all the killing, of course. Even after that, I still remember the feeling of her patting me on the head and telling me I've done well." She looked up with wide, pleading eyes. "What sort of broken person must I be to still feel that way? What's wrong with me?"

Slowly, carefully, Poppy walked over and sat at Roisin's feet, resting her head on those absurdly knobbly knees. "Oh, petal."

"I'm so ashamed."

"Not about this. Never about this." Poppy rubbed Roisin's thighs as though she were bringing blood to the surface. "That woman twisted your brain."

"It isn't mesmerism that has me feeling this way. I'm sure of it."

"There are other ways to infiltrate a person's head."

Roisin reached down with trembling fingers. Slowly, she pushed Poppy's hair from her face. Traced her nose. Crooked a finger to stroke her cheek.

"You have no idea how good it is to see you alive," she whispered. "I thought—"

"Shh. You do too much thinking. Be daft like me."

"You're very intelligent, Poppy. You were clever enough to resist eating those humans."

"Not clever enough to keep my feet on."

And there it was. That thin, silent line of a laugh, frustrated and fond. "Are you hale enough for a hunt?"

They blew clouds into the December night. The moon, too, breathed out hazy air, was wreathed in it. There were fewer hidey-holes for the hares, not as much green cover. They were sleeping, sluggish, deep in their burrows, and didn't even scream when they were pierced. They barely woke to know they had died. Poppy licked their summer-hot blood from her lips and knew it would never be enough. She would never not yearn for something fuller and richer, something transformative and bright. But she also knew, with the same sort of certainty that accompanied the facts of her birth and undeath, that if she were ever to indulge, there would be no going back.

Some drunks could drink. Some claimed that one sip would be their

117

undoing. Poppy knew that her first taste of human blood would call the underground spring within her to rise to the surface, burst from its banks, and drown everything.

So she swallowed her hare and wondered whether, as the years passed, it would get easier. Roisin had accused Poppy of assuming everything she desired was her due. Poppy wondered, as she watched Roisin drink, if she still felt that way. If she still looked at Poppy and saw a spoiled, wanton girl. Or had her restraint changed things? Had the stumps of her feet or the collapse of her ribcage changed the way Roisin saw her?

Roisin had changed in Poppy's eyes. Her picture was fuller, with more colors, more light and shadow. The murky bits were clearer, the parts Poppy had averted her eyes from now demanded her attention. There she was: fallible. Restrained. Frightened. The woman who had now brought Poppy back from death twice. Who had cleaned her hair of blood, and her stomach and breasts, and would throw herself before the gates of hell to murder a woman she still loved, though she wouldn't name it. Though she couldn't.

"Carmen bought new beds for the upstairs bedrooms," Roisin offered sheepishly. "I suppose I ought to have done that months ago. I'll trance upstairs if you—"

"Oh, come to bed." Poppy wiped the blood from her lips. "I promise I won't do anything untoward."

They lay together like their first morning, stiff and far apart. When the trance took her, Poppy welcomed it as an old friend.

Chapter 16

They had a small Christmas. There was no holly nor ivy to be found, so Poppy yanked up a tree with her bare hands, a wee thing with bald patches and sticky blisters of sap. Still, she preened.

"I could make a fortune at Astley's." She held the sad plant over her head. "See?"

Roisin gave her a withering look. "It's good to have aspirations."

They were limited in their gifting due to Poppy's inability to visit the village. She could get closer, nearly touch a toe to the main street, but the thrum of so many heartbeats still overwhelmed her. She requested Roisin buy her a set of watercolors in advance of the holiday, and spent a full night sequestered with the paints, paper, and ink. On Christmas Day, she proudly handed over her masterpiece: a bit of carefully written text, surrounded by daisies and daffodils and all manner of delicate, feminine flora.

"*Life, although it may only be an accumulation of anguish, is dear to me, and I will defend it,*" Roisin read aloud.

Poppy had expected a laugh. That was the whole intention of this Christmas gambit. Instead, Roisin looked at her very seriously, said "Thank you," and nailed the paper to the wall just next to the hearth.

"It was meant to be comical," Poppy protested. "The flowers, and the, you know, moroseness—"

"It's my present," she insisted, "and I may do with it what I wish."

Most days were too bright to attempt a trip into town, the white snow reflecting light up into the parts of their faces they revealed to the world by necessity. They went by night instead, peering into the windows of sleeping shopkeepers and grocers, Poppy staring longingly at the baker's display of buns and loaves of bread. His middle-of-the-night arrival was their cock-crow; when the baker lit his fires, they went back to Covenly. But his footsteps were light and he was hard to smell with so much blood around, and with a dusty layer of flour insulating his richness.

"Miss."

Poppy yelped, spinning to find him right behind her. Roisin was farther away, hidden in the shadows, ready to save Poppy, should the need arise. The sight of her somewhat relieved the terror, but not much.

"Miss, you look hungry. Here. From yesterday but still very fresh."

"Oh." The odor of his blood was heavy in her sinuses. "I couldn't."

"I insist, miss. And if you come back in the day, I'll give you a pie."

"I mustn't take from you, sir. You're too kind."

"Think nothing of it." He slipped the loaf into her arms and patted her on the shoulder. "Me ma always said to be kind to witches. I figure you'll like this far better than the milk what the old ladies leave on their windowsills."

Poppy laughed all the way home.

"Good god, Poppy, it wasn't that amusing," Roisin chided, but her flat mouth slipped from one side of her face to the other like a seal in the waves. Poppy took the loaf home and smelled it and watched it until it went stale, and when it did, she took out her watercolors and painted on it, little pictures of daisies and thrift and ferns growing from the beautiful slit at the top of the brown, hearty thing that had once been wheat from the ground.

They went to town during the day after that, Poppy drunk on confidence. She smiled at the grocer and the tailor and the cobbler and, of course, her friend the baker, whose name was Ben and was one of the few who didn't fear her.

"Verna—that's the cobbler George's wife—she says I oughtn't talk to you lest ye take me to your horrible lair and steal my entrails for your terrible potions. But I says to her, what would a young, pretty witch like Poppy want with my old entrails? If she wants entrails, there's always your son. Better that than what he gets up to with the Cobbe girl." He laughed, low and wheezy. "She didn't much like that, but she doesn't much like anything. Anyways, I tells her you don't have an eye on my entrails. Here,

120

have a sweet roll."

"Ben, you're far too generous. I've told you I can't eat any of it."

"Then give it to your familiar. Your black cat. See if I care. Or your ghost." He pointed at Roisin, loitering by the jam. "She could do with a little sweetness."

"I can't disagree," she told him conspiratorially.

Roisin didn't like Poppy's new friendship.

"The more they know about us, the more they'll suspect," she said when they had returned to Covenly. "People like that don't enjoy a foreign element in their town."

"I'm not foreign. I grew up in a place just like this."

"You're not human. Where you grew up is immaterial."

"I disagree." Poppy held the sweet roll up to her nose. "What would happen if I ate this?"

"Poppy, be reasonable. It's one thing to practice your restraint by visiting a shop now and then. It's another entirely to have the whole town gossiping about us. They'll think we're, we're . . ."

"Sapphites?"

"That's the best scenario."

"What's the worst?" She wrinkled her nose. "What if I just licked it a bit?"

"The worst is that they come up here and burn this place to the ground."

"Nonsense. Imagine how boring their lives would be if we weren't in them. A bit of the icing, maybe."

"I used to be able to go about my business without the old ladies of the town surveilling me. Now I can feel their eyes on my back while I pick up the post." She shivered. "And I don't like how they pull their children from us in the streets. Makes me feel like a pederast."

"Bit rich of you to call someone old," Poppy observed and took a bite of the sweet roll.

Roisin stared at her, aghast. "Did you actually eat that?"

"Tastes a bit off," she said, and projectile vomited blood clear across the kitchen.

It was February before guilt forced Poppy to tell Roisin about Carmen's instructions.

"She wants you to kill Cane," she admitted haltingly. "She wants me to convince you to do it."

"I don't need convincing." Roisin was sprawled in her chair, feet dangling off the edge. "It's what I plan to do."

"And what of me?"

"Did you like Carmen? I'm sure you're welcome to stay with the Brood."

"I could go with you," Poppy suggested, feeling a bit needy, a bit sheepish. "I can't fight, but I could do wonders for morale."

"No."

"I could be your drummer boy." She demonstrated on her knees. "I'm afraid I have no aptitude for the fife."

"Poppy, stop."

"Don't go. But if you must go, don't go alone. Let me come with you."

"You're a liability."

She pressed a hand to her chest, where genuine hurt bloomed. "That's unkind."

"You'll find it is extremely kind. You are not immune to Cane's mesmerism. I am. There are many things she could do to you with that sort of power."

"Kill me? Do you think I didn't consider that as a possibility?"

"She's far more creative than that. She could make you kill yourself and have me watch. She could puppet your body and use it to kill me, knowing that I would never raise a hand against you."

"You would, in that circumstance." Poppy brought up her knees, hugging them, attempting to disguise her fear under a cloak of nonchalance. "You would have to."

"I would rather not be in that position if I can avoid it. And I can avoid it by keeping you far away."

"And what if you didn't do it at all?"

"Didn't pursue her?" Roisin appeared to genuinely consider this, which was more than Poppy deserved, as she had asked the question out of pure, wheedling selfishness. "I cannot fool myself into believing she'll let me be forever. This was a brief respite. I am certain she still believes me to be her property."

"You aren't anyone's property," Poppy said fiercely.

Roisin's flat smile pressed into her cheek. "Well observed, Poppy. Aren't you clever."

"Be kind to me or I'll throw Ben's old loaf at your head."

"Maybe I ought to bring you along if you're so skilled at projectile bread-based combat. Tell me: how do you fare with the penny loaf cannon?"

In the day, they tranced side by side. Poppy closed her eyes and willed herself to think of something other than closing the distance between them and grazing her lips along Roisin's stark jaw. Leaving light kisses on her slender throat. Licking along the length of it, letting her fangs drop and drawing pink lines into her white flesh. Cupping her small breasts, rolling the hard nipples in her hand. Palming her quim, finding it hot and wet and wanting. She wondered, as the afternoon's light burned outside, what Roisin would sound like. Was she the sort who kept all her sweet noises trapped behind her tight lips, held deep in her throat? Or was she one of the buttoned-up, prim ladies who wailed loud enough to wake the dead? What did she taste like—like her blood, a bright star with a lightning tang? Sweet, like a hug from someone who wasn't accustomed to the practice? Would she want to give pleasure to Poppy, to lay her down and use her long fingers for the purpose God intended?

Poppy slipped from bed before nightfall sometimes, tiptoeing to one room or other, pulling up her skirts, and bringing a hand to herself. It was easier than crossing that invisible boundary in the bed, easier than tossing her and Roisin's hearts into the sea and hoping they floated. Time was precious now. Soon, Roisin would be gone, and Poppy would be elsewhere, and it wasn't fair to throw their last weeks together into turmoil.

And yet.

What if they could have something? Something small and precious and brief, and be better for it? Or was to invite that sort of tenderness to put their souls under the butcher's cleaver?

On the longest days, Poppy went to the small room with the portraits and looked at Roisin's long life. The girl with soft cheeks. The youth in periwigs. The centaur with its hair in a cruel goddess's fist.

Poppy imagined a painting of her and Roisin together, surrounded by flowers and young, sprouting things, lit by the cool graces of the moon.

"What will I do without you?" she asked Roisin's many silent faces. They didn't say a thing.

Chapter 17

It was a different sort of spring than their last. What had once been cold and miserable now stood bright and proud, the day resting under a blameless blue sky, the night stretched out beneath a feast of stars. It was as though Covenly were giving them a parting gift. Poppy received it with ill grace.

"We can write to Carmen. Let her know to expect you," Roisin suggested, not for the first time. She was shuffling their writing supplies and selecting a clean sheet of paper, which she did with the utmost ceremony. "You're perfectly capable of going to London."

"Hm." Poppy held a poker from the hearth and listlessly stabbed the ashes. She had been in a foul mood lately. It wasn't her fault. Whenever she thought about what came next, a frantic wrongness seized her jaw and squeezed until snippy things came out. She was having a bad time, was all, and if she were to have a bad time then it was only fair Roisin should suffer commensurately.

It wasn't brave. If Poppy were brave, she might have stretched open her mouth and vomited all the true, terrible things she wanted desperately to say: that Roisin ought to stay. That Roisin ought to keep her close. That she was certain, from her scalp to the soles of her feet, that she was hopelessly in love with a woman who had always been halfway out the door.

So instead, she said, "I'm not certain."

"Not certain about the Brood?"

"Not certain I can handle London. Do you have any friends in Bath?"

Roisin, frustratingly, looked mildly entertained. "Don't you want to see Lizzy again?"

"What will I tell her? How will I explain that the funny scar on my bum is gone?"

"You have a funny scar on your bum?" Roisin's brow knit, molding logic from the nonsense. "Lizzy is aware of this scar?"

"*Had*. And yes. She said I must have been bit by an eel."

"Have you tried . . . not showing her your bum?"

"I like it here." She abandoned the poker and threw herself into her chair. "What if I stayed?"

"Alone?"

"I could always visit Ben. Maybe Verna could be coaxed into friendship."

"Poppy." Roisin came to kneel at her feet. "We knew this day was coming."

"You don't have to seem so pleased about it."

She raised her eyebrows. "You think I'm pleased?"

"You aren't weeping," Poppy complained, stroppy and shitty and too shameful about it to change course now.

Roisin's nowhere smile shifted and slid. "You'd like me to weep?"

"Yes." Poppy poked her in the shoulder with a pointed toe. "To weep and scream and bang on the floor."

Roisin assessed said floor, head cocked. "It's a bit much for me."

"Do you even care for me?"

Roisin's expression was too kind, too patient. Too maddeningly forgiving. "Have I ever given you the impression that I didn't?"

"You're indifferent."

"*Poppy*."

"You've lived too many years to care about the one you spent with me."

That, it appeared, was a bridge too far. Roisin's expression cooled. She rose abruptly and brushed off her trousers. "I refuse to do this with you."

"Above it, are we?" Poppy sneered. She, after all, was far from above it. She was so far below it she could see right up its skirts.

"Why are you trying to goad me?" Roisin asked. "Is it really so distressing to part amicably?"

"Yes."

Roisin turned her back. Her linen tightened over her slender shoulders. "I understand you want more from me, but your way of going about it is unkind."

"Your indifference is unkind."

"I am not," Roisin replied tersely, "*indifferent*."

"You haven't—" Her voice caught. Damn humiliating. If she wasn't going to take the high road, she had at least expected the low road to provide proper hiding spots. "You haven't once tried to kiss me."

"Nor have you tried to kiss me," Roisin replied, tart as an unripe berry.

"You didn't exactly make yourself available. Leaving me after my tree climax."

"I don't know why we're arguing," she deflected curtly. "I'm not angry at you for not trying to kiss me."

That nearly brought a tear to Poppy's eye. "You *aren't?*"

Roisin sighed, plainly exhausted. "What is it you want, Poppy?"

The list was too long, or maybe it was too short. Maybe it just said ROISIN in big, clumsy letters, the only sort Poppy could write.

Poppy scrambled for a hidey-hole. "When I woke up from my month in bed, you said you had finally figured out what it is that *you* wanted. Why don't you tell me that?"

"Oh." Roisin paused, silent, then bustled over to the table and busied herself shuffling papers. "It's immaterial."

"Please." Poppy looked at that hunched, skinny back. That crisp linen. Drank in the sight, memorized it, because this would all be over soon. She didn't want to part as nothing. Enemy combatants would be better than nothing. "What is there to lose?"

"Don't say that. There's always something to lose." Roisin's shoulders slumped, defeated—or, more likely, aware of Poppy's powers of irritation and choosing to avoid them. "If you want this from me, that's fine. But you have to settle."

"Hmph."

She lowered herself into her chair warily, her eyes locked on Poppy, warning her silently not to make any sudden moves.

"I remembered my mother recently," she began. "I don't think I properly explained that to you. I remembered her voice. The way she held—erm, the way she was with me." Her toes curled in discomfort. Even

126

after all this time, she struggled with anything that meant something. "Her language. Her stories. There was one she often told me about the great warrior Oisin and his love, the immortal princess Niamh. Niamh was from Tír na nÓg, the fairy world. It's a beautiful island, and the people who live there are gods called the Tuatha de Danann. In Tír na nÓg, they write poetry and feast and play music all day long, and they never get old."

"Sounds familiar."

"Not quite." Her jaw worked. "Niamh brought Oisin there, and he became the king. They had three children and were very happy. But one day, Oisin became homesick. He told Niamh he wanted to visit Ireland. Niamh let him, but she warned him not to touch the ground. Only three years had passed in Tír na nÓg, but three hundred had passed in Ireland and it was dangerous for him to touch the ground." She shrugged, as if to say, *What can you do?* "He went anyway."

"Did he touch the ground?"

"Yes." She propped her chin on her hand. "He fell off his horse. And when he did, all three hundred years caught up with him and he died."

"That's a terrible story."

She frowned. "It's one of the most well-loved stories where I come from, so I'll thank you to keep your bad opinions to yourself."

"And what you discovered that you wanted was . . . to go to the magical land?"

"No." She stared into the dark hearth. She had not changed in a year. She had not changed in a century. "We're not meant to stay in this place for long, Poppy. It's not for us."

"You said it was a place for immortals."

"I said it was a place for gods." She took a deep, steadying breath. "I haven't earned this. I am not allowed to be this happy."

Shame settled in Poppy's stomach. This was a woman to whom the world had been unreasonably cruel, and here Poppy was, kicking dirt in her face.

"Oh, petal."

"Don't call me that," she snapped. "Jesus wept, Poppy, don't you know what that does to me?"

"Obviously not!"

"Don't feign ignorance." Roisin crossed her arms over her chest, clamshell-tight and thin-lipped. "You know exactly what you're doing. You can goad me and manipulate me all you like, Poppy Cavendish, but I thought you would be kind enough to let me part without entirely debasing myself in service of making explicit what we both know to be true."

"We may never see each other again, do you know that?" Poppy pleaded, watching it all unravel, helpless to stop it. "She could kill you, and you won't allow us a moment of open affection because you're afraid."

"Of course I'm afraid!" Roisin cried. "But I have to subdue that fear, or I'll never get to her. I'll never have the strength. I've discovered what I want, Poppy. I don't want to kill her. I want to be done with killing her, so I can actually live my life."

"That doesn't sound particularly revelatory."

"Not to you, maybe. Tell me, do you know what it's like to be indifferent to your own existence?" Roisin might have laughed. She might have wept. "I will find her and kill her, and in doing so, I will keep her from you. If I succeed, I earn peace. Regardless, you will be able to live free of all of this. You'll be able to enjoy the life I cursed you with—"

"*Roisin.*"

"You've done nothing wrong." Her eyes shone. She kept them moving, a hummingbird landing on every ledge. "You can go on and—and fall in love, if it pleases you."

Poppy's stomach gripped. "You want that?"

Roisin aimed her hard gaze over Poppy's head, her eyes fixed on something only she could see. "Yes. I owe you happiness."

"*You* make me happy."

"You may think that," she said, conciliatory and shaky, "but you've only been with me for one year. We've been alone for most of it. Close quarters and all that. You had no choice. You're built to love, and I was here."

"No."

Roisin did not appear to take that in. "You're built to love," she repeated, "and I was here. And I'm the least deserving thing, the absolute least, after what I've done to you, and what I kept from you. And after my whole life, the whole wretched span of it, the last thing I deserve is to be cared for by someone as joyous as you. You deserve to be fulfilled and loved by someone who is capable of it."

Poppy's lips were numb. "You don't think you're capable?"

"How can I be? I've lived with half my memories for most of my life. I didn't have the early ones. The *human* ones. They were gone and now they're back and only for a handful of months have I known what it feels like to be loved by a mother. How in the hell could I love you if that part of me was gone for so long? It's like a language I can barely speak."

"Motherless people fall in love every day."

"Humans." A wistful word, from a faraway place. "I'm not human. I have lived more years than you've been alive not knowing what it's like to be human. Don't you understand?"

Understand? How was she meant to understand Roisin when the woman barely understood herself? Even now, her fangs were dropped, her control fraying, her fingers flexed to grip any still object, any anchor, that might keep her from flying off into the reckless, bare frenzy of unguarded emotion.

Oh. *Oh.*

"I understand." A strange certainty laid itself over Poppy's shoulders. She was calm down to her bones. She smiled.

Roisin narrowed her gaze. "Why are you looking at me like that?"

She was light as a bubble. She was a fairy. She could pull glasses from high shelves and dance on frozen grass. "You're amusing."

"Don't laugh at me."

"I'll do as I please."

"If you're committed to—to *frivolity*, I'll take my leave."

"Oh, sit down, mate. You're not going anywhere."

Roisin pursed her lips, her face gone lemon-sucking sour. "Don't speak to me that way."

"I'll speak to you as you deserve." Poppy leaned back in her chair, regarding Roisin through half-lidded eyes. Roisin visibly bristled. "You don't know what you're on about."

She reared back. "Pardon me?"

"She likes a good rule, our Roisin. A sensible, hearty truth. She can't love. She must go. She isn't human. Our Roisin doesn't like when things get murky."

"Don't talk about me as though I'm not here."

"Our Roisin." Poppy rose, stalking past the hearth, one careful footstep at a time. Roisin gripped the arms of the chair, eyes flicking left and right, an animal in a trap. "She talks like the rules are written in some big book. She talks like she knows best. And then truth is—are you ready for this, petal?"

"Stop."

"The truth is she's as unsure as the rest of us." Poppy stood stock still, shoulders straight and proud, hands on her hips. She had only a few inches of height over the seated Roisin, but she took them as her advantage and her due. "What a frightfully convenient skill she has, to say something and declare it as true. She says I can't love her because she's all but trapped me in this musty old pile. She says it and—poof! It's true."

"Stop this," Roisin said, her voice rising in pitch.

"There were a lot of rules she had, our Roisin. Only, one year ago, something happened." Poppy licked her lips. "She disobeyed herself."

She looked like a horse spooked by gunfire, jumpy and wild-eyed. "No."

"You've never turned anyone before me, have you?" Poppy knew the answer. She just wanted to see Roisin squirm. "How terrified you must have been, petal. How frightened that you had done something you'd never done before. For the whole year since, you've been grasping onto permanent things by your fingernails. *You can't. You mustn't. I am this* and *I am that* and *these are the things I deserve because of the sort of person I am.* Do you think just because you're terribly old you've earned some sort of permanence? You changed the second you bit me, and my only contribution was a resemblance to Clover. You must have been so frightened, to have done something so very new. So much the opposite from who you considered yourself to be. You poor, new thing. You wee babe."

Roisin's mouth worked. "You have no idea what you're talking about."

"And then," Poppy went on, "only months later, you began to remember all of the years you had been forced to forget. Suddenly, you realized that all the very true things you kept in your pockets weren't jewels. They were stones, and they were weighing you down. All this time, you had been *wrong.*"

"I'm done with this, Poppy." She scowled, tuppence eyes molten with liquid fear. "Stop."

Poppy did not stop. "You thought you were one sort of person, but you've got a whole other bit, too. Only it was deep inside. Hiding, just like you are now. Did you protect yourself with these assurances? Is this so no one can ever hurt you again, like Cane did?"

She felt the pain before registering the clap of sound, the zap of lightning before thunder. When she looked up, it was to find Roisin wearing a dazed expression, staring strangely at her own outstretched hand.

"Oh," said Roisin, in the vertiginous, slurred manner of the recently head-injured. "I've slapped you."

Coda

Roisin knew that Oisin and Niamh's story was a good story. Of course it was good; people had been telling it for centuries. Innumerable generations had loved this story so dearly that they had kept it alive through tellings and retellings, writings and teachings and songs. They told it in times of war and misery and joy, too, and it had held them up, a stable constant tying together a people squashed under the boot of a powerful, relentlessly violent neighbor.

And yet, Poppy had turned up her nose at the tale. This could not have been the fault of such an enduring story. Therefore, the only conclusion was that Roisin had bungled the telling.

This was unsurprising. She hadn't the facility to weave a tale. Her imagination was weak. Maybe that's why the future looked like nothing but fog.

There was a fundamental disconnect, in Roisin's mind, between Now and Next. Connecting the pieces was constant work. Days ahead were iron spikes and railroad ties in her hand; she laid each new bit as she hung off a moving train. If she didn't keep her eye on the track ahead, she was sure to derail.

Her eyes left the track. She slapped Poppy. She derailed.

Here she was, floating through the air, abandoned by a body that chose its future without her consent. She hovered through time, back to the horrified moment when she realized she had made her first vampire. Nauseated, head throbbing, blinking uncomprehendingly at blood-stained hands that might have belonged to a stranger, her tongue coated in the metallic taste of a changed life.

She could taste it now. Blood and iron and acidic panic, and the strange peace of weightlessness, of surrendering to a fall.

Why had she turned Poppy? Why had she lied to her about it? And, for heaven's sake, why had she slapped her? The simple answer was the defining correlative figure: Poppy. But for Roisin to blame Poppy for Roisin's own transgressions was to act as the biblical elders who punished Susanna for their own lecherous desires. Like Susanna before her, the only crime Poppy had committed was to exist. It was Roisin's own lust that had perverted her heart. She was the old relic of wicked days, and her sins had now come home.

She had started to remember Bible verses. They popped into her mind fully formed, filling her with the thrill of recognition. The *aha!* of a brick slotted into a glaringly empty slot. It was only after their return that she remembered how much she hated them.

She oughtn't blame Poppy. In truth, she ought to *thank* Poppy, because the correlative figure was the only reason Roisin hadn't perished of shame. Poppy had surprised Roisin each time: first, by who she was, so lovely and so strange. Then, by forgiving her for her greatest transgression, which Roisin still was not convinced she deserved. And finally, for laughing.

That was what happened after the slap.

"Oh," Roisin said. "I've slapped you."

"Oh, well, I suppose you did." Poppy rubbed her round cheek. "Not the best I've had, mate. You need to put more muscle in it."

"I'll, erm, take that under advisement."

That's about when the laughing started. It was Poppy, of course, who set it off, cheerful giggling wrapping around them both, loosening Roisin enough to join in. But something went wrong, or perhaps she had been loosened too far, because soon Roisin's laughter transformed into miserable, humiliating sobs. She was shaking all over and she couldn't stop, and she must have looked a terrible fright because Poppy scooped her into her arms, gathering her up on the chair and rocking her as though she were a child. Roisin couldn't even protest. Dignity dictated she ought to, but even if she could stop trembling long enough to shove out a word or two, she didn't want to. This closeness fed a deep, wailing bit of her that had starved for decades. So she wept and she shook and eventually they were in the bed and she continued on, because Poppy had done something, or loosened something, or been the correlative figure in several somethings that had turned Roisin into something entirely new.

Poppy had been right about all of it. Roisin was terrified. She barely recognized herself. She lived in fear of what her next mistake might be. Yet as much as Poppy derided Roisin's rules, Roisin had created them to keep herself safe. Now, she was concerned with Poppy's safety, too. If Roisin didn't cling to her principles, what might she bungle next?

Were she a more imaginative person, she might have provided a list. That she lacked the imagination to do so proved her point entirely.

And anyway, the rules served a functional purpose outside of providing Roisin comfort. They were stopgaps, put in place to prevent her from falling into another life like the one she had had with Cane. A life where someone had told her what to do, and Roisin, like a needy child, had begged to be told.

"Girl, bring me ale."

That was the first thing Cane had said to Roisin. And Roisin, desperate to please, had obeyed swiftly, spilling a few drops in her haste. Cane had marked her as a target from that very moment. She had seen how eager Roisin was, how biddable and wanting. So she gave more orders, good and bad and strange, and Roisin felt a surge of calm warmth whenever she did them right, and a correctness when she was punished for getting them wrong, like all the crooked paintings in the world had simultaneously gone straight.

Cane acted in much the same manner during coupling, and Roisin's stomach flipped at each blessed directive. Her mind was smooth, her body alive, and she thought she had found bliss. It was freeing to place herself entirely in someone else's hands. Until, of course, it wasn't.

Roisin had always known that she herself was to blame for how her time with Cane had ended. It was her hand that laid the track, so transparently greedy was she to serve. Of course Cane had been shocked at Roisin's disobedience. It was not in her nature to rebel.

A fundamental truth of Roisin's life was that she had a hole in her, a great, gaping thing, that wanted a firm hand. Roisin's wants could not be trusted. *She* could not be trusted.

Poppy had wants. She trusted them. She thought Roisin was good.

It was unbearable to feel so new.

Roisin didn't know how long she cried, shamelessly allowing Poppy to soothe her. Grabbing at the care and comfort with both hands.

"Cane will come for you if she knows what I feel for you," Roisin said, when she could finally speak again. "I *will* attempt to kill her, but I *must* follow her. T-to give her the attention she desires. And to keep her from you, a-and to convince her that you mean nothing to me."

"You'll be miserable for her benefit and mine."

"Yes."

"And what of your life?"

"I want you to be h-happy," Roisin mumbled into the material of Poppy's dress, tightening her arms around that wonderfully soft body. "If I owe you anything—"

"I thought we were through talking about what I'm owed."

Not until I give you everything I have, everything I am.

"Let me do this for you." Roisin touched her small, sweet nose. Watched her lips twitch in a knowing grin. "What?"

"For now."

"What do you mean 'for now'?"

"I mean you'll go off now and we'll see what happens."

"I tend to stay the course."

"Experience proves otherwise."

So it did. Which was why Roisin snuck out the next morning to post her letter before she could think better of it. Poppy was still deep in her trance when Roisin rose, her mouth lazily open, her eyelids twitching. Her eyes were so large and round that her eyelids didn't fully cover them, leaving a strange little slit of white exposed to the elements, shielded only by pale, curling lashes. It was an odd feat, a bit remarkable and a bit disgusting and if Roisin didn't move she would kiss those strangely hemmed eyelids, so she moved.

The weather finally matched the mood: appropriately gray and foggy, the clouds a low, thick boundary, cutting off the earth from the celestial. She gave over the letter with a curt word and stomped all the way home.

Poppy was awake when she returned.

"Where did you go?" She sleepily pushed her hair from her face. It always got so tangled during trances, a terrible mess of unspooled gold thread. She moved constantly. She made a fuss. She made a ruckus. She

135

was messy and demanding and ruined absolutely everything.

Roisin could barely speak, for the love of this absurd woman. "The posting inn."

"Oh," Poppy said. Roisin would have preferred her to scream.

They went back to bed and Roisin couldn't help but sob once more, her body shivering, her eyes aching. "I'm sorry. I'm sorry for this."

Poppy stroked her hair, and she felt it in her ribs. "I did say I wanted you to weep for me. Besides, you haven't wept in a century. This is more than appropriate."

"We ought to be doing something fun."

Poppy wrinkled her nose in thought. "Do you fancy a bit of reading?"

They read *The Monk* because he got what he deserved, and life was so rarely that way. In the day, they lay together, silent and exhausted, examining one another's hands and faces. Sometimes they laughed and talked of nothing. Often, Roisin cried.

Poppy didn't kiss her. Perhaps she sensed Roisin was too fragile for such a gift. The abstinence was a mercy; no doubt that after one kiss, Roisin would do whatever Poppy asked of her, and love it. She was meant to preserve Poppy's life, and Poppy seemed concerned with preserving Roisin's dignity. Neither could take the risk.

And yet, Roisin wanted desperately to be kissed. To be held down and desired, teased and tortured and loved in the way she was certain only Poppy knew how. A creature built to love, with joy spilling out from every bit of her. Joy braided into her golden curls and threaded through her large, round eyes. They were the damp blue of twilight, the time of day when vampires awaken. To stare into them was to arise.

Now and Next. Poppy had asked her what she wanted, and Roisin had said to be done with killing so she could live her life, and that was true, but it was even simpler than that. Roisin's long life was nothing but Next, Next, Next—trying to outwit a woman cleverer and stronger and older than she was, who never failed and never rested. Becoming so indifferent to her existence that a desire couldn't take root. What Roisin wanted was Now, a big fat feast of it. To glut herself on the plenty of Now, to sit and be idle and think of nothing but how the cool night breezes felt on her unblemished skin.

And if Poppy were there, she wouldn't mind terribly.

No. That was unkind, and impossible. Not only did it have the stink of Pygmalion upon it, but to love the immortal she had made was exactly what Cane had done to her, and look how that turned out. Besides, Roisin was still mostly certain that Poppy's love for her would atrophy in her absence. Poppy would get a great big Now and Roisin would prop her body between the woman she loved and the unceasing blows of Next, Next, Next.

And if Roisin killed Cane, and Poppy still carried a torch for her, well, they would cross that bridge as it came.

It wouldn't be that way.

If Roisin managed to kill Cane, she would afterward find herself in a world in which Poppy was happy with someone else. And if not that, Poppy would surely have come to her senses and learned to hate Roisin for what she had done: for turning her, for leaving her—Poppy could have her pick. Roisin would take that world and be satisfied. She would take whatever world she deserved and have a nice, long seat outside in the dark and appreciate the gift of having hands free of iron.

She'd have to swallow a lot of longing to get there.

She did this, as days passed. She ate her tears instead of letting them fall, and willed her trembling to still. She felt less, and tried to forget how maddening it was to be inches from Poppy and still unkissed.

"Don't do this," Poppy pled. "You're hurting yourself."

"I'm preserving myself."

Poppy couldn't argue with that. Roisin's stomach twisted with guilt. She ate the guilt too, a bit of tonic for her persistent, human ailment.

Packing was horrible. Poppy's things looked so little in the dusty trunk Roisin had unearthed for this purpose. She had only a few garments, some paper, and a couple of books.

That was all there was to show for their year. A full year, round as a ball, no sharp edges, with a good heft when held. When Roisin was with Cane, Cane had lavished her with gifts. Their trunks had always been overfilled. They had to sit on them to close them.

Poppy shut the mostly empty trunk with her foot and gave it a little desultory kick.

"Do you want to bury my flower loaf in the garden? It's starting to mould."

As they lowered the loaf into the earth, Poppy offered a miserable dirge of a psalm, delivered with such fussy pomp that Roisin had to hide her laughter behind her hand. As turnabout was fair play, Roisin contributed a bit of a funeral song she was beginning to remember. It had to do with spending money in good company, and drinking health from a parting glass. She had expected a laugh from Poppy. Instead, Poppy just stared. She was blinking very fast.

"That was lovely, Roisin."

Roisin had to duck her head. "No." She wasn't sure what exactly she was refusing.

"Roisin, you don't have to—"

"You're so stubborn." So vexingly stubborn, so insistent on what she wanted, so certain that she wanted Roisin. It was only a matter of time before Poppy realized there was nothing there to want. What vital twenty-one-year-old immortal would tie herself to the bony ghost woman that time forgot?

The sorry truth was that the only times Roisin felt like there was something worth loving in herself were the moments Poppy looked at her with those carelessly big eyes, otherworldly and lovely and aglow with misplaced tenderness. Those nights when Poppy twitched her nose and brought up her round, rosy cheeks, and said something absurd and irritating, her mouth like a damned sweet pea. When she laughed, which was often, and Roisin got to be near her and made good in the flickering nimbus of her light.

"I'm not stubborn," Poppy protested, stamping her foot. Roisin might have laughed, if her laughter hadn't been pinned under a blacksmith's anvil of misery. Instead, she smiled as best she could. As best she knew how. Poppy rolled her eyes.

Roisin floated, the days ahead too glowing hot to touch, molten hot—hands off lest she burn and burn and burn until there was nothing left but a pile of ashes and a plaque beside it reading, "Whatever this thing was, someone loved it."

The carriage came the next evening. Carmen's footman emerged with a bow and some quick words. Roisin didn't hear his name, but Poppy said, "Thank you, Freddie," so he must have introduced himself. Roisin could barely move. Around her, things shifted. Trunks placed in the carriage.

Poppy putting on a bonnet. A rabbit ducking into a hole. A door closing.

She closed her eyes and breathed. When she opened them, Poppy was beside her.

"This is my home." That lovely, small chin held high and proud. "By rights and by lawful occupation. It's mine, and I'll have it." She reached out, grabbed Roisin's hand, and squeezed it. "You're mine, Roisin. I'll have you, too."

The breath punched out of her chest. "You can't know that," she whispered, airless, succumbing to the reflex of placing a cold denial where something nicer might have fit just as well. There were cracks in the windows in front of her, in her house. That's where the bees got in.

"We'll see," Poppy said.

Roisin was sick with longing. She wanted to relax into the surety of this small, strange woman and be carried off. Her awareness of danger kicked in, like the jolt of falling as she slipped into a trance. She swallowed, and she swallowed again.

Now and Next.

They got into the carriage. Behind them, Covenly got smaller and smaller, until they could see nothing but wildflower, shrub, and clover.

Part II

London, 1838

Chapter 18

Poppy smelled London before she saw it. The air was reliably fetid, tinged dusky with the fog of commerce. The Thames gave off its usual, unmentionable odors. And through it all, the people. Blood-rich as ticks, their many hearts cricketing in a beckoning susurrus. Her mouth watered.

Roisin opened the door of the carriage, and the red smell slammed into Poppy like a wall of seawater. She choked, covering her face with a quivering hand.

"Poppy."

"I'm fine." She steeled her jaw, stemming the ache. "Fine."

Roisin gazed at her with concern, quickly discarded. "Here we are."

Poppy nearly tripped over her skirt. "*Here?*"

It was the sort of Mayfair redbrick so grand it could only be one of a collection, along with a country manor, a shooting box, and perhaps a set of apartments meant for a lesser son or dowager aunt. The type of place that stood empty for half of the year, if one didn't count the cadre of servants paid to keep it ever ready, should the master follow a whim and demand comfort. The whole thing was frosted like a cake in detailed stonework and frothy wrought iron, an absurd assortment of ornamentation dripping from every visible inch. Poppy felt sickeningly drab in its shadow.

Freddie the footman knocked. In short order, a gray-haired, middle-aged butler—human and smelling richly of blood—welcomed them into the grand foyer.

"The mistress is in the sitting room with Master Valentin," he informed them with a put-upon air. "Not that either of them are sitting."

"Thank you, Godfrey." Roisin didn't wait for the butler's lead, pressing past him with the confidence of a woman intimately familiar with her surroundings. Poppy followed dizzily.

"The last time I was here he was seventeen," Roisin whispered when Poppy caught up, blinking away the afterimages of a garishly bright Pierrot painting she spied on a far wall. "He was ginger."

She pushed open a door. Behind it stood a naked man, very pale and very blonde, holding a bunch of grapes over his delicate parts.

"Finally," he drawled, dropping the bunch. "Some blasted entertainment."

"*Valentin.*" A groan floated up from a corner of the room, its origin blocked by a massive canvas atop an easel. "I told you not to move."

"Terribly sorry, *cherie*, but I've been standing here for hours. I may be immune to fatigue but I am certainly not immune to boredom."

He strode forward, entirely unbothered by his state of undress, and opened his arms to receive Roisin in a warm embrace. His glacial gaze roved over her shoulder as he stroked her back, and he caught Poppy's eye.

"Well." He pulled off, placing his hands on his slender hips, a framing that dared her to look. "You must be *la nouvelle.*"

"Don't frighten the poor girl." The figure behind the canvas finally emerged. There was Carmen, tall and willowy, dark hair half-piled atop her head, her eyebrows thinly plucked. Deep blue skirts swirled around her, crinkling like the sparks Poppy had always loved to call up as a child by rubbing her feet on the rug. "So good to see you again, Poppy. This is Valentin. We do hope you'll be comfortable here."

"We understand you won't be staying with us, Roisin." Valentin pouted. "A terrible shame. You ought stay for a few nights, at least. To sit for Carmen, if nothing else. Let's have you painted without that awful woman leering over you."

"That awful woman is why I must go." Roisin's affable mien was a fresh betrayal. "It's time she and I finally settle our differences, don't you think?"

"I have new pigments." Carmen placed an imploring hand on Roisin's shoulder. "We could finally do you as Dionysus."

Roisin smiled, flat and reliable, and demurred, and the conversation went on, pleasantries and well-wishes and requests for tales of the time they were apart. It went on, and Poppy's eyes watered because it was ludicrous. How could they all speak so calmly? How could Roisin betray her with ambivalence, after she had wept so freely and so heavily? Where was Poppy's hearth, her flags, her chair?

"I have to—I'm sorry." She sped off towards the door, her simple shoes clacking on the marble floors. As she stepped out into the street, an arm hooked her elbow before she could take off running.

"Hello, Poppy."

Disappointment surged in her chest. Not Roisin, but Carmen.

"I'm sorry. Your home is beautiful. But I can't—"

"I know this isn't your first choice, but may I offer you some enticements?"

It wasn't as though she had anywhere else to go. Ahead of her, the city sprawled, corridors and corridors of shut doors. "I suppose."

"Well, first I ought to tell you that we don't often take in new members. If you care about exclusivity, you've accomplished the impossible." She made a seat on the stoop, leaving room for Poppy beside her. Reluctantly, she sat. They were feet apart, but Carmen's skirts still managed to spill over onto Poppy's lap. "We're all of us queer, in case Roisin hadn't made that clear. Being careful with new members is as much for our pleasure as it is for our protection."

"You're vampires."

"Well spotted."

"I only mean, is it not harder to be a vampire than queer? Or, rather, can't you escape whatever scrapes you might end up in—"

"Newgate, but continue."

"—by virtue of, well, your gifts?" She blinked. "Wait. Newgate?"

"I trust you've heard of it."

"I never heard of a woman going to Newgate for sapphism, mate. I reckon we're safe."

"You might be," Carmen replied coolly. "But if a magistrate were to strip me, he wouldn't see what he would consider a woman's body. Do you understand?"

Poppy could have slapped herself for being so tactless. "Of course. Yes. You know," she said, because she felt like she had to, "I've had friends like you. Erm, you know. Like *you*. And I think they're lovely. And you! I think you're terribly lovely . . ." She took a deep breath, words juddering to an uneasy stop. "I didn't mean to be rude."

"No. Of course you didn't." Carmen eyed her with plain assessment. Poppy felt very small.

"I don't care about your little friends," Carmen said firmly, eyes fixed across the street. She fingered the necklace at her throat, a large, blue stone set in rows of diamonds. A breeze blew back her long, dark hair, teasing the there-and-gone sparkle of matched earrings. A *parure*, Poppy remembered vaguely. A Frenchified word for a thing she had never dreamed of being so near. "Don't break your back showing me I'm acceptable to you. I don't require your approval."

"Yes," Poppy said at once. "Yes, of course."

"To answer your previous question: Why don't I use my abilities to skirt the law? I've lived for a very long time. I must run because I am a vampire. I refuse to let anything else chase me. Do you understand?"

"Yes." She paused. "May I ask you a question?"

"Of course. Though whether or not I answer is under my discretion."

"Do all the humans who work for you know what you are?"

Her painted lips turned up at the corners. "Oh, yes."

"And you're not concerned they'll reveal your secrets?"

"If they do, they may deal with the consequences," Carmen stated simply. Poppy shivered. "But why should they? We pay them exorbitantly. The best paid household in the city, and that is saying something, as you can probably imagine. Massimo—you'll meet him tomorrow night—has a very interesting gift. He shields us all. So while we live among society, they think we all are terribly boring. That appeals to most of the mortals in our employ."

"They're like us?"

"Some. Our dear Godfrey is as much a left-handed man as anyone in this city, bless him. Others bear their own secrets, none of which I am free to tell you."

"I wouldn't ask."

Carmen granted her a small, skeptical squint. "Of course you wouldn't."

Across the road, a linkboy led a man through the night, the golden glow of his torch lighting up his face like a painted cherub. Neither head turned toward the grand dame and her companion, hunched on the stoop like beggars.

"You got what you wanted," Poppy said after the boy's golden light had disappeared around a corner. "She's going after Cane."

Carmen sighed heavily. "So she is."

"Don't act so pleased."

"Don't make assumptions." Her skirts rustled. "Just because I wanted this doesn't mean I am blind to its tragedy."

"She'll be alone." Poppy's eyes ached. There were no stars here. "She's leaving me."

Carmen reached out slender fingers and gently pushed a lock of Poppy's golden hair behind her ear. It was too tender, and it made Poppy shake.

"I cannot imagine the pain you're in, *pobrecita*. Come live with us. Perhaps we can make you happy."

Poppy gave a thick chuckle. "I don't see that as a possibility."

"Well, then consider us a safe haven in which to be sad."

She imagined herself walking through the halls in her country clothes, muddying the marble floors with her misery. "I'll lower the value of the house."

"Would you truly choose to be a sad little wastrel? We have orgies. Doesn't that sound fun?"

Poppy replied with a reluctant grin. Carmen mirrored it, her smile wide and knowing. In an instant, the smile melted away. Poppy was left to wonder for only one moment, just until Carmen brought a long-fingered hand to Poppy's face, catching the sudden onslaught of tears.

"I'm sorry," she choked. "I didn't mean—"

"Don't apologize. My dear, there is nothing to apologize for."

Arms came around Poppy's shoulders, dragging her against a sturdy, sweet chest. Poppy let herself weep, soaking the costly weave of Carmen's frock. She sobbed and she choked, and barely noticed when Carmen scooped her up in strong, slender arms and carried her back into the house. Soon, she found herself deposited in a soft bed, Carmen's warm body curled around her.

"Come, now. Let's trance together."

"You trance in diamonds?"

There was some movement behind her. Then, a cool weight fell over her chest.

147

"No, *pobrecita*. Tonight, you do."

She gulped, fingers finding the tiny, harsh corners of the necklace. The stones cost more than her life. The bed was soft, the bedclothes fresh and whole, without any moth-eaten edges or thin spots from wear. She was an interloper, someone from a world of dullness and gray tones dropped unceremoniously into one of the vivid paintings in Cane's secret room. "I can't—"

"Quiet, now. You'll feel better tomorrow."

Reluctantly, she let her eyes fall shut.

In the sort of dark that is sweeter for the press of light outside its bounds, Poppy felt a kiss on her forehead, and with it, a few soft, sad words.

By the time the moon rose the following evening, Roisin was gone.

Chapter 19

In her first month with the Brood, Poppy rarely left her room. Carmen helpfully supplied her with rabbits—they kept a hutch in the back garden—as well as company, but eventually even Carmen's patience thinned. At the moonrise of Poppy's fourth Friday in London, Carmen informed her that she refused to aid in what she had correctly identified as self-indulgent moping.

"You haven't even met the others, *nena*," Carmen chided, brandishing what she made clear would be the final rabbit-in-bed. "Massimo's taken to calling you *La Traviata*."

"What does that mean?"

"Nothing good. Make yourself decent, now. It's time to join the Brood."

Miserably, Poppy conceded. Even if the moping were commensurate with the grief (Lizzy had once told her that a jilted lover was due a moping period equal to half the duration of the relationship), she was being a piss-poor guest. It was a testament to her misery—and, perhaps, the strangeness of spending a year in a manor home that had been her property—that she hadn't known the urgent need to scrub Carmen's floors and kiss her toes the minute she set eyes on her new quarters. Naturally, the room was exquisite. Carmen had called it the Rose Room, and it was an apt enough title to be redundant. The walls were papered in a floral toile, a repeating pattern of looped roses climbing from baseboards to molding, a vertical garden equal only to Briar Rose's prison. Two layers of heavy hangings draped the tall windows, pea green and dusky pink, fastened to a brass rod with metal flowers blooming from either end. A criminally plush oriental rug of spring green and faded reds cushioned the parquet, which itself was smooth as glass. The bed was canopied and grand, sculpted from, well, *wood*—Poppy had never developed an eye for wood identification, but she could have been convinced it had been retrieved from a fairy forest, it glowed so warmly.

Opposite the bed, the vanity reflected her personal wreckage: a tuft of yellow hair under the many pink and green blankets that shielded her. It was minor chaos, all told. Poppy had seen herself after nights on the lash, rolling out of bed with a sandy mouth and a head full of sleigh bells. She had spied her swollen face in the middle of spring two years prior, when hay fever turned her eyelids into apricots and filled her nose with algaenous sludge. This was nothing like that. From forehead to chin, she looked as she always did, ever since the change. Here, in the full, unbroken and fastidiously cleaned mirrors they had been deprived of at Covenly, Poppy was at her loveliest, with the smooth, vampirically glassy skin that was the closest thing she had to a new family resemblance.

It was an indignity. If a woman were to be miserable, she at least ought to look the part. But vampires didn't take on eye bags and burst capillaries. They didn't bite bits of flaking skin from dry lips, exposing raw, red flesh. Vampires didn't soothe their sorrows with custard and gin, summarily vomited as a uniquely painful and humiliating ritual of cleansing. Her heart hadn't even properly broken—how could it, when it didn't beat?

So she rose, and she grumbled, and she allowed Carmen to button her into what was undoubtedly her best frock.

"This is a rag." Carmen traced the path of pink ribbon with a long finger. "We'll get you nicer things."

"I haven't any money."

"I put away my first funds in the sixteenth century. Believe me, they've had plenty of time to accrue." She clicked her tongue, observing herself in the looking-glass opposite Poppy's bed, fussing with her earrings. "You'd have learned about our finances already, if you had bothered at all to come out of your blasted room."

"Would an apology be worth anything?"

Carmen thoughtfully pushed a pin into the dark, heavy mass of her hair. "Maybe to you."

Chagrined, Poppy followed the mistress of the house down the grand staircase and through to a warm sitting room. There, sheepishly, she introduced herself to the assembled parties.

There was Valentin, of the nude portrait session. He was French originally, she learned, and hadn't lost his general disdain for all things English.

"The d'Orsay style," he informed Poppy tartly when he caught her staring at his painfully dandyish waistcoat and cravat. "Just because this entire island has fallen under the spell of that miserable Brummell doesn't mean I have to follow suit."

There, the fabled Massimo, a wide smile stretching his strong, dark features. He greeted her with a booming *"Buongiorno!"* followed by a riot of cheek kisses and one generous pinch. He wore an embroidered blue mantua over a yellow petticoat, which he explained was the sort of thing a woman might have sported a hundred years prior. From the corner of the room, Valentin's eyes tracked his every move.

There, Karol and Zahrah. Karol was Russian, she explained, which is why she enjoyed sipping from humans drunk off of vodka (this, apparently, was a longstanding joke). Her face was round, her features Asian, and her manner comfortingly direct. Beside her stood Zahrah, apple-cheeked, dark-skinned, and incredibly warm, with a froth of curls shoved under a silk top hat. Both women wore frock coats and trousers, and held heavy snifters filled with brandy purely for effect.

"Should I have worn a frock coat?" Poppy asked. "I feel horribly out of place."

"Impossible," Zahrah assured her. "You look lovely, my friend. Is that pink ribbon? If you found yourself a gown of that exact shade, I'd fall right over."

The Brood chatted like only lifetime friends could, with private jokes and unfinished thoughts, seamlessly completed by the next person. Stories were passed around like morsels of food, touches of affection like sips of wine. Despite the lingering embarrassment of her month in hiding, Poppy found herself drawn in. Massimo was genial, Carmen steady, Zahrah jovial, and Karol frank, and they all made room for her. Valentin was in turns acerbic and taciturn, but never outright hostile, and his presence cut through the nearly stifling attention like vinegar over fish and chips. The hours passed companionably. Poppy should have been delighted.

How would Roisin be in a group like this? Would she dazzle the room with her wit? No, of course not. She would sit beside Poppy, their hands pressed together. She would let Poppy sparkle, and they would go home together, and Roisin would tell her she had been charming. And Poppy would tell Roisin that it all had been for her, every last bit of it.

Poppy found she didn't have much to say.

Near dawn, a group of human maids and footmen entered the room.

"Ah, thank you all for joining us." Carmen stood in welcome. "Poppy, these are our friends. We will be drinking from them today. The rules are as follows: drink from the wrist, swallow your mouthful before taking the next, and stop as soon as you feel a tap on the head. Jane and I will demonstrate."

A maid peeled away from the pack, hopping up to Carmen's side with obvious anticipation. Carmen leaned down and kissed her on the mouth, slowly and tantalizingly. The girl's knees softened, and she eagerly held out an unclad arm. Carmen gave a wicked grin, fangs dropping. She held the girl's wrist, slowly smelling the flesh from palm to elbow, her nose dragging across creamy skin. From across the room, Poppy could see the girl's pulse rabbiting. It made her mouth water.

"Good girl," Carmen cooed, and bit.

The effect on the girl was immediate. She moaned as Carmen sucked, helplessly groping her sex through her skirts. She shivered and trembled, thrusting against her own hand. Another maid, moved to action, grasped the girl from behind, keeping her upright while feverishly stroking, pinching the maid's nipples and licking her neck. As the convulsions began to die down, the girl raised a hand and tapped Carmen on the head.

"Well done," Carmen told the girl, who smiled lazily up at her. She carefully carried the spent human to the rug and laid her by the fire, leaving her with a gentle kiss before returning to the assembled, eager staff.

Poppy choked. The air smelled red. Her chest heaved. In her mind, tuppence eyes flashed.

"I'll have a rabbit," she heard herself say. "I'd prefer that."

Carmen cocked her head, concern narrowing her gaze. "Are you sure?"

"Yes, I—yes. Thank you."

Valentin looked up from his dark corner. "I'll show her the hutch."

"You needn't—"

"It's all right. Come along, *nouvelle*."

She followed him into a moonlit back garden, where a rabbit hutch housed a number of fat, squeaking beasts. She reached in and drew one out, biting it with relish, sublimating her desire and sorrow in its hot blood.

"Aren't you having one?" she asked, dictated as much by politeness as nerves because Valentin was looking at her in a knowing way that was not altogether comfortable. He had light eyes, blue as springtime. In them, she could finally understand how some eyes might be described as "piercing"—needles, not swords. A bouquet of them.

He shook his head. "There's a man in there I like to bite. It makes him spend in his trousers."

"Delightful."

"Immeasurably." He perched on a bench, his gaze poking holes in her frock. "Do you not drink from humans?"

"No.

"Why not?"

She licked her lips and swallowed. "Perhaps I'm afraid I'll enjoy it too much."

"Ah." He arched an eyebrow. "Denying yourself pleasure for fear it will consume you."

"Is that not better than being consumed?"

"English." He made a derisive little sound. "Absolutely no self-control."

"I suppose you're the expert." She cast down her drained rabbit. "How can you stand to be near him?"

His eyes widened, but he didn't dispute her. "How? Or why?"

"Either. Both."

"Well, the how is easy: I would rather be with him than apart from him, so I refuse to let myself be broken by my desires. That he considers me a friend, his *greatest* friend, is enough because it must be. As for the why?" He shrugged. "*La même chose.* The very same thing."

"How can you stand it?"

"How could I stand the alternative?" He rose, brushing invisible dirt

153

from his trousers. "I'll give you some advice, *nouvelle*. Our lives are long. Terribly, hideously long. You, *ma chérie*, may never stop loving her. Perhaps she will return for you. Perhaps not. Regardless, you have a life to live." He dusted off his shoulder, looking exceptionally bored. "I suggest you live it."

Chapter 20

She did her level best. She went to society functions, introduced as Valentin's cousin from abroad, spending the night with him hissing in her ear to keep her mouth shut lest she give away their game with her, as he called them, *barn manners*. Karol and Zahrah took her to special clubs where they were welcomed clothed as gentlemen or as ladies, one night dressing Poppy in a frock coat and laughing uproariously as her bosom nearly burst the seams. Massimo took her dancing, twirling her through music halls, his wide smile sparkling like diamonds. She laughed and she laughed and she laughed.

Carmen was the easiest company. They went to the opera and to the molly's clubs, to the secret, high-stakes card tables and to dingy public houses. Carmen knew everyone, and was well received in nearly every room. She largely avoided the balls that constituted the season ("too dangerous," she explained, gesturing at her elegant jawline) but went seemingly everywhere else. She also enjoyed a night at home, and soon began teaching Poppy to paint. Poppy, as it turned out, had no real talent aside from drawing flowers, but enjoyed listening to Carmen explain the pigments and the oils, the stretched canvas and the careful ways to manipulate the brush hairs so that a blob of white became the crest of a wave, a dab of yellow transmogrified a carmine-leaning red splotch into a sunbeam. It reminded her of long nights at the hearth, carefully picking over *The Monk*, learning the shape of the words as she went.

She read feverishly because it reminded her of Roisin. She stopped reading because it reminded her of Roisin.

She looked for tuppence eyes and shining, dark hair in every room she entered. She listened for the rolling poetry of a faint lilt. When she entered her trance, she found herself back at Covenly, in the arms of a woman who had lived and lived and lived.

Sometimes, she watched Lizzy. She was secretive about this.

"Where are you off to?" Valentin asked, watching Poppy tiptoe toward the door one Tuesday evening. "You're free to come and go as you please, you know. You don't have to act like a child with a curfew."

She tightened her bonnet. It was the darkest item she owned, an undignified dove gray that would not camouflage her, but wouldn't draw attention.

"Why do you want to know?"

"Do you have a lover?"

She tipped her head, a coy little move she hoped would convey that this was a distinct possibility. "Perhaps."

"No, you don't. I can see it in your eyes. You're too sad."

"Maybe my lover makes me sad."

"You only have room for one tragic love at a time. You're not a complicated enough person for more."

She wasn't sure whether she had been insulted. "Don't you have somewhere to be?"

"Where might you suggest?" He rested a hand on his hip, entirely at ease.

She was losing her patience. "Up your own arse, for a start."

"I scarcely need your invitation," he murmured, admiring his manicured nails. She scoffed and quitted the place, trying not to slam the door behind her.

Gas lamps led her out of Mayfair, but the streets dimmed as she stepped into her old haunts. Here, the fine gentlemen who visited the working women paid local linkboys for the twin services of a lit way and unmolested pockets. Poppy didn't need gas or flame to see anymore, not with her new eyes. Nor did anyone pay her much attention. This was Massimo's gift in action, shielding her even on her own, so far from the rest of the Brood. But maybe her appearance helped too: the unremarkable dove gray, her bosom tucked away, her hair entirely hidden, her face free from paint. She was not a whore, not a patron, not a beggar, not an innocent. Not maiden, nor mother, nor crone. A no one, navigating the warren of streets with quiet footsteps. After a series of familiar turns, she ducked into an alley, scaled a wall, and hoisted herself onto the flat roof of a building that housed a mean bookshop and a handful of sorry rooms. From her nest atop the world, she could peek into a window and watch a ginger head duck this way and that. A pale woman paint her face in the vanity. A friend go about her work. And in the morning, as the sun began to rise, she could sneak through the window, drop a small pouch of coins on the table, and be out before anyone could spy her.

On her third night's vigil, she realized she was not alone.

"This is inconvenient," said Zarah, straightening her waistcoat and laying down her cane. "Couldn't you have selected a lovely park bench instead?"

She wore a deep blue frock coat with fawn Cossack trousers and gleaming, coffee brown hessians. Her journey up the face of the building had dirtied her; light, chalky stains striped her coat, while darker smudges adorned her trousers. She, along with the rest of the Brood, dressed fastidiously. That she braved this ghastly sullying to join Poppy was unexpectedly heartwarming.

Poppy hadn't spent much time with Zahrah alone; she and Karol were a matched set. Poppy liked Zahrah, though. She had clever things to say and a sonorous voice to say them in. She didn't have an accent so much as a different rhythm, a musicality to her voice. Some words were high, some low, and some fell as though tapped off a table by a mischievous cat.

"Why don't you go talk to her?" she said now, low and crooning.

"Why did you follow me?" Poppy demanded, both irritated by the intrusion and glad for the company. "I'm not doing anything wrong."

"No, no, of course not." Zahrah removed her top hat. Her hair was plaited down against her scalp in lines, braids slender by her forehead, thickening as they reached her nape. A plaited bun sat at the base of her head, tight and smart. "I was only curious where you were going. I used to be a tracker, you know."

"You tracked me?"

She shook her head, unrepentant. "Nah, but I did follow you. I've been wondering where you were going."

"You might have asked."

"This seemed simpler." She sat, propping her hat beside her. "Carmen told me to leave you alone."

"You didn't think to listen to her?"

Zahrah had quick, dark eyes, the kind that seemed specially crafted for sly, silent communication. "My reasoning is, if you're free to do as you please, I'm free to do the same. And if you want me to fuck off, you can tell me to fuck off." She waggled her eyebrows. "Shall I fuck off, *nouvelle?*"

It was a rare occurrence that someone could charm their way into Poppy's company, especially by being a little bit annoying. That was typically Poppy's purview.

Well, it was always nice to be in the company of another artist. "You were a tracker in the military, then," Poppy supplied, predicting the exact triumphant grin Zahrah gifted her in return.

"In several militaries," she confirmed. "I was a soldier of fortune, until I met Karol and dedicated my life to luxury and sin. Do you know of Amina?"

"No. Should I?"

"Everyone should." She leaned back, eyes fixed somewhere in the distance. "My queen. I served her and the nation of Zazzau for years, until I was turned. Never a more fearsome warrior, nor a more powerful leader. But your tiny bloodless mass of a country could never understand." She pursed her lips, letting fly a *tsk* of derision. "She was a world of a woman."

"Did you love her?"

"Of course. She was my queen."

"As a lover?"

She chuckled, enjoying a private joke. "I valued my life more than that."

"Why did you leave?"

"Well, England does have something Zazzau did not."

Poppy watched a thick, sulfurous plume of smoke belch out of a nearby chimney. "Oyster Rooms?"

"Clouds." She held the word in her mouth, pink tongue grazing a fang. "Not that I mind the night terribly much, but I like a lovely, gray afternoon."

"And the fog?"

"It's revolting." She squirmed in pleasure. "I adore it. Now, why won't you greet your pretty little cocksucking friend?"

158

"Oh, I don't know." She drew up her knees and rested her chin in the vee between them. "What am I meant to tell her?"

"Whatever you want to," Zahrah said, as though this were the simplest thing in the world. "There used to be rules about that sort of thing. Ways to keep humans from kicking up a fuss. But the Immortal Council is long gone, so everything is at your own discretion. Can your little ginger friend stomach the truth?"

"I think so."

"Can you?" she asked softly, and Poppy had to turn her face away.

"I don't know what you mean."

Zahrah waited to speak, leaving space for the sounds of the street to waft up like steam off a boiling pot. "I remember grappling with this myself. Explaining to my mortal friends what I am. Knowing that I no longer existed as a human to them. It was the closing sentence in the story of my mortality. Dry ink." She picked a bit of detritus from her pant leg. "It's been so long since I've been on surveillance duty. I forgot what a filthy business it was."

"I don't hate what I am."

"Nor do I," Zahrah assured her. "But you are still something new, are you not? You've changed."

In more ways than one. "What if she doesn't like me now?" She had been only fifteen when she met Lizzy. She felt that way now, small and frightened and thirsting for closeness. "She's the only one who cared for me when I was human. I wish I could be the same to her."

"You could tell her you're the one who's been leaving her money. That would certainly endear her to you."

"Mercenary," Poppy scolded.

"Oh, a very good one." Her eyes went soft. "I can't tell you what to do. You're still a baby, gumming on the world, crying when your new teeth come in."

"Fuck off."

"You're meant to make mistakes. You will. And I understand that your memories with your ginger friend are too precious to waste on a mistake. But consider." She spread her hands. "You're still very pretty."

Poppy gave her a good-natured shove. "Zahrah?"

"Yes, my dear?"

"Will you sit with me for a while?"

"Of course." She glanced into Lizzy's window, and her eyes went wide. "I think I'm in the presence of a master. Tell me: do you do that sort of thing? Because there's a party planned for next month…"

Chapter 21

One month later, there was an orgy. Carmen purchased Poppy a pink silk dressing gown for the event. It was the loveliest thing she had ever called her own. It was also, without doubt, the costliest.

"A bit silly, you buying me new clothing for an orgy."

"It isn't clothing." Carmen was wearing a robe of her own, a deep sapphire thing that clung to her hips like ocean water. "It's a dressing gown."

"But I'll be undressing, yeah? That's how I always did it. Or is there some new sort of fashionable fornication sweeping the upper classes?"

Carmen gave her a long-suffering look from the doorway. "Just wear the dressing gown, Poppy. The party has already started downstairs. The more time I waste up here, the less I waste down there."

She swept out, leaving Poppy alone in her room. Poppy considered staying there for the duration of the evening, holing up with her pink wallpaper and her small collection of things. She had a few perfumes and cosmetics now, including the Turkish rouge that she and Carmen both wore. The little bottle had pride of place on her vanity table, as it had earned its role as a faithful friend. Beside it, hairpins rested in a small cup, a few adorned with pearls, sisters to Lizzy's gift. Lizzy's was undoubtedly the cheapest of the bunch, but it was Poppy's favorite, and she wore it most nights.

These things, albeit small, were her very own, and she could have more. Carmen had set up a meeting with the Brood's man of business, a bald, bland fellow called Robinson, who had patiently explained the details of a dizzying fortune. Before, Poppy had never had more than a few pounds to her name. Now, she had access to the Brood's funds, as well as an account of her own for smaller purchases. The numbers made her head spin.

"How?" she demanded, and Robinson had told her that Carmen had acquired most of the Brood's sizable fortune by holding on to pieces of art and fine furniture for centuries and then selling them for unthinkably large sums. She had invested sparingly ("Too often I've accidentally funded another person's exploitation," she had said later that evening) but she occasionally put money behind a restaurant or play or seditious printer, if the mood struck.

Also, according to Valentin, Carmen smuggled and fenced works of fine art. This, above everything else, earned her Poppy's admiration.

Poppy did not need this money, comfort though it was. She already had everything she wanted—at least, everything she could buy. In descending order of priority, those were: a place to sleep, pins, rouge, and a dressing gown. The amount of money now accessible to her was only conceivable in the abstract, a number so high she had no idea how to count to it. What was she meant to do with that sort of wealth? Buy jewels? Her entire adult life, albeit brief, had been spent counting pennies. One couldn't covet rubies and sapphires when one was busy coveting a warm coat. Poppy couldn't help but see those shiny rocks as equal to vats and vats of bone broth and at least one warehouse full of Stilton wheels.

She stared at herself in the mirror. Her hair hung unfashionably loose and wild. She barely painted. She looked beautiful. She looked miserable.

"This is why you came here," she imagined Roisin saying behind her. She could almost see the watery reflection in the mirror, tall and slender, wrapped in a black silk dressing gown, her hair draped around her angular face. "To buy things. To have things. To spend time with friends. I want you to be happy."

"How do you suppose this will make me happy?" she asked the specter.

"You haven't changed that much." Poppy imagined long-fingered hands smoothing the slick material across her shoulders. And above those hands, a flat, shifting smile. "Don't tell me you stopped liking this."

"You can't even say it."

Imaginary Roisin's mouth tightened. "*Fucking.* There. Are you pleased?"

"Even in the version of you I dreamed up, you're pushing me away."

She reached up to touch a hand and felt only air. "I don't know how to dream you beside me."

"Head up, *mo cuishle*. Try to be happy, just for tonight."

It wasn't as though she had a better idea.

Barefoot, she strode down the stairs, the bottoms of her feet slapping against the wood, then the cool, veined marble of the hall. The orgy was being held in the ballroom. In a normal household, the ballroom would be used to host grand events as part of the season, welcoming the *ton* to marvel at the architecture, the costly dishes and spirits, and the eligible daughters. The Brood, for obvious, undead reasons, could not do such things. Therefore, orgies.

Poppy pressed the doors open. At first, her ears pricked to music, but when her mind swallowed the sound, it spat out a clearer picture; the only music was that of bodies coupling. Slaps of flesh against flesh, moans and pleas rising up to fog the windows. Figures undulating together, vampire and human alike. A massive, writhing animal made entirely of decadence. The beast with—she took a quick, muttered count—*twenty* backs at least. She spotted a few familiar faces: Massimo, gently stroking the hair of the man who knelt before him, swallowing him down. Karol and Zahrah, holding a sweating, panting woman between them, grinning rakishly to one another. Carmen, holding court on a settee while a woman rubbed her feet. Valentin, reaching crisis in the arse of a bent man, his eyes squeezed shut.

A creeping sense of overwhelm shrank her. Feeling tiny, she grabbed the lapels of her robe and lowered herself onto an empty daybed to watch. Her thighs tensed to stand. She sat. She would rise and enter . . . now. *Now.* She would get up, strip herself, and walk over to those two kissing women right . . . this very . . . second . . .

"Gathering your courage?"

She flinched, recovering quickly in order to glare at the man now seated beside her.

"Why is it that you always seem to be naked?"

Valentin's laugh was thin from exertion. "Who can keep up with the fashions, these days? Far easier to abstain entirely."

"I assumed you'd be with Massimo."

His smile faltered. "May I be honest with you? Or would you prefer a clever remark?"

"Why would I want a clever remark over the truth?"

"I know my value." He tipped his head back against the wall, closing his eyes. "I'm meant to be dry and entertaining. The minute I give you my honesty, the illusion is broken."

"Have I made you feel that way?"

He lifted an elegant shoulder. "I've done it to myself. I find comfort in distance." He winced. "I'm sorry. There's something about spending that absolutely ruins me. Perhaps my schoolmaster was right in saying it would turn me into an imbecile."

"My schoolmistress thought I was simple."

"Are you?"

She gave him an incredulous look.

"What?" he sniffed. "I haven't known you for a particularly long time. Perhaps you're simple and just remarkably good at hiding it."

"Perhaps I am," she said on a sigh. After all, she was at an orgy, speaking to a man she had no interest in fucking and, if her assumption was correct, had no interest in fucking her. "So why aren't you with Massimo? The truth, please."

"Oh, it was his decision." There was a touch of well-fought boredom in his tone, stretched thin over the pain. "We used to. But I loved him and he didn't love me and he thought, for my sake, we ought to keep apart. That it wasn't kind to me to give me scraps, as they would never satiate me."

"Let me guess: you told him that you could decide for yourself and he disregarded you."

"Of course you speak from experience. Left here like Moses in a basket." He threw an arm across his face. "Poor wastrel, picked from the weeds! The most beautiful babe in Egypt."

"And here I was, having fellow feeling for you. I suppose I *must* be simple."

"Who have you been sent to free, I wonder?" He rubbed his chin. "Not those chaps over there. They seem to have requested specifically to be put in bondage."

She nudged him with her shoulder. He nudged back. Unbidden, a smile crept across her lips.

"So, will you be joining the party?" He gestured to the beckoning waves of bodies. "Or will you loiter by that bowl of grapes over there? Pretend to eat them. Fondle a stem."

"I'll call down a plague instead. Cover you in boils."

"If you're doing plagues, you ought to turn the Thames to blood. Imagine how easy it would make things."

"Bring a ladle by for cheeky scoops? But then your friend would never get the chance to spend in his trousers."

"There are other ways, *nouvelle*."

She snorted a laugh. Carmen strode over, open robe trailing behind her, and planted herself on Poppy's other side.

"Having fun?"

"I am," Poppy said. "I'm having fun with a naked man."

Valentin rose. He had very little arse to speak of. She wanted to poke it, make the meager flesh jiggle. He turned before she got the chance.

"*Adieu*, ladies." He bowed, eyeing a smiling human man perched on an ottoman. "There is an urgent matter that requires my attention. Let my people go and all that, pip pip."

"How are you, really?" Carmen asked once Valentin had taken up with his paramour. "Bit overwhelmed?"

"Roisin ran away and took my cunt with her."

"Some might say," Carmen mused, after a few silent moments, "that an orgy is the best way to return to physical pleasure. That the anonymity of it, and the distance of multiple partners, would keep you from your pain."

"I didn't say anything about pain."

"You didn't need to." She smoothed her dressing gown. "Perhaps avoiding the pain isn't the answer at all. Maybe you need another emotional connection. A different one."

"I'm not likely to love someone, if that's what you mean."

"I didn't say love. Or, rather, are you familiar with the ancient Greek words for love?"

"Carmen, do I look like I'm familiar with the ancient Greek words for love?"

"I wouldn't presume. There are six."

"Bit excessive."

To her credit, Carmen went on undeterred. "*Storge*, the love of parents for children. *Philautia*, love for oneself." She gestured at the woman splayed over Karol's lap, two fingers curled inside of herself. "*Philia*, the love of one friend to another. *Eros*, erotic love." She gestured again, rather unnecessarily. "*Xenia, Agape*. There are many types of love. Perhaps you need the love of a friend."

Poppy's stomach flipped. "You?"

"If you like." She lifted a shoulder, confidence and boredom and nonchalance swirling together, the melange doing something remarkable to Poppy's nerves. "Or Karol, or Zahrah. Or Karol *and* Zahrah, if you prefer. Do you like men? Valentin has no appreciation for women, but Massimo might be interested."

"No men," Poppy said, with a little quake in her thighs. "You." Carmen was beautiful and kind, and the most elegant woman Poppy had been this near. And she was patient. Understanding. Poppy knew she could lower her guard with Carmen. Perhaps together they could turn this dance from a recollection of the steps into something more joyous.

"You. Now," Poppy said. Carmen raised an eyebrow. "What I mean is, erm, now? Would you be amenable to . . . now?"

Carmen laughed and rose, leading Poppy from the room by her arm. She peered back behind her as she left, catching Valentin's eye. He winked, baring his fangs and dropping them into the arm of his favorite human servant, whose face immediately creased in bliss.

They took the stairs one at a time, their pace sedate, but Poppy longed to leap across the steps. Her skin was aflame. For the first time since leaving Covenly, she had an awareness of her body. It was the difference between a morning with tea and a morning without. She had been groggy, before. Now, she was awake.

They stepped into Carmen's room, the door closing behind them with a gentle *snick*.

"I've never been in here before," Poppy said. The space was immaculate, the sort of clean that Poppy could never accomplish, even if she dedicated hours to a mop and a rag. There were maids in the Brood's employ, of course, but Poppy had a nigh on magical way of dirtying a place with her very presence. Carmen's aura was bright and fresh, daring dust to settle.

A large, proud bed stood in the center, with deep blue bedclothes laid crisply across its substantial width. "Everything's blue here."

"*Evidentamente.*"

"I assumed—I mean, it's pink in my room. I thought all the rooms would look the same."

"Ah. They do not." Carmen took a long, slow breath before speaking, choosing her words. "Roisin requested you go in the Rose Room. She said you would like it best. I thought it was a bit odd, considering."

"I do like it," Poppy said, though she had no idea what was odd about it, and had no interest in asking. Instead, she busied herself looking over the dressing table, its surface laden with trays covered in cosmetics and perfumes. Locked jewelry boxes housed Carmen's many splendors. The walls bore paintings of cool-toned ocean scenes, some above water and some below. In one, a squid swam through an icy sea, whitecaps hovering above on the freezing surface. A posy of amaryllis rested in a porcelain vase, alongside a small tree, dirt and all, in a large clay pot by the window. Everything was perfectly undamaged, save for a tattered tapestry that hung on the far wall.

"My mother made that." Carmen came up behind her, skating her hands along the soft fabric of Poppy's dressing gown.

"Your mum did all that?"

"Not alone, of course. In a workshop."

Poppy peered at the faded stitches. "Is that a unicorn?"

"It is."

"They're not . . ." Poppy bit her lip, the pressure of Carmen's fingers shifting the silk, teasingly soft.

"Not real?"

"Are they?"

"I've never seen one, but that doesn't mean they don't exist." Carmen parted the dressing gown over Poppy's sex, stroking her curls with the back of her hand. "Is that all right?"

Poppy groaned, leaning back against Carmen's warm chest.

"Poppy," Carmen chided, moving her hand away. "I'd like to hear words."

"I think unicorns are real."

"Not—Poppy, was touching you like that all right?"

"Yes. Good. Go back to doing that. Please."

Carmen chuckled against her hair. "Well done. But before we begin, there are a few things I would like to say." She grabbed Poppy by the shoulders and spun her around so they were facing. "I have a cock."

Poppy grinned at the arousal tenting the elegant silk of Carmen's robe. "So I see."

"I am a woman. It's a woman's cock. So if you use any words to imply that you are fucking a man, this whole thing will end very abruptly. Do you understand?"

Poppy dragged her eyes up to Carmen's face. Her mouth was set and a furrow had appeared between her brows.

"Yes," she said, gathering her scattered focus. "I understand."

"I won't fuck you with it. Not in your cunt or your arse. You can suck it, if you ask nicely."

She made to sink down to her knees, but Carmen shot a hand out, grabbing her by the chin. Her clean nails pressed into Poppy's face. "You know, you're already in a far better state than when I found you downstairs."

"You were right about all that Greek business." She forced her words past her cheeks, squished together between Carmen's strong fingers. "Stork. Philomena. Eric. Erm . . ." She thought hard. "Zebra. All them loves."

"Well done," Carmen drawled. "Model student. Now, tell me what I need to know about you."

"Me? My name's Poppy and I'd love to suck your cock."

"Poppy." Carmen squeezed harder, then let go. "You ought to tell me if you have any limitations, or any particular desires. We're here to enjoy one another. I want this experience to be as enjoyable as possible."

"I'll let you know." Poppy tugged lightly on the tie of Carmen's dressing gown. A request. "I promise to let you know."

"Good." Carmen stepped back. In one fluid movement, she slipped off her dressing gown, exposing her body to the dim light. She was slender, her thighs softly curved. Her long, dark hair spilled across her shoulders, kissing her clavicles and framing her elegant neck. She crawled onto the bed, laid her head against a plump pillow, and brazenly spread her legs, knees bent, feet planted on the counterpane. "Now, I believe there was something you meant to ask me?"

"Carmen." Poppy undid the knot at her waist, letting her robe drop to the floor. She felt Carmen's hot gaze trail up and down her body. "May I please suck you?"

Carmen lifted a lazy, acquiescing hand. In this grand bed, with her regal bearing, she never looked more the queen.

"Proceed."

Poppy hurried over to the bed and positioned herself between Carmen's slim legs. Her skin was smooth and clear, welcomingly soft. At the center of the valley, she strained from a bed of dark curls, long and elegant as a wax taper. Poppy's teeth dropped in welcome pressure, the sharp tips caressing her lower lip. She dragged them across the perfect expanse of Carmen's creamy thigh, drawing up pink lines. Carmen gasped above her, arching slender hips off the bed.

There was a chair in the corner of the room with dark blue upholstery and spindly wooden legs. In it, a specter crossed her legs and raised her gaze.

Poppy squeezed her eyes shut, tethering herself to the earth in the feel of Carmen's skin, hot on her lips. The warm, musky smell of the room. The baubles of the worked counterpane pressing against her knees. The taste, when she lowered her mouth to lick Carmen's crown, bitter and familiar and strange all at once. The spread of her lips to receive her gift. The pressure at the back of her throat. The water in her eyes from the blessed choking danger. From fullness, and from giving. Only giving. No more tears to spare for what was taken from her.

Carmen shuddered above her, tangling her fingers in Poppy's hair. Pulling for guidance, and for a little pain. A welcome, generous pain that rooted her to the bed and sent brightness across her scalp and down her shoulders. Poppy skated her fingers lower, across pebbled skin, and below, to a tight, waiting entrance. Some noise above her, then something smacked into her head. She lifted off with an unceremonious pop, somewhat dazed.

"Oil." Carmen gestured to the little bottle that had ricocheted off of Poppy's head. "I trust you know what it's for."

Carmen's tan skin was flushed, her eyes dark and heavy-lidded. Her regal composure slackened, the bejeweled facade cracking.

"Listen to her," said the specter. "Do what she asks."

"Poppy?" Carmen's brow creased with concern. "Are you well? We can stop if—"

"No." She fetched the bottle, daubing her fingers with shaky hands. "I'm fine. I swear it."

"Poppy." Carmen eyed her carefully. "I don't want you to be thinking of someone else when you're fucking me. It isn't kind to either of us. Will you need to stop?"

Poppy helplessly stared down at her glistening fingers. "Talk to me," she whispered.

"What shall I say?"

"Anything. Just your voice. Your words. Keep me here with you. I want to know it's you."

"Oh, *pobrecita*." She lay back down, dark hair spilling over the pillow. "I won't let you forget."

She was as good as her word. Her voice was mellifluous, a bardic narrator's voice, telling the tale of their coupling. It wasn't praise so much as chronicling, but it was perfect. Carmen spoke as if everything Poppy gave was entirely her due, Poppy her willing supplicant. It spread Poppy across her own skin like oils, drew out the part of her that thrilled to serve. She sucked and stroked, curving and pumping her fingers until the words began to trip and tangle. A quick, cursed warning, and her mouth was filled with the tang of Carmen's release. She swallowed, licked her lips, and grinned. Her sex ached with need, and in her chest, a prideful bloom of accomplishment spread its golden petals.

"Come here, *mi amor*. I want my hands on you."

Carmen's touch was tender until it wasn't, firm, knowing strokes with slender fingers, kisses with painted lips, bites with drawn fangs. She was long, dark hair and strong, slender limbs. She was crystal cut cheekbones. She was pride and care.

"This is what I gave you," said the specter. "I wanted you to have joy. It's my gift."

"Carmen." Poppy panted. She throbbed. She wanted. "She's here."

"It's all right." Carmen kept her hand close, cupped over like a hug. "Let her come."

"But you said—"

"When you were fucking *me*. Now, I'm fucking you." She circled her fingers in demonstration. "Let her be here. Remember what I said?"

"What you . . ."

"Different love. Love for me. Love for her. All of it true. Feel all of it, Poppy. Let go."

She closed her eyes and sank.

"You made me remember," said the specter in that level voice with the fading hint of a lilt. "You did not clear my cobwebs. You did not light my path. You were more forceful than that. You were violent in your care for me. You ripped me from myself. I became who I used to be, with you. You changed me, and I changed you too, Poppy. Didn't I? I did, didn't I?"

"Yes," Carmen cooed. "That's it."

Tears streamed down Poppy's face, hot on her eyelids, cool on her cheeks. Carmen's fingers strummed an unrelenting rhythm.

"I'm in you," said the specter, wheedling and defiant in turns. "I'm in you. Inside you. You're different now. Lizzy may remember you from before, but she only knows you live because I can write. I made you. And you made me. I feel everything now. I feel everything. Come for me."

"Now, Poppy," Carmen commanded. "Come for me."

Sharp teeth sank into her neck and she shouted her pleasure, a scream ripped from somewhere deep, tearing through her body like cleansing fire.

Later, they lay together, Poppy's head splayed across Carmen's chest.

"I'm sorry," Poppy said, tracing the exposed hint of each rib with her finger pads.

"Whatever for?"

"For not being free from her." She kissed the hollow between Carmen's small, graceful breasts. "She's everywhere I am. She's chasing me. I can't be rid of her."

"*Pobrecita.*" Carmen pushed a yellow curl from Poppy's sweaty forehead. "You never claimed to be."

"But you thought this would work, and—"

"Did it work for you?"

Poppy unstuck her cheek from Carmen's warm stomach. "Well, I came."

"I want your attention when it's on me. When I attend to you, go where you need to, as long as I'm along for the journey. Maybe it will help you heal."

"Maybe I'll never move on, as long as I allow her into my head."

"Perhaps." Carmen dragged a fingernail down Poppy's nose, softly poking the tip. "In my years of life—and there have been many—I never came upon a circumstance in which the best solution was to stifle an impulse."

"Sneezing at the opera?"

"Well—"

"Passing wind in church?"

"All right, I understand—"

"Pissing in a pub?"

"Yes, Poppy, you absurdly literal creature. Some impulses are meant to be curtailed. But not love." She tapped the area above where Poppy's heart once beat. Poppy held back a snort. *Literal, indeed.* "Perhaps she'll fade with time. Perhaps not. But I see no reason to sabotage our time together worrying about whether a feeling you cannot help but feel is appropriate. Love her, love me, take another lover, or two, or a dozen. But don't punish yourself for having a heart, *mi amor.* We have years ahead of us. I would love to see you survive them."

Chapter 22

"You need an occupation."

Poppy rolled onto her back. She had retired to her bedroom an hour or so earlier, pleading a need for rest. It was a generous fiction that the entire Brood indulged. Well, all members but one.

"You need a damned occupation," Valentin repeated.

"Did I not say," Poppy groaned from under her pillow, "that I was not to be disturbed?"

"I'm not disturbing you. I'm providing you company."

She peeked out from behind her pillow, squinting against Valentin's bright colors. He stood resplendent in a violet waistcoat festooned with gold brocade. A butter yellow silk cravat revealed a sliver of creamy skin at his throat. She could smell the perfume of his lavender gloves. He was, she had to admit, quite appropriate in her rose-papered bedchamber, a butterfly dandy of the highest order at home amongst the flowers.

"An occupation, eh?" She found an ungainly seat within the thick covers. "Am I not earning my keep?"

"I didn't mean a monetary one."

"That's lucky. I'm not good at anything professional."

"Save one impeccable skill. Unfortunately, you're presently giving it away for free."

"Aw, you're just jealous I haven't given you a ride." She opened the blanket for him. After a moment's hesitation, he wriggled in beside her. He was stiff as an alley cat new to the tender mercies of indoor living. She stroked his raised hackles, the hairs of his nape like grass after a frost. "Am I ruining everyone's mood?"

"Yes."

She barked out a laugh. "Don't sugarcoat it, mate. Give it to me straight."

"Shut up. We tolerated the depressing stint after your arrival. That you've succumbed to a new brown study is too tedious."

She shuddered. "I've always hated that term. Brown study. It sounds like I'm wallowing in my shit."

"Crudeness aside, that is, metaphorically, a rather apt descriptor."

"You really know how to bolster a girl's self-regard."

"I . . ." He stiffened even further. "I'm not known for my gentleness. I apologize for—"

"Shut up." She curled against him. It was akin to snuggling a silk-wrapped fire log. "Must I?"

"You must." He patted her with a flat hand. "There's a soiree tomorrow evening and I need you with me. Lord Throckmorton—you remember him—he's invited an opera singer I'm dying to see. A soprano. She was supposed to sing Norma in the debut, but something happened. Something tragic, no doubt. I've forgotten already. Perhaps you will like her very much and decide to spend some of that lovely money you're ignoring on becoming a patron of the arts. We'll dress you in one of your new gowns. Won't that be pleasant?"

Ah, yes. The gowns. Six in total, made especially for Poppy. The Brood had brought in a very accommodating modiste who was willing to work odd hours and didn't bat an eye at the chill of Poppy's skin against her quick fingers. With her came two large men, each carrying rolls and rolls of fabric. With a flourish, they had unrolled lengths of shot silk across the parquet, colors of every hue shifting impossibly, each its own puddle of magic elixir. Poppy had gasped at the plenty, eyes watering against a brightness that rivaled daylight. She had poked at pinks and blues, and in due course found herself covered in crinoline and corseted so tightly she was grateful she no longer needed to breathe.

A fortnight later, the finished gowns had come. There were so many, a sea of yellow and rose and violet. And other garments, auxiliary yet no less carefully made, small stitches clinging to the curves of daytime frocks like goats on a mountain ledge. These were things Carmen referred to as "simple" yet were so far from. Even the undergarments were finer than

174

anything Poppy had yet owned.

"How much have we spent on this?" Poppy had asked Carmen, warily observing herself in the glass. In the fair floral of her new gown, she reminded herself fiercely of a porcelain figurine Minna had kept in her bedchamber. The abbess had treated the thing like Aladdin's magic lamp, her greatest treasure. In Minna's eyes, a girl might soil the thing simply by resting her gaze upon it.

If Minna saw Poppy now, she'd have an apoplexy.

"Never mind the cost," Carmen had replied, smoothing an invisible rumple in Poppy's skirt. "We can afford much more than this."

"You don't like the gowns," Valentin remarked now, wriggling down into the irrepressible comfort of Poppy's bed.

"It isn't that I don't think they're beautiful. I do, of course."

"Naturally."

"It's only that the cost of one could have fed and housed me for five years. *Easily.*"

"Jolly good that you have a higher standard of living now."

"You're missing my point."

"You're missing mine," he said. "You lived miserably. Now you don't have to." He stroked her counterpane as evidence. "If you stopped resenting your good fortune and started appreciating it, you might find something to enjoy."

"Such as?"

"*Nouvelle,*" he drawled. "I have done you the great service of identifying your problems. Must I solve them, too?"

She pouted. "What use are you anyway?" And then, a moment later, "Help me pick out what to wear to this damned soiree."

The next night found her in a pale blue frock with a pale, blonde Frenchman on her arm. The Throckmorton house was within walking distance, a mere two streets away from the Brood's Mayfair redbrick. As the sun was waning, and as Carmen had insisted each of Poppy's gowns come with a matching parasol, they elected to walk, Valentin dodging rays under his hat. Even so, a few stubborn sunbeams found them both, sizzling bits of skin that healed as soon as they found shade. Poppy removed a glove and watched in wonder as her exposed fingers blistered and bubbled, then healed to pristine smoothness. Blistered, healed. Blistered, healed.

"Stop that," Valentin hissed.

She halted. Valentin's voice was worryingly thin. "Do I offend?"

"Don't do that." He ducked his head, the brim of his hat shading his eyes. "Not in front of me."

She ran a soothing hand down his stiff arm. "Come, now. It's harmless."

"Don't get in the habit. I know you've already found life tedious, but I won't have you become one of those tragic vampires who enjoys seeing how far they can stretch their immortality. There are better ways to feel something."

"Oh," she said, and replaced her glove. "Oh."

He let out a long-suffering sigh. "Just try to enjoy tonight, will you?"

There was, on the surface, much to enjoy. The room to which they were led was magnificent, high-ceilinged and grand. Garlands hung over sconces bearing the faces of lions, their tails wrapped around curled bronze paws. The company was remarkably attired, skirts of wild pattern and color roving along the floor like aimless beetles, each bracketed by puffed-up mutton sleeves and topped with layers upon layers of frothy ribbon. And the *food*. Never mind that Poppy couldn't eat, she could at least stare at the petits fours and biscuits, the sweetmeats like spilled jewels. The best champagne, glistening in crystal glasses, forbidden as fruits of the goblin market.

Arm in arm, she and Valentin sauntered through the crowd. Massimo's odd gift covered them like gauze. A nodded hat here, a gloved hand there, raised in welcome. Dear Valentin and his cousin, once met at a parlor or racetrack, or some other lovely occasion. Nice to see, entirely unfit for matchmaking. Why? To examine such a thing would be nonsensical. That is not what Valentin and his sweet, plump cousin were *for*. They were for a turn about the room, a look, a taste of witty repartee, and, once out of sight, to be entirely forgotten. Only the memory of pleasantness remained, a vague face, the shape of a throaty laugh. Jolly good company, that. Ever so welcome.

It was a bit grating, if Poppy were honest. Small talk was already small enough. With Massimo's merciful spell casting overhead, the whole business shriveled into a teeny-tiny waste of a decent evening.

Not that she had any particular desire to be known, or any great illusions about her impact on those she encountered. She felt purposeless

176

here, that was all. When her company was bought, she became whatever the man with the purse desired her to be. That, at least, was something. That was easy, an identifiable transaction with careful rules, its own tiny pageantry. Life with the Brood was more complicated. She was someone in their home, surely, but she couldn't put her finger on who. She could only manage cheer for short stretches. Otherwise she was a drain. A specter in a locked room, like a jilted bride in a ghost story, perished by a broken heart. Ghastly maudlin, and not even particularly original.

There had been only one year, one moment, one person who had turned Poppy from a collection of pieces into a whole, and the grip of that memory nearly dragged her right back to her bed.

"Valentin," she whinged into his shoulder. "Must we stay for much longer?"

"Are you not having a nice time?"

"I wish I could eat a petit four."

He looked her up and down. "Cannibalism."

"Even so."

"Don't fret. We are about to be rewarded." He pointed at a small stage on which a number of musicians waited with instruments of gleaming brass and wood polished to mirror shine. "*La dama* has arrived."

A woman stepped up onto the stage, clad in a white gown with a long, spilt milk train. A garland sat on her dark hair, intertwined bright begonias, pink at the heart with red trim so perfect fairy seamstresses might have embroidered the petals. Around the woman's waist, a belt of shimmering bronze fabric hugged her curves, the same material that graced her short sleeves and delicate wrists. Her eyes were large and round, her face a picture of tragic piety, hands clasped before her breast.

"What's she here as?"

Valentin shushed her on instinct. "A druid priestess."

Oh, shitting fuck, of course. "And what'll she be on about?"

"Appealing to the goddess of the moon to keep peace."

"Between whom?"

"The Gauls and the Romans."

"Who are the Gauls?"

"I'm the Gauls."

"You're French."

"You're tedious." He clicked his tongue, a brief consideration before surrender. "I'll give you a translation. I think you might like this." He paused. "I'd *like* you to like this."

Poppy was touched. "Because *you* do?"

"No, because maybe the opera will get you out of that damned bed. Now hush."

The musicians lifted their instruments, signaling a quiet that curled, smoke-like, over the room. The woman stood at the center, tall and white as a Greek column. She took a deep breath, ducked her head in a small nod, and the musicians began playing, eyes cutting to a man with gently waving hands. He had to be some sort of sorcerer, pulling sound with fingertips and wrists, casting it behind him like skirts. The strings played a rolling cadence, reminiscent of green hillocks, gentle and expansive. Atop, the flute soared as a dove might, not swooping, but gliding, moving inexorably towards a far-off sun.

Poppy had nearly forgotten about the woman until she opened her mouth and breathed in, eyelids fluttering, nostrils flared. The first note was clear as sunrise, subtle as a sharpened blade, correct as the closure of a garment with a single button.

"Chaste goddess," Valentin whispered into Poppy's ear. "Who covers with silver these ancient sacred plants."

The melody changed, hardened. A request. A demand. "Turn your beautiful visage to us," he said. "Without cloud, without veil."

The hair rose on Poppy's arms. On the stage, the woman swayed, arms wrapped around her shoulders as if to humble herself in the presence of a moonlit deity, a goddess of women. Poppy could almost see the fingers of silvery, coruscating light kissing some field, some strange nowhere place where the wild earth grew undeterred, unmanicured, untamed. Where feet slapped against clover and daisy, dodging rabbit holes and gorse needles. Where sylphs filled the night, kissing under stars that shivered at the maddening touch of their lips, stars that were so very, very far away, and so very, very jealous.

"Lovely," Roisin might have said, were she there beside Poppy. She might have been dressed in black like a mourner, rapt, staring at the druidess. "Oh! How lovely this music is."

"Temper, oh goddess," Valentin translated. "Temper the ardent hearts, temper still the audacious zeal. And spread on earth the same peace . . ."

"A bit furious for peace," the specter observed. "She isn't waiting for peace, is she? Or courting it. She's *demanding* it. She needs it. She can't live without it. We know that sort of longing, don't we? To long for peace in a terrible storm. In our own heads. In our own hearts."

"Spread on earth the same peace with which you reign in heaven," Valentin finished, as the heavenly music faded to silence. "Oh, dear. Are you weeping?"

"I need to meet her." Poppy received Valentin's handkerchief and dabbed her eyes, too stunned to join the applause that filled the room. It was jarring, of another world. "I have to talk to her."

"Settle down, *nouvelle*. She'll change into something more appropriate and join us presently."

She sulked, wiping her nose. "I liked the vestments."

"I can't put my finger on why," he remarked drily, "but that is rather *saphique* of you. Ah, there she is."

She wasn't as tall as she appeared on stage, but Poppy had had her fill of tall women. She had a soft, oval face and wide, brown eyes, so round and full that a strip of unbroken white showed between her iris and lower lid. She had forgone her ornamental floral crown and was now bareheaded; the flowers had hidden a braided bun, now on full display at the top of her head.

There was a scrum of people eager to make her acquaintance, but due to Massimo's magic, or perhaps Valentin's complete disregard for anyone else's comfort, they managed to get an audience.

"Pardon me, La Greco." He sketched an elegant bow. "May I present my cousin, Poppy Cavendish. Poppy, this is Miss Orsola Greco. Miss Greco, my cousin has become an ardent admirer."

"I've never heard anything like that before." Poppy received the woman's hand and pressed. "Your talents are extraordinary."

"*Grazie*, Miss Cavendish." Miss Greco had a thick accent, like Massimo's but more generous, round vowels and percussive consonants. She pursed her lips when she spoke, kissing the words as she sent them off into the air. "You are too kind." She touched a hand to her clavicles in what could have been read as a gesture of humility, but was clearly pure, unselfconscious pleasure. Poppy adored her for it. "Do you frequently attend La Scala?"

"Never." Valentin delivered a swift elbow to her waist. "Er, not in a while, I'm afraid."

"Oh, you must return. I will be singing Anna Bolena next season."

Poppy felt a crush of disappointment she was too raw to hide. "Does that mean you'll need to return soon?"

A knowing smirk spread across Miss Greco's face. "Not terribly soon." Other admirers cleared their throats and shifted forward, making their presence known. "Miss Cavendish, would you care to call on me tomorrow evening? I am staying at Brown's Private Hotel, on Dover Street."

"Close to us," Valentin offered. "My cousin is honored to accept your invitation."

"Until then, Miss Cavendish." Miss Greco pressed her hands once more, then turned to accept the admiration of an eager man with a sweating face.

"Visit her at her hotel?" Poppy hissed as Valentin dragged her away. "What am I supposed to say to her? I don't know a damned thing about opera."

"I doubt you'll do very much talking." He yawned behind his hand. "Let's go home. I've done my good deed for the night and I'm entirely depleted."

Chapter 23

It was not unexpected for a woman to step into Brown's Private Hotel. Unlike the rest of the clubs in London, women were not actively shunned from the premises. Poppy did not consider this a triumph. She did not aspire to become clubbable. In her limited knowledge of these institutions, clubs—aside from those blessed havens that catered specifically to mollies—were places where men could gather to congratulate themselves for being well-born. It was in this rarefied air that landed gentry discussed their exploitation of the working classes and celebrated their penchant for adultery, all over brandy that cost more than Poppy's life—her old one, anyway. It was possible—nay, probable—that all political decisions were made in these well-appointed rooms, crackdowns on reformers and seditionists all but ratified over a game of billiards. If she had her way, every club would be fucking leveled.

It was possible she was nervous.

At least she looked smart. Massimo had helped her select a gown—yellow, his favorite—and had laced her into it himself.

"The skirts are a hindrance," she whinged. "It'll take an age to get out of this stupid frock."

"That's part of the dance." He pulled hard on the lacing, and the air whooshed from her lungs. "It draws out the seduction."

She was grateful for the layers of petticoat now, as well as the lavender pelisse she wore. They were distance from the bustling throng. She didn't need armor, but there was value in it, especially as she was alone. Especially as everyone around her was human and filled with rich, red blood she could nearly taste. The underground stream rushed through her bones.

She thrummed, muscle and skin trembling at the invisible speed of a hummingbird's wings. She was a violin string, wound too tight. Were someone to pluck her, she'd shriek.

To be here, outside her comfortable realm, set her teeth on edge. It was one thing to fuck a friend in one's own home while an orgy raged downstairs. It was another to visit an unknown woman in her dwelling for the express purpose of bedding her. And furthermore, it was one thing to live amongst vampires in a city of humans, yet another to be in the company of a human, without another vampire to step in if she made a mull of things.

And! It was something else entirely to do two new things, in a new locale, with a specter at her back.

"You look well here," said the specter, running insubstantial fingers against a marble wall. "Maybe you ought to join a club."

She could join a club. It would, after all, be something to do. Just as this, whatever it was—this *assignation*, was something to do. The magic of La Greco's druidess song had melted away since the previous night. The thrill Poppy had felt in that ballroom, listening to that demanding tale of summoning peace, was gone. She wanted it back. She was here to chase it, to feel something, damn it, because Roisin had been indifferent to her own life and Poppy would not let herself succumb to the same tedious fate.

A ghost of a servant led Poppy up to a room and rapped gently on the door. Poppy knew she had been spoilt by the elegance of the Brood's home, but it struck her afresh in this nominally elegant suite. La Greco's accommodations were, for lack of charitable descriptor, plain. Simple papered walls, a coffered ceiling, and soft furnishings of dull hues. There was a desk for writing, supplied with paper, a letter opener, a pen, and ink. There were windows for looking out of and drapes for draping. Two years ago, Poppy would have believed she had stepped into a palace. Today, she was bored.

La Greco was easily the most vibrant thing in the room. Her gown was a jarring crimson, with a bubbling, repeated pattern crawling up the sides, as if the modiste had taken an impression of a ruby dropped into a glass of champagne. She leaned elegantly on an indecipherable piece of furniture, its distinguishing features swallowed almost entirely by her frock. Her lips were painted red—unfashionable these days, but somewhat

182

acceptable for a theatrical type. This flouting of decorum was, Poppy had to admit, very endearing.

"Miss Cavendish." La Greco rose, hands outstretched. Poppy received them, as well as a light kiss to each cheek. "How lovely it is to see you once more."

"Please, do call me Poppy." She removed her pelisse and held it in her hands. There were no servants here to sweep it away, and she scolded herself preemptively for even flirting with the idea that this was due to a lack of consideration. She was here for a discreet tryst, after all. Not everyone had a cadre of servants to keep their secrets.

"Then you must call me Orsola." The singer retook her throne, pulling back her voluminous skirts and gesturing to the newly revealed space on what turned out to be a settee. "Sit, please. I thought to ring for some tea, but, of course, you don't take tea."

Poppy stiffened halfway into her seat. "What makes you say that?"

Orsola smiled conspiratorially. "We do not need to play these little games, Poppy. I know what you are. I know what your cousin is. It is not the first time I have encountered your kind, nor do I presume it will be the last."

Poppy's throat was tight. "I'm not certain what you mean."

"Ah, of course. My mistake." Orsola's hair was pulled back from her face, a shining sweep of brown. Her jawline was knife-sharp. "You are not, in fact, a blood-drinking creature of the night?"

"No." There was panic on Poppy's tongue, hot and acidic. No one had prepared her for this. They ought to have done. Her fear morphed into anger—why hadn't Carmen or Valentin or any of them told her what to do when a human made insinuations? She longed briefly for Cane's powers of mesmerism, and immediately felt sick.

"What a preposterous assertion," she said, desperately.

"Not an immortal being? No?" Orsola pursed her lips. "Not a woman with the fangs of a snake?"

She could leave. She wanted to leave. She wanted it viscerally—to go home, crawl into bed, and converse with a ghost woven from mad loneliness. Her first time out alone and she'd been discovered immediately. Were she not in the center of this dense, stinking city, she'd scream.

"I ought to take my leave," she said instead.

183

"Oh, dear. I fear I've overstepped." Orsola frowned, pretty red mouth as pluckable as a begonia. "I don't wish to make you uncomfortable. Quite the opposite, in fact."

"O-oh?"

"I do not wish to see you hide yourself from me. This is the only reason I mentioned it. We cannot be comfortable with such an untruth between us. Krylov's elephant, yes?"

Poppy had no idea who Krylov was, or how an elephant figured into it at all. "I see."

"So please," Orsola went on. "If you do not wish to tell me, know I understand this. But if you speak truth, I will do you no harm. I only wish to know you."

She thought of Lizzy, stumbling around in her room at Minna's, completely oblivious to her captive audience. Would she want to know Poppy, too? Was it possible to be seen entirely? Could Poppy's cold skin and silent heart not be things she'd have to explain away?

"Yes," Poppy said, cringing through the admission. *Fuck it.* "You have the right of it."

"Aha!" Orsola clapped her hands in triumph. "I knew it!"

"Is that why you've invited me to your hotel? To confirm a theory?"

"Do not think me so—how shall I phrase it?—limited in my investigative means." She reclined, regarding Poppy through thick lashes. "I could have inquired after you. I did anyway, just a little. It seems the *ton* believes you to be pleasant and not much else. I assume this is by design. Is it?"

With the initial fear dissipating, she was able to examine what made Orsola so intriguing. This was a woman who would so willingly sequester herself with her natural predator. A thrill zinged up Poppy's thighs.

"Frankly," she murmured, "I'm not sure whether I ought to tell you."

The singer pouted prettily. "You are no fun at all!"

"You say you've met people like me before. Of whom do you speak?"

"Oh, well." Orsola spread her frock across her knees with a performer's unmistakable thrill in advance of a show. "I had a patron in Milan. An older man by the name of Signor Blanco. He came to hear me sing night after night, sitting in a box alone. I could feel his eyes on me every time I went on stage. I knew he'd succumb soon."

"Succumb?"

"Let go of whatever kept him in that box and out of my dressing room. After a month, I found him there with roses in his hands. His skin was . . ." She shivered pleasantly, sucking a thin stream of air through her teeth. "His skin was so perfect, like silk. Like porcelain. Almost unreal. The way he moved, like a wild cat. The slow movement of a fast animal. I knew he could crush me in his hands if he wanted."

"Oh," said Poppy, then winced. Orsola was giving a performance. The least she could do was show some appreciation. "How . . . invigorating."

"He became my companion," Orsola went on, undeterred. "He took me around the world with him. His bite was . . ." She shivered once more. "It was the greatest pleasure I ever received."

"What happened to him?"

Orsola's cheeks stiffened. "Inconsequential." She straightened a fold of Poppy's skirt with an appraising pinch. "Let us not speak of him anymore. You are here now. That is what matters."

"Yes. And to that end . . ."

"Mm?" Orsola dragged her fingers over Poppy's bodice. There was so much material there, so much boning. Poppy couldn't feel a thing.

"Why in particular did you invite me here?"

Orsola's lips tipped up. "Is it not obvious?"

"Of course, only—are you looking for a night of pleasure? Or something more?"

"Why must we be so serious?" Orsola skated a fingertip across the seam at Poppy's bust, her nail skimming the tops of Poppy's breasts. "We are here for companionship, no? Is that not what everyone desires?"

"Of course." She exhaled, fighting through her own tension. Seeing the star of pleasure in the distance. "Come, show me how songbirds kiss."

Orsola had soft lips, willing and pliant. Poppy could read a kiss, and this one was written in letters ten feet high: *Take me. Lead.* This was no trouble; Poppy took either part of the dance, or neither. The greatest joy was to give her partner pleasure. This was a luxurious woman, used to fine things. Poppy could be a fine thing, for tonight.

She kissed down Orsola's neck, realizing the danger as it arose. There was blood here, and it pressed against her senses. Orsola did not appear bothered, proffering her unbroken skin. She moaned, the sound vibrating beneath Poppy's lips. For nearly two years, Poppy had been so cautious, so careful. It was perilous here. Orsola's perfume smelled of it: belladonna and hemlock and deadly nightshade. Bitter foxglove. Lords-and-ladies. A daffodil bulb swallowed whole.

The quiver of danger bubbled in Poppy's blood. Her mouth watered.

"You will bite me tonight," Orsola murmured.

It was as though shock grew fingers to pull Poppy back by the hair. "I won't."

"Do I offend?"

"No." Her skin sang. She needed to calm herself. "I don't partake in human blood."

Orsola cocked her head. "It is the lifeblood of your kind."

"Not necessarily."

"So what do you drink?"

"Rabbit's blood." She needed to leave. She needed to get up and quit this place. She looked to the specter for direction, but it had gone. Of course it had, the fucker. That was what it did best. "If a bite's what you've invited me for, then I must disappoint you. I should—"

Orsola's hand darted out, quick as a snake, and grabbed Poppy by the arm. "You are a jumpy one, aren't you? Tell me why you will not bite me."

Poppy was a fair liar. Not a master of the art, but no slouch. But something about this moment—the blandness of the room, or the intensity of Orsola's gaze—stripped the skill from her entirely. "I cannot."

"Cannot?"

"I will not. There are other things I will do . . ."

"Wait." Orsola watched her. The hairs on Poppy's arms lifted. "I sense this is a subject which causes you discomfort."

"Yes. I think it would be best if I returned home."

Orsola shook her head, bringing her tongue to her soft palate to volley a handful of low tutting noises. "Please. Allow me to apologize for being untoward. I was eager to host another *vampira*. In my enthusiasm, I forgot that you are all individuals, are you not? None like the other."

"Thank you." She mirrored Orsola's smile as best she could. "You're very understanding."

"Perhaps." Orsola rose, walking to the place by the window where the specter had stood. She gazed out over the narrow street. "If you would prefer, we can carry on as friends."

Oh fuck, thank Christ. "I would like that very much."

"Will you permit me one final question on the subject of your, eh, *abstinence?*"

It wasn't worth the effort of objecting. "Of course."

"Why have you made this choice? Ah—I see I've bothered you. I suppose it is not *a* question, rather *the* question."

"It is." Yet Orsola didn't retract it. Silence reigned. Eventually, Poppy gave in, as the only way out was through. "I don't have self-control when it comes to drinking human blood. Were I to drink from you, I don't think I would be able to stop."

A slow smile spread across Orsola's face. "*Buona.*"

"Pardon?"

"I must apologize to you once more, Poppy. I wasn't entirely truthful earlier."

A chill spread across her back. "Whatever about?"

"About not having any motive other than companionship." A wolfsbane smile, all teeth. A frock as red as a holly berry.

"If you're hoping for a patron, I'll happily discuss it," Poppy offered thinly. "An intimate relationship is not a requirement for—"

"No, no. This is not what I am after." She pulled out the chair from beside the writing desk and sat in it. Poppy was glad for the distance. She wanted more. She wanted a city between them, an ocean. "Signor Blanco made me a promise. He did not fulfill this. I am looking for someone who will."

"What sort of promise?"

"Immortal life, of course." She drew the back of her hand across her neck, her breasts, her nape. "My Signor said he would make me his *sposa*. His queen. And then, one day, he disappeared from my life. I still age, Poppy."

The walls drew in, bloating at the middle, windows warping. "This is a very large request."

"Is it?" Orsola leisurely tapped her fingernails on the desk. "You heard me sing. Imagine that voice never fading. Never dying. The public could listen to me for hundreds of years."

"And what about when you aren't singing?" Poppy's eyes cut to the door. "What about when you can't go out in the day, or you can no longer eat food?"

"My Signor lived splendidly without such trifles. I have been denied my gift."

"It's not your due."

"Pardon me?"

She longed for the specter. It might have had something to say about the irony. "I am sorry you were not turned by your Signor Blanco, but I cannot do that for you. I don't mean to be unkind." She didn't give a fuck about kindness, but she'd been a whore long enough to know a careful word was the difference between a handful of coins and a slap to the face. Of course she could tear this woman to shreds, but the defensive instinct was too deep to recognize its own obsolescence. And besides, bloodshed would be indiscreet.

The blood. There would be so much blood.

"Only, I don't know you," Poppy said. "I don't know what sort of vampire you would be. I don't know if you're gentle, or you're patient, or you can exercise restraint. I have nowhere to take you to teach you to control your urges. I must refuse you. I will take my leave."

La Greco moved with horrible, near imperceptible speed. Poppy blinked, and the letter opener was in the woman's hand. Light shone off the metal as it sliced through the skin of La Greco's own wrist, where the green veins wriggled. Blood shot out from the wound, spraying across the white paper and polished wood. It sounded like spit landing in the street and looked like a feast.

"Deny me now," she growled, the red dripping into her dress, staining it black. "Drink from me. Drain me. Change me."

"*No.*" The smell burned her throat and eyes like smoke, like living fire. She was hot and trembling, her hands reaching out, moving beyond her control. She could drink. She could drink from this woman, drain her to near nothing, and revive her with her own blood. She could skip the last bit and suck her dry, leave her a husk for her hubris. For revenge, for she had taken her dousing rod and commanded the stream from where Poppy had buried it deep. Orsola Greco wanted to sing forever. She would never sing again once Poppy was through with her. Poppy would drink from her and take her voice and sing so beautifully the angels would weep to hear it. She would sing her blood into the night and demand peace from the chaos. From the bloodshed. She would be a goddess of the night. *Temper the ardent hearts. Temper still the audacious zeal.* She would command to see the visage of the goddess, without veil, without cloud.

"You don't know what you've done." Her voice was a thick, feral rasp. "You've damned yourself."

"Damn me," Orsola wept, high and keening. "Damn us both."

They were together. Poppy must have moved, because she was close to the window, by the chair where Orsola still sat, her hand clamped around the dry side of the bleeding limb. It leaked with the pumping of Orsola's hurrying heart, sloshing out over her sleeves, soaking them. Poppy could pull the fabric into her mouth and suck, stain her lips like Turkish rouge and be so pretty with it, with the blood in and on her. She could be beautiful, and call to the goddess, and claim it all.

"Yes!" Orsola shouted. "Drink, *vampira*! Drink of me!"

"Where are you, specter?" Poppy whispered frantically. "What do you think of me now?"

No one answered. She hated to be alone. She hated, hated.

She was across the room, by the door, and she had knocked something over, some glass or ceramic, something big and bland, and it fell to the floor into a thousand shards. Her face was wet. Her eyes were bleeding. The room was a red haze, and it was beautiful, so much more vibrant, so much less plain.

Orsola's face shifted, rage contorting her mouth and flaring her nostrils. "You will not deny me, monster."

There was blood between Poppy's legs and blood dribbling down her mouth, streaming from her nose. She was growing weak. Orsola was growing close.

"Stay back," Poppy warned, lips trembling. She wondered if they were turning blue. There was so much rabbit's blood over them. She was not going to die here.

God, she wanted Orsola's blood. She wanted it so badly. She could have it. She could let it consume her.

Roisin was gone. Orsola was here, close now, so close. There was an arm before her and it bled the red smell, the human smell. Poppy opened her mouth and licked.

Chapter 24

Before God said, "Let there be light," there was nothing. The rector had read from the Bible about it on a hot Sunday in the little parish church on the hill. As the sun beat blue, red, and gold streaks through the stained glass, he had said, "And the earth was without form, and void." He had said, as a dusty beam of white light spread across the pulpit, "Darkness was upon the face of the deep."

And then He had said, "Let there be light," and there was light, and it was good.

There was light inside of Poppy. Bright, febrile light, blazing through prismatic glass, and it made her formless and void, a being of screaming, brilliant flame and forever-replenishing fuel. Gasses and sparking ammunition and the shrieking, unmoored divine, light and light and light and everything together, everything that was good ever, forever and ever, amen.

She closed her burning eyes and lapped it up. A red suck, another drink of the meaty tang and her eyes stopped weeping and her ears popped and she could hear the world scream in joy for her in a voice made of many mouths with many teeth. *Our sincere congratulations! You've remade it all!* She thanked the world and drank the blood from the marrow of it, the juice and the pulp, and she licked the pit, knobby and at the center of everything. She kissed mouths and mouths and was bit by the teeth of the pit, the great chasm at the center of it all, gnashing. She opened all of her eyes and closed them again.

And then it was gone.

She bellowed. There was no more of the light, no more red in her mouth. Someone stole it, her teeth yanked out, falling white and nerves dangling. Someone who touched her, some monstrous thing of fingers and flesh and two eyes in its mean, human head, so she flung it, and it went with a crash. The red had given her strength and teeth and so many eyes, but she'd leaked out the bad blood for it, and she was fading. Not too fast, not too fast at all, because she threw another monster away (two eyes, no wings, no voice but to shout in pathetic fear) another shriek and crash and something rent to slivers and shards. Maybe a nice pot or bowl, or a window, because she could smell air and taste fog, and it wasn't red, it wasn't blood, because someone had taken it from her with hands as small as splinters.

"Hold her down! Damn it, man! Get the other woman out!"

"Miss Greco, you need to see a doctor immediately! Come with me!"

The smells were fading and so was Poppy, and this wasn't fair, because she was their God. She was their God, and here were her people forsaking her. How dare they, small maggots, two hands and two ears and teeth like sheep, baa and baa and useless. She'd take their world from them, take it and smash their temple and throw them all into the sea.

If only she could. She'd had just a suck or two of good red and there was nothing in her anymore, nothing, except the knowledge of what she once had, now lost. Apple-eating beasts, they were, all of them, and she'd lost it all, she'd lost and she was done, done for, and the night was dark black and formless void around her, and she slept . . .

Darkness, for a while. And then.

She was vaguely aware of a jostling. The floor shook beneath her. She lay on her side, her body pressed into itself by bands so tight an inhale drew an ominous creak from her ribs. Under her cheek, she could glean the motion of carriage wheels on road. She might have been on her way to Newgate, except for the odd odor out there, a little cleaner and brighter than it ought to have been. There were fewer people to smell here than the filthy hordes quartered in the Old Bailey. No one rode in the carriage with her. No one in their right mind would, after what she had done.

She searched for a feeling, and came back with weariness pooled in her limp grasp.

Thirst ached in her throat. The river was in her. It wasn't quiet. She couldn't examine it too closely, couldn't press on it for its uncomfortable tenderness. It was a bruise, or the place that remained when a milk tooth fell. She tongued it and it ached. She was so fucking thirsty.

What a fool Poppy had been. In that room, as Orsola Greco lazed inches away, Poppy had betrayed her every instinct. Her stomach had told her to run a half dozen times, and in no uncertain terms. She had once trusted her instinct beyond all else. Now, they were barely on terms.

This body was still an unfamiliar home. She rattled around in it.

She tried to free herself from what she surmised was a strait-waistcoat, but it wouldn't give. The ties must have been a hearty leather, or her weakness was more profound than she'd realized. Either way, she wasn't getting anywhere by brute force. Her only choice was to rest here, on some strange floor in some strange carriage, going who knows where, until something changed.

She fell into a trance, or perhaps just faded away for a while. When she came to, it was daytime. The smell of clouds hung heavy and wet, leaking a steady drizzle that tapped against the carriage roof. A muffled call for the horses to halt, and the wheels stopped below her. She caught the shape of an argument outside, something that might have been *It's worth more than my life, mate. You get her.*

Eventually, her door opened. Despite the miserable weather, she squinted into brightness. The form at the door was shape and shadow, backlit by the weak sun. It might have cocked its head.

"Oh, you're just a little thing aren't you," he said, for it was a man. "Tetchy, wee thing. Let's get you inside, shall we?"

He reached in with long arms. She smelled them as they approached.

"Don't," she warned. "No. I can't."

"Oh, tut, can't believe what they're saying about—"

The warmth of his skin against her neck. The odor, red and throbbing. The wanting of what he hid. She snarled and shook, her teeth searching fruitlessly for his flesh.

"I'm sorry," she roared, and it didn't sound like an apology at all. "Don't come closer," she begged, licking her lips, beckoning him closer.

"I can't help myself," she moaned, knowing no one would help her.

The man stood in shocked silence, then fled, feet kicking up mud that splashed into Poppy's face. She convulsed hopelessly, thrashing, her skirts wrapping around her heels, her saliva leaking from her mouth in a viscous stream.

Eventually, a new person came. He held out some sort of cane like a rifle. A rag was tied to the end. Poppy caught the sweet, acrid scent of ether and could have wept.

"Thank you." She breathed deep, welcoming oblivion, dimly aware of a sack being put on her head. "Thank you, thank you, thank you."

Chapter 25

She awoke in a cell. There was no lamp nor window, but the darkness couldn't hide the squalor of her surroundings, not to her cursedly capable eyes. The walls were dark brick, so wet and slimy that they seemed amphibian, dripping muck from low ceiling to uneven floor. All was equally dank, uniformly gray-black and bubbling with filth.

Her ears pricked to a squeak and shuffle. She attempted to reach for it, discovering as she did so that she was still in her strait-waistcoat. She flopped to the ground instead, worming her way across the floor. The stone scraped her face, the shallow wounds filling in with cold, wet slime. She noticed this vaguely, in a small, distant part of her mind. She was too hungry to care.

By the time she reached the source of the squeak, it was gone, undoubtedly scared off by the shambling, squirming thing that had tried to corner it. No bother. There was a small hole in the wall. Poppy knew where the beast lived. She could wait.

Her starved mind wandered. Would she die here? Could she? Or would she waste away to nothing except a stubborn shard of life, a husk of a vampire who was once quite plump and lovely? A vampire whose arse cheeks were once so round and sweet, a good slap turned them rosy. Would she live, grayed and desiccated, until the building was demolished and she was squashed between the living bricks? Was she to become the wetness?

The squeaking was back. She pounced—flopped, really, but it did the trick. The rat's blood was greasy and thick, with the lingering, cheesy taste of butter that had long since turned. She licked her lips and exhaled.

"Did you have a family?" she whispered to the corpse of the rat, lying dead an inch from her face. It was gray and shining with filth. She might have been crying. She might have been lying in a puddle of her own tears. "Will they come for you? Will I eat them too? Will I swallow your babies whole?"

She tested the strength of her strait-waistcoat. It barely gave. Maybe after a few more rats, she could make another attempt.

And then what? Return to the Brood? Her actions had no doubt put them in danger. It didn't seem likely she would be welcomed back.

She thought about lazing in bed with Carmen for hours. Sparring with Valentin, earning laughs and half-hearted admonishments. Sitting on a roof with Zahrah until sunup and watching Lizzy work. She hiccupped.

Another rat made its presence known. Poppy caught its tail in her foreteeth and reeled it in, slurping the appendage like a noodle. This time, she was more aware of the animal as she bit it. Its hard, wiry hairs bristled against her lips. Its plaintive squeaking rang as she drained it. Its dark eyes dimmed. Its unfortunately lovely little ears, like petals, like fairy cups, stopped their twitching. They were pink.

The blood was filthy, but it worked.

A specter lowered itself to the ground.

"It wouldn't be fair to ask how you are."

"Would this be different," Poppy asked the specter, "if you had just introduced me to human blood? Would I not have attacked her?"

"Perhaps." The specter shrugged. "I didn't want to."

"It's always what you want."

"It seems that way," the specter agreed. "And yet, I am miserable."

Poppy could taste rot. "The miserable are always selfish."

"That's unkind."

"I can't do this anymore," Poppy told her knees. She tried to draw them up, but her binds were too tight. Two dead rats were very close to her face. "You need to leave."

"Is that what you want?"

"I want to go home." She didn't know where that was. She couldn't feel it. "Oh, god. Oh, god. I want my mother. I want to go *home*."

Time passed weirdly. Minutes bloated and burst. Hours shriveled to bone and skin. She might have drunk more. A cockroach might have crawled across her open eye. A fly might have alighted on her lip and laid eggs.

Poppy hadn't realized there was a door to this place until it swung open with a heavy squeal. If it had never opened, she might have believed she'd been bricked up in this place.

"Hello," said a man. He had his hands clasped behind his back and spoke with a gentle, comforting cadence. It was as though he had practiced for hours how to best convey that he was not, nor would ever be, a threat. "You seem to have had quite a time of it."

Hot drool dripped from her mouth to the floor. "Where'm I? Prison?"

"No, no." He stepped in slowly, his careful feet hinting where they would land just before they did so. *And nothing up my sleeves.* "You're at a hospital."

In her mind, a hospital was a place with firm beds, clean doctors, and crisp, white sheets. "Y'sure about that, mate?"

"It's a hospital of sorts." He crouched down beside her. "I understand you attacked a woman in her rooms?"

"T'was a m'sunderstanding."

"Of course." He granted her a serene smile. "Oh, dear. It looks as though you've helped yourself to some of our pests. I ought to thank you. The rats are a terrible nuisance."

"I'll send you a bill."

"Would you like to be sitting?"

"No, m'fine here." Even with the blood of two rats inside her, she couldn't be sure she wouldn't attack him. He smelled so lovely, like a roast. If he were to touch her, she would fight him for his juice. "Wha sort of hospital's this?"

He pursed his lips, crafting what was certain to be the mildest possible answer. "It's a hospital for those whose ailments are not physical, but mental."

Exhaustion turned her bones to lead. "You think I'm batty."

"That's not a word we use here. That said, you did drink a woman's blood, and subsequently injure two men who tried to separate you from her. Do you recall?"

"Vaguely." Shame burned through her spine.

"Hm." He tapped his chin. "My occupation is to discover how best to help you. Do you have any suggestions?"

"Hare."

"Pardon?"

"Hares," she amended. "Rabbits. Raw. Alive."

"As pets?"

Her eyes flicked to the two dead rats before her. "Yeah, mate. Pets."

"I see." He drummed a nervous rhythm on his knee. "Would you not prefer some lovely soup?"

A wheezing laugh choked her. "Naw. The hares. Then you can turn me loose."

"Ah. Unfortunately, that doesn't appear feasible. Not when you might harm others."

A fresh welter of stinging tears slid down her face. "Oh."

"Tell me." He gestured at something by her thigh. "Your frock has been irreparably damaged, I'm sorry to say. However, it is very well made. You must come from a fortunate family. Is there anyone I ought to contact?"

The Brood. Their home. Their audacious parties and their quiet moments and the marvelous, fearless life they built because nothing other than the discovery of their vampiric nature would make them run.

"No. There's no one."

His eyes were green, she noticed. Green and positively leaking empathy. "Are you certain? I could ask at Brown's."

"*No,*" she insisted. "The dress isn't mine."

"Did you steal it?"

"Yeah, mate. I stole it." A hot tear dribbled down her nose. "I stole it. It was never meant to be mine."

Chapter 26

In the shapeless days that followed, no one came into her room but that one man, who she only called Doctor. She surmised there were meant to be others, but they were too frightened to approach. There was the gruff cove who stood in the doorway, tossing in her trays of gruel like skipping stones, spattering the stuff all over the walls. The shy, reedy fellow who pulled back the untouched tray with a long hook. The strange man who opened a slot at the top of her door and peered in, writing notes about whatever he observed inside, which was nearly always Poppy lying flat and doing absolutely fuck all.

Doctor seemed like a decent enough bloke. He removed her bindings when he was present, and strapped her back in before he left—this, he told her in a careful whisper, was the decision of his superiors. He brought her the promised hares and watched as she drained them, a dopey, fascinated look on his face, which turned out to be decently handsome, if a little bland. He asked after her history, but Poppy didn't have the energy to give him what he wanted. What was she supposed to say? That there was someone out there who loved her, but had left her nearly a year before and hadn't even sent her a letter? That she had had a family for a brief, shining moment, but had carelessly squandered the gift of them? That she had brattishly failed to appreciate all she'd been given, preferring the comfort and safety of her bed to the splendors of fortune?

Doctor soon realized he would not be privy to Poppy's secrets. He did not appear to be angry about this. He switched course to discussing the weather and the books he had purchased. Sometimes he read aloud from the *Morning Herald*. That was decent of him.

Poppy wondered whether she'd watch this man grow old and die. Whether she'd become his life's work. What she'd tell him, when the loneliness became unbearable.

She didn't feel much in these strange, shapeless days. It was an aggressively neutral way of being, a wool blanket between her skin and her innards. Sadness would be an effort, as would anger. She didn't have the strength. It was like floating in a pool of muck, sound and sight clouded over, the idea of breathing merely abstract.

This must be how Roisin lived. Dull, removed from her goodness. Tired and unable to sleep. Each waking hour the twin of the one before it, and the one after.

The specter did not come back.

She learned to tolerate the taste of rats. What was the difference between hare and rat, when human blood existed? Why bother enjoying what she drank when it could never compare to the blood that remade her?

One evening, Doctor bustled in with a spark in his eyes.

"Poppy, I have excellent news," he said brightly, crouching down beside her in his usual way. "Two experts in my field have come to see you."

"Experts?" She was preemptively annoyed. "I doubt they'll have anything clever to say."

"Oh, come now. This might be the solution we've been waiting for." He patted her knee in a heartbreakingly earnest sort of way and opened the door. "Poppy, may I introduce Doctor Spettro from Venice and Doctor l'Ombre from Paris. Gentlemen, this is Poppy."

Poppy did not raise her head. It was far too heavy.

"Zank you, Doctor," said the French man. "We would like to be alone wiz ze patient, if you do not mind."

"Like hell you will," Poppy hissed, gaze snapping up, and—

Oh.

Oh, god.

Doctor's hackles raised. "With all due respect, I would prefer to be present. I'm the only person who has been treating her, and—"

The Venetian laid a gentle hand on Doctor's shoulder. The man relaxed immediately.

"You may leave us," the Venetian said, slow and comforting. "She will be well tended."

Doctor took a few dazed steps toward the open door. "Yes," he mumbled, shuffling out. "Yes. She'll be well. Good show."

Valentin slammed the door and grinned. "Did you miss me?"

Poppy couldn't speak. She made some noises, shocked and shameful. Everything was blurry. Through the ordure of misery, a strange light burned. In its glow, she became aware of herself. The filth she lived in. The disgusting slurry of rat guts and hare blood in her stomach. The grayness that she had accumulated in her caked hair and on her itching skin. The graveyard of pests.

The strange light burned and burned. She named it happiness.

Happy. Fuck, so fucking happy. And happy enough to know she ought to be ashamed of what she had done. Of her mistakes, and her piteousness, and of not being what they had wanted her to be. Of being miserably deficient.

"You poor thing." Massimo huddled down beside her, undoing the buckles on her strait-waistcoat. "The barbarians, keeping you in this terrible contraption so long. This is a torture chamber."

Her teeth were chattering. "What are you doing here?"

"Taking you home, of course," Valentin told her tartly. "What else? First thing, I'm scrubbing you down completely. You smell like a charnel house."

"Why?"

"Probably because you ate rats. I don't know. I haven't been here, have I?"

"No." Poppy shook her buzzing head. "Why are you here now? I fucked it all up. I put you all in danger."

"Oh, *piccolina*, we've all done worse." Massimo unbuckled the final strap and freed her arms. He grasped one and rubbed it back to life. "I'm sorry we couldn't have found you sooner. They brought you to the strangest place. Do you know," he leaned in close, "we're in *Essex?*"

Valentin twitched his nose in distaste. "Exotic."

"I'm not going to stay here." Thick tears were rolling down her face. She was embarrassed by them, ashamed and small and needy, and lit up like daytime under a blazing sun of joy. "You're taking me."

"Far away," Valentin said. "That Doctor's a bit of stuff. What sort of fellow is he?"

"A decent one, so don't go sniffing around." She licked her lips, savoring the aftertaste of words that felt like her own. Her hands were blessedly free. She wiped her nose with them. "What about Carmen?"

Massimo handed her a handkerchief. "What about her, love?"

"I-I made a mess at Brown's. She can't want me back."

Valentin let out a loud laugh. "*Nouvelle*, she's been combing the city looking for you. She's been on a rampage. When she found out you were here, she cooked up this whole plan to get us in. She's outside in the carriage with Zahrah and Karol."

"You're all here." Her voice cracked. She was shaking again. She thought she might be sick. "I thought I was going to be alone."

"Never again," Massimo said. He held a hand to her face, cupping her cheek. "You're one of us now. You're family."

Family.

She missed her mother and father. She missed Roisin. Christ, she missed Lizzy.

Three of those people were gone, beyond her grasp. But one was so very near.

I'm going to see her, she thought, a triumphant, golden bubble swelling in her chest. She'd been given another chance. She wasn't going to waste it. Not this time. *I'm going to see Lizzy. I'll have most of my heart back.*

Feeling rushed back into her body like a sat-upon limb finally freed, welcoming its blood. She hurt, pins poking into her skin, muscles throbbing.

She was cared for. She was remade—every cell, every atom.

"Are we ready to leave?" Valentin tapped his foot. "This place is horrendous. Have you seen the abbey next door? It's enough to give you nightmares."

"I'm ready." She rose unsteadily to her feet, knees clicking from disuse. "I can't wait to see my room again." Her wallpaper garden. Her soft, plush bed. Her little bottle of Turkish rouge. The things she didn't allow herself to miss because she thought she'd never see them again.

Massimo squirmed. "Did I not mention? We're going to Wiltshire."

"Wiltshire? Why?"

"Because you kicked up a fuss, *nouvelle*," Valentin explained. "It took a great deal of coaxing to silence Miss Greco, not to mention the small fortune she—"

"He's *saying*," Massimo interjected, "that while we did our best to minimize the damage, we have still attracted some unwanted attention. It's best we travel abroad."

"Wiltshire isn't abroad."

"Always our clever Poppy."

"*Stai zitto*, Valentin. Poppy, we're going to Wiltshire to secure our passage and make arrangements."

So she wouldn't see Lizzy after all. "Oh." Her stomach hurt. "I see."

"Don't look so pitiable," Valentin scolded. "I'll buy you some lovely perfume in Paris. And a nice hat. Do you want a hat?"

"Y-yes. A hat would be . . . Massimo, what about Doctor?"

"What do you mean?"

"I'm concerned he'll be axed if I go missing."

"Shall we say he was overpowered? Leave him a nice bruise?"

Massimo clicked his tongue. "Carmen will arrange a large donation, contingent on the good doctor maintaining his position. Does that please you?"

Poppy's eyes burned. "I've caused so much trouble."

"Yes," said Valentin, kindly. "You have."

She had once collected pennies. Now, she had money. She had family. She had everything, and she could miss Lizzy freely because it was safe to do so. It was safe, and she could love Lizzy, and she could cry, so she did, in fat tears and great, childish gulps, snot running down her face, carving rivers in the muck. People loved her and not everybody left her, some people stayed and she had left Lizzy and wasn't that sad, wasn't that something she could cry about?

"I'm going to spend some money," she told Valentin thickly as they shambled out of the hospital and into the wet night. The air tasted so marvelously fresh. She stuck her tongue out.

"Felicitations." He kissed her on her forehead and immediately gagged.

The rest of the Brood were waiting in the coach outside, as promised. They hugged and kissed her despite her filth, and her mistakes, and all the bits of her that were lacking. She fell into their arms and wept from the plenty, from the feast of what she had.

She was filthy. Filthy and free.

202

Coda

In a middling part of town, abutting a worse-but-not-terribly-so part of town, there stands a very regular building. It is constructed of brick, with eight street-facing windows composed of unbroken panes, no bullseyes. The ground level is equipped for a business. The stories above are residential. The building's twin is to the left, their triplet to the right, and siblings fill not only the street on which it stands, but the next, and the one after that, in three directions—north, south, and east.

It is a plain building, notable for only two reasons. The first is the residents' entrance: one must take an alley into the mews, pass the backs of two similar buildings, and unlock the heavy bolt of a subtle door to gain entry.

The second reason is even more singular: this building has been a gift.

London, 1839

"A building?" Lizzy gawped at the bald man across the desk. "Naw, pull the other one."

"I am not deceiving you," said the man, whose name might have been Robinson. "It belongs to you, now."

"This can't be for me."

"Are you Elizabeth Green? Then yes, it absolutely can."

She narrowed her eyes, donning her most fearsome face. "Is this some sort of trick?"

"You can see all the legal language here," Robinson replied, entirely placid. "I was told you could read?" He looked to her for confirmation. She nodded. "You are free to look it over."

A slew of inscrutable words mocked her from the page. "Mate, reading isn't going to help me with this. It ain't even English."

Robinson winced apologetically. "I agree, the language is a bit, shall we say, *specialized*. I'll explain." He cleared his throat. "You have been given a house and a small allowance, which will feed into an account at Cocks and Biddulph."

She was irritated at how much she wanted to laugh at *Cocks and Biddulph*. "I don't need money."

"Yes, I have been made aware. However, the person who is giving you this house and this account is doing so to give you the freedom of choice." He pushed the papers an inch farther toward her. "Do you understand?"

Of course she did. It meant she could stop whoring if she wanted. It meant she could get some rest.

This was too lucky. It stank like fish. "Who's this generous *person*, when they're at home?"

"They wish to remain anonymous."

"Oh, fucking of course." She clapped her hand over her mouth, face heating. "Erm, my apologies."

Robinson shook his head and tutted. "Never mind. I work for somewhat unorthodox clients. Your hair would curl at the things I hear." He indicated a thick paragraph. "Here is the matter of the bakery."

Ah, yes. The trick. There was no reason to feel disappointed. "Mate, I don't have a bakery, and I won't be on the hook for one just because a baldheaded cove like you said I need to—"

"The ground floor of your building has all the equipment necessary for running a bakery," he interjected loudly. She shut up immediately, shamefully pressing her lips together. "This contract states that you and I will interview prospective tenants, and you will decide to whom you wish to let the space."

"I thought this was my house."

"It is."

"So who says I need to give my ground floor to a baker?"

"Well, the rent will sustain you—"

"I'm not talking about lending," she cut in. "I'm asking why it has to be a baker."

He shifted in his chair. "Of course, you may choose another tenant, though the stoves would be rendered obsolete. The truth is, the person who is gifting you this building, erm, trusts bakers."

Suddenly, she knew exactly who was behind this. Her vision blurred with tears. "Fat arse. A baker. Of course."

"Pardon?"

"Where is Poppy Cavendish?" She wiped at her eyes. Robinson handed her a handkerchief. It was impossibly clean and criminally soft. "She can buy me a house but she can't pop in for tea?"

Robinson was a terrible liar. "I don't know to whom you are referring. Now, if we could get back to the issue at hand . . ."

Lizzy walked from empty room to empty room, stomach swooping at the dizzying space of it all. She touched every sill, every corner, and every stair with her dirty fingers and scuffed boots. There were new windows to keep the cold out and fireplaces to keep the heat in. It was a fucking palace.

"It's not all for me, is it?" she asked the empty rooms. "Right, Poppy? It's not just for me?"

Robinson bought her a new frock in which to conduct business. She looked like an undertaker's wife in it, dour and unapproachable. She fucking loved it. She was the type of girl people always felt comfortable chatting up. Her affable, pink-cheeked face, her bounty of freckles, and her orange hair attracted the worst sort. In her new, hideous garment, it was all covered up. A sense of safety loosened her muscles.

"Well," Robinson prompted. "Do you like any of them?"

"The last one."

"Truly?" He took out a handkerchief and wiped his bald pate. "He's quite old, and can barely afford your asking price."

"He's the only one who answered my questions."

Robinson furrowed his brow. "Many answered your questions."

"Sure, but they looked at you when they did it. That last one looked at me. And he says he's got sons working with him."

"I see," he murmured. "You see this as a family business? Work with the father, work with the sons?"

She turned her face away. "Listen, Mister Robinson. I'll be a woman in a building with men. There's no helping it. The way I see it, they can hurt me or they can help me. Those that won't help will hurt. I'm hoping the father taught his sons respect, and to look a woman in the eye when she asks you a question."

"Yes." He was looking at her very closely. "Miss Green, would you care to join my wife and I for dinner this evening? She's making a roast."

The baker was called White and he had three sons, all with the same dark, curly hair and deep brown eyes. The two eldest had thick muscles from lifting bags of flour. The youngest wore spectacles and managed the accounts.

He was a miserable shit.

"You've had many visitors upstairs," he told Lizzy one morning as she came to collect rent. He spoke deliberately—a little pompous, a little snide, not even bothering to raise his head from its bent position over a haphazard stack of paper. "A lot of girls. Tenants? Guests?"

"Who I have in my home is none of your concern."

"Oh, isn't it?" An insinuating sneer dug into his cheek. Were he anyone else, she might have regretted leaving her knife upstairs. The youngest White was tall, but he was a reedy, weaselly sort. She could snap him like a dry branch. "It's my concern if it threatens my father's business."

"Your father allergic to girls?"

"He's allergic to whorehouses." He sniffed derisively. "All respectable businesses are. I plan to alert the Met."

She snorted. "Do your father think you ought to?"

"Well, what he thinks is—" He caught himself. "Never mind what my father thinks. I'm my own man."

"Ah, I see. *You're* the one with the allergy to girls, littlest White."

He flushed from the roots of his hair to his throat. "Shut up you—you *madam!*"

She doubled over laughing. "Oh, Jesus. To hear you. Oh, hell."

"Shut up!"

"It's not a bawdy house, mate." She wiped her eyes. "It's the opposite."

He drew his brows together, pompous affect dropping off like an ill-fitting coat. He couldn't have been more than twenty, putting on a show to compensate for the bald patches in his mustache. "The opposite? You mean they're—they're midwives?"

She tipped her head back and howled. "Christ alive, man. You really are an innocent."

"Well, there is something afoot up there," he said, collecting the shards of his dignity, "and I'm going to figure out what it is."

"Don't bother." She gestured to the chair opposite him. "Mind if I sit?"

"N-no." He appeared entirely back-footed by this shift in energy. Gingerly, he situated himself in his own chair, hands flat on the table as though he didn't know what to do with them.

"Some of them," she said, "are whores."

"Aha!"

"Come on and listen, littlest White."

He puffed up his shoulders. "My name is Albert."

"As I was saying, little Al." She watched him bristle. "Some are whores. Some are not whores. Some are whores today, but don't want to be whores tomorrow. Do you understand?"

"Yes."

"Do you really?"

"Yes, of course." He bit his cheek, lips canting to one side. "But say I were explaining it to someone who didn't . . ."

She sighed. "God save me from men with questions. My place is a place where a girl can get a good night's sleep." She smoothed her skirt, suddenly aware of the gamble she was taking sharing this information. But he wasn't a threat, not really. He was merely a young person, too beloved to be cruel, too ignorant of true aggression to properly emulate it. "It's where a girl can escape a violent man. It's where a girl can get fare home, or do piecework in the quiet to save up enough for her own place. Nobody does any whoring upstairs. The only thing the whores are doing is casting down their worries for a night. Do you understand?"

"Mm." He fiddled with his spectacles as he thought this over, pulling a clean cloth from his pocket and wiping the lenses clean. "We need help in the bakery."

"Pardon?"

He sucked his lip between his teeth. Lizzy noted, despite herself, that it was a very nice lip.

"Help," he repeated. "You said some of the girls are doing piecework. We pay better than that. Do any of them like to bake?"

"And what," she said cautiously, "of the girls who wish to continue whoring?"

He considered this for a long moment. Eventually, he settled upon a response.

"Do they like pie?"

In a middling part of town, abutting a worse-but-not-terribly-so part of town, there stands a very regular building. It houses a bakery, which is known for its pies. A family works in the bakery. A father and three sons, all with curly brown hair. A daughter with ginger hair. A slew of girls and women who don't resemble any of them, but appear to be family, nonetheless. An older, plainly dressed, bald man who likes to have a chat while he eats his pie. And a few children, some with orange hair and some with brown, who are very poorly behaved and very, very happy.

Prelude

Excerpted from the diary of Roisin C.

The second of March, 1852
Bayonne, France

Dear Poppy,

It's happening again. I fear I can't stop it this time.
I lost her trail in the Basque Country. I was ashamed.
I bought one of their terrible hats. You might have said I
looked fetching. I'm afraid I looked a fright.

The thirteenth of April, 1852
Lisbon, Portugal

Dear Poppy,

It happened again. In the street.
The last time I was here, the city was richer. They
had sugar and spices and the buildings were cleaner.
This is because they were slavers. Everywhere I go, there
is cruelty. I wept. I tried not to. I tried and tried.

The sixth of May, 1852
Tabriz, The Qajar Empire

Dear Poppy,

There was a Mohammedan mystic Cane enjoyed. She read his work in the original language. She said there was a translation, but it was miserable and not worth reading. I asked her to read to me, that she might translate it on her own. She never did. She didn't share anything she truly loved.

I lost her trail, but I recalled the mystic. I didn't remember whether he was Turkic or Persian, but I wanted to be farther away from you, so I came here. Maybe Cane went to where he was born, or where he died. Maybe someone could tell me.

There are so many Russians here.

I speak some of the local language now. I found an old man and told him the name of the poet.

"Born?" I asked him. "Died?"

He said to me, "I love! I love!"

"Died?" I asked.

"Long ago," he said.

"Where did he die?"

He shrugged. I thanked him. He was the first person I had spoken more than two words to in a month.

I approached more people. They couldn't help me. Days passed. I nearly gave up looking. Then, I met a woman and gave her the mystic's name. She nodded. She said:

> *"Last night you left me and slept*
> *your own deep sleep. Tonight you turn*
> *and turn. I say,*
> *'You and I will be together*
> *until the universe dissolves.'*
> *You mumble back things you thought of*
> *when you were drunk."*

It's happening again. I'm feeling everything again. I can't stop weeping. I can't do this anymore. I can't I can't I can't I can't I can't help me please I can't do this I can't I can't I can't I ca

Part III

Dorset, 1853

Chapter 27

Poppy tumbled out of the carriage, stretching until her bones creaked.

"I don't understand why I couldn't have run the last leg, Godfrey. I could have done with the air."

The butler had recently celebrated his fifty-fifth birthday and the years were beginning to slow him, though the thinning hair had only managed to enhance his constant air of put-upon propriety.

"Because you are a lady, Mistress Poppy. Whatever you may claim to the contrary."

"She's as much a lady as I am." Valentin popped out behind her, smoothing his rumpled clothes. "Now come along, *nouvelle*. We have friends to greet."

Valentin had dragged her to a weeklong fete involving a cadre of French vampires holed up in a grand Elizabethan pile. She was his preferred date for these sort of excursions. He carted her up and down the country and sometimes abroad, showing her sights he pretended to find tedious, rolling his eyes, barely hiding his fondness at her unbridled joy. Somewhere along the line, they had become the closest of friends. Largely against her will, mind, but there had been no stopping it.

"Cor." The woman behind them made an ungodly noise of discomfort. "It's a bleedin' castle."

She could practically hear Valentin roll his eyes. "It's a house."

"It's a big house. It's *the* big house."

Sarah was a newcomer to the Brood, a human maid with a foul mouth and inconveniently sticky fingers. The loss of a number of highly valued bits and bobs had turned her into *persona non grata* amongst the

Haymarket set, but that had made her a perfect candidate for the Brood's very particular household. She was either too frightened to steal from a pack of vampires, or she had been clever enough to not get caught with the silver throughout the duration of her employ. The point was moot: nobody cared if she took a few shiny things. Not when she was as loyal as a hunting dog, and nearly as ferocious.

Officially, Sarah had come along as sustenance for Valentin, as Godfrey was no longer hale enough for regular withdrawals. In actuality, she came because she wanted to.

"So what can we expect from these toff frogs?" she demanded, trudging up the expansive drive. "More orgies?"

"*Propriety*," Godfrey said emphatically.

Valentin nodded his agreement. "To that end, you and Godfrey are off to the servants' entrance." He gestured toward a line of liverymen, currently hauling their luggage away. "Follow them, if you please. Ta."

Sarah and Godfrey stalked away, one grumbling, the other hobbling. Valentin hooked his arm through Poppy's.

"Ingrate," he said fondly, blowing a kiss at Sarah's two-fingered salute.

Eight months prior, Sarah had shown up on their doorstep unannounced and rain-soaked, all piss and vinegar. Poppy had taken to her immediately. The trappings of the Brood's monstrous wealth still squirmed uncomfortably in Poppy's stomach, and Sarah's low birth was a balm. Palling around with Sarah reminded Poppy fiercely of those bright years whoring. Years she missed, when she was feeling maudlin. Many of her compatriots from that time had grown solidly middle-aged, hadn't they? Robinson had told her that Lizzy had children now.

She thought about this, felt a sharp pain, then ceased thinking altogether.

"Valentin!" A powdered, vampiric cream puff greeted them at the door, air kissing and chattering away. She wore a gown so pointlessly extravagant Poppy's fingers practically itched for the dressmaker's card; she wouldn't know whether to scold the modiste for the expense or order one in every color. The inside of the home was filled with the same sort of frippery: frocks that would have looked well alongside towers of petits fours and caviar-laden blinis, were the company different. Pink and lavender gowns floated by, followed by a cream-colored dandelion, a pale blue swath of sky, and then, near the back of the chamber, a not-quite-black storm cloud, heralding chill rain. In it was a woman. She gazed out the window toward the moonlit, expansive grounds, her head at a familiar tilt.

Poppy knew what she would see when the woman turned. Still, the tuppence eyes were a physical shock, sending shivers from her throat to her toes. She was glued to the square of parquet below her feet. Her knees gave a liquid tremble.

Years tumbled around her. Years and years and years. She smelled wild grounds. She heard a chorus of night insects.

Roisin stared back. Her mouth was tight, striving for nonchalance and telegraphing nerves. Her eyes, which could never hide a thing, were wide. She wore grayish-black, or blackish-gray, a soiled snow-drift of a dress, clogged with fog and chimney ash. Her head was bare, her smooth hair coiffed within an inch of its life.

Roisin. Oh, god.

With a large inhale, Roisin gathered herself, stacking her shoulders over her back, her back over her hips, and her hips over her feet—which had always been so maddeningly dear, so inexplicably protectable. And then she smiled. She smiled, flat and shifting and perfect, and she turned miraculous, a split rock shimmering with hidden bits of mica crystal. It was all Poppy could do to keep upright.

Fuck her. Fuck her. Fuck this.

Poppy moved before she could think, storming through the chamber, grabbing Roisin's arm and dragging her down the hall. She had no idea where she was going, nor what her hosts might make of one guest bodily hauling another away, but that was of little import. The only thing that mattered was the bright, centering flame of anger inside her, the fuel that kept her feet moving.

She tossed Roisin into what appeared to be a study and slammed the door behind her.

"Where the fuck have you been?"

"America," Roisin answered immediately. Her voice was startling in its familiarity. Poppy had strained to hear traces of it in every room she entered. She hunted for crumbs of it, a whisper of a wafting low tone or a careful, muffled lilt. And here it was, full force, a feast of sound. Almost too loud. Ringing in her ears. "That was where I went first. To the north.

217

You'd love it, Poppy. It's so much like Covenly, all wild terrain. But there's quite a bit of coastline as well. And the mountains—"

"I don't give a buggering *shite* about mountains," Poppy spat, seething. Her jaw trembled. She clenched to keep her teeth from chattering. "Did you find her?"

"No. I had heard she was in New England, but I couldn't pin her down."

"So I take it you thought she'd be here, then."

"No, actually." She perched on the edge of a divan with a weak facsimile of ease. She clasped her hands. Poppy was certain that, inside her shoes, her toes pointed and flexed. "I've gotten word she's in Sardinia, near the French border. It's horribly sunny. I can't imagine how she can stand it."

"And, what—you're here to practice your French?"

"No, Poppy," she said. "I'm here for you."

The walls trembled, watery and strange. Reality doubled over, clutching its stomach.

She'd dreamt of this. Those were cruel trances. When she dreamed of Roisin, of them running together through wild grounds or sitting before the hearth, the night was a thief of joy. She would arise and weep.

"Me."

"The beach there is nothing like it is here," Roisin said softly. Her nails were bitten short and ragged. "The water is warm."

"You want to take me?"

"I . . ." She swallowed noisily. Her fingers fidgeted.

Poppy's stomach sank. "You don't."

"How have you been?"

"How have I—" She let out a hard, heavy laugh. A laugh with spikes on. She could taste acid. "Shut up. I don't want to hear another word out of you." Her vision blurred, strange stars appearing at the corners. "I've been *trying*."

"Trying what?"

"To live without you."

Fifteen years without. Fifteen years of a heart like a haunted manor, trying to fill each room with friends and flowers, only to find that a ghost upturned the peonies and set the pianoforte on fire.

There had been joys. Giving Lizzy a home and an income. Traveling with the Brood, seeing parts of the world she could never have imagined. Developing a taste for fine things, only somewhat marred by her insistence that these things, no matter how exquisite, cost too damned much.

Joys, like whitecaps on waves. Mostly there was an ocean of salty blue longing. A massive, flat expanse that offered no thrill, nor respite. Nights that fell into one another. New parties or pals or shining necklaces and modern skirts that promised happiness in their acquisition, yet always ultimately underperformed.

Poppy had given up believing Roisin would provide the joy she lacked, but it was starting to become clear that the attainable things that made her happy only did so for fleeting moments. Boredom was a sickness she couldn't shake. She fairly hated herself for it. Through sheer force of will, she attempted to appreciate everything she had; she'd be a fool not to try, at least. But her insides didn't light up for the things they ought to. Paintings didn't move her. Music only helped for as long as it played—a moment of silence, and the magic was gone. She was trying to love her life, trying so hard she sweat. Becoming, by sheer determination, the woman she knew she ought to be. Some months, she could manage the strain. Some months, she couldn't leave her bed. She was beginning to believe she might be defective.

"It isn't fair," Poppy said. On the divan, Roisin looked chastised, her head half-bowed.

"What part in particular?"

"That I spent one year with you and fifteen years without and the one year has played the fifteen for a fool."

"Poppy—"

"I *tried.*" She sank to the floor, her skirts pooling, a moat of pale green. "I sleep with Carmen now."

"Oh." Her shoulders fell. "I'm happy for—"

Poppy waved her away. "It isn't like that. And I go to the orgies."

"Do you?"

"You expected I would, I'm sure. And I have frocks. So many frocks!" She plucked at her skirt demonstratively. "Do you see?"

"Yes. Very lovely, Poppy."

"Oh, shut up. I go to balls and music halls and—and even gambling halls! And Valentin takes me 'round to these sorts of things. House parties, you know." She gestured at the coffered ceiling. "In places like this."

"It sounds like you're living a very full life."

"It does, doesn't it?" She wasn't sure whether or not she was yelling. Roisin leaned away a bit as if blown by a stiff wind.

"It does."

"So why," Poppy began, attempting to stand, small feet working under the layers of tulle. "No, don't help me. Why, Roisin, do I feel as though there's a great big hole in my life that I am endlessly trying to fill?"

"So you aren't . . . you aren't happy?"

"Do I appear to be happy?"

"I've given you . . ." She scratched her arm, up and down, up and down. "I've given you everything I could."

"A pittance, compared to what you've taken."

"What I—" Her mouth tightened. Poppy knew a sick thrill to see that anger rise. She missed every part of Roisin: her care, and her scorn, too. "And what of what's been taken from me?"

Poppy curled her arms over her chest defensively, but poked out her chin to provoke. "I told you back at Covenly that you deserved more than you gave yourself. It's a bit rich that you should come to me now, angry I haven't properly appreciated my lot. Angry you don't have joy when I'm the one who tried to convince you to respect yourself."

"I'm not angry—"

"A likely story."

"If you'd let me finish," Roisin snapped. "I'm not angry at you for failing to enjoy your many *splendors*." Her nostrils flared like the crown of a cobra. "I had fifty years before I met you, Poppy. Fifty years of being able to drift from place to place, trying to mitigate that woman's destruction, and after one year with you suddenly every step is a damned misery."

"Oh, this again. I've ruined you, have I? Was it so cruel of me to care for you?"

"Yes! Yes, of course! It only . . ." Her voice hitched, head of steam running out. "It wasn't meant to be like this."

"Like . . ."

"I can't breathe, most days." Her proud jaw trembled. "Everything is sore."

Poppy felt sick. "You're in pain."

Roisin's brows were drawn so close they nearly touched. Her cheekbones jutted. "I'm berating myself for wasting all that time. We could have been—" Her voice broke. "Being miserable was never such a misery before."

"Are you saying you're done looking for her?"

Her silence was answer enough. Poppy's anger surged.

"Then why are you here? To leave me all over again?"

Roisin's eyes flashed, hot and dangerous. "You have no idea what I've been through. The loneliness of it. I'm keeping us both safe. I'm keeping *everyone* safe."

"Who demanded that of you?"

"I did!" she cried. "I worry about you all the time. All the—" She shuddered. A sob burst from her throat. "I can't do it anymore. I can't. I have to. I must. I can't. I can't. It *hurts*."

There had been days. Months. Years, even. Stretches of time in which Poppy could almost hate Roisin. Hours she could remember their time together as a deception, or as a cage. Moments she could curse Roisin for making Poppy care at all, as though she had done it out of cruelty. As though she had wanted to ruin the rest of Poppy's life by being absent from it. Poppy could curse her and wonder after her and tell herself that she could have had something greater, had Roisin not been so kind, and so careful, and so easy to love.

When she moped, she pictured this moment over and over again. Their reunion. Preferably, Roisin would be crawling on the ground and bleeding from her hands—in these visions, they were often, inexplicably, in the desert. Roisin would wipe the sand from her eyes, clumsily swipe her dirty hair from her face, and beg for Poppy's forgiveness.

Poppy had wanted to see Roisin crawl. She hadn't considered that Roisin had been on her knees for fifteen years.

Don't cave, she told herself. *Don't bend. Don't fold.*

"Oh, petal," she groaned, in absolute pieces.

"Don't." Roisin held up a shivering hand. "Don't come near. Y-you've ruined me. You've ruined me, because now I know what it is to be h-happy. And now, now that I've had it, I'm afraid I can't live without it."

"Roisin . . ."

"I love you," Roisin blurted, quickly and wetly and drenched in spit. "It's absurd. Terribly absurd. Only, I can't run anymore. I'm so l-lonely for you. Saints, this is so blasted humiliating."

"May I . . ." Poppy moved forward, arms experimentally spread. When Roisin looked up, her eyes were a terrifying sort of helpless.

"I don't deserve it."

"Oh, shut up."

Poppy wrapped her arms around a shaking body, her hands welcoming those sharp angles and straight lines home.

"What the fuck," she mumbled miserably into Roisin's hair, "are we going to do?"

Chapter 28

"Are you sure this is wise?" Valentin picked a bit of lint off of his trousers. He had kicked off his shoes and was reclining on Poppy's bed, mussing the pillows. "I remember how you were when you first came to us."

"How can you?" Poppy asked from her seat at the dressing table, where Sarah pulled the army of pins from her hair. "I spent the first month in my room."

He clicked his tongue. "Yes, I remember that bit. Wasting away in there. And then, when you came down, you were in a terrible state. A wastrel. A waif in the rain."

Sarah snorted. "I believe it."

"You'd know about lost waifs," Poppy mused.

"As I see it, the only reason you're in that chair and I'm standing behind is because you're a vamp and I'm not." Sarah freed the last pin, shaking out the loose, golden waves. "So don't be putting on airs." She flicked the back of Poppy's head. "Gutterblood."

"I said I'd change you when you turned twenty-five." She squinted at Sarah's reflection. "*Thirty*."

"And I told you," Sarah replied crisply, "that I haven't made up my mind yet. So stop trying to get in my veins."

"All right." Valentin held up a hand. "Whatever we say about the Roisin matter, you'll do as you please, Poppy. I'm not naïve enough to think otherwise. But I would like to share with you, while we are here, that we are your friends." He gave Sarah a meaningful look. She rolled her eyes, but nodded. "We are your friends, Poppy Cavendish, and we will be here for you however this ends."

"I know how it ends." She stared at herself in the looking glass. In only her chemise and with her hair undone, she looked just as she had at Covenly. She hoped the sight would . . . *do* something. Fix something, or break it so dramatically that it could not be ignored. "She'll go back to chasing Cane, and we will return to London, and life will go on in much the same fashion as it has for fifteen years."

"And we'll leave Godfrey to walk back by himself." Sarah smiled at the pleasant daydream. "Have him give me a lesson on propriety with mud in his shoes."

"Silence, you beast. Poppy, I know you think you're perfectly comfortable with things ending the way you say. But are you truly?" His cheeks were raised, his teeth bared in a grimace of anticipatory pain. "Consider. You've been pining for this woman for fifteen years. And now she's here. Coming to your bedroom."

"Are you worried for my virtue?"

He scoffed. "Don't play silly buggers."

"Valentin, my darling. I'm playing very serious buggers." She picked up a brush and started in on her tangled hair. "Whatever warning you wish to give, consider it too late."

Sarah joined him on the bed, kicking her legs out in front of her, scooting close. She had taken to Valentin since her very first day in the Brood's service, in the manner of cats always finding the one person with an allergy. "I can't wait to meet her."

"Who says you'll get the chance?"

"Mate, I'm not leaving this bed until I see what sort of woman has kept you maudlin for a whole bleedin' decade. Pining like that cove in the bell tower."

Valentin carefully pulled the fabric of his trouser leg away from the encroaching force of Sarah's skirt. "What cove?"

"Your kind."

"Vampire?"

"Worse." She poked him in the shoulder. "*French.*"

There came a knock at the door. All three heads perked up.

"Just a minute," Poppy called, at the same time as Valentin beckoned, "Come in!"

Roisin opened the door, stilling at the unexpected sight of two people on the bed.

Poppy couldn't speak. She'd half imagined she'd made the whole thing up, that Roisin wasn't actually here, in this house, close enough to hear, to touch. And yet, Roisin insisted on being material, flesh and bone and smiles that weren't and eyes that *were*. Oh, how they were.

"Good morning." Roisin reached up, fingers twiddling, as though she had a hat to remove. "Good to see you, Valentin."

"And you, *cherie*." He continued his lazing, giving no indication that he planned on vacating the bed. "This is Sarah, Poppy's lady's maid."

"Oh. Delighted to meet you."

"And you as well," Sarah replied, employing her often-used and horribly inaccurate imitation of the upper class. She sank back into the pillow, deliberately getting comfortable. "Fuck, you're tall."

"Yes." A flat grin played across Roisin's lips. "I am."

"You're a vamp, yeah?"

"Last I checked."

"Cheeky," Sarah said with mock reproach. "I hadn't pegged you for a brunette. Poppy said Irish. I thought ginger."

"My da had dark hair." Roisin absently pushed a sleek strand behind her ear. "Mam was ginger. Said she wept when I came out without it."

"All right. Get out, you two." Poppy stood with too much force, her chair skidding out behind her. Three pairs of startled eyes snapped in her direction. She was too loud, too stiff, but that couldn't be helped. Not when Roisin—careful, deliberate Roisin—had gifted Sarah a tidbit of family history so sweet, it made her teeth ache. Roisin had never talked about her parents on those long nights at the hearth, outside of mentioning their little pub. They had been formless, shadowy figures. Now, not only did they have hair, it had *color*.

Had Roisin remembered the color of their hair in the time she and Poppy were parted? Or had she learned, in the past fifteen years, to give bits of herself to whoever asked?

Mine, Poppy thought, noting the strange urge to pull Roisin by her hair and expose her slender throat. To bite. *That was meant to be mine.*

"Quite right." Valentin rose, straightening his shirt. "Come, Sarah. I could use a drink."

He stopped by the door on his way out, shooting a meaningful, concerned look over Roisin's head. Sarah dragged her feet as she followed, shutting the door behind them.

A whining complaint wormed its way through the heavy wood.

"But Valentiiiiin, I want to *listen*."

Chapter 29

"A lady's maid," Roisin remarked. She was standing by the wall opposite the bedstead, far enough away from chair, bench, or bed to make sitting without invitation a conspicuous endeavor. A vengeful little part of Poppy enjoyed watching her squirm. "I'm glad you're being treated well in London."

"Did you suppose I wouldn't be?"

"No, no. I mean, you've adapted. You look the part. You act the part. You're a lady, Poppy. It's lovely to see."

"You know better." She became aware of the conspicuous bareness of her arms. She wrapped them over her chest, touching gooseflesh. "I'm not a lady, nor am I attempting to be one. Nothing so honest as that."

"What are you doing then?"

"Existing. Just existing."

"What do you—"

"I'm not waiting, if that's what you think." She couldn't do this. Not with Roisin standing so still, poised to listen. What was she thinking? "I'm not waiting for you. But nothing is you."

Roisin was silent for a long moment. "Nothing is you, either."

Poppy walked over to the bed and sank onto it, curling her legs underneath her. "What do you do out there?"

"There's a great deal of travel, as you can imagine." She lifted a shoulder. "A lot of asking around. Getting information from an occultist who met a very strange woman in Tangier. Going to Maroc, only to discover that she had already gone somewhere new. Up to Spain, where I found a coven of witches, who—"

"Witches?"

She nodded. "I can't attest to whether or not they're genuine, but they did burn some things and say the smoke told them Cane was in Prussia. And then I went to Prussia and, well, you get the general idea."

It wasn't enough. Poppy wanted to know each step Roisin had taken. Every person she had seen. She wanted it like air, like blood.

"Where did you trance?" she asked instead.

"I hired rooms." Roisin eyed the bed, but didn't move. "Barns, sometimes. I carried a tent for a period, when I was outside of cities, but that became too conspicuous."

"Did you go back to Covenly?"

"No."

It stood empty. The kitchen. The room with the portraits. Their bed . . . *No.*

"Come to bed." Her lungs were tight, her face burning hot. "Standing over there like a spare prick at a wedding. Absurd, is what you are."

"You said that to me . . ." Roisin didn't move. "We can trance."

"Yes."

"If that's what you want. It you want us to lie beside one another like before, and to trance, and to rise together when night falls, we can do that."

If Poppy's heart beat, it would be pounding. "Or?"

Roisin came over slowly and sat beside her in the bed. "Anything." A plea threaded through her silvery eyes. "I'd do anything with you."

Lord, Poppy wanted this. She wanted it so badly, and the wanting felt like her skin had been ripped from her, exposing her most delicate parts. Her muscle and her bones and her stolen blood, the heart of a body both dead and alive, and never more living than in this moment.

She had to be smart about this.

"Do you truly want to be with me?" She held up a hand to forestall objection. "Wait. Let me say this. You came here to see me, as you say. And now you've seen me. I've lived in your head for these fifteen years, and you in mine. I would forgive you for being disappointed—" Roisin made a stifled noise of protest. "*Disappointed,* I said. Or, at least, that you've realized the truth of me doesn't align with the Poppy that lived in your head."

Poppy had been different in 1837. She hadn't been a person who understood that sadness could swallow up all the night's hours. That the warmth of a bed was the only thing that made the passing of time bearable. That, in the absence of a welcome tomorrow, the world lost its color. Everyone had always come to Poppy for a laugh. These days, she had fewer on offer.

"I can survive a great deal. I have." She curled her fingers into the counterpane. "But I won't have you playacting love because you've found yourself beside me and are too polite to tell me you've made a mistake. That, I cannot abide."

Roisin stared, dumbstruck. Then, slow as dripping pitch, a smile formed. It was a strange smile for her, in that it was a full, true-to-its-name smile. A real, crescent-shaped thing that exposed a mouthful of teeth. And from behind those teeth, laughter spilled like dropped pennies, a shower of tiny fortunes bouncing off of the floor.

"Well, you don't have to laugh at me."

"Poppy," Roisin gasped, wiping mirthful tears. "You *mopstick.*"

"All right, enough of that."

"You fool." Roisin bent over, hesitated, then moved, kissing her on one cheek, then the other. She was warm, her lips soft. "Of all the things . . ." She rolled off the bed and stood. "Make yourself useful and help me out of this blasted dress."

Poppy did so. She grumbled for effect, and in defense of her shrunken dignity, but she did so only for a moment. Only until her finger grazed that first inch of pale skin. At that touch, and the answering inhale, she was transformed.

It wasn't that this was new. Dressing and undressing one another was one of many of their rituals at Covenly. The only difference was that now, Poppy could finally press her fingers to Roisin's body. With a trembling hand, she caressed the dip of a shoulder. Stroked along the white nape. Shaped a hip and waist hidden under linen. Roisin swayed at every touch, her breath growing as ragged as the tattered line of the far-off Milky Way in a sky thick with stars.

When Poppy was down to the chemise, Roisin stepped away.

Poppy groaned, moved nearly to tears. "We were just getting to the good bit."

"Oh, shut up, Poppy. My Poppy." Roisin's eyes were glittering, fond and frantic. "You're mine, aren't you? Just for now. Nothing next. Just for now, you're mine. And I'm yours, aren't I? Tell me I'm yours."

"Sh, sh. Settle." She reached out and held her, stroking her back until all those little tremors melted away. "You're going to pop out of your skin."

"I feel like I could do anything," she chirped, gay and wild. "Get me out of this."

Poppy obliged, hands reaching down to ruck up the chemise, mouth pressed to Roisin's shoulder. She tasted of leaves and smoke, like a burning forest. Roisin raised her arms, and Poppy tossed the chemise away.

Skin and skin and skin.

"Shall I touch you?" she murmured.

Roisin nodded mutely. Poppy let her hands roam. There were more curves to Roisin's slender body than she could tell by sight alone. A subtle sway in her lower back. A little give to her hips. A shallow slope in her shoulders. Small, careful things that could only be discovered by feel. Hillocks that fit perfectly in the palm of Poppy's hand.

Poppy's face went up and Roisin's down and their lips met. It was a small kiss, almost dainty. Only after they parted did Poppy realize it had been their first.

Roisin's face was tight with nerves. "I'm sorry, it's been so long and I—"

"Hush, now." Poppy cupped her cheek. Drew her thumb across that sharp chin. "Can you follow me?"

Roisin nodded, looking somewhat more relaxed and entirely grateful. When they kissed again, Poppy opened her mouth. Roisin gently heeded, the seam of her lips parting, freeing a little gasp when Poppy's tongue darted inside.

Poppy could always read a kiss. It was her extra sense, her special talent. A gift that never failed, until now, because this kiss was something entirely new. This one was an entire library, pages upon pages, in prose and in verse, about how they belonged to each other. Too lengthy to read, too many words, too many stories. Tales of giving way, a shared breath of ball lightning. An embrace written in ancient runes, in lost languages. If they had done this fifteen years ago, they would never have parted.

Roisin was shaking again.

"You're in a state." Poppy gentled her, not thinking about what she herself must look like. "What do you need?"

"I—" She swallowed. "I need you to look at me."

Yes. Oh, god yes. "Step back and give me the chance, love."

There she was. Tall and simply built and perfect. Her thin arms set in wide shoulders. Subtle breasts with lovely dark nipples, small and peaked. And around her waist—

"What the fuck is that?"

Lines. Black lines drawn just above her hip, curling up her abdomen, disappearing around the corner of her back.

"Turn."

Roisin turned. The black lines turned with her, traveling adjacent to her spine, up to her shoulder. Lines of ink on the paper-white skin, like someone had taken a pen to her body.

"What is that?"

"It's a tattoo."

"Well of course it's a fucking tattoo." She couldn't help but touch. Her fingers found the curls and dots, lines that thickened and thinned. Roisin shivered, gooseflesh rising. "Who gave it to you?"

"A sailor." Her teeth were chattering. She talked through it, her voice pitched nervously high. "Nice chap, didn't even charge too much. I think he enjoyed the eyeful."

"Why? Not the sailor, I mean. What I mean to say is . . ." She took a deep breath. "Why did you do this?"

"Don't you see what they are?"

"What they . . ." They were flowers. Lots and lots of flowers, planted from hip to shoulder. She blinked and she stared as icy disbelief poured over her.

"Poppies," she breathed. They were poppies. Each one inked into Roisin's skin, forever blooming across the soft earth of her body.

"I needed you with me." She turned back around, hands clasped over her chest. "Do you know how many times I thought about coming back to London and taking you with me? But I knew how she'd hurt you, if I did. How she'd use you to hurt me. I couldn't let that happen. But how could I do what needed to be done without you? How, when I had only known I could do it because you gave me that strength?" She was rambling. She inhaled shakily. "So I got these as a reminder. That you were in London, or

231

wherever Carmen and Valentin whisked you off to, safe and warm and fed. I got this to remind me you were wearing fine frocks and wrapping pink ribbons 'round your curls. To remind me that I was going after her because of you. *For* you. Do you understand?"

Of course she did. How very Roisin, to love Poppy in a way that excluded her entirely. How maddening, how absurd.

And yet, Poppy had wondered, in her lowest, darkest moments, whether the year they spent together had left Roisin with any lasting impression. After all, the woman had been alive for over two centuries. How did one year compare to a life so vast? How could Roisin love her, yet be able to leave so abruptly? How could she, when she had not let Poppy ease her burden, to help her make the decisions that would shape the rest of their lives?

Yet here was proof. A permanent proof, in unmoving lines of darkness. Roisin, by Poppy's love and a sailor's needle, was changed.

Poppy was too full to speak, her head too heavy with unshed tears, her heart inflated like a bellows. Instead, she kissed.

A startled "oh, *god*," popped from Roisin's lips as Poppy sank to her knees and kissed one petal, then another. She wanted to count them with her mouth, catalogue every stem and leaf and bloom. Know them, like she wanted to know every step Roisin had taken in their absence. Every story of her home. Every inch of her skin.

She mouthed at Roisin's hipbone. Felt Roisin sway, knees going soft. Pressed her face to the warm thatch of hair between those long legs.

"Poppy!" Roisin squealed, scandalized and sweet.

Poppy chuckled and kissed her. Tasted wet heat. "Get on the bed."

Roisin hurried to oblige. Poppy licked her lips.

"Good," she said, testing a theory.

Roisin's body gave a little lurch. Her lips parted, eyes dark and devastated. *Good.*

Poppy started with her feet. Long and bony, with ten ridiculous toes. Old, strange friends. Then her calves; Poppy rubbed the tension from them, reveling in the feel of the small hairs below her palms. Two knobbly knees. Two slender thighs, obediently spreading when Poppy pressed them apart. And between them, dark curls, glistening damp and waiting. Poppy cupped her there, pressing in with the heel of her hand.

Above her, Roisin inhaled sharply.

"What do you like?"

Roisin's eyes were squeezed shut. "A-anything you do, I'll like."

Poppy pressed harder. "Roisin."

"Inside," she whispered, like an admission. An entreaty. A secret. "Please."

She was hot on Poppy's fingers. Fifteen years of wanting and it burned inside her like a furnace. Like a hearth, with two seats beside it. Poppy lowered her mouth and Roisin keened, heels scrabbling on the counterpane. She tasted sweet and bright, like a memory. Like a star.

Her hands were pressed to the headboard, thready arm muscles tensed.

"Keep your hands there," Poppy instructed, and Roisin nodded frantically. Poppy had wondered what Roisin would be like when they could finally be together. She had imagined a gentle loosening of Roisin's tightness, a giving way in inches. She had not expected this explosive beast of diluvian longing, drowning under the tide, clawing helplessly at nothing and gasping for air. A woman who shook and writhed and made lovely, agonized sounds that went, "ah, ah, ah," and silently shaped the word *please*, over and over and over.

"Roisin, my petal," Poppy murmured. "Open your eyes."

"I-I'm not certain I can."

She was too tense, too tremulous. A loose mote of electricity needing grounding. Poppy crawled up, scooping her in steady arms.

Roisin was gulping air. "Did I do something wrong?"

"Never," Poppy murmured into her shoulder. "You could never." She kissed that long neck, that shoulder. She held close, bodies pressed, mouth circling a hard nipple. She reached down, slipped back inside. Felt Roisin's leg insinuate itself between her own. Welcomed it. Here, tight together, Roisin was safe. They both were, in the warmth between them. In brilliant nearness.

"Poppy," Roisin gasped, fingers pressing into her back with wonderful strength. "I w-wanted. I waited."

"I know," Poppy told her, surrounded by it. Overwhelmed and held and cherished, pleasure shooting up and down her spine. There were Poppies everywhere, in dark, shifting lines. She was drunk on them. "I know, petal. Me too."

"Oh, god. It feels . . . you *f-feel*. I'm close, I'm going to, I'm—" Roisin arched her back, exploding in a shower of sparks, gasping out something that sounded like surprise. She breathed and breathed. When she finally opened her eyes, there was a look of stunned wonder in them.

"I'm such an idiot," she slurred.

Poppy pulled a sweaty strand of hair from Roisin's damp forehead. "Mm?"

"You could have done that to me fifteen years ago."

Poppy was still laughing as Roisin began to map out her body, to hold her breasts and taste them. To kiss her navel. To situate herself between Poppy's legs and stare for so long Poppy began to worry.

"Do you plan to . . . do anything down there?"

Roisin slapped her thigh, sharp and mean. "Someone ought to teach you patience."

"Mate, I've been patient for fifteen years."

"Don't call me mate when I'm about to…" She gestured vaguely. "You know."

"Say it."

Her perfect smile emerged, flat and subtle and sly. "Not a chance," she said, and did the only better thing.

Poppy melted into the pleasure of it, of it being Roisin, and laughed for the fathomless joy of it all. In response, Roisin redoubled her efforts. There was no laughing after that, only holding on for dear life, Poppy's hands in Roisin's slippery hair, each tug pulling a groan that rumbled through her marrow.

"Good," Poppy said with tears in her eyes. "Good. Give it to me."

Roisin did, and Poppy thrummed with the sensation of Roisin's clever, eager mouth. She lay and took it and grabbed at more. *Mine*, she thought, *mine*. Her desire and her due. Theirs, because the calm in Roisin's eyes was unlike anything she'd seen before. A sloughing off of sick centuries, healthy skin underneath.

"Ours," she whispered, and came like a star.

Chapter 30

Poppy would have been content to stay in bed with Roisin the entire week, making up for lost time. Instead, the next night, as the gentle moonlight slipped through the window and across her pillow, Valentin threatened to kick in the door and toss Poppy into the sea.

"I brought you here to look pretty and reflect well upon me, Poppy Cavendish. If you embarrass me, mark my words, I'll be the one you spend the next decade-and-a-half pining for."

Reluctantly, Poppy allowed Sarah to dress her in a pale pink frock that slipped off her shoulder, two halos of delicate lace hanging around the sleeves and neckline.

"Well." Roisin watched admiringly as Poppy stepped into a pair of new slippers, done in the same rose silk. "You look a lady to the manner born."

Poppy rolled her eyes. "I was born in my mum's bed. One of the sows gave birth on the same day, in the barn right outside. Dad said they screamed together, and that when mum got tired of my suckling, she threatened to have me nurse on the sow."

Sarah tipped her head back and laughed until she cried.

The party lounged in what appeared to be a large breakfast room. The walls were papered with a distinctly French cream-and-blue toile. Long windows opened to the night sky, letting in a damp, salty breeze from the nearby coastline. The furniture was pushed to the corners of the room, delicate pieces jumbled together with upturned upholstery, chair legs in the air like women receiving their lovers. A few musical instruments were scattered about, taken up in turn and played to the amusement of the group. A long-necked woman tucked a violin under her chin and fiddled, while another stretched her fingers along the keys of a small piano. Women danced, pressed together, trading off the leading position, whispering in giddy French with faces so flushed they looked for all the world as though they were flown on champagne.

And perhaps they were. Some of these women had the telltale odor of life about them. There were humans intermingling with these immortals. Not as servants, but as companions. Friends, certainly. Lovers, more than likely. On a table by the window, a large bottle of champagne was open, coupes surrounding it. One small, slender human with straight, black hair sidled over, poured herself a glass of bubbles and sipped indulgently. Poppy tried to tamp down the envy as a memory surged of sweet, shimmering wine dancing on her tongue, turning her thoughts muzzy and cloth-covered.

She stood with Roisin on her arm, noting the heads turned in their direction. As well they might; Roisin was at her smartest, dressed in slender trousers of a pale gray, accentuating the long line of her slim legs. She had forgone a frock coat, revealing a painfully white shirt with a carefully starched collar, a dark cravat, and a silvery waistcoat that turned her eyes to starlight. Everything looked terribly new and frightfully expensive, and a lump rose in Poppy's throat when she realized Roisin had probably purchased the lot just for this.

Valentin approached looking harried.

"That cow," he pointed at a bored-looking woman within earshot, "told me there would be men here."

"Bah!" the woman exclaimed, blowing air from her mouth in a way Poppy had associated exclusively with Valentin, and was now coming to recognize as characteristically French. "'Ow else was I meant to get you 'ere? Couldn't get you out of ze Brood's clutches without a, *comment dit-on?* A winkle pin."

"Oh, winkle yourself."

She winked, which was close enough. She was a plump, short, sugar plum-type woman, with black skin and round eyes the color of dark licorice. Her lips and cheeks were rouged vivid pink, her eyelashes as long as moth's wings. The tight coils of her hair were combed and styled into the approximate shape of a rococo wig, giving her the air of a queen, as well

236

as nearly a foot of height—though the top of her hair still barely reached Valentin's chin. From her sea-green gown to her meticulously painted face, she was so remarkably well-assembled Poppy might have stared. She might have, were it not for the sharp, derisive look on the woman's face that dared her to try.

"And is zis Poppy?" She held out a lazy hand for Poppy to grasp. "My name is Anaïs. Welcome to zis 'ome. It is not *my* 'ome, of course, but ze lord of ze manor is off wiz 'is racing yachts and 'e owes me a favor or two."

"Well, thank you for collecting," Poppy replied, falling back on the manners Valentin had drilled into her. "It's lovely to be here. I'm looking forward to this week."

"I was expecting to 'ave one guest fewer." She arched a plucked eyebrow in Roisin's direction. "And zen I received a letter from an old friend requesting an invitation. Impertinent. Wouldn't you say, Poppy?"

"Oh, horribly so." She slid her hand to the small of Roisin's back. "Thank you for having us both. Forgive my companion's lack of grace. She's been traveling alone for many years, and I fear she has forgotten what it is like to move in polite company."

Anaïs blew a puff of air from her nose; it might have been a laugh. "You 'ear zat, Roisin? We're polite company now."

"You've always been the height of manners, my friend."

"Polite!" Valentin crossed his arms over his chest. "Do you call inviting me here on false pretenses polite?"

"*Mon pauvre petit,* 'ow tragic, you'll 'ave to go *sans la bitte* for a whole week! Will you turn into a pumpkin like ze Cendrillon?"

"She doesn't turn into a pumpkin, her carriage does. *Connasse . . .*"

"Why don't you tell me all about it over 'ere and we'll let ze girls dance, *ouais?*" She tutted in a consolatory manner, dragging him away.

"You demanded an invitation?" Poppy asked as Roisin swept her onto the small, makeshift dance floor. The pianist was playing something soft and slow, and there wasn't much to do but hold each other and sway. "I wasn't aware you could be that forward."

"I wanted to see you."

"And you were opposed to, say, meeting me in London? The place where I live? In the home filled with your friends?"

Roisin pressed her mouth to the part in Poppy's hair, sighing against her scalp. "It's your home, now. I have no right to intrude."

"Legally, the house belongs to Carmen, so I don't see why my living there should stop you."

"Poppy." She kissed the top of Poppy's head, tightening an arm around her waist. "I feel like a villain. I want you to forget me, most of the time. I think a world in which you're free of me is a juster one. But I'm selfish and I want to be beside you."

"And that means you can't come to my home?"

"It means I don't belong there. That perhaps there are places we belong together, but they aren't in London. I half hoped you would see me here, greet me politely, and introduce me to your new lover."

"And the other half?"

Roisin said nothing, but her arms firmed on Poppy's body. The music curled around them like dew. On the wind, ocean salt tickled her nose, cutting across the blazing forest of Roisin's skin. In the corners of her vision, women's hands snuck up one another's skirts. Necks were kissed and bit. The air was peppered with the music of stifled moans. Valentin pouted in the corner.

"Roisin?" Poppy murmured.

"Mm."

"Why didn't you write?"

Her grip faltered. "You wouldn't know where to send a response."

"A sorry excuse."

"I know, I know." She breathed in Poppy's hair. Sarah had dipped her comb in jasmine hair oil to turn the locks sweet, and Poppy wanted to kiss her for the foresight. "What could I say?"

"'I'm alive' for a start."

"Would that have satisfied you?"

"Of course not." She pressed herself to Roisin's chest. "I might not have worried so much, is all."

Poppy felt Roisin's head shake. "I'm meant to worry. You're meant to live."

"That's not for you to decide."

"It's my juster world. The world where you forgot about me." Her voice shrank, until it was very small and very faint. "I thought you forgot about me."

Poppy's dumb puppy heart rolled over. "Couldn't."

"Mm." She dropped a silent kiss on Poppy's forehead. Relief might have leaked from her lips. "I ought to be ashamed of bringing us back together. I ought to be panicked about what comes next."

"Are you?"

"No." She pulled back to lay a kiss on her Poppy's nose, small as a jewel. "I'm too happy to be clever. You know, your frock is the exact same color as a ribbon I remember rather fondly."

Just then, a pair of tightly entwined women stepped over to the champagne table. The vampire was taller and thicker, her human partner small and clinging like a barnacle on a ship's hull. The taller woman gently extricated her lover's hand, biting at the wrist to open a vein and decanting the blood into a clean coupe. When she was satisfied with her loot, she gave the wrist a gentle kiss and produced a bandage, lovingly wrapping the skin and leading the wobbling human to a divan to rest. Before drinking of her lover's blood, the vampire raised the champagne bottle and filled the bloody glass to the top. The liquids swirled, turning the champagne a deep, ferocious red, the bubbles going sluggish in the thickening drink. With a smile of satisfaction, the vampire raised the glass to her lips and drank.

"What," Poppy breathed.

The vampire lowered the glass and let out a satisfied sigh.

"*What,*" Poppy repeated, somewhat louder and not entirely of her own volition.

There was no retching, no curling over an aching stomach. Just a trill of laughter as another partygoer came by to steal a sip.

"*What!*" Poppy cried.

"I don't know." Roisin was similarly mesmerized, brow furrowed in confusion. "That's *possible?*"

Anaïs materialized beside them. "'Ave you never 'ad a mixed drink?"

"Mixed drink?" Poppy asked in wonderment.

"It works best wiz alcohol. Worst wiz milk, as you can imagine. We 'aven't yet perfected it wiz food, but one can enjoy a drink from time to time. Return one of life's pleasures."

"From time to time?"

"Too much and you'll experience ze sort of affects you might expect from 'uman delicacies. But, for a party . . ." She tightened her lips and blew out a thin, flatulent gust, apparently meant as a percussive *Voilà*. Truly, the French had an entire vocabulary composed of nonverbal sounds. "Would you like to try?"

Would she? Of course she would. But where would she get the blood? She had drunk of several rabbits before leaving London and wouldn't need a meal for days yet. There were animals on the property; she had caught the distinctly verdant scent of foxes scurrying through the bushes. But she was wearing a lovely dress and was loath to spoil it chasing after the little beasts. In some of her travels, she brought along a rabbit or two in a small carrying case, but Valentin had advised her to not to do so this trip.

"They won't understand," he had said. "Frankly, I don't either. But I," he squared his shoulders, "am *polite*."

"I don't. Erm." She looked between the champagne table and Anaïs, whose painted features were beginning to show impatience. "I drink from my maid, and she's retired to her quarters."

Anaïs pursed her lips. "I'm sure one of ze guests 'ere would be willing to 'elp."

"I will." Roisin curved her fingers around Poppy's hip. "I don't mind."

"Your blood?" Anaïs raised her perfectly groomed eyebrows. "Zat 'ardly seems satisfying."

"I sired her, did I say?"

The French woman's eyes went wide. "You 'adn't mentioned! I assumed it was—"

"No, not *her*. Me." Her fingers tightened, just a touch. "When Poppy woke, her first thought was of the food she couldn't eat and the, well, the liquids she wouldn't be able to drink." Poppy tightened her lips to stem the wild, threatening laughter. "You can't imagine the guilt I felt. I would love to share this moment with her: the first time she'll drink champagne in more than fifteen years."

"If zat is what you want," Anaïs said, not entirely convinced. "Far be it from me to comprehend ze will of lovers. Go. Bleed. Drink."

Poppy approached the bottle with a strange surge of nerves in her belly. She felt oddly like a bridegroom approaching the end of an aisle.

Her first love. Taste. The richness of things, the colors she felt on her tongue. Her greatest pleasures. The fats and sweets her mother warned her against, for fear she'd succumb to excess. The world she was denied when her life had veered from humanity. Her eyes watered as much as her mouth.

Roisin selected a coupe with unnecessary care, holding it out for approval. Poppy gave a quick nod and waited.

Roisin shuffled her feet. "Are you going to . . ."

"Oh!" Poppy took in her hunched shoulders. Her tight mouth. "You want me to bite you."

Roisin froze, caught out. She quickly brought her wrist to her own mouth. "I can—"

"Stop." Poppy gently pulled her arm down, stroking the soft skin, hairless and hidden. "I haven't bitten you before."

"No."

"Will it . . . does it always . . ."

Roisin nervously licked her lips. "I don't know what I was thinking. A silly suggestion."

"Hush now." Her lips curled in a smile she knew to be wolfish. She could see its effect in the expanding of Roisin's dark pupils. The rising breaths in her chest. "You want me to bite you where everyone can see."

Roisin turned her face away, staring out towards the full-bellied moon.

"Roisin, look at me."

Her head snapped back. Her eyes were pressed closed, her nostrils flared with high breathing.

"Open your eyes, petal."

She did. Her pupils were blown wide, her silvery irises reduced to the width of a bangle.

"Oh, you *do* want this." Poppy let her lips spread, predatory and knowing. "You want it very much."

"Poppy . . ."

"You want everyone in this room to see how lovely you'll be when I bite you. Is that it?"

Roisin said nothing. She was taut as a bowstring, but her lips were slack. Readied, like the tension of holding the world up was replaced with something more urgent. Like the burdens were shoved out by a force ten times as demanding.

"I want them to see," Roisin said after a silent moment, her voice barely a whisper. "I want them to see that I'm yours. Bite me, Poppy. Make me yours."

241

Poppy swallowed her heart and bit. Roisin's blood was familiar, tickling the false memory of standing in the night with her mouth open and arms outstretched, face turned to the sky, catching and swallowing falling stars. It sparkled on her tongue and down her throat, and turned her into a glowing thing.

She reached for the coupe just as Roisin doubled over, hand slamming to the table, rattling the glasses. Her body trembled, small, agonized noises slipping from her mouth. Poppy squeezed the blood from her wrist, then lifted it to her mouth once more, licking the wound.

"It feels good, doesn't it?"

"It's too much." Roisin skated a hand from her breast to the front of her trousers and back again. "Y-you're everywhere."

"I always am. Like the poppies." She reached out, cupping Roisin's sex with a proprietary hand. "Tell me how you feel."

"Yours. I feel like I'm yours."

When the shudders subsided, Roisin poured the champagne into the glass. She swirled the liquids, then placed the glass between Poppy's outstretched fingers. The bubbles glowed like rubies.

"Do you want to have a glass, too?" Poppy asked, tingling with nervous anticipation. "I'm happy to open a vein."

Roisin shook her head, a pleased, dopey expression on her face. "I want to watch you drink it."

If that didn't send a thrill down her spine. She raised the glass to her lips and drank. It was . . .

It was.

The taste carried her through rooms of memory. To nights in London, drinking with her friends until she was sick in the street. To demanding men pouring fine bubbles over her lips and kissing her full, messy mouth. To biting into a liquor-filled chocolate and letting the syrup slide down her throat. She bubbled and fizzed and sang and filled a hole in her life that had stood empty for sixteen years.

And through it all, the familiar, foundational taste of the one year that mattered. The one person.

"How does it taste?" Roisin asked.

"Like you," Poppy told her.

Like you, like you, like you.

Chapter 31

The next night, the party ran down to the beach, the vampires in only their chemises, the humans bundled against the spring chill. They climbed down a steep hill, vampires slinging their giggling human lovers over their shoulders, and alit on the sand, spreading out blankets and passing around bottles. A few took up a game of graces that sent clacks and laughter into the air. Valentin had not yet entirely warmed to the company, but Poppy had requested Sarah join them for the night and her presence softened the sting. The two of them lingered by the back of the throng, Sarah slowly plodding down the hill, Valentin trying to appear as if his keeping pace with her was merely coincidental.

The beach was walled by rocks, culminating in what appeared to be a stacked-stone arch, though a party guest helpfully informed Poppy it had been created entirely by nature. Durdle Door, the woman called it, and she and Roisin tried not to collapse into giggles at the sound of those two words spoken in a thick French accent. They failed miserably.

The following night, the weather was less mild. For the sake of the humans, Anaïs decreed that the group would stay indoors. Roisin wrapped an arm around Poppy's waist, nodding towards the open window.

"Shall we?"

They made their apologies and trod off to the beach together. Poppy's skirts were a nuisance on the rocks, so Roisin swept her up and leapt down the hill, jumping the last few strides. Poppy shrieked, merry and vital and free. The ocean told her to hush, over and over, its waves crashing as gently as a kiss.

They lay together, watching the stars.

"People like you," Poppy said.

"It seems that way."

"*I* like you."

"I'm glad of it."

Poppy absently drew some lines in the sand. "If you're determined to leave once more, you're not obliged to spend every night alone."

Roisin was silent for a long time. When Poppy looked up, it was to find Roisin smiling at her, in her particular way: flat-lipped and noiselessly amused.

"What?"

"I wanted the same thing for you. Tell me, have you shared your heart with anyone?"

"I'm not talking about your heart, mate. I'm talking about your bed."

"Does sharing your bed make you miss me less?"

"For moments," Poppy admitted. "I can forget for moments that I'm not entirely whole without you. Fucking helps. Laughing is better." She jostled the memories like coins in her palm. "The daily stuff of living with people. Worrying for them. Sharing advice. Staffing the house. Watching Carmen paint. Remembering that life continues, whether or not I wish it to."

"That isn't something I can afford. The daily business. And while I suppose I could share my bed, it doesn't seem worth the effort." She shrugged. "Anyway, I don't want to."

"But you're so . . ." Poppy screwed up her mouth. "Is there no cure for your loneliness?"

Roisin's lips flattened and shifted like a spent wave. "Sometimes I forget how young you are." She inclined her head, a silent acknowledgment she meant no offense. Only strange, complicated fondness. "In my loneliest moments, I wasn't alone. I'm not looking for companionship, Poppy. When I can have you, you are who I want. When I can't, I make do with what I have."

"Which is what?"

She lifted a shoulder. "I keep a diary."

"Oh, a diary! Well, you're set then."

"You have everything you could possibly want. Tell me, Poppy: is it enough?"

The sea ran into the sand. *Hush*, it said. *Hush*.

In the quiet whispers of the night, Roisin began to speak.

"When I first met Cane, I thought the world of her. I had so much responsibility at my parents' pub. Mam and Da cared for me, but I was their worker as much as their child. When Cane came into my life, she said I could rest for a while. That she could make my world smooth and sweet.

"She had a way of taking away my worries. She would tell me what to do, and I would obey. I was always a nervous person, even as a child. I used to tug out my hair and bite my fingernails to the quick. But with her, my mind would go perfectly still. She told me to attend her, and I did. She said kneel, I knelt. She wanted my hand, it was hers. In bed, I wanted it. Outside of it, it began to make my life smaller. Like when she gave me her name and no room to refuse, or when she decided who would have my friendship and to whom I could no longer write. When she told me what I could eat, and that I wasn't allowed to say no. She was my whole family, my whole life. And then, she took away my free will entirely."

Poppy reached out to clasp Roisin's hand, holding it between their still bodies. It felt colder than usual.

"I had been thrilled to be obedient." She admitted this ruefully, the shape of banked grief in her throat. "If I had not given her so much, then she couldn't have taken the rest. How could it be a punishment, if it was exactly what I deserved?"

Poppy's chest hurt. Her eyes ached. "Oh, petal."

Roisin pressed on. "And then there was you. Bright like sunlight. I thought you would burn me up. And the way you wanted me." She gave a disbelieving laugh, warm in the chill sea air. "It was consuming. But it was terrifying, because I knew what I wanted. Even after everything Cane did to me, I still craved the feeling of being told what to do. Of obedience. I felt sick over it."

Poppy's heart was scooped out. "You could have said."

"I couldn't. I can barely say it now." She sucked in a steadying breath. "You make me believe I might not . . ." She broke off. For a long while, the only sound was that of the shifting, tiny rocks at the shore, the cycling waves. When Roisin spoke once more, she sounded very, very young. "Is there something wrong with me, Poppy?"

245

Poppy turned to face her. Those tuppence eyes were as wide as coins. Her cheekbones were hollow, her mouth small and tight. Her brows touched one another, huddling together for warmth.

Carefully, lovingly, Poppy kissed her brow, her cheeks. Her stark angles. Her furrows. The little lines beside her eyes that couldn't hide her amusement when it struck. The place where her soft hair bloomed.

"Nothing," she said fiercely, "is wrong with you."

"Don't lie to be kind."

"Nothing is wrong with you. Your desires are common. Mundane, even."

"*Poppy.*"

"Boring. I've seen them a thousand times over."

"Don't tease."

"I'm not. And if they're not mundane, they are spectacular, because they are yours. They're good, because they're yours." She kissed her on the mouth, warm and slow. "You are good."

"I'm not good at loving you," Roisin said thickly. "I don't know how to do it. It's the best thing I do, and it's so incredibly difficult. And the terrible injustice of it is that the worst things I've done were easy! I've done hideous things, most not under compulsion. I've killed so many people. I've hurt even more. I want to do something just, for a change. I want to make the world safe and right for you. I know you hate it, and I know I could never fully explain to you the need I have to do it. I know all you see is me leaving you. But I need to make myself worthy of living in the now, and destroying her is the only way I can see forward."

Poppy frowned. "In the now?"

"I wish you wouldn't wait for me. I wish you would. I hate myself for wishing for either. For *anything*. I ... I haven't even read any good books lately." She petulantly shoved her knuckles into the pebbles and sand. "Not in years."

Poppy cracked out a laugh. "Pathetic." She slung an arm around Roisin's shoulders and pulled them both down into the smooth gravel. Roisin was stiff all the way, falling to the earth with a stubborn *thunk*. "I've been told there's a good one out about a big fish."

"A whale," Roisin amended, arms crossed over her chest.

"A whale's a fish."

"No, Poppy. It isn't."

She drew down her brow, thinking hard. "It ... swims."

"Not all things that swim are fish."

"They *are*."

"All right, Poppy. What's a seal?"

She considered this. "It breathes, too. Whales don't."

"They do, you'll find."

"And how would you know?" she grumbled. "You haven't even read the fish book."

Roisin's subtle smile emerged, irritated and fond and exasperated and so perfect Poppy could cry.

"I missed you," Roisin said.

"Yes, well." Poppy cleared her throat, as it had suddenly gone thick. "Naturally."

"Poppy?"

"Mm?"

"As I've laid myself bare to you, would you mind telling me what it is you like?"

"You, primarily."

"In bed, I mean."

"Same answer."

"*Poppy*."

"I've known how to answer this question before," she confessed, acquiescing. "Only the truth is, I always told whoever asked what they wanted to hear. The ones that loved licking me, I said my favorite thing was to be licked."

"Ugh, Poppy."

"What? You did it earlier today on the *chaise lounge!*"

"Not the act. I, well, I actually enjoy—" She let out a small, gruff noise of frustration. "The doing and the saying are different matters entirely."

"Why should one be hard and the other easy?"

"Because I'm not brave like you." She picked up a flat rock and tossed it into the waves. Poppy lifted her head to mark its trajectory, but it went so far she couldn't see where it plopped. "I'm beginning to believe there's nothing you can't do."

This was, in Poppy's view, a somewhat dubious claim. "You think I'm ridiculous."

"Two things can be true." She chose another rock and examined it. "Look." She dropped it into Poppy's hand. "It's you."

It was small, round, and pink. "My child." She hurled the rock into the ocean, watching as it disappeared into the dark. "I never get a chance to throw things. Or jump high, or run. It's easy to forget how remarkable we are."

"I'm not getting into this with you again," Roisin said. "And don't think I've forgotten you didn't answer my question."

Poppy admitted defeat. "Fine, here is my answer: I like to be what my bedfellow wants me to be."

"To serve, you mean?"

"Not quite." She toed off her slippers and pulled down her stockings. The gravel was deliciously cool between her toes, the sand beneath it wet and dense. "If they like to serve, I like to demand. If they like backchat, I like to give cheek. If they like a supplicant, I'm a priestess in their temple."

Poppy could see Roisin roll this over in her mind. "And what if there were no one else there?"

"You mean what I do on my own? I've actually been reading. Valentin has translated some rather diverting works by a disgraced French nobleman—"

"Not like that. I mean, if you could pick your ideal . . ." Roisin visibly swallowed a few words before tasting one she could spit out. "*Amour,* what would they want from you?"

"You know the answer."

"Do I?"

"You are my ideal *amour.*" She colored the word with silly panache because Roisin looked close to dying. "You wish for a firm hand. I wish to be that firm hand."

"Poppy." Roisin nervously fiddled with some rocks. "I don't need you to be kind."

"No, you need me to be a little cruel. I understand."

"*Poppy.*" She fidgeted, swearing under her breath, then seated herself with her knees at her chest. "Don't indulge me just because my life has been difficult. It doesn't mean I don't have the strength to hear what you actually want."

"That you think I'd be so selfless." Poppy reached up to push a hair from Roisin's face. Roisin didn't shift her sightline from the shore. "Darling."

"Hmph."

"Will you look at me?"

"I'd rather not, if it's all the same."

It wasn't, but Poppy could compromise. "As long as you listen."

"Mm."

"There's a look you get," she began, her bravado dripping off like sea foam, the words gone dry in her mouth. "Like you've put your heart in my hands. Like you trust me enough with it, you can put down all the bad years and relax your shoulders for a moment. And *I've* done that. I'm the one that made that happen for you. You let me in, let me see how best to, best to . . ." She was sure Roisin was staring at her now, could feel the press of that ardent gaze on her cheek. "To be what you need. To thrill you, thrills me. To love you . . ."

"You love me?"

There was Roisin. God, she looked happy. Only, it was her sort of happy: a fragile thing, held so carefully her hands shook. Happiness borrowed from an acquaintance and due back in an hour.

Poppy couldn't love her more if she tried. "Did I not say?"

"No, Poppy." Scolding. Irritated. Smiling, a little. "You didn't."

She let a handful of sandy memories run through her fingers. "I must have."

"You *didn't*."

"Are you angry? You seem angry."

"I'm not—" Roisin shook her head, a bewildered laugh puffing her lips. "Say it."

"I love you." It tasted like the sunshine she hadn't felt since her heart beat.

"Oh." Roisin's gaze flicked down to Poppy's lips and up again. "W-what do you want to talk about now?"

"I'm done talking. I want to take off your clothes and tell you what to do."

Roisin's buckskins and shirt were quick work. She reached for Poppy's frock.

"No." Poppy swiped her hand away. "It's too complex for the beach."

249

"So it's just me nude, then? Seems unfair."

"How lovely you still believe in fairness. Step back, I mean to look my fill."

Moonlight spilled over her, a halo reflected in her shining hair. Poppy circled her slowly, feet sinking into the soft earth. She pulled the tie from Roisin's queue and watched the strands fall.

"Put your hands out, petal. Like that. There you are."

"Why?"

"You look like a goddess this way." She skated her fingers over the dark poppies, followed their line from hip to shoulder and back again. "A moon goddess, basking in the divine . . . the divine whatsit."

Roisin's breath stuttered. "This is a little embarrassing."

"I enjoy you a little embarrassed."

"Yes, it does seem that way." She shifted from foot to foot. "Is this your entire plan? To have me stand here?"

"Hush now." She reached down, smiling at Roisin's sharp gasp. "You're wet."

"You're l-looking at me."

"Is that truly all it takes?" Poppy clicked her tongue. "Tart." Roisin made a mortified noise. "Don't worry, petal. I've got plans for you yet."

They moved into the surf together, Poppy's skirts dark and heavy in the saltwater. The sea was icy, but it was a bolstering chill rather than a quelling one. Poppy dragged Roisin down into the waves so that her lower half was covered, and called her a mermaid.

"You're the mermaid," Roisin protested.

"I look like a randy sailor's drawing of a mermaid. You look like the actual thing." She caressed a breast, the nipple peaked from cold or arousal. "Like you swim all day long. Lean, like a fish. Touch yourself. Show me how mermaids do it."

She did, the water lapping by her hips. The ocean saying *hush, hush.*

Poppy settled down between her legs to watch. If her enhanced vampiric vision was for anything, it was this: to see Roisin's hands moving in the dark water, her ten white fingers a school of fish. "Two inside, like you like."

"*Christ.*"

"Get close. Don't come. Can you get a third in you, or is the water washing away all your joy? Should we get you on the sand instead? Watch you drip?"

Roisin reared back as if she'd been slapped. "You're a menace," she rasped, but her hands didn't slow, and she obediently pressed a third finger into herself.

"Good," Poppy murmured, and Roisin said, "ah, ah, ah," small sounds pulled from somewhere deep, somewhere like the dark room in her stomach where her soul took naps.

"How does it feel?" Poppy asked.

"Feels good," she slurred. "I'm c-close."

"Hands off, there's a good girl."

Roisin's tight fists pressed into the waves, her arm muscles bunching. Poppy shifted to her side and pulled her into a supine embrace, Roisin shaking finely, Poppy soothing her with gentle touches and clucked comfort. Poppy's skirts were in the surf, swirling around Roisin's spread and trembling legs.

"That was lovely," Poppy hummed. "Just lovely. Again, if you please."

She went again, louder and more frantic this time. Poppy held her, pinching and twisting her taut nipples, licking her neck and ears, tasting salt and burning leaves.

"I'm nearly th-there."

"Hands off."

Roisin fairly seethed this time, writhing in the shallows like a lost eel.

"Please," she groaned.

"Please what, my love?"

The endearment brought her breath up, short and high in her breast. "I want to."

"Want to what?" Poppy asked, unrepentant. Her own blood sang. She very seriously considered ripping her skirt to threads, crawling over Roisin's mouth, and demanding her own satisfaction. But this wasn't about her, not really. It was about the ceaseless woman in her arms, who wanted nothing more than to clear her mind of worry and grief, and give herself over to someone she could trust with her most tender bits. Roisin was an infallible woman who craved fallibility, who became a loose thing, a crazed thing, making unselfconscious sounds that shook the stars like stacked china.

251

"I want to come," she admitted, shy as a dormouse, silvery eyes averted. "Let me, please."

Poppy pretended to consider this. "One more go round, I think. For luck."

Roisin's brow knit. "For luck?" she repeated, incredulous. Breathless.

Poppy had always had a bastard streak. She wore it like a scarf today, warm and cozy.

"No point arguing. You'll do whatever I say, won't you?"

Roisin didn't answer. She stared at Poppy, her mouth set in a proud little frown, which fell away the instant she got her hands on herself. She squeezed her eyes shut.

"Open your eyes, love. Look at me."

"Can't," Roisin gasped, doing it anyway. *My brave thing*, Poppy thought, and kissed her hard, teeth clacking clumsily, Roisin's head jerking in rhythm with her quick strokes.

"Please." Her hands flew from her quim and gripped her thighs hard enough to bruise. "Please l-let me."

"One last thing."

Roisin's wrecked moan came filtered through gritted teeth. "I'm . . . I can't—"

"You can. Hear me out." She brought her mouth close to Roisin's lovely ear, licking the shell. "Tell me a whale is a fish."

Roisin blinked unfocused eyes. "What?"

"A whale," Poppy whispered, biting the lobe and tugging. "Tell me it's a fish."

"But it isn't." There was something like fear in her face, now. "You want me to . . . to lie?"

"I told you what I want." She dragged a lazy hand down Roisin's stomach. Felt it hiccup and jerk. "How do you feel? Like the sun is burning in your cunt?"

"*Fuck.*"

"Be correct or be satisfied. Be stupid for me. I'll even bite you. How does that sound?"

A strangled noise of burning want. Writhing and kicking up waves. The moon bearing down on her ancient, ageless body.

I love you so much, Poppy thought. *My avenging angel. My fountain of*

252

life. My time well spent.

"Be wrong, petal," she told the woman who remade her. "Just this once."

Roisin scrunched up her face. "Awhalesafish."

Poppy could have shouted with glee. "What was that?"

"A whale," she repeated, baleful eyes trained mutinously on the sky, "is a fish."

"Perfect," Poppy decreed, and Roisin sagged in relief. "Hands back on yourself. Tell me when."

"Now. Now!"

"Already? You really are a tart."

She bit that slender neck, her mouth filling with a universe of starlight, her skirts swirling like kelp.

When the world was set to rights, Roisin shook her head.

"My god, you're a devil," she said, bright-eyed and hopeless, and Poppy said "Fuck it," tearing her skirts in twain, ripping off her drawers and seating herself on lips that laughed against her skin.

Chapter 32

Poppy arose the next night with Roisin in her arms and a fluttering sensation in her chest that she cradled close, until she recognized it as hope.

She knew better than to hope.

She did her best to hide her flagging joy. The last time they were set to part, their final days at Covenly, Poppy had become a terrible brat, poking for proof of Roisin's devotion. She had Roisin's devotion now. She still wanted to poke.

"You're moping," Sarah observed on the sixth moonrise, combing Poppy's curls while Roisin and Valentin were out promenading on the beach. "It doesn't suit you."

"She'll leave again."

"You knew she would. Don't be daft."

"I'll be as daft as I please." She drummed her fingers on the vanity table. "Do you think there's something I could say to—"

"No." Sarah rapped her on the head with the back of the comb. "And don't try asking. We've got plenty back at home, and you'll make do with that. It's more than either of us deserve."

"Have you ever been in love, Sarah?"

Sarah let out a long-suffering groan. "I'm only bleeding seventeen, Poppy."

"That doesn't mean anything."

"I've been busy."

"Have you really?"

"There was a boy, I suppose." She abandoned her post to flop on the

254

bed. "Mustafa. A Muslim Turk, like me. I thought he was all right."

"What happened?"

"He knew I worked at a fancy house and he told me I ought to nick some silver. So I nicked some silver. And then I got caught. And now I live with a pack of vampires, combing hair and wondering if any of these bloodsucking frogs will eat me."

Poppy's shoulders curled with guilt. "I'm sorry. I shouldn't have asked."

"Ask all you like; just don't expect a jolly answer. Can I come to the party tonight? Wear one of your frocks?"

Roisin and Valentin found them cackling, shoving wadded-up stockings into the hopelessly oversized bust of one of Poppy's frilliest gowns.

Roisin cleared her throat. "If I may, I have a suggestion."

A half-hour later, Sarah was dressed in one of Roisin's smarter ensembles, with close-cut black trousers, startlingly white linen, and a waistcoat of a rich, arterial red. To complete the ensemble, a tall silk top hat rested precariously on her head. Thankfully, Roisin's trousers were made without an instep strap, as they required several turns of the cuff so as not to drag on the floor. Sarah and Roisin were similarly slender, but Sarah was a whippet to Roisin's greyhound, and everything hung a touch too long. The shoes were another obstacle—Roisin and Valentin's were too large and Poppy's too small—so Sarah went without. There was precedent for this; half the women in attendance had spent the past few nights skating around the house barefooted. The complete picture gave Sarah the look of a child playing dress-up as her father, but she didn't seem to mind. She gathered up her long, brown hair in a bun, hid it under the hat, and strutted down the stairs with the cocky gait of a nobleman's first son.

"I like her," Roisin remarked when they were downstairs, observing Sarah select a pizzelle from the tower of human refreshments. Poppy watched the little sweets disappear with longing.

"She's like me."

"She is. I'm glad you have her in London. I'm glad you have all of them."

Poppy nodded, her fragile joy slipping away like suds down a drain. "Hm."

"Poppy . . ."

"Don't. Not now. We've got tonight."

Roisin's fingers reached out for her and stopped halfway, hands lingering uselessly. "You know I would if I could, right?"

Poppy's eyes burned. "You *can*."

"Should we go to the beach?" she offered, concern tempered with exasperation. "We've both been avoiding this conversation."

"This is a party." Poppy crossed her arms over her chest, darting away from Roisin's gently approaching hand, a little humiliated that Roisin was the one who suggested they talk. "I don't want to be rude."

"Oh. All right."

Fight, damn you. "Good."

Poppy wished she could lose herself in drink, but that one glass of champagne the other night had barely touched the sides. The buckets required to get her well and truly bladdered would sour her stomach before she could get them down. Besides, she wasn't in the mood to take Roisin's blood, nor was she vindictive enough to ask another vampire for a donation, no matter how temptingly petty that would be. Instead, she flung herself into dancing with Sarah and Valentin, falling over herself with compliments for Anaïs, and perfunctorily conversing with an increasingly ferocious-looking Roisin.

Several hours later, Roisin approached, her mouth curled with distaste. "Are you having a good time?"

"Oh yes," Poppy trilled. "Anaïs is a marvelous host. How did you two meet?"

"We were introduced by a friend." Roisin gritted her teeth. "A mutual friend."

"Carmen?"

"You know it wasn't Carmen."

"How am I meant to know what you don't tell me?"

She let loose a strangled noise of impatience. "Are you determined to punish me all night, or can we skip to the part where you apologize?"

Poppy rounded on her, eyes blazing. "There you are, petal. I've been looking for you for hours."

Roisin's mouth shrank to a tight scowl. "Outside. Now."

They stomped down to the beach, Poppy pushing past Roisin so she had the lead. It felt important, somehow.

"Well?" Poppy spread her arms. Above them, the stars bore down ceaselessly. "Shall we have it out?"

"I thought you understood." Roisin's hat was long gone, her slippery hair falling from its queue. Her eyes were red. "I thought we were clear."

"I understand what your opinion is," Poppy replied, tartly. She hurt all over. "I also understand you don't give a fig for mine!"

"*Poppy.*"

"No, let me speak." Tears threatened, pressing behind her eyes. If they fell, she would be lost. "You were a wreck just a week ago."

"I was."

"And you're yourself again. *I* did that."

"Yes."

"Perhaps now you'll have the strength for another fifteen years. Twenty, even. And what will I have?"

Roisin was shaking her head. "Poppy—"

"You're better," she spat. "Bully for you. I'm worse." She imagined the warm, dark space between her blanket and her mattress. Her haven of nothingness. "For the first year, I saw a ghost of you. I can't do that again. I can't be that."

The night was still and silent. The ocean held its breath.

"I had an idea." Roisin spoke softly. Slowly. "It might not suffice."

Hope. A stupid, fluttering thing. "What is it?"

"You know I aim to kill her," she said, carefully. "That is my true intention. But I follow her to have her believe I care entirely about her and nothing about you."

"If you don't get on with it I might scream."

"God, you're a terrible brat." She ran her hands over her face. "Once a year."

"Once a year what?"

"We see one another. If you like." She hunched her back, curling in toward her middle, a touch proud of herself and entirely embarrassed about it. "Once a year."

The breath stole from Poppy's throat. She could already feel hot tears on her cheeks. "Truly?"

"I know it isn't enough. I know it isn't the life either of us deserve. But for the sake of safety—*mmph!*"

Poppy was on her, kissing her face and neck, scrabbling at her clothes.

"Wait, Poppy," Roisin laughed, halfheartedly pushing her away. "I'm not done."

A gluttonous thrill lit her up. "There's more?"

"A condition."

"Mate, you are in no position to dictate terms. I've been waiting for fifteen years. This," she licked a stripe across Roisin's neck, "is mine."

Roisin groaned, knees softening. "Poppy, wait, wait. Please."

"Fine, but it had better be easy."

"You don't like the opera."

"You want me to . . . like the opera?" Her mind was sticky with arousal. "I suppose I could try harder. Opera singers are a bit shit though, mate."

"No, I mean—stop touching my breasts, Poppy, I can't focus."

"God, I'm so proud of you for saying breasts. Let me suck them."

"I-in a moment." She ducked her head, stepping unsteadily back. "You don't like the opera because it ends. You don't like to buy frocks. You don't like to pick them out. You don't mind wearing them, but it isn't a thrill."

"I'm aware of my flaws," she retorted, ardor cooling painfully quickly. "You don't have to remind me."

"They're not flaws."

"I'm unable to appreciate the most desirable things in the world. There's nothing left to want."

"You drank champagne."

She had. It had lit up bits of her that went dark in the year 1837. It had made her more alive than she'd been in years.

But it had only been a glass of champagne.

"You want me to become a drunk?"

Roisin rolled her eyes. "Yes, that's obviously what I—Poppy, I want you to find something you like as much as that."

The stars shone so brightly. The night mocked her. "Don't you think I've been trying? I'm happy to have you, and to have food and drink, and I can have neither."

"You can have me," Roisin offered.

"If I'm good enough. If I find a little occupation."

"Poppy."

"As though seeing you is my reward alone. As though you don't want it as much as I do."

"You're right." She approached, enveloping Poppy in her long arms; Poppy kept her own folded ungraciously over her chest. "Don't consider it a condition, then. Let it be a suggestion."

"Why don't you let your arsehole be a suggestion." She nuzzled into Roisin's chest and breathed. Burning leaves. Spice. Sunshine. "If we're talking about conditions . . ."

"Anything."

"Write to me."

Roisin smiled down at her. "Done."

There was a rock under her toe. She kicked it away. "That was too easy. Let's have another."

"Fine."

"You'll visit me at home."

"Yes."

"Roisin!" She gasped, laughing, because Roisin had lifted her into the air and was spinning them both in the sand. Poppy had never felt so light. She was sure they could fly.

They landed in a giggling heap. There, on the pebbly beach, under the watchful eye of the rock formation with a silly name, Poppy took her time with Roisin's face. Pressing her cheeks forward and back. Messing up her eyebrow hairs. Petting her nose.

She wasn't sure when she started crying.

"What if you lose to her," Poppy rasped, throat full up with tears. "What if she kills you."

"Oh, my Poppy. *Mo cuishle.*"

"What does that mean? Mo coosh-la."

"My pulse." She reached between them, laying a hand over where Poppy's stood still. "When we're together, it's as though my heart beats."

"I'm so scared for you," Poppy whispered. "I'm terrified all the time. She's stronger than you. She's older, and she drinks from humans."

"She is, and she does. But." She crooked a finger to lift Poppy's chin. "I know her terribly well. She relies on her mesmerism, which I can shake off. I'm a far better fighter than she is, and I've been practicing. You should see me with a sabre now. I'm very quick." She shrugged. "And I have a flintlock."

259

"A sabre?" Poppy sniffled, wiping her nose with her sleeve. "Do you have it here?"

"I do."

"Could I ... I mean, if you don't *mind* ..."

"Poppy." A knowing glint flickered in her tuppence eyes. "Would you like to see me with my sword?"

Poppy took off running towards the house, Roisin's wild laughter hot on her heels.

Roisin, as it turned out, was fairly proficient with the sword. Not that Poppy could tell a good swordsman from a great one, but she fancied herself wise enough to discern a complete amateur from one who moved like they aimed to cause damage. Poppy lazed on the bed and watched, ankles leisurely stacked, a soft pillow under her head. Roisin was not elegant, but there was a stiff grace to her body, a confidence in her jabs and slashes. Her feet were positioned evenly; she bounced on them.

After a few minutes, Roisin dropped her sword arm. "Have you seen enough?"

Poppy stretched out her legs. "A little while longer, I think. This is doing something for me."

"Is it?" Roisin flicked the sabre out dramatically. "Well."

"Five more minutes and then I'll tie you to the bedposts and make you scream. Are you amenable?"

Roisin groaned. When she took up the sword once more, she was, satisfyingly, a little less coordinated.

Once a year. Sips, not gulps, but infinitely better than stumbling through the desert, dying of thirst.

She knew Roisin now. Knew her inside and out, and wanted her in a way that made her animal. When she returned to London, she would remember the dark poppies that patterned Roisin's body. She would run the sound of Roisin's gasp through her mind over and over, and think for hours on the way she looked at Poppy, like Poppy knew the world's secrets.

And once a year, in a time for them alone, Poppy could ease the weight of the world from Roisin's back and give her a moment's rest.

"Enough, knight," she pronounced from the bed. "Beat your sword into a plowshare and prepare to be plowed."

"That's disgusting, Poppy," Roisin said, dry as desert sand, but she was smiling with teeth and already pulling her linen over her head.

Coda

Excerpted from the diary of Poppy Cavendish

The eighth of August, 1853
London, England

1. Buy lots of champagne
2. See if the butcher has a great vat of hare blood
3. If no hare blood see about installing rabbit hooks like
   at Covenly
4. ~~Ask Sarah how to use the stove~~ Sarah does not know
   how to use the stove
5. Ask Godfrey how to use the stove
6. Buy the following books
   —Le Cuisinier Francois
   —Le Patissier Francois
7. Ask Valentin to teach me French
8. How much salt do I need???
9. How do dried things become dried? Ask Godfrey if
   stove or sun
10. Can dry blood fill me? Can it be flour?
11. Buy flour

The tenth of August, 1853
London, England

1. Buy something nice for Carmen to apologize for the kitchen

Part IV

Paris, 1868

Chapter 33

Poppy was dizzy. Poppy was never dizzy. She had thirty-one years of immortal life behind her, complete with supernaturally enhanced health, and hadn't had a single true dizzy spell since her human days of needing food and finding it hard to come by.

But now she was dizzy. Dizzy and, if she was not mistaken, looking at a corpse.

A voice rang out from the shadows, echoing against glass and tile. "Interesting place, is it not?"

"Where am I?"

"The Paris Morgue," the voice replied. "A worthy concept, I think. The bodies are displayed here, behind the glass." The *tink tink* noise of tapping. "Anyone can come by and identify the dead. A body pulled from the Seine. A frantic mother. And then: '*Mon dieu*, that's my Pierre!'" A mirthless chuckle. "Of course, it's a popular attraction, even for those not searching for a lost soul. Oh, they say they're only looking for the shock. But the truth is, every mortal person is drawn to this place, because every being on this planet will someday become just as this bloated specimen." *Tink tink.* "All, but a very special few."

Poppy's mind swam. How did she get here? How long had she been separated from Valentin? The last she remembered, they were stepping across the threshold of a smoky cafe in Montmartre, where girls sat with girls and boys with boys.

"Try not to look like such a rustic," Valentin had said, pushing her through the narrow doorframe. "Whenever we go to a place like this, you act as though you aren't a thoroughgoing tribade and, frankly, I'm sick of it."

A dark, slender woman had led them to a table so small their knees knocked. There, her ample arse balancing precariously on a spindly chair, Poppy had tried and failed to hide her open-mouthed gawping. It wasn't her first time in Paris; it was, in fact, her *fourth*. But every time, the sight of queers openly and queerly communing made her head spin. She knew sodomy wasn't a criminal act on this side of the Channel, but seeing it in person—the word that first entered her mind was "shameless," but that wasn't quite right. That word implied there was something to be ashamed *of*. This was a room devoid of shame. Shame-repellant. Shame had no home here; it would drown in the flood of genial laughter. Clinking glasses would smash shame to a pulp between them. Cigarette smoke would choke shame until it wheezed and fell. Shame would wither and collapse under the distinctly Gallic condescension of any one of the slim-hipped, expertly coiffed Frenchies breaking bread in this remarkable place.

Valentin tossed a coy glance across the room. "There's a man by the bar giving me the eye. Do you mind if I do what I do best?"

"By all means." Poppy waved him off with her napkin in her hand, the way the rest of the Brood had done for them at London Victoria. "I love to see a master at work."

A woman had claimed Valentin's seat as soon as he vacated it.

"We meet again, Poppy," the woman had said, and the world had gone very dark indeed.

And now, she was in the fucking Paris Morgue in the dead of night, with the sinking feeling that this was the last place she'd ever see.

"Cane." Poppy's fists curled, nails cutting into her palms. "Why have you brought me here?"

"You remember me!" Cane smiled, painted red lips slowly curling, revealing dropped fangs. "I was so dearly hoping you would."

She stood as tall as she did in Poppy's memories, taller than Roisin, and with a much larger presence. Her shoulders were wide, the black fringe of her epaulettes dripping over the aubergine silk of her stiff bodice. Her sleeves were done in the pagoda style, large and voluminous and ornamented with all manner of bauble. Atop her head, a spread-finger splay of black feathers burst from her jeweled bonnet. The hat itself was affixed by a dark length of ribbon, tied into an incongruously sweet bow around her sharp chin.

"Why am I here?"

"In Paris?" Cane carried a cane—*she would*, Poppy thought miserably—tapping it on the echoing floor as she spoke. "Pleasure, I presume. As for me? I travel widely, as I'm sure you are aware."

"I'm sure it's none of my business."

"Come now." Cane dragged a gloved finger along Poppy's jaw. The lace itched. "I know she's looking for me."

Panic rose in Poppy's throat, a metallic tang. "Have you hurt her?"

"No, no." Cane's face was too close. From here, Poppy could see the cracks in her lip paint, the fault lines of not-quite-red in the crimson swath. "Not as of yet. She comes to see you, does she not?"

"No," Poppy lied.

The hot puff of Cane's chuckle caressed her face. "Oh, there's no point fibbing, girl. I know about the visits."

"If you plan to use me as a lure, you're out of luck. She won't come."

This was true. Roisin appeared no more than once a year, always without warning, and never twice in the same location. After Dorset, Roisin had found Poppy in Madrid, where she had been vacationing with Zahrah, Karol, and Valentin. Roisin had been shy all over again, lovely and wanting. When they came together, she fell apart, wet and eager, frantic to be held. Swathed in Spanish moonlight, they had whiled away three nights, blissful and heartbreaking in turns, because Roisin wept so very much. And on the fourth evening, Poppy had awoken to a note bearing Roisin's apologies.

The next year they met in Munich.

"A bloody note, Rosh!" Poppy had cried, feeling entirely the fool in her stupid dirndl—a silly frock that she had to admit did wonderful things to her bosom. "I know you wanted to spare us the row, but I only bloody see you once a year and I'll spend every minute I can with you, even if we're fighting!"

So they fought in Munich, loud and soppy, and capped it off with Poppy's thighs around Roisin's ears, Roisin's tongue buried deep in Poppy's cunt.

Then Ghent, Rome, Oslo, Brighton—even London, Roisin knocking on the door of the Brood's home, her hat in her sheepish hands. They had fucked, and they had rowed, and Poppy had begged Roisin not to follow

Cane anymore. It had been years. Cane hadn't moved to harm either of them, nor had she lured Roisin to her side with a dying woman, as had been her years-long practice. It was time to consider giving up the fight.

Now, in the chill Parisian night, her eyes fixed on the cold morgue glass, Poppy was magnanimous enough to admit that she had, perhaps, been wrong.

"Are you going to kill me?" she asked, because it would be very helpful to know.

"Look at that girl right there." Cane lifted a hand. *Tink tink.* "Do you see her?"

"I'd rather not."

"Oh, do as you're told."

It was fear of retaliation that turned her head. The dead girl was nude, her bloodied clothing hung on a peg behind her. From above, a thin stream of icy water dripped onto the body, slowing decomposition. The damp spared the girl's hair, which was cornsilk blonde and well-kept, draped over still, soft shoulders. Her eyes were half shut, but her coloring was fair. Poppy could guess that the eyelids hid a pool of blue or green, vivid in life and sinking quickly. Her mouth was slightly open, pouted and round and a graying sort of pink, like rose petals hit by an early frost.

"She's very young," Poppy whispered.

"As young as you were when I found you. Not quite one-and-twenty if I recall. And the golden hair. You could be sisters, don't you think?"

"Yes. We could be sisters."

If Poppy had lived a normal life, she could easily be the girl's mother. Her grandmother even. She had never felt as old as in this moment, in the dark and quiet morgue, with only the dead and not-quite-living for company.

"I have met so many girls like her," Cane said. "Like you. Sweet and uncomplicated. Merry little things, eager to play and quick to trust. Rich and poor, thin and fat, virginal and, *well*." She gestured indicatively at Poppy. "So many of you. But only one of *her.*"

She rested both hands atop her cane, eyes wistfully turned toward something Poppy couldn't see. "Roisin is singular. I knew that the first time I saw her, in that dingy little pub in Belfast. She always looked like royalty. Like a Grecian marble depiction of Athena, while the rest of you

were Dresden shepherdesses. She's meant to be eternal. You may shatter."
A pause. "Does that frighten you?"

"Depends on whether it's a threat."

She waved dismissively. "Call it a warning. I value her greatly. When I first claimed her, she was rough. Uneducated. But I could tell that the figure of David hid under the marble, so to speak. I told her I would only gift her this life if she dropped that provincial accent, and she worked like mad. A bit of motivation and she's a stallion at the gate. She longs to be obedient." A low chuckle. "Isn't that an interesting contradiction? Such a strong, steady presence, but she melts entirely at the barest scrap of instruction. For our first century, I didn't need to compel her with my gift, she obeyed so completely. And when it became necessary to use what skills I had to force her hand, well, it was not purely for my own benefit. She longed to obey, perhaps especially when she didn't believe it herself."

Rage clogged Poppy's throat. "Don't talk about her like that."

Cane clicked her tongue, a scold and a warning. "Tetchy. Do you think she left you because you didn't know how to bring her to heel?"

"Sod off, you old crone." She tried to lift a leg and found her foot glued to the floor. "What have you done to me?"

"A touch of precaution. I wanted to speak with you, and therefore it is entirely my responsibility to ensure neither of us is injured."

"Have you said all you need to? Only I was having an excellent night, and I'm likely to be missed."

"My sincerest apologies." Cane smiled thinly. "I will not harm you tonight, girl. That's a promise."

"I don't take much comfort in your promises."

"Why ever not?" She pouted, red lips a dried bud, dead before its bloom. "I don't make them lightly. You may say a lot about me—I'm sure you do—but, for me, a promise made is a promise kept. If you die tonight, it will not be by my hand."

She didn't like the sound of that. "You wanted to talk."

"Yes." Cane drew her tongue across a scarlet lip. "Do not see her again."

"No."

"Think before you refuse. Once a year, is it? Fifteen years, at least. And in that time, do you not think I've been working my fingers to the bone attempting to bring her back to me?"

Poppy's stomach dropped. "You've seen her? You've—you've *spoken?*"

Cane shook her head pityingly. "Oh darling, I don't need to speak to win her back. She need only look at my spotless record."

"Your . . ."

"I don't kill lovely girls anymore." She squared her shoulders and puffed her chest, peacock-proud and beaming. "I have been as sweet as a berry and as neat as a pin. She'll see very soon that I'm entirely the person she ought to be with. I have pruned every objectionable habit. I'm harmless as a shrub. The only trouble," she drew her knuckle across Poppy's cheek, "is *you.*"

"Me?" She tried her feet again. They remained stuck. She made to look for an exit in case the opportunity arose, but her neck was stiff, as though someone were holding onto her nape and squeezing. As though she were a kitten staring down the wrong side of a bag.

"You are why she insists on straying from the path," Cane said mildly. "Without you blocking her vision, she would see how well I've—," she choked a little on the word, "*compromised.*"

"Do you really think that's what's happening? That she's warming to you?"

"Oh, I know she's trying to kill me," Cane drawled. "It's tedious. However, if she makes a credible attempt, I will have no choice but to destroy her. To destroy my masterwork, because she will not be compelled to reason. It would behoove all involved to avoid such an outcome. What choice have I, but to remove the rogue element? *You,*" she whispered behind her cupped hand, like a secret.

Poppy wanted to rip the woman's jaw from her face. "Why don't you *behoove* us all and step into the sun?"

"I'll forgive that cheek, as I understand I've spoiled your night." She leaned on her cane, head held at a contemplative angle. "I made her a promise, you know. When she left, I vowed she would be by my side once more."

"She'll never."

Poppy recalled the way Roisin fell into her arms each time they reunited, run ragged and half dead. The loneliness that grew over their months apart, tumorous and seeping, only excised in yearly sobs that tore Roisin's throat to ribbons. The desperate digging of her fingers into Poppy's flesh. The way she held on and whispered, "Is this real? Are you really here?"

Fifteen years of disbelief.

"Oh, she'll be back," Cane crooned. "She's spent a second with you. A moment. Her greatest years were by my side." She examined her cane, rubbing out an imperfection in the wood. "Have you noticed yet that I haven't killed you?"

"Hard not to."

She twisted her wrist with a flourish. *Voila.* "Consider my new leaves turned, or whatever you humans like to say. If it were a century ago, I would have torn you apart and kicked your head into the street to crumble. But I am older now. Wiser. Remember to tell her that when you see her."

"I thought you didn't want me to see her anymore."

"Oh, I don't." A Cheshire Cat grin exposed her sharp fangs. "Clever girl. You've paid attention!"

"Yes, well done me."

"Call her off, and I'll show her my mercy. She'll love that, I'm sure." Cane's eyes held the fervent light of a true believer. It sent chills skittering down Poppy's neck. "Call her off, and I can show her what joy she would have by my side once more."

"You're off your bleedin' nut!"

Cane was before her in an instant, so close her hot, wet spittle alighted on Poppy's lip. "That is the last time you speak to me without the respect I am due," she hissed. "I can make your life miserable, poppet, and I won't even have to hurt you to do it. Do you understand me?"

Poppy clenched her jaw. Cane scowled, and a phantom force grabbed Poppy by the back of the skull, forcing her head up and down.

"Good." Cane hummed approvingly. "For whatever reason, Roisin listens to you. I want you to tell her to end this foolish nonsense and return to me. And that if she does not heed my words, there will be dire consequences for you both. Do you understand?"

A pressure on her tongue like invading fingers, her mouth opened too wide.

"Yes," she croaked in a voice she did not recognize.

"Show her this if she doesn't believe you." Cane reached into the folds of her dress and pulled out a small object. "Put it in your cunt."

"*Pardon?*"

"You have no purse nor pocket, and I won't see you lose it. Put it in your cunt. *Now.*"

Poppy's body moved by compulsion, jerking like an Italian marionette. She grasped the object with unfeeling fingers, clumsily rucked up her skirts, and winced as her dry hand entered her quim with force, depositing the invader. It was smooth, thank god, but it had a wrongness like cancer, and she ached to pull it out.

"Good girl." Cane straightened Poppy's rumpled skirts. Poppy struggled to slap those encroaching hands away, but the compulsion pinned her arms to her sides. "I do loathe all this fuss. It used to be so easy to have her running back to me, if only for a few stolen moments. All I would have to do was obtain another Dresden shepherdess—I found one in Dresden, can you believe? I'd parade the girl around for a few days, enjoy her company, insipid though it typically was. And every time, it worked like a whistle for my most loyal dog."

Invisible forces held Poppy's mouth shut, trapping oaths and insults and—shaming though they were—sobs.

"She would have done nicely," Cane went on, tapping the glass. The yellow-haired girl was silent and still. "She might still live."

Poppy's eyes went wide.

"Oh, that interests you, does it? It was the sort of thing that got *her* attention, too. She called me a murderer so many times, yet it was she who denied the girls eternal life. Those with life still in them."

All but one. Poppy's knees began to tremble. She imagined Roisin, her stormy eyes tracking the life as it drained from girl after girl, only once doing a damned thing to stop it. Her stomach lurched.

"I wonder if this one has life enough for you to save." Cane stepped away, soles clacking on hard floor. "You'll be able to move in just a few moments, once I'm beyond pursuit. For our safety, mind."

Behind stuck lips, Poppy let out a muffled scream.

"Remember what I said. Give her my warning, and my gift." She smiled, slow and toothsome. "And my regards. Extend them to Carmen as well." She strolled toward the exit, footsteps as slow as a dirge. "Oh and Poppy? If you fail, neither one of us will particularly enjoy what happens next. Let's give it . . ." She examined her nails. "Five years? Generous, isn't it? Five years to return what you've taken from me. If she is not by my side in that time, it won't only be you that suffers the consequences. I hear you have a family. I would love to pay them a visit."

Chapter 34

Poppy stood alone in the dark palace of death, trapped in her own skin. Her eyes were fixed open and her neck was stiff, leaving her no choice but to stare at the dying woman. Minutes passed, maybe hours, an exhausting, soupy morass of shifting time. She imagined she could see the dying girl's life slipping from her body. Were her lips going grayer? Was that the movement of breath in her chest or a trick of the faint light? How much time did Poppy have before the woman was reaped beyond her grasp?

Poppy's jaw loosened first; she gnashed her teeth, groaning through the clicks of pain and freedom. Next came her neck, her eyelids, her arms. Her legs remained maddeningly frozen, manacles crafted of her own flesh. It wouldn't do; there wasn't any time. Poppy flung her arms back and forth until she toppled over onto her stomach, breasts and belly slamming into the floor with breathless force. She cried out, burying a scream in the crook of her elbow. When the pain ebbed, she reached out with her forearms, dragging herself toward the curtain that separated the living gawkers from the displayed dead. Her legs were a leaden weight behind her, her dress tearing on the stone floor. Still, she moved, cursing Cane and Roisin and their sick game of cat-and-mouse. Cursing their hands, for all the lives they had held and discarded.

She pushed herself between the curtain that divided the eager living from the restful dead, navigating a maze of table legs, gagging at the drips of moisture that found her. The air smelled of chemicals and rot, sweet and cloying and primally wrong. Braving the possibility of a droplet falling into her mouth, Poppy turned her head upward to confirm what she suspected: she had finally reached the woman, laid half-seated, too far above to touch. With an oath, she grabbed at the tabletop as a bolster, and felt the legs creak. That wouldn't do. The wall was close; she wriggled there instead, hoisting herself up by the window frame. For a moment, she stared into the empty morgue, where the living came to meet their futures, and wondered futilely on which side she belonged.

Using the window frame as leverage, she spun around, legs twisting underneath her. The table was close enough to fling herself onto. Her chest hit the corner as she went, cracking something inside. It would heal quickly, but the pain was bright and stinging and set her eyes watering. She groped ahead, dragging herself along the table. The sweet, young face was placid, and too still. Poppy didn't wait, dropping her fangs and ripping into the skin of her own wrist. Blood sprayed violently across the girl's cheeks and lips, and Poppy's own dress. With trembling care, she pried the girl's mouth open and tipped in the sticky, red fluid, watching it pool. She wasn't swallowing.

"Fuck, fuck! Come *on!*" She massaged the delicate throat, coaxing the blood down. The reflex didn't activate. The skin regained no color. The eyelids didn't flutter. There should be pain by now, shouldn't there? Poppy had turned in pain, in screaming agony that had lasted days. She wished she had asked someone, anyone, how the process was meant to go. How long would it be before the woman rose, if she was going to at all? It had already been long enough that the split skin at Poppy's wrist was mended and her rib no longer pained her. Her legs finally awakened, though they quaked. Still, nothing was happening to the girl. Why wasn't anything happening?

Men's voices came from somewhere in the building, close and getting closer. Hastily, Poppy tore a strip off her skirt and cleaned up the blood from the dead girl. There were still smudges of pink by her mouth, which was full up with blood. With a heaving stomach and a silent apology, Poppy sucked her own blood out of the girl's mouth, gagging, choking it down. It was a filthy, rotten kiss, and it tasted like death.

A window revealed the smoky cool of predawn light. She couldn't leave, not without proper protection. Were there hats she could pilfer? Could she find a coat that would cover her exposed chest? That might hide the blood that had sprayed across her lovely silk bodice?

She dropped to the floor for cover, crawling away from the displayed bodies and behind a wall, into a new chamber. This place was bigger, the smells stronger. A few bodies were laid out on tables, their clothing hung beside them. Mops and brooms rested on the walls. Tables held bottles full of chemicals, waxes, and other macabre needments. There was nowhere to hide. The voices were growing louder, the early-morning chatter of French working men arriving to ready the morgue for the eager voyeurs. There were only two or three approaching, and they were certainly unarmed. Poppy could fight her way out, but where would she go? The morgue was behind Notre-Dame, not terribly far from Valentin's residence in the *neuvième arrondissement*, but far enough that a bloody woman covered in rags lurking through the shadows would no doubt attract attention, especially as the church was besieged at all hours. There was only one option, and she hated it.

She reached for the ties on her bodice, fingers clumsy and numb. It was impossible. She was trapped in fine thread and lace. *Sarah will kill me*, she thought, as she reached down to her bosom and tore the bodice in twain. It didn't go easily, but it went, threads reaching out like lovers waving to and from a departing ship. Her skirt went next, splitting with a satisfying *rrrrip.*

The voices stilled, then footsteps came quicker, fast approaching the room where Poppy stood nude and guilty, her fine garments in tatters by her feet.

She managed to arrange herself on a vacant table the second before the door burst open. Remembering not to close her eyes fully, she let her eyelids go lax. Through her eyelashes, in the blur, three men arrived, muttering in rapid french.

"*Oh la la, lalalalalala.*" The largest clicked his tongue. "*Milo, trouves un policier.*"

"*Et aussi Marcel de La Presse, le journaliste. Elle est belle, non? Pauvre p'tit.*"

"*Eh!*" The sound of a slapped hand. "*Attends! Ne la touche pas! Nous ne savons pas comment elle est arrivée!*"

She didn't dare trance; what if she forgot herself and mistakenly took a breath? She had to keep aware, had to make sure she was as still and stiff as a corpse. To that end—should she affect the firmness of rigor? Or should she go limp, like the freshly dead, or those beginning to decompose? She couldn't fake rot, not with her body so pristine and pale, like death in its most tragically beautiful. Oh, hell—if they put her out behind the glass, someone was going to paint her as Saint Cecelia. The thought was exhausting.

More men came, poking and prodding and yelling in a language she barely understood, despite Valentin's best efforts. There were firm, impersonal fingers on her thighs and arms, on her belly and breasts. Someone washed her with a rag, and she thanked whatever gods existed that the water was not cold enough to raise gooseflesh. Behind her came the sound of rushing crowds, people arriving to see the dead. Vendors called, selling newspapers and oranges and baked treats, so a man might have a pleasant mouthful while he observed the fresh cadavers, the ink of the day's news bleeding into his chapped fingers. How many stopped by for a quick look on their way to work? For how many was it part of a daily routine—breakfast, death, work, home, in that order?

Arms lifted her at knees and back, depositing her on a wooden surface. It moved, her body jostled by the gait of the morgue workers, carrying her through to the gallery. Bringing her out to be displayed.

A gasp hushed the chatter. Then, sound burst, the voices of men and women and children raised in thrilled pitches. A woman screamed, high and wild. Men shouted. Someone pounded on the glass like an irate visitor at a door, demanding entry. A *thump thump thump* that meant "I'm here. Just try to ignore me."

For one, terrifying moment, Poppy was certain that something terrible had happened. What else could inspire such a clamor? Maybe the girl she had tried to turn was finally moving. But, no. It was all for Poppy, lovely and dead, presented to the masses like a roast pig upon which to feast. In her blurry sliver of vision, the people were figures in a watercolor painting, their red faces and pointed fingers in the place of lilies and willow trees. Pounding. Jostling. Screaming.

In her limited periphery, Poppy could spy a trace of yellow hair. She had been placed beside the corpse she had bled on and kissed, now her sister in repose. The girl had been dead all along, no doubt. If Poppy had left the corpse alone, she could have reached Valentin safely, and with darkness to spare. The body had been nothing more than a distraction, a thief of time, and Poppy, like always, had allowed herself to become distracted.

The hours passed with torturous sluggishness. Water dripped ceaselessly on her chest, growing slowly from annoyance to pain. She hoped her skin hadn't reddened underneath. In her crude vision, she thought she might have seen a familiar splotch of color, the violet of Valentin's current preferred waistcoat, but it was there and gone. It wouldn't do to hope; regardless of rescuer, she would need to wait out daylight, and preferably avoid traumatizing the dangerously thick crowd. If she shifted, someone would likely get trampled.

Her skin prickled with the slimy touch of eyes. They left trails on her, snail-marked paths, changing her flesh by claiming it. Marking her as dead, and theirs. No voice. No breath. No self. A thing to be looked at. To be catalogued and thought of. To be named in stories they wrote in their heads. Lies of her, which didn't matter, because she was dead, and she was theirs, and marked, and claimed, and silent.

Eventually, the night came. The crowds were shooed from the building, the door locked behind them. Footsteps came from the back room, picking things up and putting them down. Hopefully, whoever was mucking about back there would leave soon. Her muscles itched to move. She badly wanted a bath.

The mucker-about, one of the Frenchmen from the morning, entered the room, scooping her up and placing her on a flat, tilted surface. She was dragged, lolling, away from the gallery and into the room behind, then lifted once more and placed on a flat, chill table.

The man wasn't leaving. She could hear him on the other side of the room, pouring things, clinking metal instruments together. Oh damnation, was she to be autopsied? It didn't seem likely, now that she had surely become an attraction. But she knew her supposed death and its cause were a mystery, and mysteries needed solving.

She considered moving, be damned to the man, but she couldn't imagine anything more frightening than a corpse spontaneously reanimating. What if the man died of shock? She thought of Cane, of her careless disregard for human life, her penchant for luring innocent girls to their deaths, and redoubled her limpness.

In the cold and quiet of the morgue gallery, Cane had said that Roisin had let girls die. *Those with life still in them.* Girls who Roisin would have believed to be better dead than to spend their years in undead existence, drinking blood and living by night. Girls like Poppy.

There came a brutal crash.

"Get up, *nouvelle*. We're repatriating."

Her eyes snapped open. "Valentin?"

There was a scream like nothing she ever heard. It came from the morgue worker, curled up on the floor, his feet scrabbling madly, pushing himself deeper into the corner of the room, where his back already pressed against the wall. His mustache trembled, his watery eyes painfully wide. He crossed himself frantically, alternating between thin, agonized wheezes and loud, ripping shrieks. A dark stain bloomed at the front of his trousers.

"*Merde*," Valentin groaned. He addressed the man in rapid French, something Poppy surmised ran along the lines of "Would it help if I told you you were dreaming?" The man made no response, his sounds of terror devolving into breathy squeaking. "Shit. Well, you'll have a good story to take home. Poppy." He tossed her a wad of fabric. "Put that on. The cap, too. We need to hide your hair."

"Why?"

"Because you're famous. *Félicitations*. The papers will be full of sketches of you tomorrow, and I'm fairly certain I overheard someone in the gallery talking about a daguerrotype. Our friend over there seems to have been readying the plaster for a death mask."

"You were here today?"

"Of course I was. Where else would I look?" He made a frustrated noise. "Let me help you with those buttons. You're wasting time better spent fleeing."

His fingers weren't as quick as Sarah's but he got the job done, and soon she was dressed in the simple frock and cap of a housemaid.

"Where did you get this?"

"Sarah pinched it. Don't ask me how. She's waiting outside in the hack. We've got a boat to Dover tonight."

They hesitated by the exit. The Frenchman was tracking their movements with bloodshot eyes.

"Erm, *désolé*," Poppy attempted in her shoddy accent. Valentin spared the man a final pitying glance, then shoved her through the door.

The night was blissfully dark, lit by street lamp and a glowing half moon. As promised, a hackney stood across the street, still and silent. Sarah was sitting inside. When she saw the door open, she breathed a sigh of relief.

"What the buggering shite happened to *you?*"

"Cane happened."

Sarah covered her mouth. Valentin made a strangled noise, his lips falling open.

"You're kidding," he said. "Tell me you're kidding."

"Yes. I'm kidding. I love to laugh about Cane. Ha ha ha. Of course I'm not fucking kidding." She tipped her head back, closing her eyes. Gods, but she was exhausted. "She nabbed me at the café last night."

"Right out from under my nose. I'm so sorry, Poppy."

"It's all right. It's not your job to keep me safe."

"Roisin asked me to, once. In Dover." He rubbed his eyes. "I just about laughed in her face."

Roisin's name sank to the bottom of her stomach. "Mm."

Sarah lifted a shoulder. "Of course she asked. I'd want you seen to, if you were mine."

"I'm not yours."

"Yes, you are, idiot." She leaned against Poppy's side. Sarah wasn't a particularly physical person. Poppy figured she had to look significantly pathetic to be getting such soft treatment. "Just as I'm yours. Don't do that to me again. I was bricking it."

The carriage bounced through the streets, the night pressing in from all sides. The fresh memory of helplessness made her stomach flip. The world was caught in frantic, nervous motion. Poppy was so tired.

"Now tell us what happened," Valentin instructed. "From the beginning."

She swallowed bile and did as she was told. She talked about coming to in the Paris Morgue, the feeling of stuck legs and a mouth that wouldn't open. She talked about splitting her wrist for a dead woman, only realizing it was too late when the morgue workers showed up for their morning shift. She talked about the sick understanding of what she needed to do, and the seconds she had in which to do it. And then, she talked about the feeling of eyes on her naked body, her flesh turned to spectacle. When she was done, she was shaking.

Sarah slung an arm around her, holding her close. "The *bitch*. Roisin better get her soon or I'll go out looking."

"That man at the morgue is going to have quite a story to tell, not that anyone will believe him," Valentin remarked. "You were meant to be a big attraction. They're calling you *La Fille Morte qui Vit*."

The Dead Girl Who Lives. "Not particularly creative."

"No," Sarah agreed. "But you're gonna sell heaps of penny dreadfuls."

"Oh, fuck." Poppy shifted in her seat. "Just remembered. She made me put something up myself."

"She what?" the other two exclaimed, too loud for the small space. The hackney jostled, sending them bumping together.

"It was a little thing. Sarah, will you . . .?"

Valentin cringed away on the opposite bench as Sarah helped Poppy gather her skirts and retrieve what was inside.

"Can't fucking believe it." Sarah was peering wonderingly at the thing in Poppy's pinched grip. It was a blue glass pendant, around the size of a tuppence coin, but shaped more like a teardrop. The crude figure of a pale blue and white eye peeped from its face, a large, dark pupil looming in the center.

"You know what it is?" Poppy asked.

Sarah nodded. "It's a *nazar*."

"A what?"

"An amulet meant to ward off the evil eye. It's dead superstitious. A lot of Turks have them. I . . ." She swallowed. "I had one."

"What happened to it?"

"Pawned it, didn't I." She looked away, shrugging. "Nice one, though."

"You want it?"

She turned back, eyes narrowed in suspicion. "Aren't you meant to give that to Roisin?"

"I'm not particularly inclined to do anything Cane told me to do. When Roisin graces us with her presence, maybe you can let her see it. Otherwise, do as you please."

Sarah cupped her hands and Poppy dropped the *nazar* in, despite Valentin's scandalized hiss of "You know where that's *been*."

"Thanks, Poppy. Right decent of you." Her chin jutted out in a way

281

that suggested she was attempting not to cry. "I worried about you, you know."

"I know." She leaned into Sarah's gently shuddering side. "I know. I'm safe now." It felt like a terrible lie.

Chapter 35

The ferry captain set sail from Calais just before dawn. Belowdecks, Poppy slipped into a long crate alongside a grumbling Valentin, who was convinced he had specifically requested that *two* crates be made available. When they arrived at Dover, Sarah arranged for their box to be hauled onto the train and bought herself a first-class ticket with money she sweetly coaxed from Valentin's wallet. Poppy was exhausted, but she couldn't trance in the box. Not with Valentin so close and so miserable. Not with the rumbling of the train jostling her this way and that. Not with her rage at Roisin's futile years of searching burning in her throat.

Roisin had convinced Poppy that limiting their visits to once a year spared them both the danger of Cane's retribution. And still, Cane had found her. She had known about the visits. She hadn't been hiding. She had been waiting.

The sound of the moving train was a bit of a comfort, the rhythmic, metallic chugging smoothing out her thoughts. Valentin's soft breathing helped, too, the gentle inhale and exhale of his peaceful trance. They had been having such a lovely time in Paris. Tonight, she was meant to meet with a well-known French chef, a disciple of the great Carême. Instead, she was in a box on a train, tired and unable to trance for the discomfort that kept her miserably alert.

Alexander and Gregory, two of the Brood's heftiest footmen, greeted the casket at Victoria Station. Poppy could hear their voices from inside the dark, stiff crate, their grunts and chuckles as they loaded their master and mistress into a carriage. Then more jostling, more bumping, more bouncing against the hard, splintery wood.

"Seems as though we're almost home," Valentin murmured.

"Mm."

If she didn't get out of this box soon, the force of her irritation might set it aflame.

When they arrived, Gregory opened their crate with a crowbar in the entrance hall. Poppy hopped out immediately, tripping over her feet and stumbling onto the marble floor.

She started off and . . .

Stopped.

There was nowhere to go. There was no way to change anything. Cane had given her five years. It was foolish to think Roisin could find and kill her in that time. Roisin had devoted the last thirty years of her life to trying, and she hadn't gotten any closer. Poppy could either let Roisin carry out this farce for another half-decade, settling for scraps of her company, or force her to rest for five years, by Poppy's side. And then, after those years were through . . .

Roisin would go back. Of course she would, especially if Poppy told her the whole truth: that Cane had threatened not only Poppy's life, but the life of everyone she loved. Roisin would go back to Cane in service of Poppy, of Carmen, of Sarah and Zahrah, of Karol and Massimo and Valentin, and all of those years of resistance would have been for nothing.

Perhaps Roisin would not be able to bear it. Perhaps she would decide that the only way to protect herself and the people she loved was to greet the daylight and be burned up like a ball of paper. *Whoosh*.

"Poppy?" Sarah was by her side. "They'll be awake soon. It's almost dark. Do you want something to drink? I'll make you one of them gin and blood things you like so much."

"You hate killing rabbits."

"I'll have Gregory do it. Wouldn't that be nice?"

"I will, miss," Gregory offered promptly. "A nice Boodles and blood for you?"

"Zahrah."

"Pardon, miss?"

Poppy's face prickled with hope. She ran up the stairs. "Zahrah may have an idea. Zahrah's ever so clever."

Zahrah and Karol had left the Brood for a few years to fight in

America, in Lincoln's army. When they first came back, they had appeared committed to resuming their boisterous, prewar lives in full force, donning their velvet cloaks and dancing the soles off their shoes. This crumbled quickly; the war had changed them. Neither discussed much of what they saw. "Monstrous," they said, when pressed. "Cruel. Miserable." Fewer nights out followed, replaced with quiet, private conversation in the sitting room. Zahrah and Karol would sit on the rug, their heads close and hands clasped, an invisible bubble shielding them from the din of resumed life. They tranced together; this, too, was new. Mostly, they chose Zahrah's room, which was green and peaceful. Karol's was very red.

Poppy skidded to a stop before Zahrah's door, arm raised to knock. Slowly, she lowered her hand. After what they had been through, it would be hideous to involve them. They, more than anyone else, deserved peace.

She sank to the floor, dislodging the bonnet as she ran her hands through her hair.

"Fuck." Her eyes filled with stinging tears. "*Fuck.*"

"Poppy." Valentin neatly kneeled beside her and wrapped her in his arms. After years of Poppy's soft treatment, he was finally getting the knack. "What's wrong?"

"What's *wrong?*"

"Let me rephrase: What is the specific wrongness that has sent you to the rug outside Zahrah's room?"

"Five years. It's over, Valentin."

"Don't be stupid."

"What do you think will happen when Roisin is given the choice to go back or die?"

"There's a third—"

"No there isn't!" She wormed herself out of his grasp. "Cane will come for us. You didn't see what happened in that morgue. You don't know what she did to me there. You don't know . . ." Her breath abandoned her, her throat gone dry and aching. "You don't know what it feels like to have your body under someone else's control. You don't know what it means to be so utterly, entirely helpless. So don't tell me there's another choice, not when you know better."

Valentin's blue eyes were drenched in pity. "*Ma pauvre nouvelle.*" He drew her to his chest. "Oh, darling."

Through the press of Valentin's arms tight over her ears, she heard the sound of a door opening.

"Who," said Zahrah, leaning on the door frame, "is shouting out here?"

Karol peered out from behind her. "If you are crying because you forgot to buy me a souvenir, I forgive you. I will accept banknotes instead."

Chapter 36

When the moon rose, the Brood assembled in the sitting room. For her nerves, Poppy opened a bottle of champagne she had been saving for Roisin's next visit and beheaded a few of the brood's healthiest-looking rabbits. The glasses were a small comfort, neatly arranged on their silver tray. A miniature battalion of bloody soldiers sent ahead to clear the path.

"Onward," she whispered to her front line, and passed out the flutes.

Carmen and Massimo perched on a settee. Neither had agreed to go directly from trancing to meeting, so each wore their typical evening attire. For Carmen, this was a cage crinoline gown of a royal blue, looped up to expose a ruffled petticoat, a style she had learned from her dear friend, the Princess Pauline von Metternich. Massimo elected to wear a green silk *gamurra*, which a new acquaintance had convinced him had been in her family since the fifteenth century.

By contrast, Zahrah and Karol were in dressing gowns, Poppy in her stolen maid's uniform, and Valentin in an admittedly fashionable, though hopelessly travel-rumpled ensemble that appeared to have lost a button.

"To what do we owe this lovely treatment?" Carmen received her glass and took a delicate sip. "Oh, fantastic bubbly."

Karol lifted a lazy shoulder. "We are putting you in a good mood."

"I'm always in a good mood," Massimo offered with a smile.

"*Da*. We know." She rubbed her palms together. "Are we expecting any more?"

"Sorry, sorry." Sarah tumbled in. She had the nazar on a chain around her throat. It glittered brightly against the black of her uniform. "Any without blood for me? Cheers, Pops."

"Oh dear, Poppy." Carmen sniffed investigatively. "What are you wearing?"

"Oh. It's, erm, a long story. Part of why we're here, actually."

Massimo beamed. "I do love a good story."

"You might not like this one," she warned, and launched into it.

Massimo started crying immediately.

"All day on that ghastly table?" He held his hand to his still heart. "Oh, heavens, what a misfortune."

"We placed a stack of handkerchiefs just there for you." Karol indicated the Chippendale end table beside him. "Make liberal use, *malyshonuk*."

Carmen's lips had gone white. "Are you certain she said five years?"

"She made well sure I heard."

Massimo dabbed his eyes. "So, what happens now?"

"Well." Zahrah clasped her hands behind her back, shoulders level and feet shoulder-width apart. Poppy had never seen her during a military campaign, and was suddenly jealous of everyone who had. "That depends on what happens in this room. Karol, if you will?"

"Oh, I will." She cleared her throat. "There is a woman out there who has brought harm upon our household and we haven't done anything about it."

Carmen raised a finger. "Our household?"

"Yes, *ma truffe*," Valentin confirmed. "Not only has harm been done to our Poppy, but Roisin has suffered for decades in pursuit of Cane, in addition to the years she spent under her thrall."

"Roisin is not of our household," Carmen countered. "I have offered her quarter no less than seven times, and she has unequivocally refused."

"You know why she refused, Carmen," Poppy put in. "She wanted to spare her friends the danger."

"And it seems," Zahrah added, "that she is a member of the Brood regardless. Cane made a direct threat to everyone under this roof, and others besides. Whether or not we chose to be involved, we are."

There was an oddness to Carmen. Poppy couldn't help but notice it. An uncharacteristic tightness in her throat and jaw. Pressed lips, a thin line of defense against whatever brewed inside her.

"So what are we meant to do?" Massimo asked wetly. "We can't just let Roisin go back to her after all this time."

Carmen shook her head. "We must let Roisin make her own decisions. We can't decide to involve ourselves without her consent."

Poppy realized faintly that she was holding her champagne flute so tight it was liable to crack. She necked the dregs and placed the empty glass on the Chippendale end table, next to Massimo's quickly dwindling pile of handkerchiefs.

She strove for an even keel. "We're not making any decisions, Carmen. We're simply discussing our options."

Zahrah nodded. "And to that end, we have three."

"Who is we?" Carmen always sat so neatly, one could be excused in thinking there was nothing amiss. One could, if one didn't know her body as intimately as Poppy had come to over the years. Carmen never jumped to anger, never burst into tears. Instead, she encased every human emotion in the porcelain of propriety. This evening, Carmen was not only prim, she was brittle. To Poppy's well-trained eye, Carmen was furious.

"Poppy and Valentin came to my room when they returned and told Karol and me what happened," Zahrah answered, oblivious. "We thought we might be able to help."

Carmen whirled on Poppy. "After everything they've been through? After the war in America, you would ask them to put themselves at risk—"

Zahrah held up a hand. "If I may, Poppy did raise this issue. Yes, we have suffered. And now, we can potentially minimize the suffering of someone we love very dearly. And furthermore, does each of us not have a right to choose our own actions? To be informed adequately enough to do so?"

Carmen tossed her head, not a yes or no, but a gesture of undiluted frustration. "That's a fine enough sentiment, but think reasonably."

"If you knew but the flames that burn in me, which I attempt to beat down with my reason."

"Solnyshka!" Karol beamed at Zahrah. "You read the Pushkin! Did you like it?"

"Do you think I'd be quoting it now if I hadn't? Carmen, my love, while you are our leader, the Brood has always been a democratic organization. I move we bring this to a vote."

"What exactly," said Carmen coolly, "are we voting on?"

"Whether we intercede with Cane, of course." Karol furrowed her

289

brow. "I have been clear. Have I not been clear?"

"And how do you plan to do such a thing?" Carmen demanded. "She has gifts you don't understand. None of you have been under her power. You don't know what it's like."

"I have." Poppy straightened her tense fingers. She shook her legs, bobbed her knees. Gave herself these gentle reminders that she remained in control of her own body, despite the animal fear that some strange force still lingered between the fibers of her muscles. "I happen to know exactly what it's like."

"Poppy," Valentin warned. "Inside voice."

"I'm sorry." She was well aware she did not sound sorry in the slightest. "But it isn't as though Carmen is offering us any new information about what that woman can do. Has she told any of you anything about her history with Cane?"

She glanced at a room full of blank faces.

Carmen perched on her seat, tall and unassailable. "My private matters are my own business."

"Carmen is entirely correct."

Poppy's useless heart leapt. In the doorway, her hat in her hands and her trousers smudged with filth, was Roisin.

It hit her all at once, like crashing through the ice on a frozen lake into shocking darkness. The lonely hours on the table in the Paris Morgue. The physical press of eyes on her. The animal nature of humanity's ceaseless curiosity. The terror of knowing that whatever message Cane had carved into her flesh in that brief time, she had done worse to Roisin. Because Roisin had loved Cane, and Cane had taken that love and written baleful screeds in Roisin's bones, pressed them into her marrow.

Hold me. Hold me, and let me hold you, and let us scream until she's truly gone from our bodies.

She couldn't move. If she did, if she fell into Roisin's arms and wept, she would never stop. To move would be catastrophic. Apocalyptic. It would open her up and everything would tumble out, wet and stinking offal on the lovely rug. Not now, not when it was finally Poppy's turn to keep Roisin safe.

"We are not here to discuss Carmen's past," Roisin went on, oblivious to Poppy churning into forcemeat only feet away. She pulled a piece of paper from her pocket. "This found me in Cardiff. Cane's plans, all laid out."

Sarah grabbed the letter and skimmed it. "It's all here. Everything she said to you, Poppy. Oh, god, she's gone fully round the twist, hasn't she? *I have been as sweet as a berry and as neat as a pin—*"

Roisin plucked the paper from Sarah's fingers. "Not for you."

"She knew where you were." Poppy's mouth had gone dry. "She got that letter right into your hands."

"Yes," Roisin agreed darkly. "It is possible that she has known my location far more often than I previously believed."

"More? You mean you already knew?"

"She's very powerful." Roisin trained her gaze on the rug. "She's been able to evade me so efficiently, she must have had at least some idea."

Poppy's stomach puddled in her shoes. "You never said."

Tuppence eyes. A slim, shifting mouth. "You never asked."

Karol knocked on the wall for attention. "If we could get back to the reason why we're here. As Zahrah mentioned before we took a scenic detour, we have settled on three possible scenarios. Zahrah?"

"Indeed." She held up a finger. "The first is an all-out frontal assault. We all enter the fray, just as Roisin has, and search for Cane. Moreover, we conscript our friends to join the cause."

Roisin and Carmen's shouted objections bounced against the wallpaper.

"It is not," Zahrah continued doggedly, "a plan without downsides, premier among which is Cane's power of mesmerism. If one of us were to come upon her alone, she would certainly do unspeakable things. Alternatively, there is the possibility of raising an army against her. We don't know how many people she can have under thrall at one time—"

"A lot," Roisin snapped, weariness transmogrified into sharp irritation. "I've seen her do twenty at once. I doubt that's the limit of her power."

Zahrah tipped her head in acknowledgment. "I thought you might say as much."

Roisin was hot with anger. It popped off her like water on scalding oil, burning in her jerky hands and her shifting feet. "And you must be out of your mind if you think I'll allow more people to join this, this *fool's errand.*"

Valentin sipped his drink. "Ooh, she *does* mean business."

"This is my task," she hissed. "My burden, my lot. I refuse to see any others hurt on my behalf."

Poppy took in and let out a long slow breath. "Darling. It is no longer a choice. We have been involved."

"If I go back—"

Poppy's stomach gripped. "Don't say that. Please don't say that."

"That is option two," Karol offered mildly. "You go back. Or you kill yourself, I suppose."

Massimo gasped. Zahrah gave Karol a look for which only she understood the full meaning.

"Well, either option is suicide," Karol said in her own defense. "Is it not?"

Roisin sucked in her cheeks. Bit them. "Yes."

"What?" Poppy wheezed, breathless. "What do you mean?"

"Oh, you don't think she'd let me live, do you? Cane would only have to let her guard down for a second to give me the opportunity. No, no. She wants to see me crawl back and beg for mercy before she does the deed. I suppose caving to her demands would get me in range to do some damage, but she'll have thought of that already. She'll have backup." She stared longingly at Poppy's empty champagne flute. "The only hope was to take her by surprise. Find her when she hasn't any other vampires around to bend to her will. If I brought you along, you'd be fighting beside her in an instant. Your arms would be an extension of hers."

"Oh, god." Poppy sat heavily in an unoccupied chair. "This is a nightmare."

"*Da*, a waking nightmare," Karol agreed with undue cheer. "We will try to avoid this. Hence, option three."

"My favorite." Zahrah was wearing an expression Poppy hadn't seen on her before. An eager, animal grin, paired with a heated spark in her eyes. "I recently read a bit of interesting literature written by a Zhou Dynasty general. *He will win who knows when to fight and when not to fight.* Or something along those lines. I've only read it in French."

Massimo neatly folded a ruined handkerchief. "So you're suggesting we . . . don't fight?"

"I'm suggesting that a direct approach hasn't worked up to now. I believe there are avenues we haven't considered."

"Save the dramatics," Carmen put in through gritted teeth. "What do you suggest we do?"

"Not *we*." A triumphant smile spread across Karol's face. "*Him*."

It took a long moment for the light of recognition to hit Carmen's eyes. "You aren't serious."

"More than I typically am."

"But he's been quiet for centuries! Even if he made a decree, nobody would pay attention."

"Pardon me." Massimo wiped his stuffed nose. "To whom are we referring?"

"Count Vlad," Karol announced, with an uncharacteristic touch of dramatic flare.

Sarah raised her hand. "Erm, for those of us with mortal lifespans . . .?"

"He's the last remaining member of the Immortal Council. Back before the age of enlightenment, there was a sort of . . ." Karol held her hand out and rocked it. "Governing body. We were far more involved in the lives of mortals, and the Council was there for our safety—though some said they cared more for the humans who paid them. But then that *kozyol* Medici came into power and suddenly everybody was 'science this!' and 'philosophy that!'" She snorted. "We lost all the power we had, and retreated into secrecy for our own well-being."

"What happened to the Council?" Sarah asked.

Carmen smoothed her skirt. "The other two were killed. I heard it was vengeful humans. Something about a girl."

Karol rolled her eyes. "It always is with men like that."

"Men like what?" Poppy asked.

"Old. Titled. Knights of Christendom, fixated on Ottomans coming to take their crosses." She indicated Sarah, who made an incredulous face.

"Erm, I'm from Bethnal Green?"

"Vlad was a miserable old man," Karol went on. "Lived in a big castle in the mountains with those hulking iron chandeliers and ugly stone floors. Medieval shite, you know."

Sarah fidgeted with the nazar, sliding it back and forth on its chain. "But if the Council isn't in power anymore . . ."

"I didn't say they weren't," Zahrah countered. "Or, rather, I wouldn't say they ever abdicated. Technically, they could still be our leaders. Whether anyone follows?" She gave a noncommittal gesture. "Undetermined."

"Well a decree is all well and good," Massimo reasoned, "but if they have no power, they have no means to enforce it."

"They did." Carmen listlessly twirled her empty champagne flute in her long fingers. "They used to have immense power. Not just influence, but . . ." She trailed off. Her eyes were unfocused. "Vlad could command the seas from miles away. He could turn wild animals against those who defied him. He could flood the Yangtze from as far away as the Cuzco Valley."

A slow, sunrise smile spread across Zahrah's face. "This is why we brought you all here. We're going to go see Vlad, and we're going to ask him to remove Cane from the board entirely."

"There is only one obstacle," Karol added. "Just a tiny one."

Poppy frowned. "You didn't mention an obstacle."

"Well, you wanted us down here very quickly. And you look so sad when you cry." Karol casually shoved her hands in her pockets. "We don't know where he is."

"The castle, surely?" Massimo suggested.

"Not that simple. He was always very paranoid about his safety. When anyone came to visit him, he made sure they forgot the address. Mesmerism, you know."

"Well, how does he get post?" Sarah asked. "How was he meant to communicate with other people when he was in charge of everyone?"

"Ravens." Zahrah's eyebrow lift communicated reluctant praise. "Animal power is mostly rubbish, but the ravens are special."

Massimo had a covetous gleam in his eye. "How can animal power be rubbish?"

"Because he can turn into a swarm of rats. Tell me, could you see someone turn into a swarm of rats and ever want to fuck them again?"

"Enough." Carmen's voice held a sharp edge. "His location is a problem, but it's not the only one. The real concern is why he should help us at all."

Poppy turned her eyes to Carmen. She did not seem capable of extending Poppy the same courtesy.

"Why wouldn't he?"

"Cane hasn't done anything wrong." Carmen held up a hand to forestall protest. "Morally, perhaps. But the Council went by an ancient code. It is not forbidden for a vampire to kill a human, change a human, or harm another vampire for the sake of self-defense, which one could argue is exactly what she did."

Valentin's jaw jutted stubbornly. "How could going after Poppy be self-defense?"

"I'm not saying harming Poppy *was* self-defense, necessarily." Carmen's words were clipped, all consonant. "I'm saying she could *make an argument* that it was."

"This isn't Bow Street!" Poppy was aware that she was shouting, but she couldn't bring herself to care. "She harmed me and I didn't do a damned thing to her, save survive when she tried to off me the first time around. I could have been discovered in that morgue, or destroyed. Does that go against the code?"

Carmen didn't answer.

"Yes," Karol confirmed. "It does."

Zahrah clapped her hands together. "It's settled, then. Our next move is to locate Vlad and convince him to take action."

"Wait, wait." Roisin leaned against the wall. God, but she looked wrecked. Her nervous fingers were slowly shredding Cane's letter. One corner of the paper had become a pile of snow at her feet. "This is all very kind. I do appreciate you offering to help Poppy and me. But I beg you all to think about what you're doing. If you act against Cane, she'll hear about it. She has ways." Her shoulders lifted fractionally, a line of worry appearing between her brows. "You're putting yourself in the path of an extremely dangerous woman."

"Did you not hear the part where she will enact vengeance on any and all of us in five years?" Karol asked. "I know I sound very sarcastic but I am really asking. I am sure it was mentioned."

"What happens in five years . . ." Roisin coughed lightly. "I've lived a very long life."

Poppy saw red. "Shut up. Shut up if you know what's good for you. And you." She spun on Carmen. "When we first met at Covenly, you asked me to ensure Roisin went after Cane. She has. You owe this to her."

"Poppy," Roisin objected, "she doesn't owe me anything."

"You don't say another damn word, Roisin. You clearly are not in your right mind if you think I'll consent to letting you martyr yourself to death."

Massimo bit his lip. "I think that is how martyring generally goes."

"Not now, sunshine," Valentin murmured, shushing him. "Though very well observed."

"Regardless," Roisin went on. "Cane can do monstrous things, and you all live so comfortably. *Beautifully*. If there is a world in which she ends up appeased and alive in five years, she will not forget your involvement." She balled up another piece of the mangled letter and let it fall to the floor. Sarah watched it go with a wince. "She has a great deal of pride. Consider whether you want to do this."

Valentin was the first to speak, and he did so rather loudly. "Of course I do. I've grown rather attached to Poppy." He fingered his shirtsleeve awkwardly, surprised by his own vehemence. "And it's as interesting a way to spend my time as any other."

"You'll need me," Karol said. "Vlad speaks one of the old Romanian languages. I'm the only one who can communicate with him. Besides which, it sounds like fun."

Zahrah patted her on the back. "Good man. It goes without saying, but you may count on me."

"And me." Massimo cast down the final soiled handkerchief. "I can shield us all from Cane, if we stay together. It's not much, but it may buy us some time."

"And me!" Sarah cried.

"No," said everyone else at once. Sarah wilted.

"It's not safe for you," Karol soothed. "Poor thing, full of blood."

"Then at least let me help you get ready." She pouted. "Going off after a great old monster in a castle and I don't even get to see it."

Carmen spoke last. "I suppose I can participate."

Her head was down, face unreadable. A rush of affection hit Poppy all at once. She made to move close to her, to sit beside Carmen and press her hand, like she had done on so many nights just like this one. Nights in this room, comfortable and together, warmed by a golden fire. Sometimes painting, sometimes reading side by side. Mostly staying close and talking. Just talking.

"Carmen—"

"No. You're all correct. It's worth doing. And I've been outvoted." She spread her hands. "What else is there to do?"

"*Ma truffe*." Valentin's endearment was gentle and heavy, as though he too was only just remembering how much he cared for her. "No one is forcing you to involve yourself."

"I am old." Carmen spoke to no one in particular, her words addressed to a bare spot of wall. "I have spent centuries building a life for myself and for those I love. This house. This art. These bits of finery. Everything I have done has been in the service of keeping us safe and comfortable. Of being certain that none of us will have to run because of who we are. What we are." Her lip curled. "I hope all of you know that embarking on this path throws everything we have into tumult. We could easily lose our lives. She's more powerful than any of you, save Roisin, are entirely aware."

Poppy's mouth moved of its own accord. "I think I have a good idea."

Carmen finally met her eyes. She was stiff with anger, her cheeks in high color. "You always know best, don't you? You wanted help? Here it is. And here lies the consequence. All of your friends risking their lives."

Roisin started toward her. "Don't, Carmen."

Carmen held up a hand. "I admit, Cane is a blight that has long needed seeing to. But none of you know what I have done to give us what we have. All I wanted was rest."

"Tell us," Massimo implored. "Tell us, and maybe—"

Carmen stepped into the hall and closed the door behind her.

Chapter 37

It was Zahrah's suggestion that they wait until the following night to begin their plans.

"I think we all deserve some rest," she said.

Accordingly, the little group dispersed. Zahrah and Karol retreated to Zahrah's room, singing a warring song that went *With your guns and drums and drums and guns, hurroo, hurroo.* Massimo and Valentin hurried after Carmen, a bottle of champagne and a few squealing rabbits in their hands. Poppy sent Roisin up to her bedroom, joining her soon after with two small bowls and two teaspoons.

Roisin dubiously received her bowl. "What do you call that?" She had stripped off her shoes and stacked her stockinged feet, her head resting limply on a mound of pink pillows. In this room full of flowers, she resembled nothing more than a stone statue in a lady's garden.

"Ice cream. Have you ever had it?"

Roisin peered at the round, brown mass. "Can't say I have."

"Give it a go. It's chocolate. And blood."

She took a tentative bite. Her eyes widened. "Jesus wept."

Poppy preened. "You like it? Spent ages working out parts blood to cream. I kept having to use the escape hatch."

"The escape hatch?"

"That's what Sarah's been calling the door out to the garden." Roisin still looked confused. "Where I vomit." Roisin carefully set down her ice cream. "Oh, come now. The vomit's done wonders for the marrow I've got growing. And—ooh!" She ran to the vanity and picked up a small paper bag. "Have you tried one of my boiled sweets?"

Roisin was staring at her with a fond, dopey half smile. "You really are clever, aren't you?"

"You told me to find something to do." Poppy defensively crumpled the sweet bag against her chest. "I have."

"I mean it. Centuries of living without food, and you're the first to work out how we can eat."

"I can't be the first," Poppy demurred, allowing Roisin to coax her over, to pull her down into the soft bed. "The first you know, maybe."

"So clever. So smart." She brought her nose to Poppy's neck, nuzzling in. "My very remarkable Poppy."

"Oi!" Poppy drew back. "Don't think you can get out of this discussion by seducing me."

"I wasn't aware we were discussing anything."

"Less than an hour ago, you suggested topping yourself for the greater good. You don't think we ought to chat about that?"

Roisin sighed heavily, leaning back on the pillows. "Must we?"

"And." Poppy took up the remains of her ice cream, nervously poking the mostly melted sweet. "Not to add to a long list, but I need to talk to you about something Cane said."

Pain creased Roisin's face. "Poppy, I'm so sorry about Cane. I wish I could have—"

"Hush, now." She swallowed the last bite and set down the glass. She hated last bites. They meant there was nothing left to enjoy. "It's not your fault."

"You shouldn't have had to bear it."

"I'll bear that and more." She steeled herself with a deep breath. "She had me in the Paris Morgue."

"I know. I can't stand the thought of you there. The place gives me gooseflesh."

"Gives me a bit more than that now." She shivered, remembering. Trying not to remember. "We were alone. But . . . we weren't." The memory came to her in short bursts, flashes in the place of full pictures, her mind unwilling to dwell in dark places. "There was a corpse there of a young woman. A girl, really."

Roisin placed her hand atop Poppy's. "You don't have to talk about this."

"I do, rather. Cane told me the girl was alive. That there was still life in her to save."

Roisin's expression went blank. Such an old trick, Poppy was almost fond of it. "What did you do?"

"I tried, probably for longer than I should have. Do ghosts exist?"

"Why do you ask?"

"Because I think I desecrated a corpse."

Roisin's face crumpled. "Oh, Poppy. Oh, god."

"She did that to you, too," Poppy pressed, denying the urge to fall into Roisin's arms and scream. "She said so."

"She talks nonsense. She's not worth listening to."

"Be honest with me, Rosh. I'm not a child."

"Oh, must I?" She stroked Poppy's hair. Poppy allowed her eyes to close, to feel the familiar hand hold her together. It shook.

"It'll help me. I promise. I feel so lonely in this. Be here with me."

Roisin pressed her mouth to Poppy's hair. "You won't like this. I won't like telling it."

"Do it anyway, and I won't eat the rest of your ice cream."

"You've been eyeballing it. It's already yours." She let out a long exhale of defeat. "Cane told me that some girls were alive who weren't, and that some girls were dead who weren't. Regardless, I wasn't going to bite any of them. I couldn't bear to make that choice for another person."

"Except for me."

"Except for you."

Poppy worried the material of the shoddy maid's uniform, coarse between her fingers. "So you looked at girls who might have been alive, knew you could save their lives, and still did nothing?"

Sometimes, Roisin looked like her own portrait in that small room at Covenly. The one painted when she was still alive, and so painfully young, with soft cheeks and glossy ringlets. "Are you angry?"

"I ought to be," Poppy reasoned. "Oughtn't I?"

A small look of hope flickered across Roisin's face, there and gone. "You aren't?"

She checked. She let her senses crawl down to her shoulders, her lungs, her stomach. There, in those deep, soft places, she found nothing but pity for a lonely, unsure girl.

300

"No." The truth of it sat heavy on her tongue. "I understand you, as best I can. As best you'll let me. I understand why you did what you did, why you made the choices you made. And moreover, you've complicated my view of what's right and wrong. Is it better to turn them or to leave them be? Me, I've done well for myself, but what about someone who always wanted a child? Or believed in an everlasting soul? Or loved somebody they now had to see wither and age and die without them?"

"You're generous with me," Roisin said softly. There was a thin thread of disbelief wound around her words, cutting them off from blood supply. "You always see my good."

"It shines." She tried to hold her tongue, but the rest popped out. "Darling, were you really considering topping yourself?"

"I was." Roisin closed her eyes. Poppy couldn't blame her for it. "Not for the first time."

"Christ, Roisin."

"Every time I've contemplated it before, it felt like an inevitability. The dull end of a long nothing. A relief, really. But this time was different." She opened her eyes. They were wet and gleaming. "Poppy." An unlikely smile erupted across her face, full of teeth. "I was *terrified*."

"Then why do you look so pleased?"

"Because I *am* pleased! Can't you see? I was terrified to die. Now, for the first time, I want to live. More than I've ever wanted to. I really, truly want to *live*."

The room went blurry behind a window of tears. Through it, Covenly grew from the ground, fresh and new, wet from birth and cleansing rain. The grounds teemed with life. Two women with generous futures ran and ran and ran.

"Go on," Poppy said. "Tell me what you want to live for. Tell me about mad Roisin's long life."

Roisin drew in a breath. Let it out. Drew in another. "I know you love to travel. I know you wish to see more of the world. We can do that."

"Perhaps we can. But that's not what I'm asking." She lowered her face so their lips met, sweet and soft. When she pulled back, Roisin's small, pained moan chased her. "What life do you want to live?"

"I want to go home." A fat tear rolled down her cheek. She shuddered, and something broke, her shoulders curling over, words spilling from her

301

mouth. Rain and earth and all of it, for centuries. "I'm so tired, Poppy. I'm tired all the time. I want to go back to Covenly. I want to sit by the fire with you. I want to clean the floors and the walls and the ceilings. I want to pull up the warped floorboards and replace them with new. I want to burn the mattress and buy us a new one, the softest one, and cover it in silk sheets. I want to argue about the proper colors to paint that daft solar, and let you choose in the end. I want to pull all those paintings from the wall, and from that wretched little room, and set them aflame on the lawn. I want to spend my days beside you in our bed and my nights running under the stars, following you through the clover and the trees. I want to catch you fine rabbits and buy you bottles of wine and ale and watch you experiment with food and drink so that, one day, you can enjoy every taste you've missed. When you fail, I want to hold back your hair and dispose of the wretched food and nurse you back to health. And when you succeed, *Poppy*."

Roisin groaned, pulling her lip between her teeth. "Watching you drink that champagne fifteen years ago was one of the most thrilling moments of my life. I want to watch your face do that, over and over. Discover everything that delights you like that. And we *will* travel, Poppy. Not in the beginning, because I've been so terribly sick of travel. But eventually. I want to take you to vineyards so you can drink new, beautiful things. I want you to learn how to eat food you haven't prepared so we can dine in restaurants, or buy food from market stalls. I want you to split the world like an orange and drink the juice. I do, Poppy." She reached for Poppy's hands, her own trembling slightly. "But mostly, I just want to be at home, with you. You and I. Safe." She looked down, then back up again, through long, dark eyelashes. "Could you want that with me? Only, don't pretend you do if you don't. Not to please me. But if you do. If you could."

"If I could?" Poppy shook her head disbelievingly. She rested her forehead against Roisin's and breathed. "I dream of it every time I trance. It's what I see when I close my eyes."

"Still?"

"Still. Every day. You smiling across the hearth, my kiss on your lips and my heart in your hands."

"Five years," Roisin said, holding the sweetness of them in her mouth and swallowing.

"And more," Poppy promised. "More."

Years and years and years. Hers only because, of all the dead girls with yellow hair, she was the one who woke. Of all the cooling bodies wrapped in red-stained sheets, she stood and breathed and lived on. The footsteps of ghosts gentled her. Invisible hands stroked her hair. In the warmth of life yet to live, she made a silent promise to the dead: *I won't waste a second of it.*

From Zahrah's room, voices came singing.

"With your guns and drums and drums and guns,
The enemy never slew ye
Oh my darling dear, ye look so queer
Johnny I hardly knew ye . . ."

Coda

It occurred to Roisin so violently it pulled her from her trance.

"Poppy," she whispered. When Poppy didn't move, she tapped her. Then nudged her. Then began to shake her because she was going to scream. "Poppy, wake up. Wake up!"

"Wha?" Poppy emerged from the blankets, her hair a golden nest. "Roisin? Did something happen?"

"I don't have to leave." Her hands shook. Her whole body shook. She wouldn't be surprised if the bed shook with the force of it. "I don't have to leave. I can stay. For five years."

Poppy blinked up at her. "Petal, if we get this right, you can stay forever."

That's when Roisin started to weep. She had always hated crying. It didn't come easily to her. Cane had loved to pull it out by force, counting each fallen tear as a triumph. In those years, when Roisin's sobs had run their course, they had left behind only a strange emptiness and a great walloping headache.

Poppy had taught her how to properly weep. Now, the tears chipped away at what ailed, eroding the shame, leaving a great swath of sparkling cleanliness in their wake. Poppy was a window, through which all the mundane things Cane had turned dark could now see light.

"I need you." Roisin moved, febrile and desperate, shifting to pull off her sleep shirt and discovering she was already naked. "Please."

Please, do what she did to me and make it good. Make me weak and willing, and let it be good in the glow of you. Make me need and make me weep and get to the truth of me, the meat of me, and show me that it isn't rotten.

304

"Let me be good for you." She kissed Poppy, thoroughly and wetly, hot from trancing, perfect, perfect, *perfect*.

Poppy let out one big, dramatic yawn. A kind yawn, because she knew how Roisin enjoyed it when she seemed a little bored, a little indifferent. "Anything for you. Get my comb?"

The comb that pulled Poppy's heavy yellow hair from her face. To see it always stirred something within Roisin. Poppy had inadvertently trained her to respect this comb for its great worth.

"Yes." She scrambled out of bed and rushed over to the vanity. There it was, simple bone with a shallow pattern engraved on the face. Roisin rubbed her thumb over the grooves, feeling the pattern in her stomach.

"Oh, and Roisin? Be a dear and grab what's in the box by your feet?"

She hastened to comply, reaching in blind and gasping at the first touch of leather against her fingers.

"What is this?" A mass of buckles and leather straps hung from her finger. "Is it for me?"

"For me, you'll find. You know I like to dress in finery. The box isn't empty, petal."

No, it was not. Inside was a carved wooden cock, polished to a gleaming shine.

"It's big," she said unnecessarily. Poppy had used such an apparatus on her before, but never of this girth and never accompanied by this leather object, whatever its use.

"Too big for you?" Poppy grinned wickedly. "Or not big enough?"

There it was. That glimmer of cruelty in the kindness of her. That bastard streak that lit up her blue eyes like sunshine bouncing off a lake. In these moments, Roisin could only see Poppy as a fickle princess. A brattish, spoiled creature, treating her fellows as game pieces, thrilling in her power.

Want had always ruled the deepest part of Roisin. She had recognized it even before Cane had crooked a finger and sent her running to obey. Even in the worst moments, the sorrowful and terrifying, Roisin could easily believe she deserved Cane's treatment, and worse. Because with it came the cruelty that fitted her bones to her muscle, her muscle to her skin, and buttoned her up into the shape of a person. She only existed under Cane's thumb; of course it would flatten her. Live by the sword, die

305

by the sword, and so on. A petard. A hoist. Accepting the love of a brutish woman because only a brute could provide the right sort of love.

Until that night on the beach when, under the auspices of Durdle Door's ancient knowledge, Poppy's vicious wanting was honed to a point that ran Roisin through.

"Give me the leather bits," Poppy instructed. "And the dildo. Lay flat, arms up. There's a good girl."

Poppy hadn't told her to keep her eyes shut, so she watched. She burst out laughing.

"Oh, you try it some time," Poppy groused, hopping into the leather apparatus, her dimpled arse wriggling, her stomach lapping softly over the belt. "The indignity of this thing."

"So it's a saddle? A harness?"

She was turned away, fidgeting clumsily. "It's what will allow me to fuck you with this cock, unless you'd rather distract me—aha!"

A triumphant smile glowed gold and silver from her festival of a face. Atop her crotch, in a web of black leather that hid soft, yellow curls, the proud cock stood erect and ready to serve.

Roisin's mouth went dry. "You bought that for me?"

"Didn't buy it for bloody Disraeli, did I?"

Receiving gifts was not new for Roisin. Cane had showered her in them. Silk scarves to tie her to the bedposts. Whips and paddles and every sort of hurting thing that made her body sing. Things that, even now, she was afraid to tell Poppy she wouldn't mind a night with. Crosses and stretchers and instruments that had pushed her undying form to its limit, had brought out bruises and welts that had taken hours to heal, rather than seconds. And then, in quieter moments, gold and precious jewels, baubles from every place they tranced.

Like the *nazar*. Roisin's breath had rushed out when she spotted it hanging from Sarah's neck. On a hot, ceaseless night in Constantinople, the human rumble of their meat floating through the opened window, Cane had explained the eye's varied meanings.

"But you may forget them all," she had said. "When you wear this, think of it as my eye. Know I am watching you."

"Roisin?" Poppy's voice dragged her forcefully back to the present. "Is my cock distressing to you?"

"No, no. It's . . ." Beautiful is what it was. A beautiful delusion, because Poppy was a shortarse with small hands and small feet. Had she been born with one, her piece would be the length of a teaspoon.

Poppy ran her hand up and down the cock, depositing slick oil. "It's going in you, unless you have an objection."

And in a flash of awareness that cracked Roisin like an egg, nothing was funny anymore.

Roisin was a flat coin. On one side was the wish to be treated like nothing. On the other, it was to be made the center of the universe. Poppy took this coin and spun it on its end. She held Roisin's nipple in her mouth, bit it, treated it like it held gravitational force, and at the same time staunchly ignored Roisin's pleas to touch her quim. Adorned her skin with touches of starlight, soft when Roisin begged for hard, nothing at all when Roisin began to moan and weep. Reassuring in word and touch, yet laughing at the writhing distress. Praising Roisin for her wetness, mocking her for her eagerness. The coin spun and spun, flying out and up and away, and with it, Roisin's anxious mind.

Poppy had three fingers in her quim and one in her arse. There was mad glee in her eyes. The cock dragged threateningly along Roisin's thigh.

"Please, Poppy," Roisin whimpered, humiliated by the sound of her own desperation, hot with its damning glow.

"What do you want?"

"Don't make me say it." *Make me say it. Please make me say it.*

"I need to hear your words, petal."

"No." A flash of real fear, because no matter how much she wanted it, it remained a trial. "Please, don't make me."

"Oh, yes." She held the dildo with her short fingers, crudely stroking it. Roisin turned her face away. "You don't like it when I play with my cock?" She tapped the crown on the soft curls of Roisin's mound. "Shall I have you suck it?"

This is why it didn't matter that Poppy hadn't thought of whips and suchlike. Because even without them she could flay Roisin entirely.

"N-no. No, please."

"You're lucky I'm too eager to get inside you. Hold your knees now, let me get a good look."

See me. See all of me. "Please."

307

"Please what, my love."

The final thread snapped. "Please put it in me. Fill me up. Fuck me on your cock. Please, *please*."

Poppy paused. Not a hesitation, not by the heady, drunken peace coming off her in waves. No, a reveling, painting this moment's portrait and looking back at the image all at once. Remembering this goodness as it revealed itself.

A pressing, gentle and slow. And then, Roisin was full.

Five years, she thought, as Poppy gained rhythm. *Five years*. Whatever happened after those five years barely mattered. Not when this feast stretched before her. No running. No trancing in alleys. No fighting drunks who reached for her in dark corners. No hunting for a hint, listening to the ramblings of a half-mad old bloodsucker who touched sunlight to feel its sparks. No nights of wondering whether she was predator or prey. For five years, she could be the closest thing to human she had ever been.

"Harder. I can take it."

"Love," Poppy warned. "It's large."

"Give me it." She curled her hands around Poppy's soft buttocks and pushed. Demanded. Holding five years by its face and kissing it raw. "I need it."

"Take it," Poppy growled, trusting and wicked and wonderful. "Take it all."

Roisin cried and writhed, the finish closing in on her. "I'm going to—"

Poppy let out an animal noise. "Come on my cock. Come on, let go, my love."

It started softer than expected, the slow ebb of tide before the wave crashed, nearly violent in its force. Stars on her skin, blue eyes, and the terrifying speed of standing still.

She was crying again.

"Oh, love. Does it feel good to cry?"

"More than you'll ever know." Roisin kissed her, licking into her mouth. More and more and more.

Prelude

Excerpted from the diary of Carmen Solano

The second of September, 1868

If my mother were here, I would tell her only this: I have done as you wished. I have lived as you taught me. And if I fail in these next endeavors, I will have no regrets, for I must believe that we will be reunited.

Part V

London, 1868

Chapter 38

Poppy woke with a start at moonlight, surprised to see Roisin still beside her, dark hair spread across the pink pillowcase, the blanket tangled between her legs.

"Oh," Roisin mumbled, half awake, stroking Poppy's wrist with a tentative, disbelieving hand. "I didn't dream it up."

They were the first dressed, so Poppy elected to give Roisin a tour of her newly appointed kitchen.

"This is dried blood," she explained, reaching for a glass jar filled with brownish flecks. "It clumps unless it's very dry in here, which it isn't, so I've mixed in some potato starch. It stays fairly well. And—oh!" She scurried over to a stack of admittedly unappealing lumps. "Do you remember I told you about the Great Exhibition in fifty-one? They were making food to last on long trips. Mummy foods. Desiccated, you see? These are blood cakes. Absolutely minging, but it's possible that I could—"

Roisin kissed her, full on the mouth, in the middle of her sparkling kitchen.

"What was that for?"

Roisin looked for all the world as though she had been the one surprised with a full-on slobber. "Because I can, I suppose. And because you look so pleased with that turd in your hand."

"It isn't a turd, it's a—"

"Evening." Sarah flounced in. "You didn't ring for me to dress you."

"Roisin did the honors."

"I don't mean to step on your toes," Roisin apologized.

"Step all you like. Poppy won't boot me. She's met my ma."

"It's true," Poppy concurred. "And I'm still waiting on Sarah's decision

313

about the change."

Sarah scowled, as well she would. The only thing she liked less than doing her job was having this conversation. "They're in the ballroom waiting for you."

"Well diverted," Poppy said, following them out the door and up the stairs.

Poppy rarely had occasion to visit the unoccupied ballroom. Typically, the room was stuffed with orgy guests. Without them, a loneliness took up residence in the cavernous space, only slightly mediated by Massimo's warm presence, and Valentin's begrudging one. Carmen stood stiff-backed against a far wall, observing them all with a weather eye.

Someone had arranged the settees and chairs into an uneven half circle. Poppy took a spot at the center, patting the vacant spot beside her for Roisin. "Why not our cozy little sitting room?"

"Because of this!" Zahrah strutted in, a bundle of white fabric in her hands.

Karol hurried after her. "They can't see it, *solnyshka*. You can't just say *this!* and expect fanfare."

"Give me a moment, then."

Together, they tacked up the fabric against the far wall. It was a flat sheet, on which several items had been written. Most of the sheet was unspoiled by ink.

"There will be more to write on this as we progress," Zahrah explained, answering the question Poppy hadn't needed to ask. "For now, we have assigned you all roles."

They went down the list. Karol and Valentin, the two who spoke and understood the most languages, would attempt to locate Vlad through research. Karol had compiled a list of libraries and promising texts. Valentin, who regularly hid his bookish tendencies, tried to pretend he did not find this thrilling.

"*Reading?*" he groaned, barely concealing his glee. "That will take *ages*."

Massimo and Zahrah would focus on defense. Securing their home in Mayfair was top priority. There was discussion of decamping to Wiltshire, but travel to and from wherever Valentin and Karol went for their search would be far easier with headquarters in London. Besides which, Carmen's murderous glare communicated how eager she'd be to be shuffled around against her will.

"And what am I meant to do?" Carmen inquired sharply. "I am hardly in possession of useful skills."

"You are wrong to assume so," Karol objected. "Your skill is that of a hostess. Everyone knows Carmen. Everyone loves Carmen. Therefore, Carmen will write to everyone and see if anything can be learned." She paused. "Roisin will also do this."

"And what about me?" Poppy fairly bounced in her seat. "What can I do?"

Zahrah pressed her lips apologetically, but Karol's smile didn't fade. "You and Sarah have the most important responsibility of all."

Sarah looked dubious. "Oh yeah? What's that?"

"You two will care for *morale*."

"Morale!" Poppy sputtered, while Valentin buried laughter in the crook of his arm. "Is there nothing else I'm good for?"

Carmen leaned against the wall, house cat haughty and visibly bored. "You asked for help. This is help."

Poppy bristled. "If there's something you want to say to me—"

"Oh, there are a number of things I want to say to you."

"Carmen," Massimo interceded. "Poppy. There is a long road ahead of us and we will not succeed if we're at one another's throats."

Carmen ignored him. "I am to write letters then? I had better get started."

She left the room, unmoved by seven voices shouting her name.

Later, alone with Roisin in her room, Poppy wept.

"Why is she being this way?"

Roisin dabbed at Poppy's face with a handkerchief. "She's terrified. She worked very hard to leave Cane in her past, and now she has to revisit it all."

Poppy came to a sharp realization. "You know why she hates Cane so much."

"I—it's not for me to discuss."

"But if it would help . . ."

"It wouldn't. Suffice to say, she has built a home with all of you and she doesn't want to lose it."

"On that." Poppy sniffed, gathering herself. "Should we choose another room?"

Rosin frowned. "Another room?"

"Only, I don't want you to feel as though you're tiptoeing around my space. Perhaps we ought to pick a room that's ours."

She stretched across the counterpane. "I feel quite comfortable here, actually. It suits me."

"It *suits* you?" Poppy laughed. "Not to offend, my love, but what part of this frippery is meant to suit you?"

"The bit with the roses."

"What about the roses?"

Roisin sat up, her brow furrowed incredulously. "The *roses*, Poppy."

"Yes. I see the roses. Do you, er . . . like roses, especially?"

"Poppy." She was staring, now. "Do you not know what my name means?"

"I . . . You hadn't mentioned . . ."

Her lips twitched. "Roisin means 'little rose.'"

"It never does!"

"Jesus wept, Poppy."

"What! Was I meant to know, all this time that . . . that . . ." She fell on the bed like a marionette whose master had tripped over a rock. "Fucking hell."

"What's wrong?"

"Only that this whole time we've been Poppy and Rose!" She threw up her hands. "We're a bleeding garden, aren't we?"

The kisses that followed stemmed the sting of Carmen's anger, if only for the moment. And after that moment, well, the hunt for Vlad was distraction enough.

Roisin wrote to all of the beings she had encountered in her decades of travel, wearing out pen nibs and draining ink pots. There were vampires, of course, but not only. She wrote to occultists, who followed the movements of aberrant beings, writing papers that would no doubt get them tossed from the Academy and confined to Bedlam. Witches, who formed sacred circles in stone, chanting and burning leaves and making up poisons for just, raging wives to slip into their hateful husbands' teas. A group of men who turned into wolves when the moon swelled to fullness, living in cabins in the deepest forests, far from civilization, ensuring they killed only deer and fox and wild bird. A beautiful woman who made a home with her fisherman husband in a whitewashed cabin by the shore, who sat at the window wrapped in a pelt that transformed her into a seal.

"He loved to watch her swim as a seal." Roisin stroked Poppy's hair as they sat by the fire. "He laughed and clapped and she barked back."

It wasn't Covenly, but it was close. Poppy rested by Roisin's knees and listened to the stories, warmed by the fire and by the feel of Roisin's calves at her back. Sometimes the others joined. Mostly Sarah, who sat as silently as Poppy had ever seen her, her eyes wide and glassy, her hands still in her lap.

Karol and Valentin made trips up to Oxford to scour the volumes at Bodleian Library, to Cambridge, to St. Andrews and the Sorbonne and the University of Bologna and smaller collections, private libraries and archives in dark cellars, searching for hints of the old man's castle in histories and ballads. Valentin took to the research with alacrity, often returning home with the spark of fresh knowledge in his eyes, along with frankly disturbing levels of academic pep lighting his cheeks. He even purchased himself a pair of spectacles, though his vision was perfect. Sarah took great joy in hiding them around the house, once even hanging the pair by their wire amongst the crystals of the grand chandelier.

Massimo and Zahrah stood out in the garden most nights, practicing Massimo's gift with drills of Zahrah's devising. She set up obstacles and circled areas on maps, calling on him to hide items big and small, thus shoring up his precision as well as his breadth. In the mornings, they stumbled in, exhausted, Massimo once fainting dead on the grand marble floor with a miserable *thump*.

Carmen sent letters to all reaches, asking not only for information on Vlad, but whether anyone recalled precedent for censure. In addition, she mapped out potential routes for passage based on several possible locations for Vlad's castle, and secured transport. A boat was put on retainer, ready to travel as soon as Vlad was found. Though the orgies stopped and all frivolous travel was halted, there was enough to do that everyone was kept occupied.

Everyone but Poppy.

"Morale," Karol reminded her, packing a bag for a trip to visit a dodgy old man with a collection of grimoires. "Go do something uplifting."

With no other options, she did the only thing that came to mind: she baked. She made blood-cream religieuses and pink-tinged eclairs. Macarons that tasted of chocolate and iron and profiteroles that tasted of strawberry and meat. Stews and curries finished with blood-butter. Raw roasts. Bone broth with bones inside. *Fondue de Fromage, aux Truffes Fraiches (et aussi au sang.)* And, of course, blood pudding.

Whether her meals affected the team's morale, Poppy couldn't be sure. Some nights, the Brood gilded her in effusive praise, blessing every bite. Other nights, worn ragged from their work, they fell on the food like starved street dogs, silent but for the sound of slurping.

Their morale was inscrutable. But hers sang.

Before now, Poppy hadn't had much occasion to feed other people. Now, she cursed the years she had spent without it. Admittedly, it itched in the parts of her that resented how much playing chef for her family resembled the expectations of her sex. Women were taught to have a place in the home; as it happened, Poppy enjoyed that place immensely. Her love for her friends was made material in the nibbles she assembled, in the drinks and meals and myriad desserts she invented—and often vomited, though this was a hazard of the occupation.

Despite the threat of danger looming overhead, it was nearly blissful. She even had Roisin.

Roisin, who lost her weather eye slowly and steadily, until she looked at nearly everything with curiosity instead of fear. Roisin, who startled less, who could be tapped on the shoulder without jumping into the air. Who no longer sat as curled as a fiddlehead, but stretched, languid and unashamed. Who sank into this time like a hot bath, and smiled as she tranced. She, of everyone, enjoyed Poppy's food the most.

The only trouble was Carmen.

They didn't argue. They didn't even snipe at one another. If one didn't know either woman, it might appear that they were cordial. Friendly, even, though perhaps not in the closest confidence.

But Poppy remembered how Carmen had given her the words for love.

"Apologize to her," Valentin implored. "Take the first step."

"I don't need to apologize to her. She had the opportunity to do the right thing, and she nearly passed it by. It's only by outside pressure that she agreed to do anything."

"You're both too stubborn, do you know that?"

She did. And she knew the words. *Storge. Philia. Philautia. Xenia. Eros. Agape.*

"Only when this is over," she told him. It was a half promise. A big fat *perhaps* dressed up for church. "I will try to patch things up when we've found Vlad. I'm sure it won't be very long."

Chapter 39

Three years later . . .

In the spring of their third year of searching, Valentin burst into the sitting room with a scroll in his hands and fire in his eyes.

"We've only bloody found him," he announced, voice hoarse with thrill. "We found the bastard."

It was Karol, in truth, who had found the bastard. She had translated an ancient, obscure ballad written by a lesser Thracian poet, detailing the whereabouts of a bloodsucking man who lived deep in the Carpathian mountains.

"So here, he's talking about the Southern Carpathians. Someone drew it." She pointed to an inscrutable bit of marginalia. "And there, you see, the Apuseni."

"Mm hmm," said Poppy, who saw nothing.

"And then east from there, to, he says 'a basin hidden in a strange plateau.'"

"That's the Transylvanian plateau!" Valentin flipped through an atlas, slapping his palm down with academic triumph. "This is the bit I figured out. The basin, in there, is the Transylvanian Basin. That's where our man is hiding. On this bit exactly, per the poet."

"Remarkable work!" Poppy cried. "I could kiss you both!" And she did, dropping fat, wet kisses to both of their cheeks. "How will the boat go?"

"From Dover." He traced the route with his finger. "Hugging the coast. Round here, Spain and Portugal, the Strait of Gibraltar, Tunisia, Sicily . . ."

Roisin watched the path closely, squinting. "Where do we finish?"

"Port of Constanta." Karol placed her finger on a dot. "It's a beautiful city. The Argonauts are said to have landed there after Jason stole the golden fleece."

"I'll alert our transport," Carmen said. Poppy hadn't even realized she was there, lurking catlike in a corner. "Get packing. We'll leave tomorrow night."

Poppy followed her out of the room.

"Carmen!"

Carmen stopped but didn't turn. It was only then that Poppy realized she didn't have anything to say. Three years of calcified coldness. Three years of stubborn women who knew a great number of words, but none of the right ones.

In the stifling silence, Poppy said the first thing that came to mind. "Thank you."

"For?"

"Oh, erm. All of it, I suppose."

Carmen's head fell. "It was the right thing to do."

"I'm sorry, all right?" There was a terrible thickness in her voice. "I know there are things I'm not entitled to know. I suppose that—that there was a good reason you didn't want to do any of this."

Carmen turned slowly. "I wasn't aware I needed a reason."

"No, I only mean—"

"I was unkind. You were callous. What's done is done."

"Is it?" Her voice cracked, humiliatingly high. "Only, I miss my friend."

"I am as close a friend to you as I am to everyone who lives in this home. We speak, and we sit together, and we dine together."

"Don't be obtuse."

Carmen's nostrils flared. "Don't insult me."

"Don't insult *me*. Don't pretend we aren't better friends than this."

"This line of inquiry is absurd, Poppy."

"I was upset," Poppy allowed. "I was upset you didn't want to help. And I was unkind to you."

"But I *did* help." She gestured, indicating, most likely, a boat waiting at a dock. "Do you remain upset?"

"Yes!"

She lifted an elegant shoulder. "I would advise you to deal with that."

"*Carmen*," Poppy groaned, vexed. "I'm still upset because we haven't spoken! I'm still upset because it's been three years and you remain angry with me!"

In a breathless second, Carmen was before her. Poppy craned her head to meet dark eyes that burned.

"You ask so much of me," Carmen said. "You came into that room three years ago with a tray of champagne in your hand and a plan to get us all to see things your way, come hell or high water. You didn't even hear my position on the matter. You never intended to take advice from any of us, despite us all being hundreds of years your senior. To you, I was merely an obstacle in the way of your mad, heroic rescue." Her fists trembled at her sides. "Oh, you might have deigned to hear my thoughts on the matter— that is, only if I revealed to you my, my . . ." She swallowed noisily. "And what's worse, you've wasted years of everyone's dwindling remaining time with this *folie a sept*. What happens when it doesn't work?"

Poppy's stomach dropped out. "You don't think it's going to work?"

Carmen's mouth worked. She looked away. "Nothing in this life is guaranteed."

"It's our only choice." Spiced, acidic anger was rising in Poppy's throat. "It's Roisin's life!"

"And what about yours, hm?" Carmen demanded. "And mine? And all of our friends? Roisin had a choice. Not only did you prevent her from making it, but you dragged us all in to be killed. You've doomed us, you petulant, spoiled *brat*."

Poppy reared back, tears springing to her eyes. "I love her, Carmen. Should I have let her die?"

"She's had centuries. You have not. And yet you would risk your own life—"

"It isn't a life without her."

Carmen sighed, fine shoulders sagging. "You're so young. So terribly young."

"I . . ."

"This conversation is over."

Poppy was stunned into silence, teeth buzzing, eyes aching, skin covered in gooseflesh.

By the time she recovered herself, Carmen was already walking away. Farther and farther and farther.

They were on the ship the next night. It was called *The Laelaps,* and it was captained by a pair of lovers, one human, one vampire.

The vampire, called Carcharos, was a fair-haired, youthful man with a generous, toothsome smile and a mouth that never closed. "I takes the night, my man does day." He gestured toward a middle-aged, grizzled fellow with hooded eyes and the musculature of a heavyweight pugilist. "You can call him Henry, if you calls him anything. He's a right fearsome cove by the looks of him, but he's got a heart underneath it all, I swear on my ship."

Carcharos informed them that they would be asea for a month and a half at least. "Perhaps two, depending on the winds, and the responsibilities of matelotage, I'm begging yer pardon." He kept a loyal, brutish crew, adhering to the same hiring requirements as the Brood's staff. Which was to say, they were all filthy criminals.

"I hope they're just queers," Roisin whispered, closing their cabin door on the thickly-muscled fellow who had insisted on helping them with their cases. "Could be murderers for all we know. Did you see those tattoos?"

"Course I did. What do you suppose 'HOLD FAST' means?"

"Depends on where he had it, I suspect."

"Knuckles."

Roisin eyed her knowingly. "You're hoping it means something randy, aren't you?"

Poppy smirked, pushing past to head back up for more crates. "I have a theory or two. Once we've set sail, I'll give you a demonstration."

Sarah joined them on deck, carrying a hatbox so she couldn't be accused of purposelessness.

"You'll be useless without me." She shoved the hatbox into Poppy's hands with unnecessary force. "Can't tell your stockings from your arsehole."

"Certainly," Poppy soothed. "I'll lose my foot up my arse in less than a week."

Sarah harrumphed. "You'll miss me terribly, I expect."

"I'll wail for you in the night. 'I only wish Sarah were here to put my bits in order!'"

"You'll suffer for me."

"I will." Poppy dropped the hatbox on the deck and scooped Sarah into her arms, ignoring the frothy, pink bonnet rolling freely across the planks. "I'll come back, you know."

"Swear it." Sarah's voice was muffled in Poppy's shoulder. "Swear."

"I swear."

"Be safe." She nuzzled deeper. Poppy could feel the shape of the round glass *nazar* against her chest as Sarah pressed close. "If something happens to you, I don't know what I'll do."

"Get shirty with a Count, I expect."

"Believe it." Sarah pulled back, discreetly wiping her eyes. "Don't be an idiot, yeah?" She gave a final, watery smile, then stomped away. Poppy watched her go, that whipcord body growing smaller as she pounded down the dock, then disappeared into the crowd.

The Laelaps hoisted anchor as soon as the Brood were safely aboard, with Carcharos taking the first post at the wheel. The deck was a riot of pulled ropes and taut sails, men screaming inscrutable things from across and above. Cloth shook and thrummed, chains jangled and screamed. Rope was everywhere, wrapped on metal pegs and curled around wooden posts, stretching from the highest points of the creaking structure to the deck below. The crew hopped and jumped and ran, their loose trousers flapping after them, their hats tied fast against the sea winds.

Lanterns lit the deck, swinging wildly from posts and ropes, casting quick-moving shadows. Above, the stars shone like small, white fish, ready to plummet into the sea below. Poppy leaned over the rail and breathed in the salty air, fresh and pungent and more than a little fishy. It blew back her hair and set her eyes watering. She knew she would smell like salt, like a pickled thing, for as long as they sailed, and found she didn't mind. Any change to her person, any shift that marked passing time, was welcome in a body that didn't age. She stood, and she breathed, and she pickled.

Roisin stood behind her, bracketing her in with long arms, her fingers curled around the rail.

"I've been on so many boats," she said. "So many, and I've never sailed the sea from anywhere but a coffin or a crate."

"How does it feel?"

"Like I'm flying. Or is that too trite?"

"It's perfect." Poppy breathed deep, feeling the hardness and softness of Roisin's front against her back. "It's perfect."

She didn't want to speak the truth out loud, but it blared against her skull, tiny trumpets in her mind. The truth that this trip could be their last before returning home to Covenly. That, if Vlad truly possessed the power he had in rumor and tale, he might bring justice down on Cane from afar, with neither Roisin nor Poppy having to lift a finger against her. Hope had been easier when the trip was merely an idea. When the magical man with command of the storms was somewhere terribly far away. Now, with the lap of the sea insistent against *The Laelaps*'s wooden hull and the caw of gulls on the wind, hope was a dangerous thing.

Carmen's question stood on the deck beside her, tall and endless.

What if it doesn't work?

"I love you," Roisin whispered in her ear. "Hell's teeth, Poppy, I love you more than I can stomach, some days. You look like one of those women carved into the front of a ship. You're so beautiful like this." She laid a kiss on her temple. "Come *f-fuck* me." She still stumbled over the word. She said it quietly, like a secret. Like only they knew the true meaning. "I'm gagging for it."

Poppy laughed, following Roisin to their cabin. There, she held fast.

Chapter 40

By the third night, Zahrah and Karol had thoroughly ingratiated themselves with the crew.

"Look!" Zahrah turned this way and that, modeling her new, wide trousers. "Do you like my slops?"

"The best slops I've ever seen, mate," Poppy assured her. "The greatest slops."

"Aw, thanks Poppy. I'm going to go hoist the mizzenmast or something."

"Yeah, see that you do."

"Carmen hasn't left her cabin," Valentin said, making a valiant attempt of sidling up beside her. He, unlike Karol and Zahrah, hadn't taken well to sea travel. His stomach held and he didn't panic at the wide, blue expanses of water, but his balance had taken a considerable hit. Poppy tried not to laugh at his skidding and tumbling, nor his new habit of walking at a crouch, arms held out, planting each foot with clumsy care.

"I don't see how that's my issue," she replied uncharitably. "She made it perfectly clear that any concern of mine wasn't welcome."

"Don't be cold. It doesn't suit you. You look like a stroppy peach."

"Sod off."

"Make me." He leaned against the rail, breathing deep. He wrinkled his nose. "God, that's awful. How do they stand it?"

"The sailors? I suppose they like it."

"Must do. Did you hear, Carcharos said he was on the Argo?"

She snorted. "He sounds like he's from Norfolk."

"Maybe Jason swung 'round East Anglia. Found himself some

326

fine, British seafarers."

"Can't have been a Britain back then. Just people in caves waiting around for Arthur, making mounds and standing stones."

"Talk to her." He bumped Poppy's hips with his own. "Not tonight, if you're not up to the task. But we've got the best part of two months on this ship. And then, if Vlad proves amenable, you'll be off. And I won't be the only one who misses you."

She stared at him. His eyes were on the sea. The breeze plucked at his soft, blond hair, gently mussing his stiffness.

"Valentin."

"Don't make a fuss." His hands tightened, his knuckles going bloodless. "It's only that I love you very much, I'm afraid. I don't look forward to you leaving us. You'll be very happy, I expect. I want that for you. Goodness knows you deserve it. But I hate you a little." He cleared his throat. "I hate you for getting the love you want, when I've been pining for decades. I hate you for leaving me. I hate knowing that when you're here, with us, there's something you always miss. You're my dearest friend and I love you and I hate you. Is that what you wanted to hear?"

She wrapped her arms around him, setting her face against his stiff upper arm. "*Oh, mon pauvre petit. Je t'aime. Je t'adore.*"

"Don't be cruel."

"I'll always be back for you."

"That's what she said to you."

"And isn't she?" She pointed across the deck at Roisin, laughing with Karol and Zahrah and a gaggle of sailors, holding a long, thick rope as if it were a venomous snake. "I've had many friends—"

"Don't brag."

"Let me finish." She pinched him hard, right on the hip. He yelped. "None as fine as you. None as lovely as you. You're the greatest friend I've ever had, and I'll keep you in my life as long as you'll have me."

"Don't lie to me."

"I wouldn't." He slanted her a look. "All right, I would, but not about this. I'll visit. I'll write all the time."

"Can you?" he sneered.

"Well enough." She nuzzled closer. "I'll write and I'll visit, and you'll come to Covenly. You can stay as long as you want. We'll make up a room for you. And for Sarah, too."

"About Sarah." He pulled back to watch her face. "You need to contend with the possibility that she won't choose this life."

A thrumming fear rolled through her bones. "I've accepted that possibility."

"Of course," he replied, openly, though kindly, disbelieving. "You've never had a mortal friend before."

"What do you call the friends I had for the first twenty years of my life?"

"That's not what I mean." He took a deep breath. "She will age. She will die."

The wind whipped across the deck, suddenly bone-chillingly cold. "Why wouldn't she want this? Why . . . why would she leave me?"

"Oh, you *do* like to believe that everything is about you." He patted her arm, sticking close. "This life isn't for everyone. I don't want you to go off with Roisin and lose track of time."

"Lose track of . . ." Her lips felt numb. "Lose the rest of Sarah's life, you mean."

"Something to consider." He stared off towards the water again. "I've given you a great deal to mull over tonight. Come. *Avec moi.* Tell me again how lovely I am."

She did. Underneath each word, a cold whorl of dread rose and fell.

Chapter 41

After a month at sea, Poppy finally barged into Carmen's room. The door snapped back with a bang.

Carmen startled, tossing whatever she was holding. Something clicked against the wall before thudding onto the mattress. "What are you—"

"Quiet. Valentin has been a terrible pain in my arse since Dover. He wants me to talk to you. So here I am. I'm talking."

"You're . . ."

"I've told him again and again that you've washed your hands of me, but he won't stop and, frankly, I've just about reached my limit. So send me away with a flea in my ear and I promise I'll buzz off. Go ahead. Because I am unutterably tired of trying to tell that man that there's nothing to be done because you hate me so terribly, terribly much."

Carmen sighed. "I don't hate you, Poppy."

"Near as." She held in a frightened gasp of surging dread. "Are you in *love* with me? Has *that* what it's been about?"

Carmen chuckled. "No, Poppy. You really do think you're at the center of all things." She looked wan. Wilted. Poppy wondered whether she was trancing. "Oh, just come sit."

"Why?"

"Because I'm going to tell you about myself and I don't want you looking at me while I do it."

"Wh . . . why?"

"Because being angry at you is making me tired." The lump of her tongue emerged from her cheek. "And you're very annoying."

Poppy sat, shoulders tight knees stiff, keeping sure they didn't touch. "Talk."

"Cane is my sire."

"*What?*"

"I'll thank you to lower your voice."

Poppy chanced a look. Carmen's body was tense all over, her hands pressed together tight. Over the three years of searching, Carmen had maintained her proud bearing and careful dress, despite the fact that she was no longer, in practical terms, a hostess. Poppy knew a hot surge of guilt for taking away her favorite thing.

"I was born in the twelfth century," Carmen said. "It was a warring time, the Muslims and Catholics fighting for the heart of Spain. A darker time, as I'm certain you know."

Poppy didn't. "Yes."

"I lived with my mamá in Aragon, where your Henry's first wife came from. Cruel man. In that time . . . Poppy, you must understand, it was a different sort of society. We feared demons. Then Cane spotted me in my prettiest dress, and I became one."

She reached in the crack between her bunk and the wall and came back with a string of beads in her hand, all similarly small and round except for one wooden crucifix.

"My mamá never feared who I was," she said. "When I told her I was her daughter, she held me and told me that she loved me. I was righteous and of the Lord. If I was to be a woman, I would be a good, Catholic woman. But to turn into a creature of the night, who can only live by drinking the blood of an innocent? That was too much for my sweet mother."

She began to move the rosary beads through her fingers in a practiced way, wood clacking against wood. "My mother treated it like an illness. She prayed over me night and day. We went to the church and she doused me in holy water. Nothing happened. We tried for years. I watched her age and pray, age and pray." Her fingers stilled, the beads swinging from her hands. "She died."

"I'm sorry."

"Yes." She blinked rapidly. Poppy looked away. "After that, Cane found me and asked me to join her. Of course I did. What choice had I?

330

But I hated to be near her. I was horrified at the things she did. The things she made people do." The words stuck between her pale lips. She wasn't wearing Turkish rouge. "She bored of me fairly quickly. She said I was too devout to play with."

"*Carmen.*"

"I went off on my own. By then, Cane had taught me English and French, and I learned a few more tongues along my travels. I . . ." She took a steadying breath. "When you're alone, it is far easier to be a man. I pretended, for a while."

The sea lapped against the ship. The air smelled of salt. Poppy's mind was heavy with the certainty that, whatever words she could find, they would never be enough.

"I paid my way with art," Carmen said. "Not like now. I painted frescoes on church ceilings. I would lie on my back on high scaffolds, inches from Jesus and the angels." Her outstretched hand caressed the air, touching the soft folds of memory. "One night, I was painting Mary. And she, she *looked* at me." A small pulse of disbelieving laughter, wistful and far away. "I knew I couldn't live like that anymore. I had a long life ahead. Why waste a second of it?"

"Yes," Poppy croaked, throat dry. "*Yes.*"

"I met another vampire when I was out hunting. Not just a vampire, but a woman like me. She presented me to Catherine, our young princess." Carmen ducked her head, preening a little. "I became her lady-in-waiting."

"So *that's* where you learned it all."

Carmen blinked. She looked as though she had forgotten Poppy was there. "Learned what?"

"The, you know . . ." She mimed pouring tea. "The fancy bits."

"The fancy bits," Carmen repeated, lip curling. "You've been with me for thirty years and you can't do any better than 'the fancy bits.' I deserve worse than what you've put me through."

"Go on," Poppy urged. "What happened with the princess?"

"She was sent to marry a good, Catholic prince. Handsome, kind, gentle. Very tall. A good match." Her face fell. "He died after six months. Sweating sickness. She was a widow at fifteen."

"Oh, that's awful."

She lifted a shoulder. Let it fall. "He had a brother. She married him a

few years later, after he had become the king. He was just as beautiful but ..."
She grimaced. "Not as kind. We weren't very comfortable in England, all of
us Spaniards. It got a bit better when she gave him a child. A girl. She tried
and tried for a boy, but ..." She paused, eyes clouded with past centuries. The
beads swung gently with the movement of the ship. "Then, the king took a
liking to one of my fellow ladies-in-waiting and demanded a divorce."

A bell rang in Poppy's mind. "You're telling me you were in the court
of *Henry VIII?*"

Carmen's lips twitched. "I was wondering how long it would take."

"*Christ.* I mean ..." She cringed. "Sorry."

Carmen mercifully ignored her. "England was no longer Catholic.
Catherine was no longer the queen. Anne was ... oh, poor Anne." She
clutched the beads. "I had been with Catherine for thirty-four years."

"Hadn't she noticed you stayed the same age?"

"Of course. That was why she had me in her court." She frowned,
dexterous brows furrowing. "Do you not know?"

"Not know what?"

"Every royal has got at least one of us around."

"*What?*"

She rolled her eyes. "I'm starting to believe you don't listen much."

Poppy grumbled. Carmen shook her head in exasperation. Maybe it
was a trick of the weak light, or seasickness that had, by some strange
maritime alchemy, transmogrified into hope, but Poppy could have sworn
Carmen looked more warm than cross.

"Catherine wasn't upset when I told her I was leaving," Carmen went
on. "She gave me enough money to establish myself as a woman of means.
She was so kind. So, in gratitude, I made England my home. Now, I'm very
rich. I'm very comfortable. And I am still stubbornly, *privately,*" she glared
at Poppy, "Catholic."

Sickly guilt curled her toes. "I'm so sorry, I didn't mean to—"

"You wanted an answer, you pried it out of me. Here is another: I kept
you safe because I needed Roisin free to kill Cane. For me. For my mamá.
For my soul perhaps. When I die, I would like to see my mother again. If
Cane took my salvation, there is no punishment too great."

Carmen, kind and giving, who made a home for wanderers. If anyone
deserved salvation, she did. "I'm sure you'll go to—"

"You have no idea what will happen to my soul." Carmen tossed the words away, boredom covering an abyss of centuries-old anxiety and grief. "Do not insult me by saying anything you will regret later."

"Is that why you haven't spoken to me in three years?"

"I've spoken to you."

"*Properly.*"

"I am angry." She didn't look angry. She looked like the moments after anger, when exhaustion oozes into the jagged crevasse anger leaves behind. "I am angry at the world for being so cruel, even after so long. I have seen so many heads roll. I thought I would live to see a kinder world emerge. Your actions have prevented me from doing so."

"I'm so sorr—"

"Oh, stuff it." Carmen covered her eyes with a hand weighed down by sapphires. "It is not your fault. It is Cane's."

Poppy's feet dangled from the bed. She crossed her ankles, feeling small. "It's a little my fault."

"I have been comfortable for so long." Carmen's words were balanced precariously on a bubble of unshed tears. "It is comfort I have earned. Do you know, you terrify me?"

"What? How?"

"Because I gave you everything I had." She spread her hands. "I gave it to all of you, the whole Brood. And still, you were willing to give it up. Each and every one of you. Even Valentin."

"Believe me, no one's more shocked about that than I am."

Carmen held the crucifix between her thumb and forefinger, rubbing its face. "I feel an immense amount of guilt, Poppy. It's not easy to say that to you."

"For what?"

"I should have killed her when I had the chance." Her fingers slowed on the cross, then stilled. "She let her guard down around me so many times. I could have sliced her head from her neck. But I was too cowardly. Too cowardly even to *leave* on my own."

Poppy's stomach clenched. "Carmen."

"It's my own failing."

"The house. The Brood. Is that why you . . ." She swallowed, thinking of all the things, both small and great, that Carmen did to make their lives sweet. "Is it atonement? You and Roisin, both. You absolute *Catholics*."

She huffed out a small laugh. "Perhaps a bit. But it's more . . . despair is an eternal sin. I cultivate joy, and I keep myself from falling."

"Why didn't you tell me any of this? I could have been—"

"What, helpful? *Mi pobrecita*, you remind me of my failings. Is that something you wanted to hear?"

"Of course not."

"So why bother you with it? I kept you safe. I tried." She slackened, leaning against the planks of the wall behind her. "I can never be free of her. Not when she did this to me."

"You *can*."

"Is Roisin?" Carmen glanced at her. When no answer came, she sagged back. "Neither of us will be free until she is gone. Stupid of me to think I could have kept you safe enough to keep Roisin motivated. Now you've roped me in. Fuck you for that."

Poppy shifted an inch closer. She remembered sitting on a stoop a lifetime ago, watching a linkboy's face light up gold. Catching the twinkle of a *parure* revealed behind a curtain of hair. She had been so young then.

"I deserve that."

Carmen's sidelong glance was heavy with resignation. "If Roisin dies and Cane lives, Cane will take revenge on all of us. You've dragged me in and, in doing so, cost me my life. And I can't fault you for it, because you're an idiot and you still think this will go as you hope. A sweet idiot, who I care for and hate at the same time."

"Shall I sit here with you for a while?" Poppy leaned back against the ship, a wave of relief washing over her. "I'll be quiet."

"You'll be silent," Carmen scolded, with warmth woven through the brambles. "You're so incredibly irritating. It was for this purpose that I kept my distance. Because I knew you would force me to share the parts of myself that I cherish most deeply. That are mine and mine alone. I hoped you could go off with Roisin and live happily. You need so much, Poppy. Company and cherishing and truth. Well, I didn't want to give you my truth. And yet, here it is. All of it."

"I'll treat it well." Light burst in her chest. "My friend. My *friend*."

"Silent, I said." She clasped Poppy's hand, holding it between them.

"Yes, Carmen." She was smiling so hard her cheeks impeded her vision. "*Philia. Xenia. Agape.*"

"Oh, now you would pronounce them correctly." She scooted down to rest her head on Poppy's shoulder. "Fuck you."

"I love you, too." Poppy's mind was buzzing. "You were friends with a *queen*."

"She would have hated you."

Their laughter tasted like saltwater. Like the sea.

Chapter 42

Constanta greeted them from the shore, golden with promise. From there, they traveled by coach, switching to horseback through the mountains. Zahrah, Karol, Roisin, and Carmen rode hard and happy, laughing as they raced over rocky path and cliff. Massimo, Valentin, and Poppy sulked on their slow, old mares.

"My cunt," Poppy whined. "My cunt is deceased."

Valentin concurred with a heavy grunt. "Bury it with my balls."

"I know the horse is all right," Massimo said for the dozenth time at least, "but I can't get over the idea that I'm hurting it."

A small village welcomed them soon, offering them places to sleep and bathe, as well as loads of an enticing paprika dish, which Poppy declined with significant regret.

Karol spoke privately with an old woman, returning to the group with a bright smile on her face.

"We've found him. This is the good news."

"The bad news?" Valentin prompted, rubbing his sore arse.

"They won't take us up in a carriage. They know what he is and they're far too frightened."

Massimo patted his disinterested horse on the flank. "Do they really?"

"They think he's the devil, which is close enough."

Carmen made a harrumphing sort of noise, but said nothing.

"So we'll take the horses," Roisin put in eagerly, ignoring Poppy's groan of protest.

Zahrah shook her head. "They're exhausted, and we'll want them rested if we need to make a hasty retreat. Karol, can you arrange them a place to stay?" She held up a satchel of jangling coins. "And perhaps attempt to persuade a carriage?"

The carriage could not be persuaded for love nor money, which is how they found themselves walking to the castle the following night, a laden donkey dragging their luggage in a cart. As they walked, the cart got lighter, the donkey speedier, and Massimo, overburdened with trunks, fell behind.

"She's just one donkey!" he protested, while Valentin returned the luggage to the cart. "It's the least I can do!"

It all became moot when they encountered a ready carriage and driver. Four black draft horses stamped at the fore, each standing at what Roisin called "probably seventeen hands" and Poppy called "blooming huge." The driver sat on the box in strange leather armor, his face hidden by a hood of the same material, so tight it displayed the curvature of his cheekbones.

He said something in a language Poppy didn't understand, his words muffled by his mask. Karol replied in the same tongue. When she turned back, she looked baffled.

"He says he's for us, from Vlad. I have no idea how he learned we were coming."

"Perhaps his fabled omnipotent power?" Valentin twiddled his fingers. "I'm not complaining. Let's hop in."

The carriage hauled them over uneven ground, the dark outside so complete it seemed palpable. The wheels creaked and bumped over rocks. Tree branches swiped at the windows, scraping the walls. There were furs along the seats, the same black as the carriage and the horses and the leather armor, which might have been horrific livery. Outside, wolves howled ceaselessly.

"*Beaucoup de loups,*" Valentin sang, tapping his toes. "*Oh, mon dieu, tout est loup.*"

Poppy elbowed him. "What's gotten into you?"

"I'm enjoying sitting on something that isn't a horse's spine. *La la la loup . . .*"

The carriage slowed to a halt and the party tumbled out. Before them, a massive stone castle grew from a jagged cliff face, spires stretching ominously up toward a starless, inky sky. The massive doors were constructed from roughly hewn planks of dark wood, braced with hard,

337

thick iron. When they opened, the metal shrieked, high and whining.

A man stepped through, the dim light behind him carving out the shadows in his wizened, bony face. His skin was a powdery, chalky white. A pronounced widow's peak framed his high forehead, growing to a long, white braid that swished back and forth behind him like a horse's tail. He wore a black cloak that tied at the neck and draped down his entire body, culminating in a dramatic train so long the man had completely descended the stone steps before the fabric fully came through the doorway. Atop his lip, a heavy mustache proudly perched.

"Welcome." He held out hands with long, yellowed fingernails. "Welcome to my home. I am Count Vlad."

Karol let out a blustery noise of surprise. "You speak English!"

"I speak the tongues of man and of God. Please, enter my home. I welcome you all."

Sparing one another a few glances of apprehension, they followed Vlad into a miserably unfurnished hall entirely made of stone. The promised iron chandelier hung above them, large and stately and adorned with a spider's utopia of gauzy webs. Vlad raised his hand and the red candles all lit. Poppy felt a little thrill at the casual power, and couldn't help but grab Roisin's hand and squeeze.

Roisin seemed to interpret this as fear. "It's all right, Poppy. Never worry—ah!" She jumped as a rat scuttled across her foot.

"Forgive the vermin." Vlad bowed apologetically. "It is so difficult to staff this castle, what with it being so remote. Please. Join me."

They sat around a large table, wiggling into uncomfortable, high-backed thrones. Either the chairs were particularly low or the table particularly high, for Poppy found herself hidden by the table up to her collarbones.

"Welcome, welcome." Vlad took his seat at the head of the table, resting his hands across the top and twining his fingers together. "Some of you I know, and some I do not. Please, tell me of your lives."

They did swift introductions. Vlad was eager to learn, asking probing questions and making unbroken eye contact. No one was particularly interested in giving him more than the cursory biography. His face was too intent, his stares too piercing. Poppy wondered if it was his power that was so off-putting, or whether he was simply a needy, lonely fellow with an oddly static smile.

"And now, we are all friends." He swept out an arm, his long sleeve trailing after him. "Please. Tell me. Why have you come all this way?"

"Well," said Poppy, and off she went. She told him about Cane and her many methods of control, and of the years she had kept Roisin in thrall. She turned to Roisin, offering to hand over the thread, but Roisin only nodded, urging Poppy on. She did, speaking about Clover, and of the women Cane used to bring Roisin back. Of Cane nearly killing Poppy herself, were it not for Roisin's swift action. She glossed over Roisin's decades-long quest for vengeance, as it didn't particularly adhere to the immortal code on which they all relied. To that end, she colored the recollection of her night in the Paris Morgue with perhaps gratuitous detail.

"Interesting." Vlad drew his fingernails along his bald chin. "And you have come here to tell me all this?" He looked to Roisin. "To talk to me about your naughty, naughty sire?"

"Erm, yes?" Roisin's voice cracked. "Well, no. We came to implore you to act in the power of the Immortal Council. Cane has broken the ancient, erm, sacred . . ."

"The code." Carmen gave him an encouraging smile. "We were hoping you could censure her. Perhaps by using your great power?"

"My power?"

"To move the seas," Poppy prompted. "To call storms."

"Yes, yes." He nodded slowly, his eyes narrowed. "The storms. The seas! The storms above the seas! That sort of thing."

"You can call the storms, can you not?" Massimo asked apprehensively. "Only, we've heard that—"

"I am a being of great power." As evidence, all of the candles in the room flickered. "Whether I use that power to enact vengeance, to end a quarrel that is not my own, I have yet to determine."

"You may call it vengeance." It was a testament to Roisin's strength of conviction that the words came out fully formed and not a frightened jumble of syllables. "I would characterize it as justice."

"Justice." He chuckled, mouth pressed into a tight, lipless line. "Tell me. What is justice for a creature that disobeys the laws of nature? Of this human science? Once, we were not an aberration. Our opposition to man's meager, limited life was part of a natural balance. In society, one must

339

always be stronger, no? We were akin to man's gods. We were worshipped as the pharaoh, as the prophet. The chosen few among the wretched many." He licked his dry lips. "You know what I mean."

Poppy straightened her pink frock, hands working in her lap. Across the table, Carmen's face had a worryingly blank look.

"Yes, some believed we were in opposition to their gods. But the clever human understood our power. Our influence. We turned paupers into kings!" He flung his hands up towards the buttresses, holding them there for a few dramatic moments before letting them slowly fall. "And then, they allowed their world to become small. To relegate their senses to merely the observable. Suddenly, to take one of us as an advisor was seen as archaic. No immortals! No, no, no, they need a scientist instead! And us?" He lifted a bony shoulder. "We had to retreat to our darkened corners, lest man attempt to eliminate what he cannot understand."

Massimo's head was tilted at a sympathetic angle. "Is that what happened to the rest of the Immortal Council?"

"I wish not to speak of them." Vlad draped a hand over his face and let out a low, long groan. In a jagged instant, he was smiling again. "So you want me to help you? You want me to act in my official capacity as a Bloodbound Sire of the Immortal Council?"

Carmen nodded. "Exactly that."

"This is a large request, is it not? I cannot answer tonight. You have only just arrived!" He grinned at all of them in turn, gaze shifting from one face to the next. "Give us a little bit of time to learn from one another, yes? I shall give you an answer soon."

Roisin lifted a finger for attention. "How soon is—"

A long, ghastly noise of exhaustion wheezed from beneath the count's mustache. "I am wearied. Come. Let me escort you to your rooms."

Chapter 43

The old vampire led the Brood through his echoing castle, pointing out bits of interest along the way. There were chambers upon chambers, many of which the ancient Count gravely warned them against entering. An entire wing appeared to be off limits. However, they were encouraged to freely peruse the Count's private collection, a dusty room filled with glinting reliquaries and heavy swords, all pointing toward a monstrously large marble altar and jewel-encrusted crucifix. Carmen's eyes fell on the display and her mouth dropped open, her eyes narrowing in what for all the world looked like rage.

The final hall housed a suspiciously perfect number of bedchambers.

"You two women in there." Vlad tapped a wooden door. "You two there, and one each for both men and the lovely lady." He bowed to Carmen, who looked like she was exerting heroic effort to stop herself from recoiling. "I will see you at the following nightfall." He bowed low enough for his moustache to graze the floor, then disappeared around the corner.

Valentin opened the door to his room, silently urging everyone to follow him in. "Well, that was odd."

"He's a strange man," Carmen allowed, her face tight. "And he has a number of things that very much do not belong to him. But he's old. Imagine coming into immense power in a world you comprehend, and then watching that world change again and again."

"And refusing to change with it," Massimo added. "I'm shocked he hasn't completely petrified."

Zahrah hummed in agreement. "He'd make an excellent gargoyle."

"This is how he always was." Karol flicked a dismissive hand. "Pompous. Dramatic. The smiling, I'll allow, is new. But he must be lonely."

Massimo's eyes traveled up to the cobwebbed ceiling. "He's a creepy old chap, but I do feel sorry for the man."

Poppy did not. "Hm."

Roisin wrapped an arm around her shoulders. "I know it's uncomfortable here. We'll do our best to convince him to help us as soon as we can."

She received a chorus of muttered acquiescence and some halfhearted nods. There was time yet before the sun would rise, but, by silent consensus, everyone adjourned to their own rooms. Just as was the case in every chamber they had encountered thus far, Poppy and Roisin's room was entirely made of cold, gray stone. A grand, though faded, rug did little to counteract the chill of the floor, nor the drab monotony of the space. An iron-framed bed hulked at the center of the chamber, its clothes bearing the same forgotten opulence as the rugs. Bars stretched from all four posts, hinting at the possibility of long-decayed canopies.

Roisin appraised their surroundings. "It could be worse."

Poppy made a sound of grudging agreement. "I suppose. It's been a while since I've done worse."

"My princess." Roisin kissed her head before stretching across the mattress. "Come bunk down with me in a bed that isn't hopelessly narrow and boarded to a wall."

She did, first popping open their trunk and pulling out some nightdresses. Poppy didn't allow herself to think too much about how the trunk had arrived without her knowledge, or her assistance. Instead, she focused on the feeling of Roisin's body next to hers, familiar now after years of steady cohabitation. Her mind calmed, sweetened, bringing her trance on. She slipped down into sugary mindlessness, and halfway in flinched at a strange, scratching noise.

"Rosh."

"Mm?"

"What was that?"

Roisin blinked herself awake. "What was what?"

"I heard a noise."

"Oh." She pushed her hair out of her eyes. "Was it the house settling?"

Poppy squinted at her. "The house settling?"

"It's an old castle." Her lips quirked. It was a valiant effort at joy, as charming as it was clumsy. She wasn't a natural at joy, but as in all things worth doing, she set her mind to it with alacrity. "It can settle."

"No, I heard . . . something else." The walls appeared farther away than before, the room stretching uncomfortably large. "Do you think this place has ghosts?"

"Of course not. Ghosts aren't real."

"How can you be certain of that?"

"Because they aren't, Poppy."

"Vampires are real. And all those people you met on your travels. The witches, and the selkie—"

"Ghosts aren't real," Roisin insisted crisply. "Dead is dead. There isn't any coming back."

"Oh, darling." Poppy spread her arms. Reluctantly, Roisin shifted into them. Poppy kissed her neck, breathing in the warm, familiar scent of her. Letting the soft strands of stubbornly straight hair tickle her nose.

"I don't believe in ghosts," Roisin mumbled, head bent, silently urging Poppy to continue. "I'm sorry."

"Nothing to apologize for." Poppy ran her hands up and down Roisin's body, marking the ribs and breasts under that endearingly austere nightdress. There were poppies, too. A field of them. "Could we talk about why you're so, erm, *devoted* to this view?"

"You can probably guess."

"The girls?"

"The girls." She sagged back to stare at the ceiling. "If Clover could come back—"

"Why wouldn't she? Of course. I'm sorry for bringing it up."

"No, no. You've every right. I wondered, though. I made a choice for them—for the ones that had a chance to live as vampires, I mean. I thought it would be a mercy. I hate to think of them trapped as phantoms in an old, musty place like this."

"Me too. I always thought of ghosts as visitors. The angry, evil ones are trapped, but the nice ones get to visit from time to time."

"Do they?" There was a tone in Roisin's voice that heralded amusement. A familiar lightness that signaled a readiness to follow whatever twisting and forested course Poppy set in her mind. "From where?"

"From a place we can't conceive of," Poppy said. "Not heaven or hell or anything as simple as that."

"Of course not."

"A peaceful space, where souls can exist as they did in life, or combine together to form great, swirling consciousnesses. Where everything feels like making love and flavors are like massages. And they can peer at us down here, if they're so inclined."

"So, if here is 'down', the souls are 'up'?"

"Don't be silly." She leaned over to give Roisin's ear a little nip. "It's not as simple as up or down, or anything of the sort. It's . . . here and not here, all at once."

"Yes," Roisin said gamely. "I'm beginning to see."

"And when our friends—our friends who are souls, I mean—see we're in peril, they can intercede."

"Has that happened to you?"

"No. But it would have been nice to think that my mother was there with me in the Paris Morgue. Then I wouldn't have been . . ." Her words floated away.

"You wouldn't have been alone," Roisin finished for her. She took Poppy's fingers in her hands, stroking each carefully, as though she were cataloguing them. "We'll get her, Poppy. I promise."

Poppy's chest went tight whenever she thought of the morgue. She wondered if it would always be that way. "It won't take away that night. It won't bring Clover back."

"No." Roisin kissed her knuckles. "But when she lives, there is no justice."

Poppy wondered if any justice could be more important than this, than two bodies in a bed, holding hands and resting as the sun rose and fell.

"Do vampires go there?" Roisin asked eventually, in a very small voice.

"Go where?"

"Where the souls go. When vampires die."

"Are you . . .?"

"It's silly." Roisin fluttered her hands, turning away. "Forget I said anything."

Poppy thought of Carmen's weary face in her small cabin, heavy with centuries of sorrow. "They do. They must."

Roisin's body relaxed against hers. "Good."

Poppy was awake for a long time after that.

Chapter 44

The next night fell with the murky, swirling darkness of a lucifer dropped into a puddle. Poppy encountered the Count in an internal courtyard, snipping carefully at a topiary of what appeared to be a massive, lovingly molded quim. She cleared her throat.

"Miss Poppy!" Vlad greeted her with a wide, milky-eyed smile. "I didn't notice you there. Come, let me show you my portrait gallery. I believe you will find it most diverting."

He led her to a dark, cavernous hall, wherein he explained every image in excruciating detail—even the skied ones, which Poppy would have had no chance of seeing even if the room were lit by gas. Many of the paintings were portraits of her host in various manners of dress. In some, he appeared far younger and remarkably healthy, which had to be due to the whimsy of the portraitist and the demands of the decrepit sitter. There was no way Vlad had ever looked so soft and plump and lovely, like someone who would gladly command the elements to lighten the mood.

"What a spectacular collection," Poppy remarked, doing her very best. "Were these painted when the council was in power?"

He did not appear to have heard her. "I have heard of your Coven Elder's great talents. Perhaps she can attend to the gaps in my collection?"

"Oh, erm, I suppose. Shall I go find her?"

"That would be most kind of you." He clasped her hand with papery fingers, his long, pointed nails poking into her skin. "Ah, before you go, I must apologize. These paintings are in terrible disarray." He lifted a hand and every single portrait went crooked. One crashed to the floor. "Much better."

He trod away, Poppy staring after him.

The following nightfall, a hunched, underfed human arrived at the castle door bearing canvas, wood, pigments, and all the other oily, sticky needments Carmen alchemized into art.

"When will you paint him?" Poppy was attempting to help Carmen set up her easel in the relatively moon-bright sitting room Vlad had designated as the temporary painting studio. Carmen had given Poppy two ill-fitting pieces of wood and she was beginning to suspect that they were meant to keep her from getting her hands into anything important and breakable. "Can I watch?"

"It won't be just one sitting. Even with my speed, the paint needs time to dry."

"So how long . . ."

"A week? If the moonlight holds and the Count does what I ask." She lifted a massive, wrought-iron throne over her head and plunked it down on the other side of the room. "Maybe less, if I can skip a few steps. Do you think he'd notice if I didn't underpaint?"

"Why would you want to rush? He hasn't given us an answer yet."

"Poppy." Carmen faced away. "We have to start entertaining the possibility that he can't do what we ask."

She thought of a room filled with crooked paintings. "It's only been two nights."

Carmen finally turned around. The pity in her eyes turned Poppy's stomach. "You're right, Poppy. We have time." Carmen granted her a small, wistful smile. "Why don't you take a walk? The moon is very bright, and I'm nearly done here."

Poppy knew what it was to be dismissed by Carmen. This was not nearly her first time, after all. She toddled off, headed nowhere in particular, and soon found herself at her bedchamber. She had left Roisin there only an hour before.

She had left Roisin . . .

She had left . . .

In childhood, Poppy had a persistent fear of the root cellar of her family's farmhouse. The fear didn't keep her from entering when she was told to fetch turnips, nor as she fumbled for tubers in the dark. The fear only snaked around her ankles as she scrambled up the steps back into the daylight, little legs frantically outrunning the nebulous terror of being pursued by an entity of shadows and dust. The faster she ran, the quicker the fear-beast advanced, snarling at the backs of her boots. She would collapse at the top, stertorously sucking in the fresh air of freedom, stars dancing in her vision. It had been years since the ghoulish, hazy fright pursued her, but she felt it now, grasping at her feet with hands made of cobwebs and echoes. She ran faster, clumsily hoisting herself up on banisters and stumbling over landings. When the door came into view, she burst through it. The bed was unmade, the curtains drawn. The room was empty.

She collapsed on the flagstones so hard her knees cracked painfully. She was distantly aware she might have broken something, but she was removed from her body, floating somewhere dark and muffled. Roisin wasn't there. Roisin wasn't *there*. She collapsed over herself, pillowing her forehead on her bent forearms and letting out a low wail.

"Poppy? Poppy, my love! What happened?"

Arms on her, soft and sweet and familiar. She came back to herself in a rush. "I thought you were gone."

"Gone?" Roisin's eyes were the same color as the gray stone of the floor and ceiling. And yet, they contained so much more. So many colors, all without name. "Why would I have gone?"

"I'm silly. Oh, petal, I'm so silly." She scrubbed at her face. "Scared myself. That's all."

With one arm at Poppy's back and the other under her knees, Roisin scooped her up like she was weightless. Poppy clung to the front of her shirt, the buttons cool against the achingly hot skin of her face. Roisin deposited her atop the large, ancient bed, and Poppy tugged her in after, Roisin's chest landing on top of hers with satisfying weight. Her legs followed. When their knees met, Poppy cried out.

"Oh, you daft thing. What have you done to yourself?" Roisin didn't wait for answer, pulling up Poppy's skirts and scooting down the mattress. Poppy had forgone undergarments, so it was easy work exposing her swollen knees, already bruising purple. "You broke these. So well made, and you smashed them to bits."

"I overreacted."

"Poppy." Roisin caressed her cheek with careful fingers. Always careful. "What happened?"

"I was frightened. I got it in my head that if I didn't get up here quickly, something horrible would happen."

"To me?"

"I didn't get that far." She winced. Sometimes the pain of her rapid healing was worse than the injury, the snapping of mending bone and the ache of knitting muscle making her break out in an undignified sweat. "I thought you were gone."

"You thought I was gone." Roisin's voice was flat. "You saw the room was empty so you assumed I was gone, then fell to your knees and wailed like a Sicilian widow."

"Not my finest moment, mind, but Carmen was looking at me all pitying-like."

"Why?"

"Because I . . ." She bit her lip. "If I tell you something about Vlad, do you promise not to assume the worst?"

"But that's what I'm best at." She kissed Poppy's brow, which had tightened into a grumpy furrow. "Tell me anyway."

Poppy, who could deny her nothing, acquiesced.

"He made every portrait crooked?" Roisin asked when she had finished. "And one fallen? But why?"

"That's what I'm trying to figure out. Either he's very, uh, *whimsical* . . ."

"Or?"

"Or . . ." She sighed heavily. "He's gone round the twist."

Roisin considered this. "It's not unheard of. The years don't scramble the mind, but misery does. Boredom, too. I've seen a few vampires addicted to sticking bits of their body into the sun when they've run out of ways to feel alive."

Poppy's stomach sank. "Do you think he's . . . addled?"

"It is the worst possible scenario, so." She shrugged. "Of course I do."

"Naturally."

"What do you think?"

"Perhaps the portrait thing was a joke." She pushed herself to believe it. In an instant, lightness began to wash away her panic. "Or some sort of test. He might be trying to see whether we're worthy of his intervention."

Roisin was looking at her with a touch of awe. "Were you like this before I turned you?"

"Like what?"

"So hopeful."

"Oh." She thought about it. "Yes? Or, my circumstances were a bit shit. The hunger. Not being sure where I was meant to sleep. I had to look at some things from the side of my eye to see them as pretty. Maybe I'm just very good at delusion. What's that have to do with you turning me?"

"Some people say that when we're turned, the traits we had in life get stronger," Roisin said. "So for Massimo, the reason he can shield us is because he always wanted to protect people. Do you know his story?"

"Some." He had told Poppy, one foggy night, of nursing the ill of Venice through a late, devastating wave of the great plague. The city had relaxed quarantines during Carnival, and Massimo remembered all the painted masks as harbingers of doom, laughing and weeping in white, painted stillness. The plague had taken everyone—not just those he loved, but also those he didn't particularly like, and those to whom he was indifferent. He couldn't feel any way toward any person, because there was nobody left to let him feel at all. He tended to the ill to make use of his barren life, until the sickness seeped below his skin, rearranging his body with buboes and pus. Then, on a dark, still night, oddly silent of wailing and weeping, a pale man took pity on Massimo and bit life into him. Massimo's first act, when the pain ebbed, was to wipe the head of the dying man who lay beside him, and fetch him a cup of water. He hadn't even had the urge to bite.

"He protects," Roisin said. "But I always looked for doom. I pulled out my hair and I bit my nails. I was too skinny, like a hungry hare in winter. Maybe that's why I kept looking. Why I had to hunt."

"And why I can delude myself so thoroughly?"

"Why you hope." Roisin pressed the words into Poppy's hair, kisses chasing them from her lips. "Why you help me hope, like you."

"Oh, come off it," Poppy grumbled, loving it.

After a quiet, warm moment, Roisin asked, "What do you suppose Vlad did in life that gave him powers like those?"

"Saw a burning bush?"

"Anyone can *see* a burning bush, Poppy. That Moses heard the Lord through it is what was special."

Her lips twitched. "It is my curse to be burdened with the company of Catholics."

"Imagine what it's like for us."

They stayed in bed until smoky morning touched the dingy windows. As Poppy began her trance, the strange, skittering sound came once more. She froze, stilling her breathing to better listen. The sound was coming from the window. Carefully, she slipped from bed and tiptoed over. The lock was old and rusted. With a grunt, she pushed open the window. Meager sunlight shone on the other side of the castle. Safely shadowed, she stuck her head from the window frame. There was nothing to either side of her, nor down below, where jagged rocks jutted upward like dragon's teeth. She turned her body around, shoulders resting on the ledge, and looked upwards.

There was the Count. His arms and legs were bent, his fingers pressed into the stone. He crawled like a bug across the face of his palace, hunching in shadow, darting away from the encroaching sun. He moved with stomach-churning swiftness, a water bug over a pond. Oblivious to his audience, the Count hastily made his way along the wall, disappearing around the corner, his strange, insect noises fading as he went.

Poppy silently closed the window and stiffly walked back to the bed. Roisin was in her trance, her face smooth and peaceful. Poppy kissed her on each eyelid, and the tip of her nose. On each stark cheekbone. On her mouth. Then, she slid under the covers, grabbed onto Roisin's body, and pressed herself against it as tight as she could. In her trance, Roisin wrapped her arms around Poppy and murmured a sweet, pointless reassurance. It couldn't stop the shivers, nor the silent tears.

Chapter 45

The next night, after attempting futilely to make headway with the Count, Poppy found herself wandering aimlessly through the castle.

She encountered Zahrah, Karol, and Massimo gearing up for a fox hunt, though it was unlikely to look anything like the sport standard.

Zahrah greeted her with a wave. "They're making godawful noises under our window. We're thirsty, they're annoying, QED. Care to join us? You might want to put on buckskins. Have you packed any?"

"I haven't."

"Then we'll bring something back for you. A nice, fat one. Doesn't that sound scrummy?"

Poppy found Carmen examining the Count's treasures.

"Do you see the stain here?" Carmen pointed at a large oblong on the face of the massive, central crucifix. "What do you suppose it is?"

"Rust?"

"Gold doesn't rust." She scraped at it with a thumb. It came off under her fingernail, brown and flaky. "It's as though the thing bled. Everything here is topsy-turvy. Look."

She showed Poppy a number of glass bottles, which, when uncorked, released an upwards-drip of liquid, as though the ceiling were the floor and they all hung upside-down. She pulled down a sword with god's honest handprints in the metal, like someone made of heat had squeezed the blade. She uncovered a trunk, which sheltered decades worth of women's garments in all sizes.

"Nothing useful, I'm sorry to say." Carmen reached for her hand. "Come. A walk might clear our minds."

They walked under the moon, listening to the faint, distant sound of their friends sparring with hungry, springtime foxes. It was a half moon, perfect as a split wheel of white cheese. They lay beneath it and breathed, and Poppy tried for all the world to ignore the tense knot of her apprehensive guts, the sickly flipping of her stomach.

Poppy spent the following nightfall with Valentin. He had located the castle's dusty library and was poring through volumes, puzzling over the ancient languages and unfamiliar lettering.

"Lovely pictures, though." He pointed out an image of what appeared to be a cluster of nuns queuing up to kiss the devil's anus. "Do you think this was drawn from life?"

She didn't give him the satisfaction. "Have you found anything useful?"

"Define useful," he said, holding up a woodcut print of nuns and demons holding hands and dancing around in a circle.

"You seem pleased."

"Do I? Perhaps I feel fortunate to have had better dance partners."

Rage simmered under her skin. "If Vlad can't do it, I'll come back with you and you'll be pleased to have me miserable once again. Is that it? You're happy to see me unhappy?"

He closed the book, carefully replacing it on the shelf before speaking. "I would advise you to choose your words."

"You don't have to be jealous anymore, you know. How delightful for you."

"I'm not the one you're angry with."

"You're wrong."

"Rarely." He crossed his arms and popped a hip, leaning. His eyes narrowed to assessing slits. "Fine. Have at it."

"Excuse me?"

"If I were anyone else, I wouldn't be so kind. But I'm me, and you are you, and you may say what you wish to me, because you can't say it to her. You're lucky I'm such a gentle creature."

Her chest tightened. "You're a cold, French shit."

"You're scared the Count is merely stringing us along for company?" He raised an unfeeling eyebrow. "You're afraid to watch her go once more? Go ahead. Be awful to me."

"Don't pretend you know anything about love."

"Oh yes. Because I've been pining for the same, saintly man for a century. How pathetic I am. How small. Go ahead, Poppy. Give me all of it."

"I—" The words died on her tongue. "Fuck you."

"There it is." His lips curled into a satisfied smile. "My *nouvelle*. You couldn't hurt me if you tried."

"Shut up." Her vision wobbled with tears. "Stupid ponce."

"Stupid, French, cold, shitty, pathetic, queer. All of that and more." He approached, his arms outstretched. "You can't hurt a man who hates himself." He yanked her into his grasp, pressing her against his front. The hug was painfully tight, as much a wrestling hold as an embrace.

"Fuck *you*." Her tears were leaking into his dampening shirt. She struggled against his stiff arms. "You misery."

"I'm not happy about any of this."

"Liar." She made to kick his shin, but he stepped deftly away. "Fucking liar."

"All that and more. Give me all of it."

"You want to see me suffer."

"Do I?"

"You want, you ... Oh shit." She went limp, shame rising acrid on her tongue. "Oh *shit*."

"*Ma nouvelle*." He pulled back, meeting her gaze. "I want you to have your happiness."

"Out of the goodness of your heart?"

His mouth twitched. "Because I fear without it, you will become me."

"Misery does love company."

"It's poor company, I assure you."

"Rubbish. I ... I'm sorry, Valentin." Her stomach churned with guilt. "You're excellent company. You always have been."

"You made me better." His hold was gentle now, his hands smoothing up and down her back. "Oh, *ma pauvre petite*. I fear for us both."

A few nights later, on a lonely walk through the castle's heaving halls, Poppy came upon Roisin sitting in the internal courtyard with a thick volume balanced on her lap. Poppy peered over her shoulder to find an image of two nuns harvesting phalluses from a small tree.

"Thinking of starting a garden?"

"An orchard, actually." Roisin turned, and her face fell. "Have you been crying?"

"Yes," she admitted. "A bit."

"Alone?"

"With Valentin."

He had found her to tell her of a dream he had while trancing, of three women who demanded his affection.

"They said I'm young and strong and had kisses for all of them." He had shaken discomfort from his hands. "So I told them gently that I wasn't interested and then they ate a baby. Oh, Poppy, it wasn't that miserable. You don't have to cry about it."

She wasn't crying about it. She was crying about the pointless, frustrating conversation she had just had with the Count, in which he had sharply suggested she ought to be a touch more patient. She was crying about Carmen's open pity, which poured from her dark, painted eyes. She was crying about Zahrah's relentless cheer, about Karol's unbroken apathy, about Massimo's sticky kindness. And then, on top of it all, she was crying about the extreme likelihood that, by involving her friends in this pointless business, she would get them all killed.

But she couldn't say that, so she had taken a walk instead.

"Come sit." Roisin made to move the book, looking around for a place to set it now Poppy occupied the other half of her bench. "Er . . ."

"Give it to me." Poppy gently took the volume from Roisin's hands and shut it, taking care not to fold any of the pages. She then flung it toward the corner of the courtyard, where it collided with a pillar.

"Poppy!"

"Oh, come now. The prick bush will survive."

"It's a prick tree, you'll find." Roisin stared after the book, silent for a moment. Then, giggles popped from her mouth, yellow and fresh as chicks from their eggs. Soon, she was doubled over, laughter spilling out, shaking her shoulders. Poppy watched, transfixed.

Roisin hadn't laughed like that in 1837. She had barely smiled back then, the gesture flat and shifting, hiding her teeth. Now, her heart lived just under her skin, and she laughed and laughed and laughed.

If Poppy lost her, she would spend her whole life waiting to hear that laughter again.

"This castle is so big," she whispered, when the tide of laughter had washed out to sea. "I don't want to lose you."

"You won't." Roisin kissed her hair. "You won't."

Chapter 46

Poppy joined Carmen and Vlad for their third portrait session. Vlad sat in a heavy metal throne, his body positioned at a regal, haughty angle. Carmen had the paintbrush pinched between her fingers, laying down shapes and shadow, her golden hand moving with vampiric swiftness. Poppy sat on a wooden stool and watched.

As the painted blobs began to resemble their subject, Poppy asked the Count about his powers, and whether he might use them again. He responded in riddles about waves and whales, about the patterns of sharks in the deep. About creatures who lived inside rock fissures, getting warmth from the boiling bubbles of underwater volcanoes, crafting uncanny submarine vessels from volcanic rock. She asked about the Council, and he sang songs of friends long gone, feasts of virgins, the taste of a priest's neck, the scrape of his stubble upon hungry lips. She asked about justice, and he spoke of might. Of large hands in gauntlets, smashing oranges and cakes and heads, and how, in the end, everything was wet pulp. Wet pulp on a scaffolding of pith and sugar and bone. And then he laughed. Laughed and laughed and laughed.

The Count gasped.

"Oh." He looked up at her. His unfocused eyes flickered to alertness once, twice. For a fraction of a second, she could see in them a sickly familiar look of terror. "Oh. I . . ." He ran his long tongue over his dry lips. "Oh my."

And Poppy, who had been stubbornly looking at this moment from the side, was forced to watch as it bared its bloody face.

"Vlad," she rasped, dread a stake through her heart. "She was

357

here, wasn't she?"

Carmen's head snapped up. "What?"

"Haven't you been listening to him?" Her throat had gone thin. Her hands trembled.

"I've been painting," Carmen said. "I was too focused. I couldn't hear a thing."

"He isn't just lonely. This isn't just the madness that . . . Oh, I'm such an *idiot!*"

"Poppy." Carmen's hands moved slowly through the air, in them the suggestion of steadying breaths. "Calm down and tell me what you mean."

"It's Cane."

It had been Cane from the very beginning. The crooked paintings. The scrabbling climb across the castle's face. The strange, fractured smiling. All this time, and Poppy had been too hopeful to see it. Too cowardly. Such a fucking *coward*.

Carmen dropped her paintbrush, face going ashen. "Oh. Oh *shit*."

"Tell me." Poppy fell to her knees before the old vampire, gripping his shoulders. "Tell me what she did to you. You can do it, I know you're in there."

Blank, dark eyes. An unmoving smile. Through it came words formed from breath and spittle. "My darling, are you doing well? You are speaking nonsense."

"Cane!" She shook him. His face didn't slip, brittle as rictus. "What did you do? What did you *do?*"

The old vampire's head snapped back, a long, sucking gulp of air rattling through his thin chest. His Adam's apple shook, spinning underneath the bluish skin of his exposed throat. His body went slack, his mouth falling open. In the dark crevasse between his lips, the points of two yellowy fangs peered out like the eyes of a hiding adder.

"No, no, no!" He was limp in Poppy's arms. His jagged fingernails trailed on the flags. His head hung at a sickening angle. "No!"

Carmen fell to the ground beside her. "Is he dead?"

The Count's body jerked. Poppy shrieked, dropping her grip. He didn't fall. His head wrenched upright, his eyes vibrant with malicious light. A grin curled his livery mouth, twisting and clever. Poppy knew that grin. It sent her back to a long night in the Paris Morgue, shivering on a table, a throng of strangers thrilling over her exposed flesh. The night her body was commandeered by a vicious stranger

"Hello, Poppy," the vampire crooned in a voice that wasn't his.

Poppy skidded frantically away, her back hitting the wall.

Carmen stared. "Cane."

The vampire's eyes locked onto her. "My little song! Are thy cheeks still comely with rows of jewels?"

To her great credit, Carmen didn't flinch. "You knew we were coming here."

"I might not have, were it not for young Poppy." The invader's smile stretched the ancient vampire's wizened face. "I can see you," she sang, a discordant, mocking lullaby. "I've been watching."

Poppy's skin prickled. "How?"

"Some people have eyes on the back of their heads." The Count's spindly finger tapped the back of his skull. "And some have eyes in their cunts."

Oh, no. "The *nazar*."

"You've got it!" Cane clapped papery hands that didn't belong to her. "Here I thought you'd be obedient enough, *clever* enough, to give my eye to Roisin. But you were even smarter than I could have imagined! What a fun idea, to give it to Sarah! I've been watching you through her for years."

Poppy's lungs were filled with ice. "Where is she? Have you hurt her?"

The Count's mouth flattened into a dispassionate line. "Don't be silly. Of course I have."

Poppy rocketed to her feet, head spinning. It had been two months since they left the Mayfair redbrick. In doing so, they had taken Massimo's protection with them. Sarah had been undefended for so long, and would remain so until they could get back.

"We have to go home," she whispered frantically.

"Oh, goody!" Cane clapped the Count's hands. "I'm waiting for you there. Sarah and I, and all of your lovely staff. They've been ever so accommodating."

A pall of helplessness fell over Poppy's shoulders. Regret curdled her stomach juices. She had made so many mistakes. They buzzed in her ears and blurred her vision. They stung her skin. They swarmed over the moon, chilling her. Darkening her night to unbroken blackness.

"If you have harmed a hair on the head of any one of my employees," Carmen growled through the haze, "I will slice your head from your body."

"Oh, that *is* terrifying. How does this sound: you come here or I will kill absolutely everyone in your employ."

"Roisin and I will come. Just us." Carmen wiped the paint from her hands, readying for battle. "That's who you really want."

"Oh, no, no, no." The Count's head wobbled on a limp neck, the fulcrum an invisible grip to his skull. "I saw everything, remember? Your two military pals. Your weepy Venetian. That blonde twat who looks a fright in spectacles. You all conspired against me. You did what Poppy asked."

Mistakes, a horde of them, whispering in Poppy's ears with honey tongues. *This is your fault. This is your fault.*

"You didn't want to do as Poppy asked, did you, little song?" Cane sneered. "You've always known I chase down my debts. But that fat fool didn't listen to you, did she?" A *tsk* of derision from the Count's stretched mouth. "You need to keep your coven in order."

Poppy was going to be sick. "Please. Let them go. You can have me."

Cane cocked the Count's head. "You? What would I want with you? You're scraps. You're nothing. You are the young, brainless afterthought who killed everyone you care for. If you had merely listened to me in that morgue, all of this could have been avoided. But you wanted *everything*." The Count's tongue waggled through his words, half-dead. Cane rolled him to hands and knees and began to crawl, drawing closer to Poppy. She trembled, pressing herself into the wall. "I've seen your cakes. Will you have this one and eat it? Or will the cake eat you first?"

"Cane," Carmen snapped. "That is enough."

The head swiveled. "I'll say when it's enough."

"No. *I* will." Carmen stood tall and fierce before the fallen figure of the Count, her head high, her hands at her hips. She was always so proud, so carefully calm. That fierce peace was magnified in this small stone chamber, her regal bearing adorning the room with gold and jewels. "Poppy took a risk, and we followed. That was our choice. How you proceed is yours. No one has moved your hand. No one will face punishment for your actions but you. As for Poppy . . ." Carmen turned a beatific half smile on her. "She is forgiven."

"I . . ." Poppy choked on gratitude, her eyes filled with tears. "Oh."

"Punishment?" The count's hand pressed against his ribs. "I?"

"We will come for you," Carmen said. "Willingly. Gladly. And you will pay for your crimes."

In Poppy's memory, in a small room in a foggy place, there stood a painting of a goddess and a centaur. Through the fug of her shame-dampened mind, Poppy saw the goddess now: Carmen, warring and wise, with the hair of a beast in her clenched fist.

The beast laughed, giggling like a child. Bellowing, sobbing laughter followed, strange and high, soaring in pitch and volume until it was nothing but a cacophony of shrieks.

"Ha! Ha! Ha! Ha!"

Poppy squeezed her hands against her ears, the world growing tight and small around her. Louder and louder and louder came the laughter, prying fingers on her hands, forcing her to listen, to go mad with listening.

"Ha! Ha! Ha! Ha!"

Then, silence. The Count blinked, the light in his eyes shifting from cruelty to terror. His arms gave out under him and, bones and skin, he clattered to the floor, wrists snapping, hands twisted, fingers reaching from the earth like ragged weeds.

"England!" he shrieked. "Must go to England!"

Part VI

Transylvania, 1871

Chapter 47

Poppy remembered little after that. She only knew sound—the rough, baleful slice of her own screams shaking the castle, the sound filling the shape of tall ceilings and climbing spires as she called desperately for her friends. There were hands on her body soon. Valentin, perhaps, and Roisin, making sense of her frantic ramblings. Carmen ordering everyone else this way and that, collecting trunks and securing transport. Karol and Zahrah, heads bent together, speaking quickly and quietly. Massimo hiding his tears. Vlad, staring at her with curiously blank eyes, his mouth open and screaming, like her, shouting himself hoarse then soundless, the two of them giving agonized voice to their horror, horror, horror.

Sarah, Sarah, Sarah, Sarah, Sarah, Sarah. I'm so sorry.

A blink, then the darkness of a coach, being held in Massimo's lap as he whispered and sang to her, his sweet powers cocooning her, and she could almost believe that they were the only two people in the world at that moment. There was an absence beside her, and it called to her, and she wanted to throw herself under the wheels, but she couldn't, not with Massimo's grip on her, and she cried for that terrible wanting. To be crushed to sugar and pulp and bone.

And then, a city. A pier. A boat, a familiar boat, where she had once peered over the deck and pickled. Air that smelled of fish and salt and starlight, and a crew with removed caps, heads respectfully bowed as the Brood filed down into one small cabin and closed the door behind them.

They stayed together, for the most part. Carmen prayed her rosary and talked about colors and shapes and the smell of linseed and the feel of her mamá's hand against her hair. Valentin told dirty jokes and sang sailing songs he had learned from the crew, and he cursed Cane into the earth and through the other side with a mouth so foul it could have burned the ears off a multilingual nun. Massimo told folk stories, rich with loving details, his voice switching between characters, pitching up or down, hoarse or smooth, traipsing through a number of accents. Zahrah recounted all of her nights out, the dark ones and the bright ones, the gaslit and starlit. She spoke of war, too, of Amina, Louverture, Makhanda, and Tecumseh, all of whom she would follow into battle to this day, but only if Karol stood beside her. Karol spoke of Vlad, when he was younger. Of the parties he threw, which were stark and awful and could barely justify the definition, but in memory were special, because they were gone. She talked about how things changed and changed and changed, and how even the unending would end when the sun grew large and ate the Earth.

"You can leave," Poppy told them all. "I did this to you. I'm the one who put us all in danger. She'll kill us all. You can go hide. You can go live."

"Where else would I want to go?" Valentin squeezed her hand. "She's got Sarah. She's got Godfrey. She'll have you. If there's a chance, I'll take it."

"I won't let her go without a fight." Carmen's cheeks were bright with rouge, her ears heavy with diamonds. "I won't run from her."

"Thank you," Roisin said to all of them. "Thank you for staying with us until the end."

Carcharos came when he wasn't at the helm. He told tales of his seafaring, lies and truths all wound up together like bad knitting. He spoke of his lovers, human men all, and how he had loved them no less for the one before or after. How they died in his arms, each of them wizened and sick, and how he bore each death with aching grace because they had chosen their lives.

"I would have bit any of them," he said, wiping a tear. "Any one of my good men, bless 'em."

His mate, Henry, came one night. He sat beside Poppy, the silence surrounding them all like they were underwater. He reached out and took her hand in his. Across his knuckles were the words HOLD FAST in dark ink. Waves lapped against the ship, and Poppy wondered if this was how Jonah felt in the belly of the whale: quaking and fearful and small.

"Did you do those tattoos?" she asked.

"No."

"Who did?"

Minutes later, a man named Davey arrived with india ink, a bottle of rum, and a small bundle of needles.

"This'll hurt fierce, miss."

"That is rather the point."

Roisin pulled nervously at her shirtfront. "Are you sure this is wise, Poppy? He hasn't got any tattoos himself."

Davey slanted her a look. "And who's meant to tattoo me? Can't do meself, can I? Excepting my thighs, o'course."

"Oh, yes. Of course. I didn't mean to offend." She fidgeted, her fingers tangling together. "But Poppy . . . why?"

"When we die—"

"If," Roisin amended valiantly. Heroically. Her whole body strained against the hope of it.

"If," Poppy agreed. "If we die and we go somewhere after. If we find one another in that up or a beyond or anywhere else, I want to have a body that's changed for you being beside it."

"Oh." Roisin wiped moisture from her eyelashes. "Proceed, then."

The pain was excruciating. Tears rushed to her eyes, spilling down her cheeks so freely that Davey pulled off for a moment, waiting for her quick nod before resuming his careful work. He poked her over and over on the skin of her ribs, depositing such little ink each time that it became disheartening to watch. It would take hours. Hours and hours.

But then, the pain began to change. Perhaps Poppy had been spending too much time with Catholics, but she felt suddenly and intensely immersed in the divinely painful throes of a martyr's sacrifice. Like a saint, enduring agony that transformed into ecstatic bliss in the hands of a merciful god. She thought of Saint Bartholomew, skin flayed from his living body, shed like old rags so that he could become new once more.

Poppy wanted to become new. She wanted Roisin's love to change her as much as her bite had. To turn her hair white or give her a wrinkle. Scar her or brand her. They couldn't grow old together. This would have to do.

For the first time in years, she longed to be in her mother's arms. Her mother, who would understand and hold her as she wept out her sorrow and pain. Her mother, who would say, "You've changed. I can see it in your eyes. You're different." Her mother, who would tell her she didn't need to go down to the root cellar at all, that she would fetch the turnips herself while Poppy sat at the table eating scraps of bread.

Later, Roisin bandaged the bleeding roses and their many tiny thorns.

"Are you in pain?" she asked delicately.

"That's a silly question." Poppy was half-delirious. Floating. "Silly girl."

"May I ask you a better one, then?"

"Anything."

"Was it worth it?"

"The tattoo?"

Roisin's stark cheekbones shadowed the hollows of her face. Her tuppence eyes were wet. Her mouth was open. Her hair, slippery and dark, was a wreck.

"You know I don't mean the tattoo."

"Come here, you idiot," Poppy said, and barely complained at all when Roisin fell across her fresh tattoo.

She wandered the ship. Above, the stars dripped celestial light. The full moon greeted these stars, swallowing down their silvery glow. Poppy walked lightly. Valentin and Massimo didn't hear her come.

Valentin stroked a hand down Massimo's shaking back. "Why are you weeping, sunshine?"

"I'm sorry," he sobbed. "I'm so sorry."

"Shh, now."

"I shouldn't have said it. D-do you remember what I said?"

"It was so long ago."

"Of course you remember. You don't forget anything. You try, but you don't. You *can't*."

"It's history now," Valentin murmured. "It doesn't matter."

"It *does*," Massimo insisted thickly. "I said, I s-said that I couldn't love a miserable man. I couldn't love someone who looked at the world with boredom and d-disdain. But that's not you anymore, is it? You were always so stubborn. But you've ch-changed."

Valentin pressed a devastated noise behind his lips. "Don't apologize, *mon amour*. I was that man. You were right."

"You were never meant to change," Massimo said, full of awed wonder. "And here you are. Here you *are*."

Poppy found Roisin in their cabin, lying on her stomach, silent and pondering. When Roisin heard the door, she looked up and smiled, her stark face melting into heartbreaking ease, into a joy hard earned and infinitely precious. She used to jump at strange noises. Now, marching toward her death, she smiled.

"Stay where you are," Poppy managed, tasting the sharp-edged shards of her ruined heart on her tongue, and fell on the body of the woman she loved.

She kissed, then. Kissed the slender nape of Roisin's neck. Kissed down her arms, the soft pits of her elbows, the hidden webs between each finger. She licked at a palm, opened her mouth for two fingers, sucked. She kissed the earlobes, small and attached, and bit, hearing Roisin moan. Feeling Roisin writhe beneath her. Seeing her tremble.

"We've just barely started, petal."

Roisin blew her fringe from her face. "Oh, *saints*."

Poppy moved lower, rucking up the shirt and mouthing at the dip of Roisin's back, tongue darting into the pair of dimples there. She rolled up trousers and ran her lips against the underside of Roisin's knees. She laid a kiss on each well-turned ankle.

"We ought to be naked."

Soon, they were. Poppy stared at the person spread across her bed. The long legs and slender arms. The hips with a little give. The small breasts. The inviting thatch of curling hair. The silvery eyes that could never hide that little bit of shock, as if, even now, she could barely believe her luck.

They lay face to face, legs wrapped together, hands working between them. Roisin watched Poppy's face so intently she felt like a piece of art on display. Roisin's face was wild with disbelief, smiling and gasping, almost laughing. Joy at the end, the purple of twilight before the night settles in.

"*Mo cuishle*. My sweet Poppy. So good, so clever."

Poppy let herself be praised. Let the guilt and shame of damning her family fall from her shoulders, if only for a minute. In that freedom, her body took flight.

"Roisin, I'm close," she gasped brokenly. "Just like that. Like *that*."

Roisin grinned, feral. Her teeth dropped. Vast anticipation rushed in so quickly it starred Poppy's vision. Wild-eyed, Roisin sunk her teeth into the flesh of Poppy's shoulder. A prick of pain, and then pleasure, her body set aflame. She heard screaming, registering dimly that it was her own voice that shook the walls. When she finally returned to her body, her throat stung.

"Your turn," she said between heavy breaths.

Much later, or in the blink of an eye, they tranced on a wooden ship floating on a vast ocean, rolling around in the belly of the whale.

Sarah, cried Poppy's tired mind. *Sarah, Sarah, Sarah. I'm on my way.*

Chapter 48

They raced from the docked boat to a train, and from that train to hansoms. Zahrah and Karol laid out a battle plan as they bounced along the cobbles. Poppy couldn't hear them, her mind occupied by a singular thought, blaring like an orchestra.

Sarah, Sarah, Sarah, SARAH.

The Mayfair Redbrick awaited, its door shut, its windows drawn. From the street, no one would guess that a malevolent, ancient woman waited inside, lives spilling from her hands.

It was Carmen who took the first step, unarmored but for the finery she wore, the heavy jewels swinging from her lobes.

"Well. Let us make our last stand."

She took a bracing breath, then flung the door open so hard it cracked against the wall.

This place was where Poppy had stumbled in more than thirty years before, convinced this was not where she belonged. This was where she had trembled at the plenty, where she had hid in her dark bed. Where she became part of a strange, remarkable family. Where she fed creatures who hadn't eaten in centuries, and loved them as best she knew how.

Cane stood there, now. A tumor in the creature built of red bricks and memory, which Poppy called home. A sickness in silk, wearing a smile of sure triumph.

The gas was low, limning Cane's darkness in gold, like the sun did the eclipsing moon. She wore a gown of a deep crimson silk, cut with a neckline *en coeur*. The frock was trimmed with enough black lace that it might as well have been widow's weeds. Her hair was a long, black sheet, falling down her back halfway to the floor. Dark paint ringed her eyes. Her lips were the color of drying blood.

"You took long enough." That voice, throaty and sultry. In it were memories, shades of Poppy's body's stiff disloyalty. Her powerlessness. Humiliating, though observed only by the dead.

"Apologies." Carmen was of Cane's height, if not a touch taller. In Poppy's mind, Cane had always been impossibly larger, dizzyingly tall and forever looming. "We had to make our apologies to the Count."

"Oh, yes. Old Vlad." Cane laughed lightly. "A useful fellow."

"Certainly. Has he any hope of recovery?"

"Recovery?" Cane strode forward. "Is he ill?"

"Come now. We're beyond this sort of game are we not?"

"Fine, fine. No, the man won't ever recover his mind." Cane grinned, exposing her fangs. There was a touch of red on her teeth, and Poppy hoped desperately it was paint from her lips. "Do you know, when I met him all of his powers were intact? This entire time, he had been able to boil the oceans and gather the clouds. And he didn't!" A small, disgusted exhalation. "Our life is a great gift. Our talents greater still. And yet, he spent his years wasting away in that mausoleum, never daring to use the powers bestowed on him. He even told me he didn't have the right. Imagine! Deciding he hadn't the right to use his powers! It is akin to deciding one cannot use one's left hand, because one only deserves use of the right." She lifted her right hand in demonstration, fingers twining together, flexing and opening.

"Oh." Massimo gasped. "I—I can't move."

Valentin lunged toward him and toppled onto the floor, sleeping legs lying mutinously behind. In the corner of Poppy's vision, Karol and Zahrah joined hands.

Poppy didn't try to move. She couldn't bear knowing she could not.

"I have been blessed with my gifts," Cane declared. "You would understand that, wouldn't you, Carmen? I remember you being somewhat tediously devout."

"You never seemed particularly interested in the divine." Carmen's stance looked unnaturally stiff, but her staunch expression didn't betray her. "Though I'll allow it has been many years."

"I could say that I've changed, but, *well*. Everyone changes except for us. Even statues erode."

A voice came from behind Poppy, near the door.

"Oh, shut *up.*"

Cane's head whipped up, her face immediately transformed. The malice melted away, replaced with what couldn't be mistaken for anything other than adoration. Her eyes were wide and covetous, her hands reaching out.

"My love." Cane's voice was nearly unrecognizable, cooing and sweet. "You've found me, my clever thing. My pet."

Roisin stepped into the room, her gait strong and even. Her hair was combed and tied, her shirtfront an unspoiled white. The dim, orange light flickered off of her sabre, held aloft as though she faced a dragon. An aureole of gaslight hugged her, a painted saint in a shell of gold luster.

"I did," she said, and it sounded like a trumpet blare. "I found you."

Cane's smile cracked wide. "Have you seen how good I've been?" Her pitch climbed higher. Younger. Almost childish. "No dead girls! Not for so very long! You told me I was an unmovable brute, do you remember? But I've moved so very much!"

"Where is Sarah? Where is the rest of the staff?"

Cane's face faltered. She pouted. "Tell me you see. Tell me you see how good I've been. You were always so good for me, my love. Tell me you see how good I've been for you."

Roisin's jaw worked. "Can you be good?"

Cane nodded eagerly. "So good. The very best."

"Then free them. Show me everyone on the staff is safe."

"Of course, my love," Cane clutched at her breast, staunching the wound of Cupid's arrow. "Anything for you."

She raised her arms. A thumping noise came from upstairs, rhythmic, growing in volume. Every door opened, on the ground floor and above. From each doorway, a line of footmen, butlers, grooms, valets, and maids stomped out into the hall. Their blank eyes showed no sign of recognition. Their hands hung slack at their sides. Nearly everyone was accounted for in this parade of strangers, including Godfrey, wispy-haired and liver-spotted, standing straighter than he had in a decade.

There was one notable exception.

Roisin noticed it, too. "Where is Sarah?"

Cane rolled her eyes, her simpering affectation flickering away to reveal the impatience underneath. "She was an absolute nuisance. The mouth on her!" She tossed her hair. "Are you sure you want to see her?"

Roisin merely stared, her sabre shifting minutely.

Cane sighed. "As you wish."

The sound of footsteps trickled through the ceiling. Poppy's breath went short, her throat squeezing air. After a few desperate moments, Sarah appeared at the top of the stairs. Like the rest of the house's staff, her expression was wiped blank. Silently, she descended, her body inhumanly stiff, her feet falling upon every step with an ungainly stomp. Slow and lurching, she reached Cane's side and stood there, obedient as a hunting dog called to heel.

"What have you done to her?" Poppy growled.

Sarah's face was a livid mess of bumps and blood, purple, green, and yellow with bruising. Her eyes were swollen shut, her mouth seeping frothy, pink saliva. Her arm hung at a sickening angle. Her frock was ripped in several places, exposing strips of bloodied, punctured skin. A trail of red dripped from a wound in her neck, as well as one of her ears and both nostrils. Poppy's eyes roved over the injuries, hunting for any trace of breathing, any shift of Sarah's slender chest or the twitch of a finger. There was none.

"She was impertinent." Cane tossed this explanation into the air, careless and casual. "Like you. I can see why you get along. Why you gave her my little present." Cane pursed her lips, tutting in mock pity. "Are you excited to die, Poppy?"

And then, with a movement so swift it was barely visible, Roisin pulled a flintlock from her waistband and shot Cane in the head.

The lead ball burned through white flesh, sinking deep into Cane's thick skull. Blood splattered on the wall behind her, droplets flying onto the unmoving faces of the assembled, frozen staff. A blob of red blood landed on a gas lamp and began to sizzle and burn, acrid smoke rising into the close air. On the ruined face, the skin around the dark, gaping bullet hole bubbled, blackening. Cane blinked, dazed, as blood dripped down her nose and across her face.

"Oh, pet," she crooned, eyes holding fast to their sharp focus. "You can't just *shoot* me in the head. You're meant to slice it *off*."

Chapter 49

Roisin and Cane flung themselves at one another. Roisin sliced and hacked with her blade, her face a grimace of sheer determination. Cane was just as ardent, jabbing with a knife she yanked from her skirts. The Brood were in sudden motion, Cane's mesmerism puppeting them into strange embraces. Zahrah was in Karol's arms, Valentin in Massimo's, and Poppy in Carmen's. Hands clasped around heads and jaws, one sharp movement away from three snapped necks.

"Poppy," Carmen breathed in Poppy's ear. "Is Sarah moving?"

Her stomach lurched. "I can't look."

"Look. That is your friend. *Look*."

Sarah stood unmoving. Her head hung slightly to one side. Her eyes were closed. There was no rise and fall to her chest. Poppy's throat convulsed.

"She isn't moving. She's dead." She let out fathomless sob. "I've killed her."

"No, Poppy." Carmen kissed the back of her head. "No despair, not now."

Poppy's movements were limited, but she could lean back just a little. Feel the reliable strength and softness of Carmen at her back.

"*Philia*," she murmured. "*Eros. Xenia.*"

"*Philautia*," Carmen whispered back, heavy with tears. "*Agape. Storge.*"

Roisin and Cane did not fight like swordsmen. They fought like beasts. They jumped high, their blades catching near the ceiling. Their knives rent garments, exposing unbroken expanses of skin. Roisin's mouth was tight with concentration, her long limbs moving at speed. Cane vacillated between feral rage and unbridled glee, roaring and mewling and whooping as she gained advantage, pressing Roisin into a corner. The hole in her head closed slowly, crackling with threads of healing muscle and skin, blood oozing.

Roisin shoved Cane back. "Let them go. It's only me you want."

"Let them go?" Cane laughed, high and wild. "But of course!"

In a clever shift of her fingers, the mesmerism lifted. Poppy fell out of Carmen's arms.

"Although, if they must be free," Cane went on, "they ought to be occupied. Don't you think?"

She twiddled her fingers once more. Dozens of heads snapped towards the Brood. In an instant, the six vampires were pinned under the many gazes of their servants. In perfect unison, the staff raised their hands, pulled blades from their pockets, and shambled forward.

They had been the best-paid staff in Mayfair. Criminals and queers, who served in exchange for their protection. Who gave their blood for money and pleasure. Who lived under the same roof as monsters, and yet knew no fear.

The Brood had offered these people protection. The Brood would not renege now.

"Hold them!" Zahrah cried. "Corral them into the ballroom! We can—" A sickening gurgle. Her hands flew to her throat to pull out the knife a young maid had buried there. Blood spurted through her fingers. Massimo shrieked.

"Not now, sunshine," Valentin shouted, grappling with his valet. "Grab Alexander. Be careful, he has a cleaver."

Poppy ducked through the arms and legs of the servants, beating a course towards Sarah. Sarah, who stood still but for the bumping of shoulders, which set her swaying. In the crush of bodies, she looked liable to fall and be trampled.

Cane and Roisin clashed at the foot of the staircase.

"Did you care for them at all, my love?" Cane snarled, kicking Roisin in the knee. Her bone snapped, leg bent backward. She went down hard, a scream snatched from her throat. "Oh, my darling idiot. My special, empty-headed girl. You should have listened."

"Sarah!" Poppy hissed, getting closer. In the chaos, she fell, her hand

376

slapping against the marble floor, her frock pooling at her knees. A forest of pant legs and skirts rose up in front of her. Someone stomped on her fingers, crushing the bones. She snatched her hand back, falling to the other elbow, dragging and knee-walking towards Sarah. So far, she hadn't been noticed by the mindlessly stabbing staff, nor Cane, whose rage had whittled her focus to Roisin alone.

Poppy was close to Sarah now, an arm's length away. She reached out, hand curled to grab when a footman snatched her off the ground and tossed her away. The movement was faster than her mind; she realized belatedly that she was midair, a living projectile high above the swirling mass of livery and blood. In a juddering instant, she hit the wall, her head cracking against the wallpaper, vision swimming.

Cane's voice was drifting through the blurred scrum. "You do not have the strength of conviction to love one only, my pet. My Roisin. Your weakness has destroyed you. Perhaps it is best for us all that I shall bring about your end."

Poppy blinked away the fog. In double vision, she could see Roisin's knee, bent the wrong way. She was bowed over it, making the high, whining noises of an injured animal. Her shoulders trembled.

"Tell me, as I'm curious." Cane stalked over to Sarah and lifted her up by the scruff of her neck. Sarah's helpless body dangled from Cane's outstretched hand. "Why didn't you take back what was yours? Why did you let her have my eye?"

Roisin's breathing was high with pain. "Put her down. She has done nothing to you."

"Hasn't she?" Cane crammed a hand into the front of Sarah's dress, a casually disrespectful movement. From the torn depths, she pulled out a familiar pendant. "You let that insolent baby give her what was yours. What was mine!"

Cane's gaze flicked up, spying Poppy crumpled against the marble floor. She strode purposefully over, holding Sarah by the nape, weightless as a kitten. "Did she pull the trinket from your cunt herself, or did you take it out for her?"

Poppy couldn't respond, her bruised head caught in vicious, dizzied rapids. She managed to wrench her mouth open, freeing a slew of damning, pathetic squeaks.

Cane lowered her face, leering an inch from Poppy's mouth. Her breath was winter winds. Her mouth was the red of a headless hare's gaping neck. Her mesmerism trickled over Poppy's skin, and the dizziness no longer mattered. Not when the stiffness of mesmerism drowned out everything that wasn't terrible, clanging panic.

"I am always watching." Cane spun, darting away from Roisin, who had nearly reached her. Roisin was dragging herself across the gleaming marble, her sabre held aloft. A saint in pain. A bleeding, fighting martyr at the end of her holy trial. "It is not wise to forget that. Either of you."

Massimo was screaming, surrounded by a huddle of men and women brandishing blades. Valentin was frantically pulling away Massimo's attackers, barely noticing the knives falling into his flesh. Zahrah was shouting soundlessly, her throat cut to ribbons. Karol had her hands full of wildly slashing women, her face stoic and taut. Carmen was gently gripping Godfrey, who sank a short knife into her face.

Poppy's bound hands couldn't wipe the tears from her face.

Cane swung Sarah's limp body over Roisin, a pendulum of rags and wounds.

"Put her down." Roisin drew closer, her face pained, but her blade steady. She carefully pressed her foot to the floor, testing her wrecked knee. It gave under her. "Don't hurt her any more than you already have. Stop this now."

"Oh, you poor thing." Cane's red mouth slipped into a sickly, pitying smile. A shoe fell from Sarah's limp foot, clacking against the floor. "You think she still lives, don't you?"

And with that, Cane hurled Sarah's body into the air, toward the hard, unforgiving wall.

The moment slowed, stretching like toffee. Poppy watched helplessly as Sarah's body arced over the Brood, all too focused on their battle to notice the dying star above. Sarah looked like a vulture, all dark feathers and death, in flight to find carrion, or become it. Even if she still lived, if a tiny spark of life clung to her even now, a collision of that force would destroy her. Poppy had failed her. She had gone to chase a wild hare, leaving her most breakable friend entirely vulnerable. And it had all been a trap. All that time, all that research, all that hope—nothing but waste and wreckage, and Sarah has suffered for it. Through unmoving lips, Poppy let out a long, baleful scream, raging at the stiffness of her legs, the terror and betrayal of her body in the moment she needed it the most.

In the dark night of Poppy's despairing rage, stars erupted. They burst like capillaries, fuzzing reality and unsticking her mind. Little pinpricks of light, tiny constellations in her periphery. Golden and abstract, too far or perhaps too close to see clearly. They grew and grew: glowing fed fires, warm hearths, bonfires, barn fires, houses swallowed by tongues of flame. Rising skyward until they were suns and stars, explosions in the deep cold of space. Light that burned and burned, and shaped itself. Form from the liquid heat. Heads and shoulders, arms and torsos. Bodies that smelled of a burning forest. Bodies of scalding angels.

They were girls made of light. Women, some of them, but just barely. They had sweet faces and wide eyes, yellow hair that tumbled down their backs or wound around their heads. Braids caressing scalps, fringe that dusted their pale eyebrows. Cheeks of a blushing, ribbon pink, smiles that grew and faded, and eyes that cried with silent, joyous tears.

She lives, one gentle voice said in Poppy's mind, amplified through her clanging bones. *She lives*, said another, like the ringing of a bell. *She lives, she lives,* a chorus of pebbles skipping over rivers. *She lives*, buttons springing from tight frocks. *She lives*, and it was a game of graces, hoops and sticks colliding. *She lives, oh, she lives*, an egg dropping into boiling water. *She lives*, a door closing with the barest *snick*. *She lives*, like laughter, like a kiss.

A yellow-haired woman smiled, her form wavering in a rainbow shock of fractured light. She wore a long white frock, like an ancient priestess. Like an angel. Her eyes were the wettest of them all. She might have been Poppy's sister, or her ancestor, or her dearest friend, for the love she held in her rapturous face. For the adoration in her blue, blue eyes. She raised her arms; then all the arms were raised, of all the women and girls, up, up and then out, and towards Poppy, all arms towards Poppy, light and sound and tripping prismatic color, an arc of energy through time and through life, and all the girls were singing, they were her fellows and friends and family and they sang her favorite song, and she sang with them and she screamed, and Clover said *Now*, and they all pushed, and Poppy could move, she could *move*.

She found her feet and ran, racing against the sluggish seconds, now quickening with her every footfall. She ran, arms outstretched, her feet skidding uncontrollably on the floor. A weight landed in her arms just as she collided into the wall, her face smashing, nose breaking with a crunch and a starburst of bright blood. She slid to the floor, the bundle of Sarah resting in her lap, blissfully spared from the collision. Now, this close, Poppy could see the barest intake of breath rattling in Sarah's chest. She let out a trembling sigh of relief and raised her head, rage starring her vision.

"You nearly fucking killed her," she snarled.

Cane stared back, dumbfounded. It was only a second. Just one moment of wrong-footedness, and Roisin stepped into it like it was made especially for her. Roisin, whole and healed and standing, swift as the wind. She swung her blade and it found its target, slicing through Cane's neck with stomach-turning ease. The head screamed as it went flying, pinwheeling through the air, hair following like the tail of a dark star. It landed unceremoniously on the floor with a pathetic thump.

"Sarah," Poppy wheezed, wiping at her nose. "Sarah."

Roisin was by her side. "She's hurt. She might be—"

"She lives. Clover said."

Roisin laid a hand on her shoulder. "You hit your head."

"She *lives*. Clover *told* me. The girls, all the girls! Thank you, thank you!"

In the corner of her vision, Poppy saw Zahrah and Karol lift the body, Carmen barking out instructions to bring it, the sabre, and the head to the garden. Massimo had his arms around crying men and women, boys and girls, who remembered little, and were frightened, but free.

Valentin crouched over Sarah's body. "I'm sorry we couldn't save her, Poppy. I'm so, so—" His voice broke, a sob shuddering through his shoulders. "I can't believe she's gone."

"She isn't. She's right here, if you only look." Poppy stared, willing Sarah to move. *Please,* she begged. The yellow-haired women were gone, but maybe they still heard. Maybe they were always listening. *Please, please, please.*

Sarah sucked in a ragged breath, her body convulsing. "Poppy . . ."

"Sarah!" *Thank you. Thank you, thank you, thank you.* "Sarah, I'm so sorry—"

"It's all right." Her voice was a hoarse whisper. "I'm dying, aren't I?"

380

"You . . ." She looked between Roisin and Valentin. Their expressions were dark, tears streaming down their shocked faces.

Roisin nodded. "You have a choice."

"A choice?"

Poppy swallowed thickly. "I could turn you."

Sarah blinked up at her. "Become like you?"

"If you want."

"Is it . . ." She ran her filmy tongue over her bruised and swollen lower lip. "Is it a good life?"

"It's long," Valentin said. "Many things matter less, because mortality isn't there to give them value. But some things become more beautiful with age. You can't grow old, but you can change. You can always keep changing."

"It's lonely," Roisin said. "The nights are long and the world fears you. But there are people who will love you if you let them. If you let them see you, and make you valuable, and keep you safe."

"You lose things," Poppy said. "You lose sweetness and salt. You lose spice and wine. No matter how hard you try, everything tastes of blood, in the end. You never feel the sun on your face again. The people who knew you like this will always see you as something different, if they see you at all. But you gain so much. There is so much joy to be had in these many long years. There is plenty, if you know where to look."

Sarah stared at all of them in turn, her face swollen, her scleras lined with blood like the vines over the side of Covenly, ivy crawling into the cracks between stones, filling each empty space with red, red greenery.

"My choice," she murmured. "My choice." And her eyes rolled back in her head.

Epilogue

Somewhere Foggy, 1872

They went back to Covenly, of course.

It wasn't immediate. There was much to do in London. The staff had sustained only minor injuries, but the terror took months to fade, and they all needed a great deal of care. Some left, but a surprising number stayed in service.

"This is my home," Godfrey sniffed, hobbling on his sprained ankle. He had, according to a swarm of breathless maids, attempted to banish Cane from the house. He had received a smack to the face for his trouble, one that sent him careening to the floor. His protest hadn't had any material effect, but the rest of the staff declared him a hero for his efforts and the pride suited him down to his meticulously polished shoes.

Then there was the matter of the garden.

"She's blighted it." Zahrah sullenly kicked at an errant stone. It hopped and skipped over the baked ground. "Her last, pettiest act."

All the plants died around the stretch of earth where Carmen had sliced through Cane's lifeless body, separated out the limbs like quarters of a roast chicken, and set the drying flesh aflame. The blight rippled from the dropped pebble of the blaze to the ivied walls, baking the soil. The only bit that had been spared the fallow curse was the spattered oblong where Massimo had lost his lunch.

"Of course I was sick." He pouted. "That the rest of you didn't vomit is what's embarrassing, actually."

Valentin slung his arm over Massimo's tight shoulders. "Yes, sunshine.

We're all very ashamed."

Together, the Brood turned the earth with their hands and spades, fertilizing the soil and keeping it moist. This was upon Carmen's insistence; she said something about a king who cultivates the field, her words wreathed in the untouchable will of scripture. Poppy was the first to kneel beside her, holding the dry grains between her fingers and letting them sift out. The others followed suit eventually, though with some measure of healthy whinging. Valentin made a thoroughly Roman suggestion about what might inspire horticultural fertility, and was shot down immediately. Poppy assumed he'd make a clandestine donation, perhaps with a newly amenable Massimo in tow. The garden wasn't ready for new growth by the time the itch to return to Covenly finally dragged them back, but it was getting there, and that was enough.

Covenly's grounds were unchanged, as wild and tangled as they had been in trancing dreams and murky memory. Poppy walked through them in a stupor, feet gliding through clover and thrift and dandelion. She abandoned her trunks and stepped into the kitchen—she had never used the front entrance and had no interest in doing so. Not when the kitchen opened its door so sweetly, welcoming her to a room with a hearth and a table, dusty and mouldering and correct. Roisin stumbled in after her and gasped.

"It's so good to see you in this room." Her voice was tremulous, one ripple short of weeping. "I almost can't . . ."

Poppy didn't have words. She flung herself at Roisin, kissing and biting and grappling. Under her, Roisin's expression flitted from amusement to concern to desire, allowing Poppy to release the tides of emotion onto her willing body. Afterward, sticky and aching, they lit the hearth and watched the fire dance until morning, safe and still, marveling in the wonder of having nowhere to go.

They tranced in a bed with dust-stiffened linen. The next night, they made a list. Sheets and blankets, planks and paint, firewood. And, of course, paper and pens and ink and envelopes, because they had letters to write.

The work was long, but they were in no rush. They spent as many hours on the house as they did speaking or reading or just pressed close, kissing and touching and marveling at their momentous luck to have this home, to be these people.

"I saw Clover," Poppy said after two or so months, putting down her well-worn copy of *The Monk*, which she had grown to love. She had hesitated to speak about the yellow-haired girls, both because their appearance was unbelievable, and because it felt so very hers—a moment for a dozen lost girls and one living Poppy. But Roisin had loved Clover, and so she deserved to know.

"You said." Roisin put a strip of paper to mark her place in her Wilkie Collins—she bemoaned Poppy's many dog-ears—and readied herself to listen. "You had just slammed your head into the wall. I assumed you rattled your brain around."

"This happened before I hit the wall." Poppy said, and Roisin raised an eyebrow. "The second time, at least. It wasn't just . . . Oh, blast, I'll tell you everything, but you have to promise not to interrupt."

"I promise."

It was as sacred as any of her promises. Of course she listened silently, mouth dropping open and other-worldly eyes growing large and damp.

"Oh," she said, when Poppy was hoarse with speaking, and with unshed tears. "Oh."

"When you told me about Clover, about waking up from the mesmerism, I thought it was love that had done it."

"Of course you did." A tear dripped over Roisin's small, mournful smile. "My sweet, romantic Poppy."

"But I don't know, now. I think it might have been Clover. I think she might have been magic."

"She was. Poppy?"

"Yes?"

"I believe in ghosts."

"Me too." She left her chair and seated herself in Roisin's lap, stroking that dark, soft hair. "I wish there was a way I could thank her."

Roisin considered this. "Perhaps there is."

Their timing was perfect; they had six months to prepare. Half a year to clean and mend the house as best they could. They stripped the paper from the walls and repapered in light, airy patterns, bits of day to savor though they lived by night. The dark, looming paintings were confined to the little room at the end of the hallway that had housed Roisin's face for so many years. With some cajoling, Roisin agreed to let Poppy hang one portrait, the one in which she wore a purple frock and her face was soft, its curves generous and slopes gentle.

"I was alive when that was painted. I've been dead for so much longer."

"We aren't dead."

"What are we, then?"

Poppy thought this over. She would perhaps be thinking this over forever.

"We're something else entirely," she said, and that was enough.

The invitations went out, penned in Roisin's immaculate hand. Poppy made costumes, green and white, studded with wildflowers and ferns. Together, they felled a tree, chopped the wood, and dried it. Roisin built a shelter for the firewood, and there it remained, dry and ready.

On the day, Poppy sat by the kitchen door and waited.

"I could say something about a watched pot," Roisin remarked. "But I take it that wouldn't go over very well."

With two fingers, Poppy silently told her exactly how that would go over. Roisin laughed and, with a bit of waffling, sat down beside her.

"Might as well join you," she said, as though Poppy had wheedled her into it. "I haven't anywhere else to be."

They sat in silence for a quarter of an hour exactly, until the door burst open and Sarah stomped in.

"*This* is Covenly?" She yanked off her wide-brimmed hat and took in the kitchen with an assessing eye. "You talk about it like it's bloody Eden! The grounds are a mess. And by the way, I ain't a maid anymore, so I resent having to come in through the scullery."

She made a brilliant vampire, fearsome and fine from her very first night. Though she lay dying, Sarah had managed to let out a faint and rasped request to be turned. When she awoke three days later, still shivering from her painful transformation, the Brood attempted to press-gang her into an immediate trip to Covenly. It didn't take.

"You think that if I stay in London, I'll gobble up all my friends?" She had scoffed. "Don't be daft."

Carmen took charge, starting Sarah on both rabbit blood and human, eagerly donated by her former colleagues. Under Carmen's careful ministrations, Sarah avoided frenzies and rampages, and managed to master her cravings in record time.

"Seven months," Poppy reported to a sulking Roisin when the letter came. "Don't be jealous now. You're still very skilled at self-abnegation, my silly little Catholic."

Sarah was still less than a year into eternal life, but she carried it like a centuries-old creature. Poppy had never seen her shoulders so broad, her gait so confident. But there had been shades of this stately vampire in the scraggly little gutterblood who wore Roisin's too-big clothing in Dorset, descending the stairs like the fete was in her honor. Sarah had always had this inside her. Poppy couldn't wait to see how much she'd bloom.

More visitors came after. The Brood, of course, all smiling and eager. Carmen was vocally tolerant of the upcoming paganism, likely for Roisin's sake. A cadre of servants up for London, here not as employees, but friends. Anaïs arrived with the women from that fateful trip to the chilly beach. Then, Roisin's many acquaintances from her years of travel and search, who Poppy was not surprised to see absolutely dote on Roisin. She accepted it all, bashful and stammering and perfect. By morning light, the house was filled with vampires, humans, and creatures who could not refer to themselves as either, all tucked up in their beds.

Poppy and Roisin built the bonfire the next day, swaddled in dark clothes and hidden under big hats. Valentin, Carmen, and Sarah were pressed into service alongside them; Zahrah, Karol, and Massimo volunteered. By nightfall, the pyre was tall and proud, lying in wait like a sleeping forest giant.

They dressed, then returned. Their guests trickled out onto the grounds, stretching away the last remnants of their trances and sleeps.

Roisin raised her arms in greeting. "Welcome! I suspect some of you know what we're doing out here." She acknowledged a small group of witches with a gentle nod. They volleyed back a bouquet of kisses. "Nearly a century ago, I met a woman who told me about the old religions of this land. She loved celebrating each harvest. Each season. Each turn of the earth, as it bore new parts of itself to the sun. Her favorite was Beltane." Roisin gestured to the massive stack of wood. "This will be our Beltane fire. In days of old, everyone extinguished their home hearth and relit it with the Beltane fire. It marks movement from cold, unforgiving winter to gentle, generous summer. And we'll, erm, sorry. Forgot what bit was next. One moment."

"What are you wearing?" one of the witches prompted.

"What?" Roisin looked down. "Oh, yes. Forgive me. This is my first Beltane." She straightened her shoulders. "I represent the Green Man. He is a figure of the land. A sort of natural deity. Actually, if you look in most parish churches, you'll see a stone carving of him. It's usually his head in a sort of leaf thing. Sometimes he'll vomit leaves, or—"

"Petal." Poppy put a hand on her arm. "As interesting as this is, we have a long night ahead."

"Yes." Roisin gave an embarrassed little wriggle. "Ah. Of course."

"You're doing very well!" Valentin shouted from across the unlit bonfire. "I'm very engaged!"

"Oh, engage yourself!" Poppy shot back.

"Erm, thank you, Poppy. As I was saying: I represent the Green Man. Poppy, in her lovely flowers, is the May Queen. She's the personification of springtime and new growth. Very appropriate, I would say." Roisin smiled down at her. "She grew flowers all over my fallow life."

"That's very sweet!" Massimo called, entirely without irony. Beside him, Sarah rolled her eyes.

"Tonight, we will mark the shift of the seasons as the May Queen takes the Green Man as her consort. We will light this fire, and while we cannot take the flames back into our own hearths, we will do so, erm, *metaphorically*."

"What she means is, we're sharing in the spirit all together." Poppy waved her arms around in demonstration. "Dancing and whatnot. That all right with everyone?"

"Yes, very well!" Carmen replied. There came a murmur of agreement all around.

"For the rest of the night, we'll have a bit of revelry. Eleanor will be playing music for us." Poppy acknowledged the long-necked violinist from Anaïs's coven, holding her instrument at the ready. "The woods are filled with rabbits for your dining pleasure. We've got some lovely little cakes and treats inside for the humans, and bloody ones for the vampires. Humans: beware of anything pink. Feel free to go a-maying, if you catch my meaning." Someone whooped. "If you're at a loss, I recommend getting by a tree. Maybe giving a little thought to the seasons. Most of us . . ."

Her voice caught. Roisin held her hand and squeezed it. One quick pulse for courage. Poppy squeezed it back, for everything. "Most of us don't get to age. We don't get to have bodies that show all we've done and seen. Our skin won't show our wisdom. We won't get lines from laughing or from weeping. But we change. We must, and we do." She took a deep steadying breath. "We aren't aberrant. We aren't unnatural. We're of this world, so we belong in it. We've got to think about what that means."

"What *does* it mean?" someone asked.

"Fuck if I know, mate." The grounds rang with congenial laughter. "Maybe I'll find an answer tonight, and then change my mind ten years down the line. That's the point, isn't it? Remembering that, though we may last forever, we still get to be different than we were. There is always room to change."

Roisin brought Poppy's hand to her lips as pleasant murmurs floated from all around. "Well said, my love."

"Oh, sod off, Greentits."

Roisin kissed her, then. On the mouth, deep and slow. A powerful kiss, with thick, growing roots. Poppy had waited years for that kiss. She had dreamt of it. It was no less miraculous now she could have it whenever she wished. It warmed her from her lips to her toes, filling her mind with the rich, thick sap of love and safety, of stillness. "If you don't stop that, I'll start weeping. Go make yourself useful and light that bonfire."

Roisin snorted laughter and went off to do as she was told. Within minutes, low little fires began their steady ascent up the jumble of sticks. Cheers rang out, and Eleanor took up her fiddling. Zahrah and Massimo were the first to dance, Zahrah leading, tossing Massimo this way and that with her strong arms. Soon, others joined, Karol included, hooking arms and swinging, laughing in the growing, orange light of the Beltane fire.

Poppy took Roisin's hand, and together they walked around their fire. Small groups took to the woods, laughing mischievously, shedding their clothes as they went. The witches dug their fingers into the soil, chanting together; between their hands, a sapling rose lazily, slowly unfurling its heart-shaped leaves. The selkie sat between her husband's legs, both facing the fire, giggling together at a private joke. Anaïs uncorked a bottle of champagne, poured it over the split wrist of a dazed, grinning woman and licked up the mess from hand to elbow.

Valentin, Carmen and Sarah chatted together, watching their friends dance. As happy as Poppy was, she missed being so near to them. Maybe it was time to start spending part of the year in London. She raised her hand in greeting.

"Good party," Sarah remarked, waving back. "Liked it when you get teary eyed."

"Fuck off, Bethnal Green."

"It is quite nice." Valentin made himself comfortable in the clover, picking a dandelion and tossing it away. "My trousers will be stained, of course. I assume you'll be footing the bill for a cleaning?"

"Not my fault you dressed in gray to sit in grass." Poppy flicked the brim of his hat, sending it over his eyes. "Take them off, if you're so bothered."

"Just trying to get me out of my trousers. I know your type."

"Leave her be," Carmen murmured. "I'll buy you something nice if you behave."

"Poppy." Roisin came up beside her. Poppy hadn't even seen her step away. "May I borrow you for a moment?"

"Sorry, my loves." She doffed an imaginary cap. "The missus calls."

Roisin led her to a subdued patch of the gathering where two women sat on lawn chairs. The older appeared to be nearing sixty, her younger companion probably just shy of thirty. Bonfire flames lit up their faces, revealing scores of cheery freckles.

Roisin pushed Poppy gently towards them. "A surprise."

The older woman, noting their presence, raised her head. Her lazily coiffed hair was comprised of shocking white strands woven between swaths of orangey-yellow. A jaunty, upturned nose proudly sat above rosy lips, which bore the first hints of encroaching wrinkles. Her eyes were a vaguely familiar color, the welcoming blue of a safe harbor.

"Hello, Shit-for-Brains," said the woman.

Poppy had little respect for time. Why should she pay fealty to a force that was no more to her than a parallel traveler? But in this moment, time slammed her to her knees and made her kiss its toes.

Her hands flew to her mouth. "Lizzy!"

"Do I look so different?"

God, her voice was exactly the same. "Yes," Poppy said. "And no." Because those eyes still twinkled mischievously, eager and wicked and,

390

even after Poppy had disappeared from her life with no warning, still unduly kind.

"My god." Lizzy reached up a hand. Poppy dropped to the ground before her, allowed her to stroke the soft swells of her face. "You're still so young."

"I'm not." Poppy was crying. Of course she was crying. "Only on the outside. I'm so sorry."

"Good." She flicked Poppy on the nose. "Think you can just buy me a house and fuck off?"

"Mother," the woman beside her chided. "Language."

Lizzy rolled her eyes, but there was obvious fondness in the gesture. "May I introduce my youngest, Miss Elizabeth White."

Poppy scrubbed tears from her cheeks. "Named for you?"

"For my sins. And yours."

"Mine?"

"Elizabeth Poppy White." Elizabeth bowed her head in greeting. "Mostly Beth. I've heard so much about you."

"Only the good bits." Lizzy winked. "So, what have you been up to?"

"Not much. You?"

She sniffed. "Kept busy."

For a blissful stretch of starry night, Poppy listened, rapt, to the story of what she'd missed. Lizzy baking bread and pastries, minutes away from Poppy doing the exact same thing. Lizzy falling in love with a man who, for some inexplicable reason, was called Little Al. Lizzy caring for generations of wains, escorting some from the trade, ensuring those who stayed were safe and healthy and fed. Lizzy standing vigil at old Minna's deathbed, forgiving her for her cruelty and thanking her for her kindness. Lizzy birthing a brood of smiling children who sent her, happily, round the twist. Lizzy, years later, holding her eldest daughter's hand as the girl brought her own child into the world.

"It was only because of you." Lizzy had slid to the ground so the two of them could tangle together, heads pressed and arms squeezing. "You made it all happen for me. And all this time, I thought you were dead."

"I'm sorry."

"Shut up. Enough of that." She bit Poppy on the cheek like a mother dog to a naughty puppy. "Nearly shat myself when I saw that handwriting on a letter again. I thought Little Al had bought the cheap whisky again."

Roisin, who stood a polite distance away, smiled to herself. Poppy's unbeating heart danced in her chest.

"She gave me so many words," Poppy whispered, a secret shared between women who had been girls together. "She's still doing it."

Lizzy nudged Poppy with her nose. "Go on. She already promised us you'll visit next month."

Slowly, Poppy approached, taking her time to appreciate everything Roisin was. Her smile, which still went flat when she felt bashful, shifting from one side of her face to the other. Her hands, long and steady, that once combed the earth, now growing used to stillness. Her toes, curled protectively into the earth. Her eyes, a fortune of tuppence coins.

"Roisin," she said, and then couldn't say any more because her mouth collided hard with Roisin's and they were kissing, feverishly, desperately, as the fire burned and the stars shed their generous, eternal light.

Roisin gestured towards the woods. "Come on. There's more."

She led Poppy through the trees, stopping by a thick beech. Poppy let out a low whistle.

"As good a seduction spot as any."

Roisin ducked her head, grinning up through some fallen strands of dark hair. "We'll get to that part. I actually had something else in mind." She bit her lip, visibly working up the courage to speak. Poppy waited. She was learning how to wait, how to make space for the quiet. "There's a Beltane tradition of handfasting."

"Oh, like—" Poppy's eyes widened. "Oh."

Roisin pulled a length of pink ribbon from her pocket. "It can mean anything, really. Any sort of commitment, if you'd like."

Poppy reached out, running the silk between her fingers. "Lovely color."

"It isn't the same one. That ribbon's threads now. But it's the same shop." A small, flat smile danced across her face. "The bakery's still there, too."

"You're joking!"

"It's the same family. Your Ben's grandson." Roisin wrapped the ribbon around her pointer finger, her eager hands curled with nerves. "It doesn't have to be like marriage. It can't be, legally speaking. But perhaps we can make some vows."

Poppy impatiently held out her hand, startling Roisin back against the tree. When Roisin got her bearings, she laughed, bright and girlish. "You've no objection?"

"I've got an objection to how slow you're going. Get on with it, please."

Roisin joined her hand with Poppy's, carefully winding the ribbon around the valley between thumb and forefinger, the back of the palm, the wrist.

"Have you prepared anything?" Poppy whispered, her breath knocked out by the sight of them all bound up together, as pretty as a present.

"Hadn't got that far." Roisin was also staring at their hands, mesmerized. "Hadn't hoped."

"Daft thing." She stood on her toes to kiss Roisin on both eyelids, both cheeks. The tip of her nose. "This was one of your better ideas. Though I'm sure I'd do just about everything you asked. Bribe a priest to put our names together in the parish register. Cover more of my skin with roses. Take your name."

"Well, that would be silly."

"Would it?"

"Of course." Roisin's brow furrowed. "I've already got yours."

"*What?*"

"Do you not remember? That night at Covenly our first year, when you offered—"

"I was just being fun! I didn't think you actually—"

"You offered it to me." Her silvery eyes were stunned wide. "It felt like my name, is all."

"Of course." Poppy rushed towards her, throwing her free arm around Roisin's back and holding fast. "Of course. My mistake, not recognizing . . . please forgive me, Roisin Cavendish. Of course it's your name. Of course."

She shook her head. "If you didn't mean it like—"

"Of course I meant it. But I dared not hope."

Roisin let out a long breath, tinged pink with laughter. "Daft thing. It was one of your better ideas."

Family, all along. Hers from the start, before they had even parted. She knew now, down to the grass stained soles of her feet, that this was why she had learned to read and write. So she might put their names

393

together on a piece of paper. So she might know every letter.

They stood like that in the dark for a few long, quiet moments. Poppy closed her eyes. "Are we handfasted yet?"

Roisin let out a crack of laughter. "We haven't made any vows!"

"Right. I Poppy vow to keep beside you, and—it's quite hard to come up with this right on the spot."

Roisin shushed her soothingly. Carefully, she unbound their hands. "We'll try again soon. Give us a bit of time to write something?"

"Oh, perhaps we can do it next year! Invite everyone back for Beltane, maybe even more. Some of the people who came to the orgies might—"

Roisin silenced her with a kiss. The sounds of revelry grew and faded in the distance. Bushes and trees rustled around them with lovers stealing off for moonlit trysts. Poppy's fingers roamed Roisin's body over her green clothes, knowing that a garden grew underneath. She pressed them together, and in the warm night, she felt new.

Acknowledgments

This book would not exist if Anna Burke and Jenn Alexander had not asked me whether I wanted to write a vampire novella. Thank you for telling me we could wrap this up in a couple of months. Looks like we made it. Look how far we've come, my babies.

Thank you to Kit Haggard, the most astute and thoughtful editor imaginable. Thank you for telling me to make this book longer and more ambitious. Thank you for asking me the right questions, and helping me answer them. Thank you for believing in these funky little vampires as much as I did. You're the best of the best.

Thank you to Sylveon Consulting and LaVelle Ridley for your sensitivity read. LaVelle, your confidence in Carmen lit me up. Carmen would not be who she is without you.

Thank you to everyone at Bywater, particularly Ann McMan for the beautiful cover.

Thank you to Kati Sherrill, Kate Wilkinson, Nora Cothren, and Megan Detrie for believing in me, and in this.

Thank you to Justine Champine for reminding me that I am deserving. You picked up my anger and carried it around when the weight made me tired. What an incredible kindness.

Thank you to Alessandra Amin, to whom this book is dedicated. You read it, you noted it, and you loved it, all while walking through hell. You're superhuman. I am so lucky to have you in my life.

Thank you to my amazing wife Kelsey for your unflinching support, and your (frankly, terrifying) confidence that I can do just about anything. You're it. You're my whole deal.

The greatest gift this book has given me is the opportunity to reconnect with my twenty-year-old self. Thank you, twenty-year-old me, for being such a wild, wonderful nightmare. We got it right in the end, but what a time we had being wrong.

About the Author

Samara Breger is a writer and performer who lives in New York. In her previous life, she was an Emmy-nominated journalist, covering sexual and reproductive health. Her debut novel, *Walk Between Worlds* was full of the magic and feelings that she loves. She has a crush on *every* character.

Follow Samara here:

Twitter | @SamaraJBreger
Instagram | @yesjbreg
Website | www.samarabreger.com.

At Bywater Books, we're committed to bringing the best of contemporary literature to an expanding community of readers. Our editorial team is dedicated to finding and developing outstanding writers who create books you won't want to put down.

For more information about Bywater Books, our authors, and our titles, please visit our website.

www.bywaterbooks.com

CPSIA information can be obtained
at www.ICGtesting.com
Printed in the USA
JSHW020923060623
42737JS00001B/2